DANCING ON HER OWN

Also by Mary de Laszlo

The Woman Who Loved Too Much
The Patchwork Marriage
Breaking the Rules

DANCING ON HER OWN

Mary de Laszlo

HEADLINE

Copyright © 1998 Mary de Laszlo

The right of Mary de Laszlo to be identified as the Author of the Work has been asserted by her in accordance with the Copyright, Designs and Patents Act 1988.

First published in 1998 by
HEADLINE BOOK PUBLISHING

10 9 8 7 6 5 4 3 2 1

All rights reserved. No part of this publication may be reproduced, stored in a retrieval system, or transmitted, in any form or by any means, without the prior written permission of the publisher, nor be otherwise circulated in any form of binding or cover other than that in which it is published and without a similar condition being imposed on the subsequent purchaser.

All characters in this publication are fictitious and any resemblance to real persons, living or dead, is purely coincidental.

British Library Cataloguing in Publication Data

De Laszlo, Mary
Dancing on her own
I. Title
823.9'14[F]

ISBN 0 7472 1958 3

Printed and bound in Great Britain by
Mackays of Chatham PLC, Chatham, Kent

HEADLINE BOOK PUBLISHING
A division of Hodder Headline PLC
338 Euston Road
London NW1 3BH

For Lydia, with love

Chapter One

'This time make sure you catch my bouquet, Miranda. It's high time you got yourself sorted out, you know.' Laura was delving about in her shambolic underclothes drawer searching for the glossy tights she'd bought for her wedding day.

Miranda Farell, lolling on the huge double bed with its chintz canopy, laughed. She didn't remind Laura that only a year ago, when Laura's first marriage had ended in tears, she had railed against the 'dull and imprisoning institution' as a trap for women cunningly laid by chauvinist men.

But Laura, one of her childhood friends, guessed her thoughts and said a little defiantly, 'Oh, I know when it all went wrong with Roger I swore I'd never do it again, but Neil is so different.' She smiled blissfully, rolling her large eyes heavenwards. 'With him it won't be an enslavement. He believes in sharing everything, all the chores, money, everything. As it should be these days.'

'I do hope you'll be happy,' Miranda said, then, catching her friend's eye, added with as much enthusiasm as she could, 'Really I do, Laura. Oh, I know these platitudes sound so insincere. But what can I say? Marriage is such a gamble anyway.'

'Is that why you won't do it?' Laura asked. 'I mean, I don't want to panic you or anything, but if you want children, the old body clock is ticking away fast. We're thirty-three next birthday, remember.'

'I haven't forgotten. But I haven't met anyone I want to marry yet. Well, that's not strictly true – Andrew and I could have got married but it sort of went off the boil. Mummy said we shouldn't have lived together for so long. She thinks it's too easy to give up if you're not married.'

'It was only three years.'

Miranda sighed, looked thoughtful. Andrew was the only man she'd seriously discussed marriage and children with. 'Maybe she was right,' she said. 'But then your marriage only lasted four years. There is no answer.' She grinned and got up off the bed, flicking her blonde hair back with a graceful gesture. 'Now I must go. I've got masses to do this evening. I'll be there Saturday.'

The two women embraced and Miranda let herself out into the

1

Chelsea street. She walked down to the King's Road to the bus stop, but seeing no bus in sight decided to continue on down to her flat in Parsons Green on foot.

It was about eight o'clock on a summer evening and she walked slowly, thinking over what Laura had said about their body clocks. She'd often thought of marriage, indeed had supposed that she would marry and settle down with children and a dog like most of her friends, but it had not happened.

She'd never been short of boyfriends – she'd even been in love a couple of times, especially with Andrew – but in her heart she knew none of them was exactly what she wanted.

She was godmother to many children, and sometimes staying with their families in their large, sprawling country houses she had for a moment been seduced by the picture of family life: angelic children running excitedly round the garden gambolling with the dogs; the warmth of family meals in huge pine kitchens, with rosy-faced toddlers swinging their legs from chairs too big for them. But she had also seen the tears and the tantrums; how beautiful babies could turn into screaming monsters and pleasant husbands into tyrannical beasts. Miranda did not think she had the stamina for it.

She did not say, of course, to Laura that she thought Neil rather a wimp. He was, to her mind, a mummy's boy, wanting to play mummies and daddies for real. She had a feeling that Laura, still bruised by her first husband's infidelities, would soon be irritated by him. But she'd learnt a long time ago that people only heard what they wanted to hear and Laura, for the moment besotted with her fiancé, would only be hurt and offended if her friend said what she really thought.

But then again, she thought as she stared into the window of an antiques shop, admiring a large mirror surrounded by shells, I may be wrong. Laura may want that sort of relationship, having tried and failed with a marriage to a man whose laddish behaviour decreed that marriage meant fidelity for women but not for 'real' men, who could hardly be expected to have control over their basic instincts. Besides, once married, Neil might find the confidence to be more manly.

Miranda walked on. The truth was, she thought, she didn't want to have to put up with another person's idiosyncrasies, soften them up if they were brutes, bolster them up if they were wimps. Perhaps she was selfish, she sighed. She'd been alone now for over a year and she enjoyed it. She smiled at herself in the shop windows as she passed. In her head, she heard her mother say, 'If only you'd settle down, dear. You know the longer you put it off the more set in your ways and difficult it will be. You may be all right now, but you'll be so lonely in your old age with no children and grandchildren's visits to look forward to.'

Her mother's reasoning did not convince Miranda. No one knew if he or she would end up lonely. The happiest relationships often ended in premature death, or hideous illness, or boredom. Children, if there were any – and the papers were full of scare stories of the male sperm rate having fallen dramatically – did not always marry, or rather stay married to nice people, or have their own children. And sometimes these children turned out to be more of a burden than a comfort.

Her heart lifted as she reached her front door. Life was better to be lived just as it came. What was the point of hitching oneself to a man in the hope he'd still be there for one's old age? Anyway, she thought as she let herself into her flat, she'd known a lot of lonely married women, stuck at home with tiny children while their husbands travelled on business. As a single person you had to make more effort, cultivate friends and interests. All this she had told her mother, who had gone on about fulfilment, then become angry when Miranda had asked her, 'Whose fulfilment?'

She loved her flat. With some money left to her by her grandfather she'd managed to buy it without being burdened with too huge a mortgage, and she'd been here ten months now. The bottom half of a small terraced house, it had a living room facing the street with a tiny kitchen cleverly tucked in at the far end of the room under an arch. There was a slip of a room she called her study, a bathroom, and a double bedroom opening out into a square garden. She loved this garden and would lie in bed at night with the door open to it, listening to the night sounds. In the morning at weekends if it was fine she'd take her breakfast outside.

It also had a converted cellar that she used for painting her miniatures, which she loved doing in her spare time. She had learnt to do this at an adult education course that she'd taken up out of curiosity – having always been good at art – when she'd had a few months to spare before going to university. She had become hooked on it and painted whenever she could, capturing tiny land or seascapes, sometimes attempting portraits of people or their dogs.

Miranda put down her bag, picked up her mail which Colin, who lived upstairs, had pushed through her door, and turned on her answerphone. There were two messages, one from her friends Simon and Tessa Gardiner wanting her to go and stay at the cottage they were renting on a large estate. The other was from her brother Marcus, saying that his son had been born two months prematurely and was struggling for life.

All her feelings of optimism and pleasure with her life ebbed from her. She slumped in a chair, stunned by this sudden blow. Sally, her sister-in-law, had suffered three miscarriages and she had carried this baby the longest, so that she and Marcus were beginning to relax, beginning to hope that this time they really would have a child.

They lived in Bath where Marcus ran an antiques business while Sally commuted to a high-flying job in the City. Were they in a hospital in Bath or in London? The obvious person to ring, Miranda thought, was her mother, but no doubt she had rushed to the hospital already. The baby had been born that morning, so her mother would have had time to get to either Bath or London from Hampshire where the Farells lived. Perhaps the child was already dead.

With a heavy heart Miranda tried her parents' home. Her father answered almost immediately.

'Daddy, it's me.'

'Oh, darling, we've been trying to get hold of you. Here's your mother.'

'Daddy,' Miranda's voice was insistent, 'you tell me what happened first.' She wanted calm facts, not her mother's hysterical euphemisms and theories.

'Well,' he coughed awkwardly, 'there's not much news. The baby was born early. It's very—'

'*He.* It's a person, a little boy,' she heard her mother chip in impatiently.

'Humph, yes, dear. *He* is very small and is in an incubator in hospital in Bath. There's nothing we can do but wait. Sally's mother is with her and we – well, your mother – might go there tomorrow. But Marcus is staying at the hospital for the present.'

'I see. Poor things. So we don't know anything?'

'Not really. Now talk to your mother. But you're well, darling? Everything all right with the job and all?'

'Fine.' It was so like him to ask about her, even in the midst of a crisis.

Then her mother came on the line.

'Oh, my darling, it is such bad luck for them. Only two more months, or even a month would have been better than this. I don't know why she went into labour – rushing about too much I would say. There was nothing they could do to stop it. Poor little mite. Marcus says he is minute, fits in his hand. I can't bear it for them, this awful waiting.'

She went on at some length and Miranda had to hold the receiver away from her ear. She knew her mother meant well and would no doubt rush as soon as she could – would have gone already if Sally's mother had not got there first – to their house in Bath and be 'supportive'. Her cloying kindness would soon suffocate Marcus, who had spent much of his life trying to unravel himself from it. Miranda's older brother, Edward, had escaped altogether by living in France with his French wife and their four children. One of the reasons Julia longed for her only daughter to marry and have children was because she felt she would at least see them frequently.

'The mothers of my daughters-in-law are both rather possessive,' Miranda had heard Julia say to a friend who was describing her daughter's latest confinement. 'Now if Miranda would hurry up and marry, that would be different.'

'Can I do anything?' Miranda finally got in. 'Can I ring Marcus or anything?'

'He's at the hospital, dear. He must stay there until, well, you know. I'm afraid the baby's so little and . . .'

'I understand, Mummy.' Miranda felt more and more unhappy. She longed to ring Marcus, could imagine his pain, both their pain. She was afraid too, not knowing how to deal with this raw side of human tragedy.

She heard her father say, 'That's enough, Julia. Let us just wait and pray.'

After a few more tales of disaster, and giving her the name and address of the hospital where Sally and the baby were, her mother rang off, leaving Miranda feeling exhausted. After a few moments she wrote a short letter to Marcus and Sally, telling them she was thinking of them and she would come if they needed her.

She felt restless and unhappy, and tried to settle to some chores, putting in a load of washing, making herself a mozzarella and tomato salad, making up a new lot of salad dressing to keep in the fridge. She was about to start on one of her paintings, hoping it would soothe her, when the telephone rang. She rushed to answer it. It was Tessa.

'Just checking to see if you got my message. I do hope you can come. It's such a sweet little cottage. You remember I told you, we're renting it from the Gillard-Hardings' estate. The house is magnificent – we can just see it from our top windows. It's owned by the National Trust but the family still live in the west wing.' She prattled on and Miranda began to feel better. When Tessa paused for breath she told her about Marcus – Tessa had been rather fond of him at one time – and how she felt rather in limbo at the moment, unable to phone or do anything to help.

'Oh, how dreadful. What a worry for them, for you all. But you know they do marvellous things these days, and these tiny babies do pull through.'

'I know they do but it's so scary. Mummy is bursting to be there, but you know how overpowering she can be.'

Tessa laughed. 'But at least she cares – not like my mother, who makes us feel that every drama any of us have we've had expressly to make her ill. But do try and come, Miranda. It's so pretty down here and we'd love to see you. I know there's Laura's wedding this weekend, but we can't go. Well, the truth is that Simon so loves it down here the last thing he wants to do is tramp up to London at the weekend, so we thought the one after, unless of course you've got to be with Marcus.'

Miranda fetched her diary and they fixed on a date a couple of weeks ahead, all being well with Marcus and Sally.

'Who does the estate belong to?' Miranda asked. 'I know you told me, but I wasn't taking it in.'

'The Gillard-Hardings. The old boy's still alive, very old school. Insists that every man does his duty. It's rumoured that his only son, Ralph, prefers the chaps, though he has married . . . an American girl, not that I've met her. They have one pale little daughter, ignored by the old boy, who is frantic that they produce a son before he dies.' She laughed. 'Not that I think he'll ever die; he couldn't bear to leave his estate to the unfortunate Ralph.'

'If he's so frantic for sons why didn't he have more himself?' Miranda asked.

'It's rumoured half the men in the village are his sons,' Tessa giggled. 'Wrong side of the blanket, of course. I think he's got some legitimate daughters, but they've escaped abroad.'

They talked some more and by the time Tessa had rung off Miranda felt more cheerful. She went to bed but when she slept she dreamt of babies, all helpless and calling for her. She woke and lay in the dark, thinking of her new nephew struggling for life, unless he had lost it already, and the little girl Tessa had told her about, not wanted by her grandfather as she was the wrong sex to be his son's heir.

The awesome responsibility of bringing children into the world overwhelmed her and she felt relieved that it was not something she was compelled to do. Being single it was her choice alone; once married it would be hers no longer.

Chapter Two

Jack Lambert fought to keep his irritation from his voice as he regarded his son. 'But, Tom, this won't do. Surely you can see that?' He tossed the ink-stained and generally blotched exercise book down on the table between them. 'A boy of your age surely should be able to do better.'

Tom flinched at his words, his pale, young face set hard. He would not cry – that would upset his father more. He knew he was a failure but he just couldn't make words do what he wanted. They were meaningless, like jumping spiders, especially when he wrote.

'This is illegible with all these crossings out. And your pen – surely you have a pen that doesn't blot so?' Jack lost his fight to remain calm and understanding. The pain and fear he felt when he saw his son's difficulties made him angry. He'd also heard his wife, Sonia, returning home late again, which annoyed him, as he was sure she didn't have to work such long hours. Seeing Tom slouching on his chair, his dark hair unbrushed, looking so like his mother, except that she was always spotless and elegant, made the hurt anger Jack felt with his wife worse.

He burst out, 'It's not as if you're an idiot, Tom. But you must pull yourself together. Look at your hair, and the buttons of your shirt!' He wailed in anguish: 'You're ten years old and you've done all the buttons up wrong, and your shoe laces are undone.' He could not bear it that his son could be so slovenly, could not bear that he was so behind with his school work.

The most shaming thing of all was when the school had suggested that Tom be tested by an educational psychologist, as if he was mentally defective. Jack had found that very hard to cope with. It filled him with a sense of panic, closely followed by one of compassion. He adored his son and could not bear to think of him as in any way 'different', or at risk. Life, at least the one he was used to, had no time or patience for people who were different.

Sonia had sighed heavily at this news. She loved Tom but her job in a smart PR company seemed to take up more and more of her time and energy, so she frequently left him with a succession of girls or au pairs.

'But surely,' she said to the headmaster of his preparatory school, 'it is your job to sort him out. After all, we're paying enough and we are hardly trained to know whether he finds it difficult to learn, or is just badly taught.'

At first, Jack had been appalled at her reaction, had blustered and explained to the headmaster that he understood and of course they'd have Tom tested. He later realised that Sonia was frightened too and felt intimidated by the headmaster's pronouncement. She felt inadequate, as indeed he did, over being unable to help Tom with his school work. Jack was so afraid that the school would chuck Tom out and the boy's future for a good education would be ruined. These days no child or parent could afford to slip behind for a moment. Mindful of the league tables, many private schools weeded out fast those who let them down, or those they thought might let them down.

Tom, who had retreated more and more into himself as his parents quarrelled, was tested and found to be dyslexic.

'He is very intelligent, but he does need a lot of extra help,' the educational psychologist had explained.

'I can't give him any more help, I really can't,' Sonia had said, leaning forward towards the middle-aged woman who had tested her son. She'd smiled and Jack had felt even more let down. He knew that smile: she used it when she'd been up to something – usually spending too much money or working longer hours than he liked – and wanted to curry favour with him again. The smile that used to smite his heart now made him feel uneasy.

The psychologist had explained, 'I mean special lessons with a teacher specifically trained for helping dyslexic children. Of course you must offer him support, both of you. Dyslexic people are often highly intelligent. Look at Leonardo da Vinci, Einstein . . .' she'd said encouragingly. 'And they are so often wonderful scientists, mathematicians, artists, good at Lego.'

'Lego?' Jack had asked rather weakly, not taking in the other attributes his son might possess. How could being good at doing Lego have any value at all for a grown man having to earn his own living? But after more encouragement and assurance that his son was not mentally deficient Jack had felt better. He was determined to help him.

But when he told his grandfather, General Callendar, an elderly man whose courage in the war was legendary and who, with Jack's mother, had brought him up when the boy's father had died, the general had snorted contemptuously, 'Dyslexia! There's none of that in our family. Work harder, that's what he needs. Dyslexia is a middle-class excuse for stupidity and he's not that. It's common or garden laziness, my boy,' he'd boomed at Jack, going quite red in the face with disgust. 'It must come from Sonia's Italian blood, a lying-in-the-sun mentality.'

'Oh, no, what rubbish!' Jack had felt fury at his grandfather's antiquated ideas and hurt that he did not believe that there was a valid reason for Tom's failure to do well at school.

'All these excuses trotted out these days. Discipline is what they need. Put the modern young on a battlefield and see how it takes them. Haven't time for excuses then,' General Callendar had blustered, impatient with the soft world that had come out of the hardship and courage of the winning of the war; impatient with his failing body, but above all sick at his grandson coming to him with these theories about why his great-grandson wasn't top of his class as he and his own son, who now lived in America, had been. If only he was younger he'd teach him a thing or two. Dyslexia indeed!

Jack had been eleven when his father had died of peritonitis. He'd been a clever, exacting man who'd married in his early forties. Having lived abroad a lot on business, he'd always seemed to be moving on just when he got close enough to a girl to propose marriage. He believed in working hard and had ignored the pain of a poisonous appendix until it was too late. Cynara, his young widow, went back to her father, himself now widowered, and the general, as the stiff military man was still known with much respect in the village, was the chief male influence in Jack's life.

Jack had always been impressed and a little in awe of his grandfather. As a child his favourite treat had been to be shown his military regalia, especially the shining sword. Had he not broken his leg rather badly skiing he'd been going to follow him into his regiment, a failure on his part for which he felt his grandfather had never really forgiven him. That he was a fund manager in one of the world's most prestigious financial institutions, the general thought secondary to commanding men in the army.

His grandfather's attitude towards Tom, while infuriating Jack, also left him with doubts. Perhaps Tom was not working hard enough. After all, whenever he came home from work, Tom was always slumped in front of the television, or glued to a computer game. So although Jack had willingly paid for him to have extra help, he found himself becoming increasingly strict over the amount of work the little boy did, and the quality of it.

Perhaps Jack had never taken much notice of it before, but compared to the other children in his class Tom's work was poor and he found it shaming on open days, when the parents went round the classrooms looking at their children's work, to see his son's sad efforts pinned up on the wall with the other neater, more mature work. He couldn't understand it, as Tom appeared so much brighter than half of the other children in his class. He knew that by the way he spoke, talked about things he had seen and done. He was far more articulate than some of the others, who seemed hardly to be able to string two sentences together. He hated it when other parents gave him pitying glances when they saw Tom's smudged work next to their own child's neat pieces. He hated the smugness in their voices as they talked of the top schools in the land that had offered their child a place. No such school would welcome Tom.

Sonia came into the room smiling. 'Sorry I'm late, darlings, the traffic is murder. Think what it will be like in another few years: we won't be able to get out of our street, I suppose.' She kissed Tom and threw a kiss in Jack's direction.

'Homework done, darling? Was there lots?' She ruffled Tom's untidy hair.

Tom muttered and Jack said, 'It's not good enough. I mean, his writing is disgraceful. Hasn't he got a decent pen?'

He caught sight of Tom's face and felt unkind. He hadn't meant to go for him, but for Sonia, who he felt should have been here ages ago, with her son, helping him. He had nothing against women having careers but he did feel that Sonia should be home before he came back from the office. He knew that he was being unreasonable, but he couldn't help but feel jealous at her, to his mind, overcommitment to her job. It wasn't as if she was saving lives or caring for people; promoting cosmetics and scents could surely be done during normal working hours. He and Tom needed her here and he resented the fact that she was so often late.

He told himself it would be a sign of weakness to delve constantly into exactly what she was doing, would show a lack of confidence that she would despise. He accepted her explanations, often given with a long moan at the inadequacy of her colleagues. But if he was ever angry about her frequent absences she would be extra loving and passionate later in bed, saying how lucky she was to be married to him, sometimes saying they should have another child when her work calmed down a bit, and sometimes he believed her because he so desperately wanted to.

Sonia was an extremely beautiful woman. Her grandmother had been Italian and she – and indeed Tom – had inherited her creamy skin, dark glossy hair and expressive dark eyes. She was like a beautiful, spoilt child, loving the attention her looks gave her. Jack had known this, understood this, but had thought that the security of marriage and children would have curbed her restless spirit.

They had been married twelve years. At first it had been blissful; he had never known such passion and such love. His grandfather had disapproved, of course.

'Latin blood, too excitable, had enough of that in the war.'

Jack had explained that it was only her grandmother who was

Italian, the rest of her family and especially her parents were as British as they were. They had a lot in common: she too had lost a parent, her mother, when she was young. It was her being spoilt and adored by her father and an older brother that had probably had far more to do with her sometimes thoughtless behaviour than her few drops of Italian blood.

Cynara, Jack's mother, was determined to like her. 'I'm going to be a good mother-in-law, darling,' she'd said. 'I shall make no comments at all. After all, it is your life.' She had been as good as her word, but it had helped that she had married again and gone to live in France. But when Tom came along she absolutely adored him and Jack felt guilty that he didn't take him to see her enough.

Despite his prejudice General Callendar grew to like Sonia. He'd always had an eye for a pretty woman, but he censured his grandson for giving her such a free rein.

'Women, like troops, need to be kept in order,' was one of his favourite sayings. 'She should be at home when you return, with the dinner simmering on the stove.'

Jack's annoyance at Sonia's lateness, misdirected at Tom that evening, was making the child even more introverted. His dyslexia teacher asked Jack and Sonia to come and see her, and suggested that it might be better if he went to a boarding school especially geared for his needs.

For some time, though he had not discussed it with Sonia, as talking about it somehow made Tom's weakness seem more real, Jack had felt in his heart that something more had to be done to help his son than just a couple of hours' extra tuition a week. He felt that in some way he was letting him down by sending him away to a special boarding school. But to Jack's surprise Sonia, and later Tom, agreed to the idea.

'We aren't really qualified to help him, and he'll be home most weekends,' Sonia said. 'He may find it easier too to be with other dyslexic children, not have to try so hard to keep up. After all, he's not going to get Common Entrance without a lot more work and his school is only keeping him on as a favour.'

Jack reluctantly agreed with her. They had originally chosen – against his better judgement at the time, though it had proved a godsend – to send Tom to a private co-ed school that kept the children until they were thirteen. The boys, unlike at more conventional private schools, did not have to leave at eight.

The school suggested to them was in Gloucestershire, Pilgrim's Court. They arranged to go and see it one weekend.

'It's right next to my eccentric relations, the Gillard-Hardings, you know, the ones that live in Chandos Hall?' Jack said. He was studying a map of the county.

'Do I know them?' Sonia said, flipping through *Harpers* and seeing who she knew in the photographs of various social events.

'No, you don't. They never came to our wedding. It's so complicated, another branch of the family really, on my father's side.' He frowned and tried to remember how they were related. He barely knew them; they had taken little notice of him after his father's death.

Sonia was not showing much interest but having been reminded of them and knowing a little about them from his mother, Jack went on, 'My great-grandfather changed his name to Lambert. I can't remember why, some family drama, no doubt. Quentin, the present baronet, was my father's cousin. He must be at least seventy by now. He has a son, Ralph, older than me and rather . . . well, it is said he is gay.'

Sonia put down her magazine. 'Isn't there a title and a huge estate?'

'Yes. I told you, darling. Quentin's a baronet, lives at Chandos Hall,' he said a little impatiently, annoyed that she had not really been listening. 'But the house was given over to the National Trust. I think they still live in it. I must ask Mother. I think she went there quite a lot before my father died. I vaguely remember going with them sometimes.'

'So who will it all eventually go to, if Ralph is gay?' Sonia said, looking intently at him.

'He's married, got a child, I believe. I think it's a girl, though. I don't know much about the setup, but if Tom likes the school and goes there, we could visit them. I think you'll find them pretty peculiar. I don't remember liking them much. I used to see Ralph from time to time at parties and things. I haven't seen him for ages,' Jack said.

He put away the map, looked at his watch. 'It's eleven o'clock in France, bit late to disturb Mother. I'll ring her in the morning and ask. Remind me.' He smiled fondly at Sonia. Sitting there, her feet curled under her on the sofa, head bent over her magazine, she was so very beautiful, so very desirable. Then, thinking to prolong her interest, he got up and took the heavy blue Debrett's, dated some years before, from the bookcase, sat down close beside her and opened it to look up the Gillard-Harding family and show her.

Chapter Three

Miranda tried hard to keep her mind on her work. She was occupied in a fashion accessory shoot for the magazine for which she worked. The photographer had suggested that they photograph the shoes, bags and belts nestling among conkers bursting from their prickly shells, and autumn-coloured leaves, and Miranda's editor, preoccupied with something else, had agreed. It was a difficult, if not impossible effect to achieve in July. Miranda, busy with other things in the office and this week overcome with emotion over her new nephew's precarious hold on life, had not thought about the autumn theme seriously until the day before. She had managed to find some almost ripe wheat on her way home from Bath, a few fir cones, some nuts left over from Christmas and some coloured leaves, but Spike was not happy with them. He fiddled about with the shoes and the wheat sulkily, like an offended adolescent.

'It's not at all what I envisaged,' he kept saying, disdainfully lifting a stalk of corn between finger and thumb, or looking down his nose at a Brazil nut. He sent his assistant out to the local park to see what he could find. 'Do you think a flower shop might have some fake conkers?' he asked at last.

'I've no idea,' Miranda said, near to tears. She had spent yesterday with Marcus and Sally and their tiny baby and it had been a harrowing and emotional experience, like nothing she had ever encountered before.

'Oh darling, do think of something to improve this fiasco. We haven't all day,' Spike said petulantly, turning one of the shoes round to a different angle in case it would miraculously solve the problem.

Miranda took a deep breath. Spike was a wonderful photographer but he liked his own way on the location and the setting, and if this differed to the editor's he could be very difficult. She could see that these brown and tan accessories would look good dropped among golden and red leaves and glossy conkers and autumn seeds, but there weren't any at this time of the year so he'd have to think of something else. Or *she* should have thought of something else; asked Stella, her editor, where they would find golden leaves and conkers in July, and what she wanted instead if they couldn't, but she hadn't. If it went wrong Miranda knew it was her own fault. Features had to be photographed three months before publication and if they waited until the autumn these accessories would probably be sold out or replaced with the next fashion craze.

'I thought this wheat, maybe some red apples – you know, mellow fruitfulness' – she smiled at him encouragingly – 'would look good with them.'

He looked at her pityingly. He'd got his idea and he wanted to carry it out. Surely there was somewhere that made fake autumn leaves and conkers bursting out of their cases?

Miranda took a red apple she'd bought for her lunch from her bag and put it among the wheat, and the coloured leaves she'd snitched from her brother's garden. She uncoiled a belt a little more and pushed a handbag a couple of inches into the centre. She hardly saw these objects, but saw instead her minuscule nephew wired up in an incubator, fighting for life.

With three nieces and a nephew and various friends' babies she'd seen many new-born infants, had marvelled at their smallness, been amazed at their tiny limbs and eyes, their perfect features, their whole series of facial expressions. But the knowledge had in no way prepared her for this.

She had gone down to their house alone on the day after Laura's wedding, her brother having asked her to come without their mother, who had been to see them but had been sent home again as surely even she could see there was nothing she could do.

Miranda met them at the hospital. She was shocked at how haggard Marcus looked, almost old. She held him in her arms, bracing herself to hear that the child had just died.

'We're still hoping,' he said with a faint, brave smile. 'He's had a couple of crises but he's still with us.'

'Oh, Marcus.' She didn't know what to say, what to do. 'Waiting is the worst,' she said at last. 'How is Sally coping?'

'Doing her best,' he sighed. 'She seems to think it is in some way her fault that he was born so early. She was held up in a meeting, and rushing to another she slipped flying out of the office. She felt fine at the time but it may have dislodged him, started him off.'

'That's hardly her fault,' Miranda said, though despite having heard endless gruesome details about childbirth from her girl friends, she was rather ignorant about it all. 'I mean,' she added quickly, thinking that discussing who was to blame for his early birth was a dangerous road, 'lots of women do all sorts of things when they're pregnant. Surely it's just bad luck, and she has always had problems keeping them.'

Privately she had been surprised that Sally had insisted that she keep going with her high-profile career in the financial market, especially when she had had three miscarriages already. But Sally had been determined. 'Goodness, today we women can do everything,' she'd said. 'I can afford a nanny, and anyway Marcus is there to cope.'

Marcus had stopped in the hospital corridor, put his hand on Miranda's arm. 'You'll find her changed but, well, we're trying to be positive.'

She hugged him, feeling afraid at confronting Sally's anguish, wishing fervently she could escape, wishing there was something she could do to help.

Sally was in her room, curled up on the bed, still in her nightclothes. She seemed listless and defeated. She allowed Miranda to hold her a moment but she felt dead in her arms. She said with a note of hysteria in her voice, 'Have you seen him?'

'Not yet.' Miranda knew now she didn't want to. If she was shocked at her brother's appearance she was doubly shocked at Sally's. Sally, usually so vital and pretty, so efficient and in command, was now slumped in her bed staring empty-eyed in front of her.

Miranda put down the flowers she'd brought and said, 'Shall I find a vase, put these in for you?' She longed to escape. The atmosphere of pain and fear in the room could be cut like thick cloth. It was suffocating.

'Someone will see to them. Mummy will – she'll be back soon. Thank you, they're lovely,' Sally said, barely looking at them. 'Do you want to see him? You can. We go often, but . . .' Her voice drained away, her eyes filled with tears.

'Shh, darling, he's doing as well as can be expected,' Marcus said, stroking her shoulder.

'Have you a name for him?' Miranda blurted, really to shift the burden of the terrible pain in the room.

'We thought Roland,' Sally said.

'Roland, that's a good name. I like that,' Miranda said encouragingly.

But seeing him so small, with tubes and wires seeming to come from everywhere, a tiny bonnet on his head to keep him warm, nearly finished her. How could a baby so small possibly survive? She'd often thought full-term babies seemed too fragile for life, but Roland surely didn't stand a chance. She felt the tears running down her face as she stared at the almost insect-like scrap of humanity.

Marcus, who'd come with her, took her arm and led her away. 'I've never seen anything so small either,' he said. 'But they tell me that even smaller babies have survived and are well and normal. We have quite a good chance. He's nearly a week old, but it's still touch and go.'

'I'm sorry.' Miranda wiped away her tears. 'I'm not being much good at being strong for you. I just feel so helpless.'

'So do we. I look at him sometimes and think, this is my son and I'm meant to protect him, fight for him, but all I can do is leave it up to the medical staff – who I must say are wonderful – and fate. It is very hard.' He bent his head, too exhausted for tears.

She took his hand and they sat in silence for a while, knowing that words could do nothing. She knew he was grateful for her silence and wondered how he had coped with their mother. After a while she asked him.

He gave her a faint smile, said with a sigh, 'She tried, poor thing. Had endless stories of people she'd known whose babies had pulled through. Seemed to think any baby from *our* family would make it.' He paused, then said heavily, 'I've had to face up to the fact that death does happen to young people, and no doubt to babies in our family. We're no different to anyone else, though Mother seems to think we are. That we possess some superior gene that will protect us, and not other less worthy people.' He almost laughed.

'I know. It's like when people say so and so "lost their fight" for cancer as if it is somehow shaming that they did, and that another person would not have done so.'

Talk became easier between them and she knew she had in some small way been a comfort to him. She went to his house with him later and helped him to answer letters, do a few chores, things she did willingly, that were helpful, yet she felt they were useless in the face of their concern. When she left him she felt despair at their pain, although she did her best not to show it. All night she had been haunted by the tiny baby covered in tubes and wires, and now Spike's artistic ideas for a few shoes, bags and belts seemed somehow pointless.

'I don't feel you're with me, darling,' Spike said acidly. 'What's the point of one apple? Hardly fruitfulness with one, and a rather small one at that.'

'I'm sorry,' Miranda said impatiently. 'Look, surely we can make something out of this. I'll go and buy some more apples if you like.'

'And a pineapple, and perhaps a coconut, bananas, why don't you?' Spike said waspishly. 'Really, this is too bad.' He flicked the apple on the floor where it rolled across the studio and settled in a corner.

'Spike, it will have to do. I've had a terrible weekend, and . . .' she burst out, fighting not to cry.

'Haven't we all had a terrible weekend? I can't tell you how terrible mine was.' Spike rolled his eyes heavenwards. 'But I don't want fruit. I'm not doing a commercial for Sainsbury's, dear.'

Miranda struggled with her tears, but he saw them.

'Don't blub, dear, I can't bear that. Oh, go and buy your apples if you must, but let's get on with it. I thought it would all be organised and we'd go straight through it.' He sighed heavily and called for his assistant, who had returned from the park and was hovering nervously.

'Where are those leaves, Clive? Let's see what we can do with them.'

Some time later the shoot was finished. The accessories, nestling in an assortment of wheat, dried grasses, leaves, fruit and nuts, had been duly captured on camera and Spike, as he always did, commented with a huge, exaggerated sigh, 'Well, I suppose that's the best I can do with such tat. I mean really, darling, next time we must do something better.' These remarks often hurt models, who took them personally and swore never to work with him again. But when they saw the quality of his work, saw how wonderful he made them look, they always came back for more.

Miranda, with a thudding headache, was thankful there were no models' feelings to bolster up now. She was so tired she could hardly pack up the accessories. She knew she had to take them back to the office before she could go home and collapse.

'Not like you, darling, to become tearful,' Spike said suddenly. 'Love life gone sour on you?'

'No.'

'Lucky you. I had a terrible row this weekend with Paul. What is it then? Someone died?'

She swallowed the lump of tears in her throat, then found herself telling him about the baby. She sat on the floor among the shoes and the grasses and told him. She hadn't had time or indeed the emotional strength to tell anyone else yet. But it poured out of her, all her fears of how long the baby would last, what would happen when it died, how they would all cope.

Spike sat very still listening to her. At last when she had finished he said, 'What a pig, darling. What a pig, and then I'm bloody to you. I was premature, would you believe? Now look at me. Or perhaps you'd rather not.'

She smiled in spite of herself. He was large, muscular, with a shaved head, but kind eyes, she thought, looking at him.

'Let's have a drink,' he said, and called for Clive. 'Have hope, it's the only thing. Are you religious?'

'Only when things get tough.'

'Me too. Sort of talisman against the evil spirits. Primitive, aren't we, when we're up against it?'

Clive appeared with a bottle of wine and some glasses. Spike opened it and gave her a glass.

'Here's to the baby. What's his name?'

'Roland.'

'Oooh, nice.' He kissed the air. 'Here's to Roland. May he win his fight to stay in this miserable world.' He touched her glass and she drank, thinking how odd it was, yet strangely comforting to be sitting here on the floor of Spike's studio, drinking the health of a premature baby who had little chance.

This was real life, she thought, though her mother would hate it, hate Spike and his, to her, rough ways. But he meant to comfort her and in his own way he had. There was a hope, she thought, while there was life and all that. And for the first time since she had seen Roland fighting for life in his incubator she felt better.

'I've been lucky,' she said. 'Nothing really terrible has ever happened to me before. Or what has seems very tame after this.'

'Then you're exceedingly lucky, darling,' Spike said. 'I could tell you a few tales that would make your hair stand on end, but seeing that you're in a fragile mood, I won't.' He poured her out some more wine.

Miranda felt suddenly ashamed, guilty that she had had such an easy life: a stable and happy childhood, good friends, a good job, no real money worries. No boyfriend at the moment, but she wasn't bothered about that.

'I'm sorry, Spike. Misery makes one so selfish, introspective, as if one is the only person with a problem.'

'I know, dear, but I expect he'll pull through. At least he has loving parents and a home. My mum was single, couldn't cope. Don't know why they bothered to save me really, just to put me in a home.' For a moment there was deep pain in his eyes, then he brightened and laughed. 'Oh well, must be some point to it somewhere.'

'Of course there is.' Miranda felt devastated for him, imagining a childhood without love. 'Look what a marvellous photographer you are, one of the best.'

'It worked out,' he said, and she could almost see him shutting the doors of his soul in front of her. He got up. 'Got to push you out, dear, got a date.' He winked.

'I must go anyway. Thanks for everything, Spike.'

Once home again Miranda telephoned Marcus and found that the baby had had a good day and everyone was a little more optimistic.

There was a rap followed by a quick ring on her doorbell and when she opened the door she was surprised to see Davina, one of her best friends, all dressed up as if ready for a party.

'Aren't you ready, Miranda? Oh, you've forgotten, haven't you? Anna and Jonathan's party . . .'

Miranda's face fell. 'I have. I've had such a day. Oh, I . . .' The last thing she felt like was going to a drinks party, shouting to people in a hot, crowded room or garden, not being able to hear what was being shouted back to her.

'Come on, do you good, and you know I hate going on my own,' Davina said. She came in, dressed in a short, slinky black dress and pearls, her blonde hair newly washed. 'Please come. Their parties are always fun. They're having it in the garden and you know how heavenly Anna's made that.'

'All right.' Miranda gave in and while she was getting ready she told Davina all about Roland and why she felt too tired to go out.

'Go for just a little. If there's no one fun there, then come home!'

'I'm not looking for anyone,' Miranda said. 'It's quite nice to be on one's own for a while. I can enjoy the flat without some man wanting to put his mark on it. Keep my own hours, do my own thing.'

'That way selfishness lies,' Davina said, who was engaged to be married but whose fiancé served in a submarine and was often away for months at a time.

'I know and I shall wallow in it,' Miranda said, thinking that she didn't look too bad now she had put on some make-up and changed into her lace Caroline Charles dress. It fitted her slim figure as if it had been personally made for her, emphasising her long legs.

They arrived at Anna and Jonathan Corrin's party and were swept up into it straight away. In the garden, Miranda was relieved to see a lot of her friends. A group of them finally decided to go out to dinner and Miranda was just leaving when James Darby, a man she knew from her university days, called her over.

'Say hello before you go, Miranda. I've only just got here. I'm dreadfully late, I know. Haven't seen you for ages. Everything OK?'

She kissed him, smiling. 'Fine, and you?'

'Got a new job, I was just telling Sonia here.' He gestured towards a beautiful, dark-haired woman standing beside him. 'Sonia Lambert, Miranda Farell.'

The two women nodded politely to each other. Sonia lifted her glass to her lips and Miranda saw the glint of her wedding ring on her finger.

'I've got this amazing job, good salary, company car,' James was boasting. 'I was head-hunted, would you believe? Didn't know anyone knew of my talents.'

'You sing them from enough rooftops, James,' Miranda laughingly teased him. James was an old friend and though they'd never had a romance they were fond of each other.

'That's not strictly true,' he laughed back. 'How about you then? Editor of the magazine yet?'

'Hardly.' She told him about her day's work, camping it up a bit, and as they laughed together she realised that Sonia was looking annoyed. Thinking she had been rude to exclude her from their conversation she turned to her.

'I work for a women's magazine and the photographer wanted my feature to have an autumn theme, difficult in high summer.'

'I suppose so,' Sonia said archly, barely interested. She turned back to James, giving him a dazzling smile. 'Tell me about your job, James,' she purred. 'It does sound so interesting.'

James blushed, obviously smitten by her attentions. Miranda thought she'd leave him to it; her friends were calling to her to leave. She touched James's arm, said goodbye and left. Something made her turn round as she reached the house and she saw the back view of a tall, brown-haired man who had come up to the pair and was talking animatedly to the woman, who just shrugged and moved closer to James.

'That's her husband, poor bugger,' Jonathan, her host, whispered. 'She's such a flirt, but beautiful, don't you think?'

Miranda just smiled at him, then thanked him for the party. Sonia was not her type at all and of no interest to her. Smiling, she joined her friends at the gate, putting the woman completely out of her mind.

Chapter Four

It was late October when Miranda was finally able to stay with Simon and Tessa in their long, narrow cottage tucked away in the grounds of Chandos Hall. She had spent some weekends with Marcus and Sally, Tessa and Simon had been on holiday, and various other commitments had kept them apart. She'd arrived late on the Friday night, tired after a long week's work, and Tessa spoilt her by bringing her up breakfast in bed the following morning.

'You can just glimpse the Hall from here, but when all the leaves are gone from the trees we'll see more of it.' Tessa pointed the house out to Miranda from the window of her bedroom as Miranda pottered round the room finding clothes to wear. 'Us lesser mortals are kept firmly in our place down here, almost out of sight,' she joked. 'But I hope when the big house opens to the public in the summer, our garden won't be infested with coachloads of foreigners looking for further historic sights.'

'That would be dreadful, but you're quite far away from it. Is the family nice?' Miranda asked, looking out through the trees to the magnificent turreted house that seemed somehow mysterious and majestic half hidden by the trees.

'We hardly see them. Today's the first time Simon's been asked to shoot. I think they needed an extra gun at the last minute and he does shoot, though he's a bit rusty. Off the bed, Henry,' she admonished her small son, who was jumping on Miranda's bed. 'There's no need to see them really, we don't even use the same drive. The little girl is older than Henry, and the old man is not very sociable.'

'What about his son and his wife?' Miranda pulled on some jeans.

'Ralph – he's there – he seems rather nice, what we've seen of him. But we haven't seen the wife for ages. There are rumours that she's left him, but I don't know. I don't think we're meant to fraternise with the family,' she laughed, 'just bring them in some extra income by renting this cottage from them.'

'It must be a nightmare owning a marvellous house like that but not having enough money to live in the style it was meant for.' Miranda looked out of the window again at the curly chimneys.

There was a slight mist which made the house seem more ethereal, a mirage through silk.

'Have the same family always owned it?' she asked Tessa.

'I think so, father to son, but now there is a real problem that Ralph will be the last in the line if he doesn't produce a son. There may be more distant relations, of course, but the direct line is in danger of dying out.'

'If he's produced one child, surely he could have some more?' Miranda said. 'Even if I loathed my husband I'd force myself if I had a house like that and all that for my son to inherit. Wouldn't you, Tess?'

'Of course, but he can't if his wife's not here. It is said that she married him for the prospect of his title, to be lady of the manor, but when she found out he didn't much care for women, fled back to America,' Tessa grinned, and fielded Henry, who, bored with all their gossiping, was now trying to climb on to the top of the wardrobe.

'Come on, Henry, let's go out,' she said. 'We'll take your godmother for a walk before it starts raining again.'

They set off in wellingtons and Barbour jackets, keeping away from the wooded land where the shooting was. They walked down the lane and past the flint church, burial place to many Gillard-Hardings, on down to the village. Henry ran ahead with a stick, shooting one minute, poking a rabbit hole or stirring a puddle with it the next. The two women walked more slowly. Tessa, who was in the early stages of pregnancy, was fighting waves of nausea and lethargy.

'Tell me about Marcus, Sally and the baby,' she said.

'He's home, just. I never believed he'd make it,' Miranda said, remembering the anxious days, the enormous battles the baby had had to fight. 'They have to take extra care of him, but they've got him home.'

'What a relief. I always feel lucky that having Henry was such a cinch, but there's always a worry, right at the back of one's mind, that the next one might not go so well.'

'I don't think I'm brave enough to have children,' Miranda said. 'I never really thought about it until I saw the agony Marcus and Sally went through when Roland was born so early. Edward and Nicole never had any difficulties with their lot. Until things happen to people close to you, you don't really give it much thought, do you?'

'I know. But Sally has had the bad luck to always have problems with her pregnancies. Didn't she have miscarriages before?'

'Yes. But who's to know what I would be like? I just don't think I could go through with it. I mean, Marcus and Sally are probably going to worry about Roland for ever now, and what if they want more children? Will the same thing happen? I know I couldn't bear it,' Miranda said firmly.

'Nonsense, you'll be fine.' Tessa linked arms with her. 'You've just got to find yourself a nice husband, then it will just happen. You'll see.' She smiled at her affectionately. 'Have you anyone special in your life at the moment?'

'No, I haven't anyone, special or otherwise. Since this business with Roland I feel I've changed. Life seems more real somehow, not to be wasted. Before I just muddled through, not really thinking about much more than whether I should go to so-and-so's party, go skiing for Christmas or not, or whatever.' She shrugged. 'That all seems a bit pointless now.'

'That's because you haven't anyone to share it with. We should have had a dinner party tonight; there's a nice eligible farmer in the next village. He's charming.'

Miranda grinned. 'Don't matchmake, Tess. You sound like my mother. She's dying for me to marry, breed like a rabbit. I told you I just want to flop with you all this weekend, not make an effort with strangers, however nice, especially eligible farmers.' She laughed. 'Besides, I don't want to exhaust you with having to lay on a feast, especially when you feel ill. It's no fun having people to stay if you have to go to endless trouble to entertain them.'

'That's true. You're one of our few friends that can just come here and flop. Everyone else seems to think they must play the "weekend-in-the-country" part: meeting the locals, drinking in the pub, dashing round the sights. It is nice sometimes to just idle about and gossip.'

They reached the crossroads to the village and Tessa called to Henry to come back and hold her hand.

'Can I have an ice cream?' he asked hopefully, seeing that they were to pass the village shop. 'Or sweets?'

'We haven't had lunch yet, Henry,' his mother said, shepherding him across the road.

'For after then?' he persisted.

Miranda caught Tessa's eye and said, 'I'll buy you something for after you've eaten up all your lunch. OK?'

'Yes . . . yes.' He jumped about, in his excitement landing in a puddle and splashing them.

'Henry, stop it – and what about saying thank you?' Tessa said.

'Thank you, thank you, thank you,' Henry chorused, running into the shop, almost knocking over a woman who was coming out of it. She looked archly down her long, elegant nose at them and swept past them, leaving a trail of expensive scent.

'Sophisticated smell for the country,' Tessa laughed when she'd gone. 'Scent before dark, very daring. I wonder if she's off for a secret tryst in a hay barn.'

Miranda smiled, looked thoughtful. 'I've seen that woman somewhere before.' She watched her walk up the lane.

'She's very beautiful. Maybe she's staying at the Hall. She doesn't seem to have a car, and apart from the Hall and the church there's nothing up that lane until the next village four miles away,' Tessa said, watching the receding figure.

'She's at the Hall all right,' Mrs Peabody, who owned the shop, said. 'She and her husband and son. Mr and Mrs Lambert,' Mrs Peabody, nicknamed Mrs Busybody by Simon, went on.

Henry thrust his none-too-clean hand into an open jar of bright red jelly sweets.

Tessa said, 'No, Henry, not unwrapped sweets. Have some Smarties or jelly babies.'

'Want these.' Henry pulled out his hand, clutching the wormlike rubbery shapes tightly.

Tessa shot an agonised look at Mrs Peabody to see if she was watching but she was busy quizzing Miranda on how she was enjoying it down here, how long she was staying and what her relationship was with the Gardiners. Tessa managed at last to extricate the sweets from Henry and put them back in the jar, whispering frantically that surely there was something nicer he could have in a packet on the counter.

Henry was not convinced, but Miranda, bored with Mrs Peabody's interrogation and sensing trouble from Henry, picked up a box of fruit pastilles and said she'd buy them for him.

'I want those red ones,' Henry tried again, then saw some long green sticks with white middles, also unwrapped, and made a lunge for those. With much commotion they finally left the shop with the packet of fruit pastilles and some M&Ms.

'I can't bear those unwrapped things. Dogs sniff them and probably lick them, children and old men cough over them. He's bound to catch something disgusting from them,' Tessa said as they walked up the lane again, quite unconcerned that Henry had added his own bit of dirt from clutching on to them with his muddy hands.

'I know where I saw that woman before,' Miranda said suddenly, and she told Tessa about the party in London in July. 'She was talking to James Darby. How funny to see her here.'

'James Darby, now there's a man for you. You've always been friends; you could marry *him*,' Tessa said.

'Oh, Tessa, why won't you believe that I'm in no hurry to get married? I love my job and with luck I'll take on bigger and bigger features, and thanks to my grandfather I've got my flat and little garden.'

'But love,' Tessa said, 'surely you want love?'

'We all want that, but it's hard to find. I loved Andrew, he loved me, but in the end it wasn't enough. It fizzled out.' She didn't say that she didn't feel suited for marriage and though she was awfully fond of Tessa and Simon and of course Henry, she thought she might be bored staying at home all day looking after small children.

Even being here a short time had shown her that Tessa didn't have much time to do anything else but cope with the cottage and Henry, and when the next baby came it would be even worse. She'd boasted that she hadn't read a proper book or a decent newspaper from cover to cover since Henry had been born. Before Henry she and Miranda had vied with each other over who had read the most Dickens, and Trollope, then Tolstoy and Chekhov, as well as modern literary works. Now Tessa read nothing.

'My time will come again,' she'd said, 'when the children are at school. All I seem to be able to concentrate on at the moment is the family. I'm going to stay at home until this one' – she tapped her stomach – 'goes to nursery school. Then I'll get a job and get my brain back.'

But Miranda wondered if she herself could give up so much of her life and for so long to bringing up children. She did so enjoy curling up with a good book. And what about her miniatures? Any baby would surely eat the paint and poison itself, even if she'd got the time to do any painting. She probably wouldn't be able to afford a proper nanny, and didn't think from the horror stories she had heard from friends that she wanted one. But each to their own, she thought, watching Tessa smiling at Henry, encouraging the tired little boy up the lane.

Miranda woke up early the next morning. The house was silent, everyone asleep. The day was clear so she decided to go outside for a wander. She put on her coat, let herself quietly out of the door and walked up towards Chandos Hall. She decided that as it was so early, just after seven, no one would be about and she could go close to the house and have a good look at it. It had rained again yesterday afternoon so after their walk in the morning they had not gone out any more.

She came to a struggle of outbuildings and decided to skirt round them and get nearer to the house. A noise made her stop and look round apprehensively, thinking she had been seen by a gardener and would be told off for trespassing. She heard a dull hammering sound, wood against wood, then a cry, a sobbing breath, then more hammering and scraping. Curious, she went back to the outbuildings, towards the sound, and looking over the half-opened door of a disused stable saw a little boy hammering and scraping at a piece of wood. He was crying, the tears dripping down on to the wood. There were dirty streaks on his cheeks where he had tried to wipe them away.

'Are you all right?'

Her words made him spring round; he looked at her fearfully.

'Are you all right?' she repeated, thinking what a beautiful child he was with his dark hair and dark eyes.

'Yep.' He hid his face from her, furiously scrubbing at his eyes with the back of his sleeve.

'What are you doing?' She could feel his misery from where she stood. She looked at the chipped log of wood on the bench in front of him. 'Making something?'

'Yep.' His body shuddered with a suppressed sob.

'What?' She pushed open the half-door and went over to him.

'A mask.' He didn't look at her but she felt his whole body was tensed, waiting for her to say something, to scold him, criticise him perhaps.

She looked at the chipped and marked log. It didn't seem at all like a mask. The wood was too hard to carve with the tools he had with him.

'It looks very difficult to do. Have you no better tools, a chisel perhaps? But even then it will be hard.'

'I know,' he sniffed, then he burst out, 'I've got to make a mask for school. Daddy said he'd help but he hasn't had time and I've got to have it done by this evening. I don't know what to do.' His eyes were agonised, swimming with tears.

Miranda's heart went out to him. She remembered her own school days and the terror she felt when she had forgotten to do something on time.

She heard herself saying, 'I know how to make a mask, but out of papier mâché. It may not be quite dry by this evening, but we could try.'

He looked at her keenly. 'What's papier . . . whatever you said?'

'Paper – paper and glue. Look, I'm staying at the cottage with the Gardiners. I can start you off with it, then you can finish it. OK?'

He looked amazed. 'Could you really?'

'Of course.' She looked round the disused stable. It had been turned into a rather glorified tool shed. There were shelves on the walls with jars and tins of nails, paint and such. 'I'll go back to the cottage and get some old newspapers, wallpaper paste if they have it.'

'We've got that here.' The boy went over to a corner and picked up a box. 'They've just done up the study. There's wallpaper too if you want paper.' He pulled out some dark blue flock paper.

'No, that won't do. While I'm getting some papers, you could make the paste. Do you see how to?' She pointed to the instructions on the back of the packet.

He peered intently at it, but seemed to be having difficulty deciphering the words. He looked uncomfortable, glancing at her fearfully as if expecting her anger.

Feeling another stab of sympathy for him, she smiled. 'Just fill a jar with water, sprinkle some of the powder in and stir it until it turns into a sort of thick jelly,' she said. 'Don't let it be too wet.'

She was soon back with a pile of old newspapers Tessa had put out for re-cycling and a couple of balloons she'd snitched from a packet she'd seen in a drawer in the kitchen. She'd scrawled a note for Tessa and Simon, saying she was helping a child make a mask, and would be back soon.

As she went back to the outhouses and the boy she wondered why on earth she was doing this. She assumed that the boy was the son of the woman they'd seen coming out of the shop; he certainly looked like her. Surely his parents would help him? They might be annoyed, wonder at her motives for helping a strange child make a mask. But there was something about the boy that touched her deeply, something about his anguish that reminded her of Marcus and his pain over his tiny son. Since Roland's birth she had changed, she thought. She'd become more compassionate – well, anyway towards children.

When she got back she found the boy had tidied away the wood and the tools and had found a stool for her to sit on. A jar of wallpaper paste and a brush stood ready on the bench.

'Well done, now let's start. Tell me your name first. I'm Miranda,' she said, giving him a friendly smile.

'Tom,' he said, smiling shyly back.

'Right, Tom. Blow up this balloon to the size of mask you want.' She handed him the balloon.

He looked puzzled, but did what he was told. He tied a knot in it and she began to tear up strips of newspaper. She pasted a piece and laid it on the balloon, then showed him how to layer it on, building it up over one half of the balloon.

'When it's dry we'll pop the balloon and you can put the mask on,' she explained to his delight.

He quickly got the hang of it and she showed him how to make slits for eyes, build up a mouth and then, when he said it could be a mask of anything, she suggested they make a punk with a Mohican haircut. That would be simple but effective.

'Yes,' he said laughing, 'and an earring.'

With a piece of thin card torn off the back of a packet found in the wallpaper box she showed him how to shape a ridge on the top of the head for his coxcomb of hair. They covered it with more paper, easily moulding it with the glue into shape. They were both laughing over it when a male voice made them jump.

'There you are, Tom. I've been looking for you everywhere.'

'Oh, Dad, look, my mask.' Reverently he picked it up and held it out to the man who approached them.

'It's wonderful, but . . .' He looked at Miranda.

Miranda felt suddenly rather claustrophobic. Tom's father was tall with brown hair and light eyes, quite unlike the child. He was half smiling, looking curiously at her, and for a moment she felt quite overwhelmed.

Then she found her tongue and said, 'Hello, I'm Miranda Farell. I'm staying at the cottage and I came across your son—'

'She helped me. The other mask wouldn't work. We hope this is going to be dry in time. She said she'd fetch her hair dryer and we hope to dry it off, even give it a coat of paint before I go back.' Tom was breathless with excitement and pride.

His father appeared not to know what to say.

'It's great,' he said awkwardly. He looked again at Miranda.

'I'm Jack Lambert, by the way,' he introduced himself. 'It's so dreadfully kind of you. I meant to help him yesterday but we were shooting and then people came in for drinks, and anyway, I'm no good at artistic things. I leave that to my wife.'

Miranda smiled at him, wondering why his wife hadn't helped Tom. Instead of being in the village shop, couldn't she have helped her child? Jonathan Corrin's words came back to her. 'That's her husband, poor bugger. She's such a flirt.'

She's a dreadful mother, too, she thought now, remembering with compassion how upset the boy had been with his feeble efforts earlier. How awful for such a young boy to be so tortured over a school task that he got up at dawn to do it as his parents hadn't the time to help him, or concern themselves over his anxiety.

Her impatience must have shown in her eyes, for Jack formally thanked her again and apologised for her having to give up her time.

'I had great fun doing it,' she said firmly, smiling at Tom, who looked uncomfortable at his father's words. 'I studied art at school, did "A" level, and haven't done anything like this for ages. It was my niece who taught me how to make a mask. We had a great weekend once, making things from papier mâché.'

'Will you fetch your hair dryer?' Tom asked tentatively.

'Now, Tom, I'm sure . . . Miranda,' Jack hesitated over her name, 'has other things to do. Your mother will have a hair dryer. Ask her.'

'I'll bring it over later. Leave it here for you.' Miranda had managed to get away from the close proximity of Jack and Tom, and near to the door.

'No, please—' his father protested.

'I'd like to. Goodbye.' She turned and left them, letting their thanks carry on after her. As she walked she thought how selfish some parents were, yet as she'd admitted to Tessa yesterday, she didn't feel she had the patience to give so much of her life to a child.

She found Simon, Tessa and Henry having breakfast in the kitchen.

'So what were you up to? Do tell,' Tessa said laughing.

'Give her time for breakfast first, darling,' Simon said, getting up to cook her some eggs and bacon.

As he cooked it, Miranda told them about Tom and the mask, but even as she protested about Tom's anguish and her compassion for him, it was his father she saw in her mind. He too, she felt, was suffering in his own way, though why she should care she could not tell.

Chapter Five

The west wing of Chandos Hall was shabby and draughty. Here and there stood wonderful pieces of furniture, some faded and cracked by the sun and needing attention. Oil paintings from various Italian and Dutch schools hung on the walls. The sofas and chairs were threadbare and the carpets – some Persian – were worn and badly patched. An atmosphere of melancholy, of memories of better times, lurked in the passages and in the dusty corners.

The family too, Jack thought, seemed like the last survivors of a dying race, tenaciously clinging on to their fading past with ever weakening fingers. Fate had played a mean trick by giving the last of the true Gillard-Hardings only one son, and one that preferred his own gender.

Some people, Jack knew, would rejoice at such a thing, would rather that Chandos Hall be turned into a refuge for battered women, or asylum seekers, than open its doors and lay out its treasures to be gawped at by the public. All the best treasures were in the main part of the house, now being done up by the National Trust ready to open to the public in a few months' time. The family made do with the remnants, beautiful remnants by most people's standards, but there was no money left to make their surroundings more in keeping with the elegance and grandeur of the house itself.

Sonia had been appalled at the place. She had thought that they would be staying in the main house, sleeping in a majestic bedroom once furnished for visiting royalty.

'It's so uncomfortable, like a boarding school, and the bathroom is icy. The bath water was cold before I'd even got undressed,' she complained the first time they went there. 'No wonder Ralph's wife left him.'

'There is no money, only land and possessions, and those they want to keep with the house as long as they can,' Jack told her. But there was something about the place that appealed to him and he felt a little irritated with her for making such a fuss. After all, many an otherwise comfortable country house had icy bathrooms.

He had written to Sir Quentin reminding him of his visits to Chandos Hall when his father was alive. He told him that they were looking at Pilgrim's Court as a school for their son, and could they drop by for a visit? Sir Quentin had written back a curt note stating they could come between two and four on the Saturday.

'Between meals,' Sonia said waspishly, who had imagined having lunch served by liveried staff in a sumptuous dining room, just as it had been when Jack was a child.

'It's probably difficult for him without a wife,' Jack said. They had gone and it had been an awkward visit with just the old man. He had looked at them keenly, reminding Jack of a bird of prey scrutinising the land with gimlet eyes, for a victim.

'Pilgrim's Court?' he'd said with disgust, glaring at Tom as if he expected him to go into a manic fit at any second. 'That's for simple children, isn't it? What's wrong with Eton? Never did us any harm.'

His heart sinking, Jack tried to explain about Tom's dyslexia. Sir Quentin was just like his grandfather, quite unable to understand such a condition. To them boys were either stupid or clever and in either case lazy, but there were no 'weaknesses' in their part of the family. Any that appeared – Tom's dyslexia, Ralph's homosexuality – had come from elsewhere, no doubt from some suspect relation on their wife's side.

Sir Quentin had listened to Jack's explanation with a disbelieving expression, but he never talked about it again. He'd asked them to stay the next time and again this weekend, and though he left them very much to their own devices, Jack thought that he liked to see them. He was probably lonely, with his few old retainers still hanging on like fossils of another age, his elderly dog and a son he despised. But now that the weather was getting colder, Sonia would probably refuse to come again.

He took Tom back to the Hall for breakfast, suggesting that he leave his mask on the bench to dry. He was tortured with a mixture of emotions. He felt ashamed that he hadn't helped Tom himself the day before, or hadn't noticed his obvious anxiety that made him wake up so early and struggle with making one on his own. Though that in itself, he argued to himself, surely showed that Tom had initiative and purpose, and had tried to do something on his own, instead of just opting out. But if he was honest he knew that his son's action had more to do with terror of not doing something he'd been set than initiative. Also, it was finding a stranger helping him that caused him concern. She, Miranda, a complete stranger, had recognised Tom's panic and had immediately come up with an easier way to make his mask. He had done it, no doubt with her help, but it was his pleasure, his joy in such an achievement, that smote at Jack's heart. One small gesture on the part of a stranger had unlocked for him doors that they, his parents, had not been able to open. He wondered if Miranda was a teacher, possessing skills he and Sonia did not have.

'Is she a teacher?' he asked Tom.

'No,' said Tom, scuffing his feet in the drive.

'What is she then, an artist?'

'No. Well, she paints sometimes when she has time. Tiny pictures, she said.' He would not look at Jack and Jack felt even more excluded. He wished he could get closer to his son, but he always seemed to blow it, not be there when he needed him, not be able to say the right thing. He felt jealous – yes, he recognised that – of this woman who in the course of one meeting had struck up such a rapport with Tom.

'I don't think it's fair to bother her any more over the mask,' he said firmly. 'After breakfast I'll help you dry it, whether with your mother's hair dryer or by putting it near the boiler, or even in a low oven in the Aga,' he said, suddenly thinking that a good idea.

'But I've got to paint it. Miranda thinks we might be able to paint all of it if I do it with water paints. I can varnish it at school.'

'We can do it here,' Jack said again.

Tom gave him a defiant look. '*She* said she wanted to help me. Not that she does really help me; she shows me how to do it then leaves me to do it on my own.' He ran through the door into the dark passage and on down to the dining room before Jack could answer him.

His mother and Sir Quentin were sitting together just finishing breakfast. Sir Quentin looked at him severely from under his bushy white eyebrows.

'You're late, boy. Been lying in bed?'

'N-no.' Tom looked quickly at his mother for moral support but not getting any, helped himself quickly and clumsily to corn flakes, spilling some on the table and the floor, which he desperately crammed back into the box, hoping no one had seen, before sitting down.

'He's been out, making a mask,' Jack said behind him.

'A mask? Whatever for?' Sonia said.

'I had to make one for school, you know I did,' Tom said desperately, keeping half an eye on the terrifying old man who was apt to erupt like a live volcano whenever he was displeased.

'There was a very nice woman helping him. She's staying at the cottage,' Jack went on, suddenly wanting to know who she was and hoping that Sir Quentin would tell him.

'Don't know who that can be,' the old man said. 'Don't see much of them, thank goodness. Thought it a good idea to ask the man . . . what's his name . . .' he frowned, 'Simon Gardiner, up to shoot, but I made it clear it was a one-off, not an invitation he could rely on.'

'I thought him very nice,' Jack said.

'Tolerable fellow, I suppose,' Sir Quentin said, and got up slowly and left the room, his ancient black Labrador, Troy, lumbering arthritically after him. In the passage outside he came across Ralph. Through the still open door the Lamberts heard him say, 'So when is that wife of yours coming back?'

'I don't know.' Ralph's voice was quiet.

'I want her back by the end of the month. You must insist you have your daughter back, here in her home and with her mother. Time doesn't wait, you know. You need a son and you need one now.'

Sonia and Jack exchanged glances. The first time they had heard Sir Quentin go for his son this way they had been horrified and embarrassed. But Sir Quentin seemed to carry on with his life, saying whatever he felt like, regardless of who was there. Ralph seemed used to it. He appeared to be so downtrodden that the only reason for his existence was to be the butt of his father's wrath.

Tom, who was used to being criticised too, always looked a little afraid and cornered himself when he heard these rows, shooting out frightened glances of sympathy towards Ralph, but never saying anything. Often he would creep away as if he were the next in line for Sir Quentin's anger.

Tom finished his corn flakes. 'They taste so old and dusty,' he'd confided to Jack the day before. 'I'm sure they've been there for ages. Did you see how faded the box is?'

'Have toast then,' Jack had said. All the food tasted dry and bland, boiled for hours by the elderly cook-housekeeper, who, Jack had discovered, put the lunch and dinner in the ancient Aga at breakfast time, taking it out when she remembered during the day.

'I'm going back to my mask. Miranda might be there,' Tom said, getting down from the table.

'Who is Miranda?' Sonia said, looking up from the newspaper.

'This person who helped me, I told you.'

'Oh, well don't be long and don't get dirty,' Sonia said.

'I really think, Tom—' Jack began.

'I won't be a nuisance,' Tom said, leaving the room quickly, squeezing past Sir Quentin and Ralph, who still stood in the passage – Ralph cowering against the wall and Sir Quentin demanding that he call his wife back to Chandos Hall at once.

Jack poured himself another cup of coffee. It was cold and sour.

'How long till church?' he asked Sonia, really more to make contact with her than because he wanted to know. He knew the service was at eleven o'clock and that the first time they had stayed here Sir Quentin had made it very clear that he expected his weekend guests to attend the service with him, 'to make up the numbers,' as he'd put it.

'I don't think I'm going,' Sonia said.

'But you must. We don't want to upset the old man.'

'It's too cold and that vicar's too boring. I'll make up the fire and stay here with the papers. I'll say I have a headache,' she said airily. 'Take Tom, though. He's nothing else to do and I don't want him hanging round asking me to entertain him.'

'He's busy with his mask and I feel badly that a strange woman is helping him, not us,' Jack said. 'I know he came out with us for a while shooting yesterday, but you should have known he had to make it and helped him.' His voice showed the annoyance he felt with himself.

'Don't be silly, Jack. No doubt this strange woman, as you call her, is bored too. Or is one of those insecure do-gooders who spend their lives helping others more insecure than themselves.' She shrugged. 'I'd leave her to help him.'

'She wasn't like that.' Jack had an instant picture of Miranda unfolding her elegant body from the stool she was sitting on, tossing back her glossy hair, giving Tom a dazzling smile. 'She—'

'Oh, Jack, leave it. I'm no good at messing about with paint and stuff,' Sonia said irritably.

'You are. Look at those pictures you used to do . . .'

'They are very different to the sort of thing a child makes for school,' she said scathingly. 'You go and help him if you feel you need to. But if I were you I'd leave him to this woman and be thankful he's so occupied.' She got up, folded the newspaper under her arm and left the room.

Jack felt let down by her, hurt that she did not want to help their son. Well, he would go and see what he could do. He finished his coffee and got up.

Ralph came in.

'Morning, Ralph,' he said cheerfully, pretending he hadn't heard the row going on outside.

'Good morning.' Ralph gave him a thin smile. 'I suppose everything's cold,' he said wearily as if he thought he didn't deserve anything better.

'It is a bit.' Jack didn't like to complain in someone else's house.

'I'll go and ask Mrs Pierce to heat it up for me,' he said, helping himself to some congealed bacon and egg that looked and tasted as if it had been cooked the night before.

Jack was about to leave and go in search of Tom when Ralph suddenly said, 'It must be rather awkward for you hearing my father go on so about Bunny, my wife.' He stood there, a slim, frail-looking man in his early forties, his pale brown hair thinning and greying, and more like soft fur than hair. His pale blue eyes, slightly bulbous, looked intently at Jack.

Jack looked away, embarrassed. He said, 'It must be awful for you putting up with it. Why do you live with him, not go and live somewhere of your own, or with your family?'

Ralph gave a sour laugh. 'Money, old chap. There isn't much. We had to give a hefty amount to the National Trust to take over this place, but it was the only way we could keep it. I have to help Father with the estate, and this seemed like a good home for my daughter.' He bit his lip, looked ashamed. 'The truth is, I'm stuck here.'

'But if you wanted to you could surely move . . . into the village even, or one of those cottages on the estate. You have a job in Salisbury, so you have a salary.' Jack couldn't understand the apathy of this man. 'You could practise as a solicitor in London just as well as here. Get right away.'

'I could, but I want to keep an eye on the place. I will inherit it, after all, and I love it.' His eyes went soft. 'I know Sonia doesn't think much of it, nor does Bunny. It was all right when we lived in the main house, though she complained about the cold and the bathrooms, but now we've been forced to move here. She doesn't like it at all.'

Jack smiled sympathetically, but thought that probably Bunny had also wanted a heterosexual man as a husband. He said, 'Will she come back, and your daughter? How old is she?'

'Amelia is seven. She spends her holidays with me, but we have to look for a proper school for her now. Bunny will bring her back herself – she'd never let her travel alone – and stay a few days, but I don't think she'll live here again.' He stared at his plate of bacon and eggs as if they held the key to his life. 'Father is difficult to live with too, so there is a lot for her to put up with.' He looked straight at Jack as he said this as if to challenge him to ask him about his sexuality.

Jack hadn't the nerve. He said, 'It must be a terrible strain feeling you have to produce a son. It's ridiculous in this day and age that a daughter can't inherit. Often a girl would be far better to hold everything together than her brother or some distant male relative that doesn't know and love the place.'

'It is mad. Amelia is a serious child and she loves it here. I might even produce a son who is a gambler or a drug addict and loses it all, or wants to live abroad, sell up. She wouldn't, I'm sure of it.' He sighed. 'Still, there it is.' He waved his plate at Jack. 'Must go and get this heated up or I'll be late for church.'

He left the room and Jack heard him calling for Mrs Pierce, his voice sounding lonely in the dark passage, like someone calling out for reassurance rather than a hot breakfast.

Jack walked slowly back to the outhouses to find Tom. There had been talk over the years from various governments about changing the law of inheritance to include daughters if there were no sons in the immediate family. The law may well be changed in time for Amelia to inherit Chandos Hall, or Ralph might yet succeed in having a son.

When Jack had told Sonia about the family she had said, 'Might not you inherit it? Your father was their cousin, after all.'

Jack had laughed and pointed out that apart from Ralph, who being just over forty, had plenty of time to produce a son, there were two other male contenders, one living in Australia, who must be quite old by now but had probably got sons, and another cousin not much older than Jack himself, whom he'd never met but knew existed.

'Funny you never bothered to keep in touch with them,' Sonia had said, rather bored now, knowing that her husband would never be a baronet.

'I told you, there was a family feud and my great-grandfather changed his name. The Lamberts have never had anything to do with the Gillard-Hardings, except that Quentin was kind to my father,' Jack had explained. 'I think it was his wife who liked him but after she died and my father died, the invitations just petered out,' he'd smiled, 'and now we're reviving the link. Funny how life turns out.'

'I hope Tom will learn enough at Pilgrim's Court to pass Common Entrance into some normal school. Then there'll be no need to go back there,' Sonia had retorted. She didn't like the place or the family, and seeing that there was no hope of Jack inheriting it, she saw no point in enduring it all.

Now Jack reached the old stable and went in. To his surprise his heart gave a little lift when he saw Miranda sitting there, holding the mask while Tom waved the hair dryer at it. A small boy was fiddling with something in a corner and Jack's heart sank back. No doubt it was her child. No wonder she was good with children if she had one of her own. He smiled.

'How's it going?'

'Very well, Dad. Miranda thinks we'll be able to paint it. She's got some paint from the people she's staying with. Quick-drying emulsion. It's white but we're going to mix in some red and yellow from my paint-box.'

'We hope to do a coat before you go to church, but it is still quite damp,' she said, smiling up at him.

Jack swallowed. She had such an open, honest face. Pretty too, with large blue eyes and a wide, smiling mouth. The room felt suddenly rather cramped, crowded, yet he felt drawn to her, wanted to sit down beside her. He looked away, disconcerted at these feelings.

Tom said, 'Do you like it? Dad?'

'Very much.' Jack gave him a tight smile. 'It's very good. So kind of you to help him when you must be so busy,' he said, half looking at the small boy in the corner, not liking to use her name in case he made it sound too intimate.

'I'm not so busy,' she said. 'I've enjoyed it. Turn it off now, Tom. Let's see how dry it is.' He turned off the hair dryer and she stroked her hand over the paper mask. 'It's still a bit damp, but we'll risk it. Have you mixed the paint? Good, I'll leave you to do it then, with your father.'

She got up and called to Henry, who, stuffing the bits of wood he'd found in his pocket, came over to her. 'Just paint it all over in that colour. You can paint the lips and hair bit and eyebrows over it when it's dry. That should be by this afternoon.'

'Will you help me?' Tom said slightly desperately, as if he didn't want her to go.

Jack felt he didn't want her to go either, but he said, 'Now, Tom, we can finish it together. It is so kind of . . . ummh, Miranda to give you so much of her time.'

'Not at all, but if you do finish it and have time before you go, pop over to the cottage and show me. The Gardiners won't mind, but we're going out to lunch and won't be back much before four.' She gave a wave and was gone, holding Henry by the hand.

The stable seemed empty and chilly when she'd gone, and Jack sat down where she had been sitting as if he could catch a little of her vitality and keep it, but he could not. He tried to show an interest in Tom's mask.

Tom splashed the paint over the paper, making Jack jump away and exclaim, 'Do be careful, Tom! Don't ruin my trousers.'

'Sorry, Dad, but don't you think it's good?' Tom said carelessly, swishing paint about over the mask, the bench, the floor, his face glowing with excitement.

Watching him Jack felt a surge of love for him, joy that he had found something that pleased his son so. The love seemed to surge over into warm feelings for Miranda, then they were hastily shot down by guilt. He was overreacting, confusing gratitude for something more. He was married; so, no doubt, was she, or anyway romantically involved. She was just a kind woman helping a child, that was all.

To his surprise, Miranda was not at church which disappointed him. They sat at the front in the Gillard-Harding family pew and each time he heard the heavy door of the church open, Jack found a reason to turn round, hoping it was Miranda. It was, he told himself firmly, a good thing that she was not here. He was making too much of his feelings of gratitude. If she had been plain and the wrong side of forty, he wouldn't have given her a second thought.

Tom worked on his mask all afternoon. Jack had to agree it was wonderful: a pale-faced man with red lips and a blue and green coxcomb in the centre of his shaved head. Tom had even painted in tiny black specks as stubble on his bare scalp. Jack was as proud as Tom was as they showed it to Sonia, Ralph and Sir Quentin at teatime.

'Very, very good,' Ralph said. 'What a talent you have, Tom. You could make special effects for films.'

Tom blushed happily. 'I could, couldn't I? Make all those space monsters, and dinosaurs like in *Jurassic Park*?'

'Absolutely,' Ralph said.

'Very good. Is it a clown?' Sir Quentin said.

'No, a punk.'

'Oh. I know, those painted layabouts who disfigure themselves. Waste of space, they are, if you ask me,' Sir Quentin barked as if by making one, Tom approved of that way of life.

'Did you do it all by yourself?' Sonia said.

'Yes. Well, Miranda showed me how to do it, but she said I must make it by myself or it wouldn't be fair on the others in my class. Do you like it, Mum?' Tom held his breath.

'Was it her idea? I mean, you could have done an animal, or the sun or Medusa with her snakes for hair,' said Sonia, feeling guilty that she hadn't helped him herself.

'I think it's wonderful,' Jack broke in, knowing how Sonia sometimes hated someone else to have the limelight and, apart from feeling guilty at not helping Tom, she was also feeling jealous at the attention and admiration Miranda was getting, on account of Tom's achievement.

Tom said, 'I'm just going to the cottage to show Miranda. She wanted to see it.' He paused, gave Jack an agonised look. 'Want to come, Dad?'

One of the symptoms of Tom's dyslexia was finding his way about. He often got confused, taking wrong turnings and getting lost. Jack knew this and realised that the only reason Tom wanted him to come with him was so that he wouldn't get lost.

'Oh, darling, you don't need to go out again,' Sonia said.

'But I promised,' Tom said.

'I'll take him. We must leave soon, so I'll see he doesn't stay long,' Jack said at the same time.

It was dusk now as they walked together through the garden, then the yard with its outhouses and on in the direction of the cottage. Neither of them talked until they saw the lights from the cottage up ahead, and asked each other if that was the right one. Tom knocked on the door.

Simon opened it, then said with a smile, 'Jack, Tom and a mask, come in. Miranda said you might call.'

He took them into a sitting room. No one was there. 'I'll call her; she's packing, I think. Do sit. Sorry about the mess, Henry's been playing. My,' he smiled at Tom, 'that's some mask.'

He left the room and they heard him calling for Miranda. Jack looked round the warm, book-lined room, littered with toys. Henry must be that small boy he'd thought was Miranda's. He felt a strange sense of relief, but he wished suddenly that they hadn't come. She was leaving, about to go back to her life; the mask-making had been a pleasant diversion, not something she would think of again. She would be irritated by their intrusion, delaying her departure.

They heard footsteps coming down the stairs, her voice say to Simon, 'Thanks, Simon. The boot's unlocked. I'll set off straight away and hope not to be caught in any jams.' She opened the door and came in smiling.

'Oh, that is wonderful! Well done, Tom.' She smiled at him, then looked again admiringly at the mask. 'You have a great talent,' she said. 'You must do more of it. You know you can make all sorts of things from papier mâché.'

Tom's face was radiant as he looked up at her. 'Thank you for helping me,' he said.

'I loved it, and you are so talented. Are you often staying down here?' She glanced up and caught Jack's eyes, then looked quickly back again at Tom.

'I go to school nearby, at Pilgrim's Court. We come here sometimes, if I only have a short weekend,' Tom said.

'Well, next time you come tell Tessa and Simon how you're getting on and they'll tell me. I'd love to know,' she smiled.

'Won't you be here again?' Tom asked the question Jack longed to ask.

'I have so much to do I might not be here again for ages, or it might be a weekend when you're not here,' Miranda explained. 'I'll send you a postcard to Pilgrim's Court, telling you next time I'm coming.'

'Thanks, I'd like that.'

She smiled at him, said, 'I must go now, back to London. Good luck and well done.' She patted Tom's shoulder, shot him another smile, calling as she went, 'Don't forget to tell Tessa and Simon how you get on.' She went out into the night with Simon and Tessa following her to see her on her way.

Jack, who had known it would be like this, felt bereft. He saw that she had left some of her radiance with Tom, who glowed with a pride he hadn't seen in him before.

Chapter Six

It was during the Christmas holiday that Miranda realised that her father no longer loved her mother. The cold realisation that it really was true and not something in her imagination hit her like an iceberg as they slumped in the drawing room after lunch on Boxing Day.

There was the feeling of anticlimax often experienced after the Christmas festivities coupled with indigestion after too much feasting. Marcus was asleep in his chair. The baby kept them up most nights and Sally was away somewhere feeding him yet again. Miranda's mother was reading and her father barely sat down with them to drink his coffee before getting up and leaving the room without saying anything.

It was during lunch – cold turkey, ham and baked potatoes, a diet they would follow in some form or other for many days to come – that Sally, in the bright voice people use when they know what they are going to say will cause controversy, announced, 'I've decided to give up my job. Since having Roland and so nearly losing him, I want to stay at home and look after him.'

'But . . . ?' Miranda looked from Sally to Marcus, knowing that their large house and the antiques business relied heavily on Sally's hefty salary.

'Quite right, a mother should be at home with her children. There wouldn't be nearly so much crime if mothers stayed at home and looked after them,' Julia said. She had stayed at home herself, really because she had married young with no qualifications and somehow had never thought it worth her while to acquire any.

'Really, Julia, what a ridiculous, old-fashioned idea. The women of today have a good education, want to do more with their talents,' Richard, who had, Miranda realised, drunk quite a lot, snapped at his wife, acute dislike for her in his eyes.

Miranda was shocked at the derisory tone in his voice. For a moment she thought she'd been mistaken but he went on, 'The rise in crime has many causes: bad education, poverty, lax morals, the weakness of the Church. A mother can still be a good mother if she works, and after all Sally was going to employ a nanny, a proper one. Sally is a very competent woman; she could have done it all.'

The way he said it sounded as if he thought that Julia was at fault for *not* doing it all.

Sally, not expecting this reaction, said quickly, shooting agonised looks in Miranda and Marcus's direction: 'I think Julia is right, children should be looked after by their parents if possible, for a while anyway. When Roland starts school I may go back to work, but just now, after all the trauma and worry that he . . .' she paused, her eyes filling with tears, 'that he wouldn't make it, I just don't want to leave him to someone else, however good they are. Marcus has to be in the shop. He can't be with him all the time.'

Julia looked hurt, her mouth going sour. She said defiantly, 'Children need parents. If they're left to run riot in the streets because their parents, or at least these days more likely their unmarried teenage mothers, are elsewhere, they commit crimes.' She glared at Richard as if the only reason their children were not behind bars was because she had stayed at home with them.

Richard shot her another look of dislike, sighing heavily. 'There have always been families like that, who can't cope,' he said wearily.

Marcus, who hated scenes, said quickly, 'I'm glad Sally's made this decision and it was hers entirely. It will be tough financially, not that money is everything, but we'll cope.'

'You could do bed and breakfasts, your house is big enough,' Miranda said quickly to steer the conversation away from her parents' animosity. She felt quite ill at the look of dislike in her father's face. She'd known about his changed feelings for her mother for ages if she'd been honest with herself, but she'd hidden the knowledge away carefully in the recesses of her mind like something shameful.

Her father had become increasingly bored with her mother since he had become semi-retired. Being stuck together so much, without the children around, grated on him. He was irritated by Julia's constant fussing; her theories and platitudes, the way she tried to include him in such mundane activities as doing the weekly shop in the supermarket or getting involved with the village politics and scandals.

Since he had stopped taking the train every day to the City he had become more and more bad-tempered, and her mother had counteracted this by becoming more and more convinced that he needed to be occupied. But changing the cut and thrust of the stock market for the dreary excitement of cut-price offers in the local supermarket, or debating what mourners could put on the tombstones of their departed relatives, was hardly in the same league. Both of them were suffering dreadfully, though both were too proud to admit it. Miranda realised that it was wrecking their marriage.

She looked now at her mother, who was reading the Christmas issue of *Tatler*. She peered at the photographs of the parties and weddings, every so often saying to no one in particular things like, 'Goodness, doesn't Susan look old? And what a hat!' Or, 'Pity William's daughter has inherited his looks. Her mother was so pretty.'

Miranda assumed that her father was in his study, which as far as she could see was almost where he lived. He had been touchingly pleased to see his family and had hoped that his son would go shooting with him, play a round or two of golf, talk with him, but Marcus, exhausted by fatherhood and trying to run his business on a few hours' sleep, and now not so much money, had not the energy nor the time to give to his father.

Julia had offered to feed the baby one night but to her Christmas was a great event: the house had to be painstakingly decorated; enormous meals prepared; the neighbours asked in; the carol singers from the local church accommodated with mulled wine and mince pies. Sally had been afraid that Julia would sleep through Roland's cries and she knew that she would hardly sleep herself, worrying over this, so she declined as tactfully as she could, thinking it less trouble to feed him herself.

Miranda, rather ashamed at being so tired just because she'd been to so many parties, offered to do her bit, and tonight she was to have Roland in her room. She felt rather afraid as he was still so small, and images of cot death and his choking on his bottle filled her mind, but Sally and Marcus were so tired and so needed one whole night's sleep that she said nothing of her fears.

'How long can you stay, darling?' Her mother put down her magazine and looked at her.

'I must go back Sunday night. I work on Monday. Then I'm off skiing the week after.'

'But what about New Year? I'd hoped you'd stay until then.'

'I can't, Ma.' Miranda felt guilty, believing that perhaps if she could stay longer her parents' marriage might recover. She would be there as a buffer between them, as an interest they could both focus on instead of their boredom with each other. 'I'm going to a party. You remember James Darby? He's giving one.'

'I knew his mother. Such a nice young man. Is he married?' Julia pretended nonchalance, but Miranda wasn't fooled.

'No, but I think he's got a girlfriend,' she said hurriedly, not wanting her mother to start on why she didn't marry him; such a nice young man with a good job, and so on, as if that was all that mattered for a marriage partner.

'Oh, anyone I know? Most of your girl friends are married now with children.' She could not hide the disappointment in her voice.

Without thinking Miranda said, 'Oh, some married woman, I think.' She had a sudden image of Jack Lambert and remembered how his wife, Sonia, had monopolised James at that summer party. The gossip had filtered down among her group of friends that James was having an affair with Sonia.

'A *married* woman!' Julia looked shocked. 'Are you sure? That's not like him at all. I can't imagine his mother putting up with it.'

Miranda sank inside. If only she hadn't mentioned James. Her mother would now not leave it alone. She would demand why James wanted a married woman when she, Miranda, was single and would suit him far better. She would want to know every detail of this woman's marriage. Miranda threw a sharp glance at Marcus slumbering in his chair, willing him to wake up and change the conversation, but he slept on.

'I don't know anything about it, Mummy. It's none of my business,' she said firmly. 'Now tell me about the Patons. Did they buy that house in the end?'

'Yes, full of dry rot,' Julia said impatiently. 'But, dear, as such a friend of his, isn't it your duty to say something? I mean, has this woman children? And what about her husband? Where's he in all this? Having an affair too, I suppose. Really, today people have the morals of the farmyard.' She was tired after all her hectic Christmas arrangements, disappointed that her pretty, clever daughter was not married, nor even had a steady boyfriend. Even that plain Paton daughter had married and was now expecting a child, and her mother kept boasting about it in her smug way as they did the church flowers together.

'It is none of my business, and maybe it's over. I don't know, nor do I care. I like James, but that's it. I'm not attracted to him in the least.'

'There's too much emphasis on sex these days,' Julia went on, her mouth tight. 'There is so much more to marriage, and that side of things, well . . .' She looked awkward and Miranda felt ill again. She really didn't want to discuss sex with her mother.

'What are you two talking about?' Marcus yawned, sat up.

'Not much,' Miranda said, relieved that he was awake.

'It's James Darby.' Julia, now with her teeth in the matter, held on with the tenacity of a terrier with a bone.

'Oh, James, haven't seen him for ages. What's he up to?' When Marcus had lived in London he too had seen quite a lot of James.

'He's having an affair with a married woman,' Julia said disapprovingly.

'Trust old James. He hates commitment,' Marcus said.

'That's no excuse,' Julia went on, about to launch into a lecture on morality and the value of commitment.

'Anyone we know?' Marcus said, stretching out his legs.

'Not really . . . They met at Jonathan and Anna Corrin's party, and I met the husband and child at the Gardiners',' Miranda said to him, suddenly wanting to talk about Jack, but knowing if she showed any enthusiasm about him her mother would pick it up at once. She'd liked him, found herself often thinking of him, though she hadn't seen him again.

She'd written to Tom and had a scrawled letter back that she could hardly read. She'd told herself she was writing to him because she'd promised and he was a child and you didn't let children down if you could help it. But really it was Jack she'd thought of, wondered if he would read her postcard and think of her. Though of course it was only a foolish daydream, a fantasy as she had no other man to concentrate on at the moment. Although she was irritated by her mother's views on morality, she did not believe in infidelity in marriage, nor would she ever have an affair with a married man, especially if there were children in the marriage.

'So who are they?' Marcus asked her.

'I think they're called Lambert,' Miranda said slowly, feeling that she shouldn't have mentioned their name. She suddenly wondered if her mother knew them and would somehow make trouble by informing their parents as if they were underage children.

To her relief Julia did not seem to know them, but Marcus said, 'I knew a Lambert at school. Brilliant cricketer, could have played for England. John, no Jack. That's right, Jack Lambert,' he smiled, remembering. 'He played cricket like a dream. He almost won all our matches single-handed.'

'It may be him. Have you seen him since?' Miranda asked, feeling a sudden closeness to Marcus as he knew Jack too.

'Don't think so.' He frowned, trying to think. 'Nice chap, year older than me.'

Miranda waited for him to say more, but Julia broke in, 'I think it's a disgrace, and if you know James, Marcus, perhaps you should say something about him having an affair with a married woman.'

'Mother, I haven't seen him for years. Heavens,' he laughed, 'London, parties and scandals are another life. I can't help what they get up to, nor do I care.'

'What don't you care about, darling?' Sally came in with the baby. Marcus held out his arms to them. Sally put Roland in them and sat on the arm of his chair leaning against him.

'He drank four ounces,' she said fondly, putting her finger in Roland's tiny hand.

'Good boy.' Marcus beamed at his son.

Seeing them sitting there, this small devoted family, Miranda felt a pang of love, of envy. For this moment they were happy, content, she thought. After so much pain and anguish they had a living child; they were complete. But nothing stayed the same, life moved on and changed like the seasons of the year. Had her parents once loved each other so completely, sat in an aura of wonder with their babies? And if they had, how had it broken, where had it gone?

Dimly she heard them all talking about London and past scandals. She suspected that her mother's high moral tone was now exaggerated by her unhappiness at her failing marriage. If she'd behaved herself in difficult circumstances, why shouldn't everyone else? Miranda felt saddened by it, suspecting this attitude would make her mother more unlovable to her father and possibly to people further afield who, perhaps ashamed of their own weaknesses, did not want moral teaching from their neighbours. Love was so elusive, Miranda mused sadly. Once caught it could never be relied upon.

She thought again of Jack and Sonia, wondering if they too had once loved each other, still loved each other. She felt suddenly depressed at the difficulty of relationships. She railed inside herself over why they couldn't stay static, stay as they were at their best, why such intense feelings could so easily be lost. It was as if they disappeared without one realising, as if the stress and activities of life took over and suffocated love, until it was too late to find it again.

She was better on her own, she thought, not for the first time. She had good friends and a loving family. Even if her parents' marriage seemed to be floundering, she knew her parents loved her. She had nephews and nieces, friends' children to watch grow up without the heartache. Surely it was better to be like this than watch a love disintegrate, become dead and dull through the mundane passage of domestic life.

Marcus said suddenly, 'I want a walk. I've eaten far too much. Anyone coming? Is it too cold for Roland?'

The mood broke as if a pebble had been thrown through the skin of a pond. They discussed whether the air was too damp for the baby, where they would go, whether Richard would come. Miranda embraced the new topic with relief, chasing away her feelings of depression: life was for living, not for analysing. Let it take what course it would with her.

Chapter Seven

The snow in Verbier was good, the air sharp and clear. Passing aeroplanes left white trails like chalk marks across the blue sky. Miranda felt exhilarated as she followed her friends down the busy slope. She paused for a moment, smiling at Davina, who had stopped and was tipping her face up to the sun.

'I know I'll look like a crocodile and probably get skin cancer but I do like to go back with a little colour in my face,' she said.

'We looked so white and drawn when we first came out,' Miranda agreed.

A group of children shot by after an instructor. One stopped, pushing up his goggles. He stared at her, then said tentatively, 'Miranda, it is you, isn't it?'

She squinted into the sun, staring back at him. It was Tom Lambert. Involuntarily her eyes shot up the mountain as if expecting to see Jack coming behind him.

Tom said, 'How funny to see you here. Where are you staying?'

She was tongue-tied suddenly, thrown by the unexpectedness of meeting him here. Then seeing the group of other boys he was skiing with all jostling and ragging with each other, she supposed he was with a school party. This she put to him.

He laughed. 'No, it's the holidays. I'm here with Mum and Dad and some friends. We're staying at the bottom of the Rouge in a big chalet. Will you come and see us? It's called Le Golf.'

'Tom, Tom, 'urry up,' the ski instructor called to him.

'Got to go. Do come.' He pushed down his goggles and with a wave was off chasing the others down the slope.

'Some young admirer of yours, Miranda?' Piers, Davina's fiancé, joined them.

'Just a boy I met when I stayed with Tessa and Simon,' she smiled, but realised that her heart was thumping. She looked again at the white slope crowded with skiers in their bright clothes, hearing the scraping of ski boards and skis against the snow. She wondered if at any moment she would see Jack. For the rest of the day she looked for him although she pretended to herself that she was not. Tom had said he was here with both of his parents so no doubt they were together.

She knew that James Darby wasn't out here, but maybe he'd moved on from his affair with Jack's wife. He never stayed with the same woman for long.

At the end of the day Miranda's party ended up at the bottom of the Rouge. There were quite a few chalets scattered here. Miranda looked out for Tom's, half hoping to see Jack arriving back from his day's skiing. Piers and Davina called for her to hurry as the bus was coming down the road so she had no time to look properly. Just as well, she thought, as she took off her skis and ran across the road to the bus stop. Sonia might have been there and it would have been awkward having to explain who she was in the absence of Tom and Jack.

'You're very quiet this evening, Miranda,' David March, single and, Miranda suspected, invited to join the party by Davina and Piers for her benefit, said to her as they all sat round in the living room, finishing their wine after supper.

She smiled at him. He was nice enough, but not someone she wanted to start anything with. 'I'm just tired. We had a pretty good day today, didn't we?'

'That we did.' He launched into a description of his day. He had got up early and skied off piste with Piers, then had joined the girls for lunch.

'Anyone feel like going to the Farm Club?' Piers said.

Miranda, who felt deliciously lazy after her day's exercise, did not feel like it but she wondered if Jack would be there. Then she thought, even if he was what good would it do? She wished now that he wasn't out here. There was no point in seeing him. He had been pleased and grateful when she had helped his son, that was all. It was ridiculous not being able to get him out of her head. She must stop at once behaving like some moony teenager, imagining there was or ever could be anything else between them. He was an attractive man, why not admit it? But the world was full of attractive men and it was unfortunate that so many of them were spoken for already.

'I don't think I will, I'm for an early night,' she said.

'Me too,' Davina said, cuddling up to Piers. 'Come on, darling, let's go to bed. We want to get up early tomorrow.'

'I think we'll go,' Michael and Carol said. They had met recently and loved to be part of the scene wherever they went. Miranda found them rather exhausting.

'I'll come too,' David said. 'Can I really not persuade you, Miranda?'

'I won't be much of a companion. I really do feel tired,' she smiled, not wanting to hurt his feelings but determined now that she didn't want to go and risk seeing Jack. She also admitted that she didn't want to see him dancing close to his wife.

'I'll come,' Jane, another single girl, said.

'So will I,' Fergus said. He was also single but rather keen on the chalet girl, Emma, instead of Jane, who had her eye on him. He went into the kitchen where she was washing up the supper to ask her if she'd join them.

Miranda left them all to do what they wanted and went to bed. She lay there in the dark wondering if she would see Jack, and how the meeting would go if she did. There were two days left until she returned home. Verbier was enormous, and although many of the British went to the same places to eat and dance, many others, especially if they had children, stayed in their chalets or visited other friends' chalets. She might easily miss him. It would be best if she did, she thought – stopped wasting time thinking about him. If only she could fall for someone like David, or even Fergus, then she'd forget about Jack altogether. But the truth was she hadn't met anyone she felt attracted to since she'd split up with Andrew. Perhaps too, she thought, the gilt on her new independent life in her own flat was wearing a little thin, especially seeing all her girl friends happy with their men.

To her annoyance her mother's voice broke into her thoughts: 'The longer you wait to settle down the more difficult you'll find it. All the nice men will have been snapped up and you'll be left with the dregs.'

Although she knew by 'dregs' her mother meant divorced men and men from, to her mind, dubious families, which Miranda herself would not mind if she loved them, she felt there was some truth in the remark. But there was no point in starting to worry. Love didn't happen to order. She put the thought firmly from her mind and went to sleep.

The next day dawned brilliant. The sky was dazzling and the snow crisp and sparkling. Miranda was glad she'd gone to bed early and looked forward to a long day's skiing. Those who had been to the Farm Club the night before were rather the worse for wear but they all managed to get on the ski lift and up the mountain before the ski schools arrived and held them up.

They went all the way up to Mont Fort and finished with a few runs on the glacier, the snow like silk under their skis.

'This is magic. Let's have a late lunch at the Cabine de Mont Fort,' Piers suggested, and they all agreed.

The wooden cabin was set on a ridge in a nest of peaks with wonderful views. It was small and rustic, with some benches outside, and simple food. To get up the hill to where it stood meant skiing very fast down the slope before it rose up to the restaurant, so arriving as near to it as possible without having to walk.

Miranda caught an edge as she was shooting down the slope,

which made her wobble but not fall, but it slowed her up enough to make her have a long and hot climb to the top. She was exhausted in the thin air, red-faced and breathing heavily as she at last arrived at the restaurant. David greeted her.

'What bad luck. It's a tough climb. Let me help you with your skis.'

'Thanks,' she gasped, grateful for his arm. She took off her skis and he stacked them for her with the others that stood like coloured pencils in the snow.

He linked arms with her and they made their way to the benches behind the cabin to join the others.

'Let's hope there's some room. I'm starving,' he said.

'I'm so thirsty,' Miranda gasped. Her chest still hurt from her laboured breathing; she was not as fit as she thought. They rounded the cabin to look for a table and the first person she saw was Jack.

He was sitting at one of the wooden tables with a group of people, the debris of a meal around him. He looked up just as she and David came round the side, arm in arm, she, in her exhaustion, slightly leaning on him. For a long moment they both stared at each other. Miranda felt herself blushing and turned away a moment, annoyed with herself but hoping she was coloured enough already from her climb for anyone to notice.

Piers had got them a table and called them over. David answered him and pulled her with him.

Just before she passed Jack she heard him say, 'Miranda.'

She stopped. 'Hello.'

David stopped too and looked at the people at the table, who were now all studying them. 'Friends of yours?' he said.

She didn't answer him and David let go of her arm and went over to Piers, calling out for him to hurry up and order some drinks.

'How nice to see you again,' Jack said. 'Tom said he'd met you yesterday.'

'Yes, I was pleased to see him,' she said, firmly taking herself in hand, telling herself that her breathlessness and thumping heart were due solely to the hectic climb she'd just had to the restaurant.

'Jack, introduce us, do.' She saw it was Sonia, remembering her from the Corrins' party, who turned round and faced her. She looked wonderful in a cherry-red suit, her hair glossy, so neat, as if she was just a model posing for a fashion shoot. She made Miranda feel even more dishevelled than she had before.

Jack said nothing, just gazed at Miranda, so she said, 'I'm Miranda Farell. I know Tom.'

'Really?' Sonia said, looking her up and down coldly. 'Of course, you helped Tom with his mask. He went on about it yesterday.' She smiled at her friends in an amused way as if to ridicule the foibles of a child.

One of the men sitting at the table smiled at her. 'He seemed very fond of you,' he said.

'She did a wonderful job,' Jack said, also smiling at her.

'What do you want to drink, Miranda?' Piers, who was rather loud, called over to her.

'I'm coming.' She gave them a quick smile, not looking directly at Jack, and moved to join her party.

Jack said quickly, 'Do come in for a drink, if you're passing. Tom would love to see you. Are you free tonight?'

'I don't suppose she is and you know Tom, darling, he'll be out on the toboggan with the others. It will be so boring for her.' Sonia threw out a smile to everyone as if to say that they too would be bored having to have Miranda for a drink.

But the man who had spoken before said, 'Yes, do come, even if Tom is not there. We have a sort of open house before supper. Bring your friends too.' He gestured towards her table. 'Any time after seven. Gives us a chance to get back and have a bath. Do you know where we are?' His smile was genuinely friendly. Sonia looked furious.

Jack said, 'Do all come. Benedict loves a party.'

He smiled towards Benedict, who said, 'Too right I do. So you'll come, I take it?'

'Thank you, I'll ask the others,' Miranda said.

'Even if they're busy you come.' Benedict winked at her, and began to tell her exactly where the chalet was.

David came over to her and smiled at everyone. 'Let me order for you,' he said to her. Miranda noticed that both Jack and Benedict looked a little enviously at him. Sonia gave him a huge smile.

'I'm sure we've interrupted your plans for tonight,' she said. 'Benedict is such a party animal, he's invited you all for a drink with us, but I'm sure that's the last thing you want to do.'

'Oh, how kind. I can't speak for the others but,' he turned to Miranda, 'are you going?'

'Yes she is,' Benedict said, and before Sonia could say any more Benedict had got up, introduced himself to the rest of Miranda's group and got assurances from them all that they would come for a drink that evening.

The Lamberts' party left soon after, calling out cheerfully to Miranda's friends as they went.

Piers said immediately to Miranda, 'Friends from home?'

'Not really,' Miranda said, and explained about Tom.

She was aware that Davina was watching her carefully and later, when they went to the loo together, Davina said, 'I didn't know you were so interested in doing handicrafts with children, Miranda.'

Miranda blushed. 'It was just one of those things. I came across him and he was so desperate . . .'

'So, I think, is his father. His father was the one nearest to us, wasn't he? The nice-looking one with brown hair?'

'There were two men nearest us,' Miranda said lamely. 'The one called Benedict fancies himself with women, I could see that at once.'

'So could I. I mean the other one, who was looking at you so intently. Are you sure there's not more to this, Miranda?' she asked smiling.

'Of course not,' Miranda snapped, putting on more lip balm in front of the tiny mirror. 'He's married, his wife was there.'

'So?'

'I do not believe in affairs with married men, Davina,' she said primly. 'Anyway, it's nothing like that. His son is dyslexic and I think Jack feels guilty and unhappy about it, and was pleased that I discovered, quite by chance I may say, something that he was good at.'

Davina gave her a hug. 'OK, OK, I'll say no more.'

'Please don't,' Miranda said firmly, imagining the commotion if Davina made everyone think there was something going on between her and Jack. 'I hardly know him and really there is nothing between us, so don't make out there is. It's the boy I feel so sorry for.'

'Be happy, you deserve it,' Davina said to her, touching her arm. She left her, and Miranda could hear her calling for Piers, asking him where he had put her skis.

For the rest of the day Miranda felt rather queasy. She was nervous of seeing Jack again this evening and dreading seeing Sonia, who she realised had taken an instant dislike to her. She wondered if she disliked her because she was one of those women who did not like their own sex, who saw all other women as threats and did not bother with them, or if she was jealous of the help she had given her son.

She thought of Sally, who, quite understandably in the circumstances, didn't want to give over her precious baby to another woman to nurture.

'It's also a bit of jealousy too,' Sally had said to her, when they talked further of her giving up her career, 'I just don't want him giving his first smile, his first word to another woman. It's something that never occurred to me before, but I can remember my nanny saying to my mother, "Show Mummy your picture. Tell Mummy what we've done today," in a sort of smug, boastful way. I couldn't bear that to happen with my child.'

Perhaps Sonia was jealous of Tom liking her. Perhaps she felt that it should have been her to have helped him with his mask. Then why hadn't she? Miranda thought crossly. What had she been doing all that weekend?

They arrived at the Lamberts' chalet just after seven. Benedict seemed to be in charge, introducing everyone, thrusting drinks at them. Tom hung about in the corner of the room and when he saw Miranda he came shyly over.

'Tom,' she smiled, 'it is so nice to see you. How's it all going?'

He wrinkled his nose, scuffed his feet, looked at the floor. 'All right, I s'pose.'

'I thought you skied awfully well,' she said, guessing that he didn't want to talk about school.

'Thanks,' he flushed, looking pleased.

Benedict came up with a bottle of champagne which he tried to force on her.

'No, really,' she said, 'I've got plenty.'

'Don't like to see a girl who can't drink,' he said petulantly. Miranda realised he had put away quite a bit himself.

'So,' he said, pushing himself closer to her, pushing out Tom, 'how long are you out here?'

'Just until the weekend.' She tried to move away but the room was full of furniture and she was penned in against him and a huge dresser laden with heavy pewter pots. She felt overwhelmed with his bulk and the large furniture trapping her. She tried to move into the centre of the room, but he stood in front of her.

'Shame. You must come out with us, dancing, drinking. Have a good time.' He waved the bottle at her. 'Drink up, there's a good girl.'

She felt nauseated by him. She recognised the type, unhappy, no doubt, but determined to drown it by snatching at what he could from life, craving attention with bluster and copious alcohol.

She turned back to Tom and said, 'Done any more with papier mâché, Tom?'

'Papier mâché? What's that when it's at home?' Benedict roared, making Tom look terrified. Miranda edged past him and stood on the other side of Tom.

'He's brilliant at sculpting,' she said, smiling at Tom.

'Really?' Benedict looked bored.

Tom, looking agonised at her, mumbled, 'Got to go, meeting friends. 'Bye,' and shot off before she could stop him.

'Can't think why he stayed. Best place for children is at home. That's where I've left mine,' Benedict said, coming closer to her again.

'What about your wife?' Miranda said sternly.

'She's back in England looking after the kiddiwinks, of course. Can't ski as she's just had another.' He lurched towards her, waving the bottle of champagne in her direction.

Miranda, doubly shocked that he had left his wife so soon after childbirth, was just about to push past him again and go and join the others when Jack, seeing her predicament, came over.

'Go round again with the champagne, there's a good chap,' he said to Benedict, taking his arm and propelling him on his way.

'Spoilsport, just when we were getting on so well,' Benedict said, planting his sturdy frame firmly beside Miranda.

Sonia came over, smiling pointedly at Jack. 'Darling, do come and talk to Davina. It's such a coincidence, but her brother has just bought Toby Mansfield's house.' She took Jack's arm and started almost to drag him across the floor.

'Come too,' Jack said to Miranda. 'Perhaps you know the house as well?'

'I don't,' she said.

'Good, then we can continue with our conversation,' Benedict said, rocking on his large, flat feet.

Miranda suddenly couldn't bear any more of him. He made her feel suffocated after the day spent outside in the endless expanse of snow and mountains, and the clean air. She made an excuse to Benedict and went over to talk to David. He was heavily occupied with another man, talking of the City, so, tired of them all, she slipped out on to the veranda into the cold night air.

There were many lights about and she could hear the children, no doubt Tom among them, calling to each other and swooshing down on their toboggans. She leant over the wooden rail, listening and watching what she could in the dim light, and wondering when she and her friends could leave. It was their chalet girl's night off so they were going to eat out, so it didn't really matter when they left. She hoped it would be soon. The meeting with Jack had been every bit as terrible as she'd imagined.

She heard a movement behind her and, turning, saw Jack coming through the door.

He smiled shyly at her. 'It's a bit of a bun fight, I'm afraid,' he said.

'That's all right. It's just so nice out here in the fresh air. Are the children safe, do you think, tobogganing in the dark?' She added that for something to say.

'They are not allowed to go very high. They must keep beside the chalets where there is light,' he said, coming to stand beside her.

'I saw Tom for a minute,' she said.

'Yes, I noticed. I'm sorry if . . .' He laughed awkwardly. 'Well, Benedict can be rather a bore when he gets some drink on board.'

'I felt he chased away Tom. I'd have liked to talk to him some more.'

She felt him look at her but she did not turn towards him.

'You're good with him,' he said. 'I do try but I find this dyslexia thing hard to take, to understand. I mean, he's so bright when you talk to him. A bit forgetful sometimes, and not good at finding his way around, but I have to admit,' he paused, said in a rush as if he had been bottling it up guiltily for some time, 'I find it hard to accept that he won't go to a top public school, or possibly even university.'

'Does that really matter?' Miranda said. 'If he's bright, which he obviously is, and so good at making things, he'll surely find a place for himself in life, once he's left school. Especially with your support.'

'I wish I could believe you,' Jack said, sighing. 'But the world is so tough now. Once you only needed a talent and enthusiasm, now it seems you need a degree even to make the tea in most places.'

He sounded so anguished she put her hand on his arm without realising it. 'It must be hard,' she said. 'It's something I don't know about, not having children, but surely these days there is so much help that can be given to dyslexic children?'

He turned to her, put his hand over hers as it lay on his arm. 'You're right, of course, but you see, my grandfather . . . My father died when I was a boy and he and my mother brought me up. My grandfather has made me rather too conventional, educationwise. He refuses to believe Tom is dyslexic, doesn't even know what it means. Though I try to dismiss his misguided ideas, I can't help feeling deep down influenced by them.' His laugh was raw with pain. 'Why do we let what influenced us as children, which we hated and fought against then, affect the way we feel about our own children?'

'I know we do, but we mustn't,' Miranda said. 'It's like my mother's misguided ideas about women not marrying. Don't let him make Tom feel worse.'

'I'm doing my best not to, but sometimes it's such a losing battle. It's the same with the Gillard-Hardings. They all seem to think Tom is just lazy, and sometimes when I see him slumped hour after hour in front of the television or glued to his computer games, I feel like agreeing.' He bit his lip. 'I'm sorry to bore you with this. You were so good to him. I'd never seen him so pleased with himself after you'd shown him how to make that mask.' He smiled at her, his eyes searching into hers.

She said quickly, afraid of the warm feelings she felt for him, 'It was just luck on my part. One of my nieces had shown me how to do it. He'll be fine. He seems to have lots of friends.' She gestured to where she supposed he was with the children and the toboggans.

Jack was silent a moment, then he laughed sourly. 'H-he doesn't really fit in with them,' he said. 'You see, the other children in this chalet party are all at top prep schools, on their way to Winchester, Eton, those sort of schools. They all . . .' he swallowed heavily, 'rather ridicule Tom. It just hurts me so much that he can't keep up with them, is always left out, though he does his best to join in.'

'But he skis so well.'

'It's not that.'

Then Miranda realised what Jack was trying to say. His child did not fit with his peers. One could laugh at it, say what did it matter? Who wanted to be like people like Benedict anyway? But she knew how people like Jack – like her too, if she admitted it – did all conform to some degree. The children were all cloned at their top public schools. It had been the same at hers. You had to be on the 'right side' to be popular, to be accepted. You may say you didn't care, didn't like the people on the 'right side', but it was very lonely if you were not part of them.

She knew it still went on through her friends' children, the language, the 'in' words, the way of behaving. All of them desperate to belong, be seen to be having fun, doing what everyone else did, ridiculing, out of fear of being out of it oneself, others who were not the same. People like Benedict never grew out of it. At school you had to have enormous self-confidence to rise above it, something hard for a child to achieve, especially one struggling already with dyslexia.

She searched frantically in her mind for something to say to comfort Jack, but before she could think of anything there was a thump outside and Tom came round the side of the chalet dragging his feet. His body was slumped, his head down. Jack and her hands shot away from each other as if they were on a burning surface.

'Hello, Tom. Had enough?' Jack said. Miranda could tell he was forcing cheerfulness into his voice.

'Yup,' Tom said, not looking at him.

On the still night air a wave of laughter reached them from the children still tobogganing. Miranda saw Tom's mouth clench, his shoulders sag and she knew that they had not wanted him. She felt a great wave of sympathy for him. She could feel the tenseness of Jack beside her, knew that he too was suffering for his son's rejection. She ached to say something to comfort them when the door to the chalet opened and Sonia came out.

'What are you doing out here?' she said bossily. 'Jack, we need more to drink, and Tom, get out of your wet clothes and go to your room until everyone's gone. You'll only be in the way, mooning round.' Miranda flinched at her sharpness with Tom, but almost immediately recognised it as jealousy at her being alone with Jack. Perhaps it looked like a prearranged meeting.

Jack said, 'We'll be in in a minute, and Tom, you could help me pour the drinks.'

'Don't want to,' Tom said, going inside.

Benedict lurched out. 'What's going on out here? Am I missing something? Oh, you old fox, that's where you've been hiding her.' He stood in the doorway, swaying a little. Miranda fled back inside to get her coat, made an excuse and left, not able to bear any more.

Chapter Eight

'So, darling, how is dear Tom?' Cynara smiled at Jack. 'I'm so looking forward to seeing him again. He must be enormous by now.'

'He's fine,' Jack said noncommittally to his mother. He had just picked her up from the City airport and they were having lunch together. He was pleased to see her and thought how good she looked: slim and elegant, her hair discreetly kept golden brown, her make-up impeccable and her pink and grey suit feminine but not fussy.

Cynara watched Jack carefully, suspecting he was worried about Tom but determined not to pry. She adored Jack, her only child, a palpable memory of her beloved husband, but she'd been determined not to be a possessive mother, clinging to him too long, making him as dependent on her as she was on him.

'Good, and Sonia?' Again she watched him. She knew that Sonia was a difficult woman, having been hopelessly spoilt by her father and used to having his undivided attention. With her extreme beauty she had no trouble in being the centre of attention with men, and Cynara suspected that Jack was not enough for her; no man would be. Sonia was, surprisingly, very insecure though this was not always apparent. She wanted every man to adore her. Cynara never said anything against her. She loved her grandson and she knew that if she made difficulties with her daughter-in-law she might not be allowed to see him. She was going to be especially careful this visit as for the first time she was going to take Tom back with her to France for two weeks of his Easter holiday.

'Fine,' Jack said again, pouring her another glass of wine. 'She's working quite hard at the moment, and I've got this long trip coming up so it's so good of you, Mother, to take Tom. He's longing to come.'

'And I'm longing to have him,' she smiled fondly. 'He'll fly back with Daddy, who's coming out for the second week. So it's all fitted in perfectly.'

'And Etienne doesn't mind?'

'Of course not. We've got his daughter and her two boys staying for a few days. Tom will have a lovely time.'

'Lucky chap,' Jack said, thinking of how he could do with a few days in the beautiful château his mother lived in with her second husband. It was in Normandy, surrounded by rich green land, and trees. It seemed a long time since his skiing holiday, and London had closed in on him, making him long to get away.

He also knew that it wasn't just London, which in fact he loved. He felt trapped, hemmed in by the problems of his home life. Tom seemed to be turning in on himself. He barely uttered more than a few monsyllabic grunts. His school report was not good, as apparently he was not working hard enough.

But almost worse than this was having his suspicions about Sonia's infidelity confirmed.

Two days ago, he'd received a tearful phone call from a woman he barely knew. She told him that Sonia was having an affair with her husband.

'I saw them going into a restaurant. She was all over him, and he . . .' Her voice had dissolved into tears before she rallied. 'He was obviously enjoying it and was on very intimate terms with her.'

Jack had done what he could to pacify her and then, with a sinking heart, had confronted Sonia.

Sonia had just laughed. 'Oh, darling, Anna Johnson, poor thing – she's just so neurotic. It was only lunch! Why didn't she come up and say hello to us instead of jumping to such absurd conclusions?'

'I don't believe you,' he'd said. 'There have been too many rumours about your behaviour. And why would this woman make it up? Or ring me to tell me? It didn't look like "only lunch" to her.'

'She's imagining it,' Sonia had said, coming up to wind herself round him. But he pushed her off, knowing from the defiant look in her eyes that she was lying and he must face up to it.

Jack was aware of how Sonia craved to be the centre of attention, almost like a precocious child. He had found it rather touching when he'd first met her, that longing for love, her grateful delight as she basked in his love. But now, especially as she had a child herself, he found it wearisome and destructive. Tom's difficulties, he thought, made her feel her confidence was threatened, as indeed he felt his had been. Instead of being able to talk about their problems, they had both suffered in their own way. Now he knew, with jealousy and anger eating holes in him, it was true that she was finding comfort in the arms of other men. Proving to herself that although her child could not take his place with their friends' children at a top public school, she had not lost her success with the men. But Tom's welfare was paramount and he was about to go away; so for the moment he would not confront her further.

Cynara, seeing the tortured look in his eyes, said brightly, 'How was your skiing holiday, darling? Was the snow good this year?'

'It was great, we had a lot of skiing. It was cold, of course, at that time of year, but the sun shone most days. We stayed in a large chalet with some friends and a few people we didn't know. You know what these parties are like.'

He thought now of Miranda. He hadn't seen her again since that disastrous party in their chalet. He'd looked for her for the remaining days of their stay, but he hadn't seen her. He could not stop thinking of her, of her kindness and interest in Tom. Of the way she had laid her hand on his arm and the feel of it, soft and small, when he had covered it with his own. But it was pointless thinking of her, he knew. She had a boyfriend, that good-looking man he'd seen her with at the Cabine de Mont Fort. A girl like that was bound to have a boyfriend, dozens. He was surprised she wasn't married.

Seeing the sudden softness in his face, Cynara said, 'Did you meet some nice people out there?'

'Yes.' He looked at her, smiling. Then suddenly he heard himself saying, 'I've met such a nice girl. She was so kind to Tom; she showed him how to make a mask out of papier mâché.'

'Tom wrote something about that to me on his postcard. Is she one of his teachers?'

'No.' Jack told her everything about Miranda, and Cynara, watching him, thought, oh, no, don't let him be in love with her. Don't let him hanker after something he can't have.

She had always had the feeling that Sonia, although she suspected her of having affairs, would not leave Jack. She knew that in her own way Sonia was devoted to Tom and Jack. Or maybe – a sliver of unease crept into her – it was the life Jack gave her that she was devoted to. She knew it was unfair on Jack, but having been left a widow with a small child to bring up without a father in the house, she did not want her grandson to suffer the same fate. Better by far, she thought, to have both parents living together, especially as Tom had extra problems with his dyslexia. He needed the security of an intact family.

Having lived in France for a few years she knew they thought differently about fidelity in marriage there. They were, on the whole, discreet and did not let affairs affect their marriages. They didn't want to leave their spouses, their homes, their ways of life, to set up with someone else and possibly take on extra children, quite apart from the burden of the financial blood-letting of divorce.

She hoped Jack, busy with his work and perhaps finding the comfort of an occasional woman on his trips abroad or even here, would put up with the situation at least until Tom was grown up. But if either he or Sonia fell in love with someone else then there was the danger of their breaking up and Tom being hurt irrevocably.

'She sounds a kind and nice person. Do you see her often?' Cynara said nonchalantly, spearing a piece of fish with her fork and putting it in her mouth.

'I haven't seen her since Verbier. I don't know where she lives.' Jack felt hot as he remembered the scene with Tom when he'd asked for her address and Tom had said he'd lost it. It had been conducted in furious whispers as he didn't want Sonia to hear.

He'd said to Tom, 'I wonder if you could give me Miranda's address. Benedict wants to get in touch with her.' He'd felt dreadful lying to his child, but he couldn't say he wanted it for himself. Tom would ask why and might easily say something to Sonia.

'She wouldn't want *him* to have it. He was drunk and horrible. She'd hate to see him again,' Tom said, his eyes stuck to his computer game. He was jerking a joystick about, trying to score a goal.

'He doesn't want to see her, just send her something,' Jack said lamely, knowing that Miranda wouldn't want to see Benedict, nor would he want her to.

'I'll ask her,' Tom said, still jiggling the joystick. 'Wow, goal, great.'

'How? Do you know her telephone number?'

'Mmm, goal again. Brill.'

'Tom, will you please stop your game for a moment and tell me if you have Miranda's number and her address and give them to me?' Jack said quietly, wondering where he could look for them.

'I haven't her telephone number.'

'Her address then.' Jack felt himself getting frantic. Tom could be so annoying.

'In my pencil case, on the chair, I think.' Tom did not turn away from his game.

'I wish you showed as much concentration on your school work,' Jack muttered, irritated and feeling guilty at wanting Miranda's address and using these stupid excuses to get it. He knew he should not make any attempt to contact her. He looked on the chair, covered in clothes, an old teddy bear, a couple of posters, both torn, a football boot, some CDs. There was nothing remotely resembling a pencil case among this muddle.

'This room is so untidy, and it's not here.'

'In the cupboard then,' Tom said, still not taking his eyes off the screen.

Jack flicked off the computer, shaking with suppressed fury. 'Find it for me, Tom!'

'Dad!' Tom screamed. 'I was winning. How could you?'

Sonia had called out and Jack had told her it was all right and had then continued his demand in a frantic whisper. The pencil case was found, but there was no address inside it.

Jack had left him, furious with himself for being so unfair to Tom, furious with Tom for losing her address. He knew he couldn't write to her care of the Gardiners. It might easily get to his cousin Quentin's ears and start off all sorts of complications.

Now telling his mother about her he suddenly felt very sad as he did not know where Miranda was. They lived in the same city, no doubt moved in the same circles, but though he had looked for her at parties, in restaurants, in the street, on the tube, he'd never seen her. He was wary of asking among his friends if they knew her or where she lived, knowing how they would tease him, make something of it. It might get back to her and cause endless embarrassments. He wondered if he would ever see her again.

He told himself that it was stupid wanting to see her, unfair to burden her with his anxieties over Tom. She had a boyfriend, might even be married by now.

'She's the only person, apart from you, who really understands about Tom. Who sees only his talents,' he said to his mother, guessing suddenly that she might be getting the wrong end of the stick over this.

'But what about Sonia? She is his mother and has given him a lot of support,' Cynara said, a hint of warning in her voice. 'I mean, dear, it's a mistake to get advice for Tom from all and sundry. Far better to talk to his special teacher. After all, they're trained, and must understand what effect dyslexia has on the whole family.'

'I've lost count of the times I've tried to discuss it properly with Sonia. We never seem to talk any more, really talk as we used to,' he said, with exasperation. 'I have tried, believe me.

'Anyway, Miranda is not all and sundry. She's just so sweet. You should have seen Tom's face when he showed us his mask.' He smiled, remembering; remembering Miranda's face too.

'I'm so glad, darling.' Cynara put out her hand and took his as it restlessly fiddled with the stem of his glass, a piece of bread, the prongs of his fork. 'I know how difficult it is for you and Sonia. May be she won't talk about it because she finds it difficult to face up to.' She squeezed his hand reassuringly. 'I know how silly Daddy is about it, but you have to make allowances for his generation. They didn't know about dyslexia in his day, and he's being particularly male in refusing to face up to the fact that Tom, his great-grandson, has a genuine problem—'

'I know, Mother. It's not that,' Jack interrupted, wanting her to like Miranda, not think she was some crank.

'But this Miranda,' she watched him as she said her name, having noticed how much Jack enjoyed saying it, letting it slip round his tongue as if it gave him pleasure, 'is not a teacher, you told me. She may inadvertently do more harm than good, as kind, good people sometimes do by mistake—'

'Mother, she's hardly going to perform surgery on him,' Jack broke in, feeling rather exasperated now. 'She just showed him something he became good at. Now he makes lots of things in papier mâché, other materials too. He got top marks for art.'

'Good, then he sounds as if he doesn't need her any more. What a bit of luck for him to meet her when he did.' Cynara thought it was time for her to stop sending out cryptic warnings about this girl. She felt rather tired suddenly. Emotion was the most exhausting thing. She did hope Jack would think over what she had said and that he wouldn't find Miranda again. He was an adult and must use all his resources to get through his life. Tom was still a child and needed his parents to stay together.

'He is so fond of her,' Jack went on lamely, knowing that his mother disapproved. He wanted suddenly to grind the tablecloth in his hands, tear it to shreds and throw the plates and glasses to the floor. He wanted her to understand, to find Miranda for him. But he did nothing but call for the waiter to bring the menu so Cynara could choose a pudding.

Cynara came to stay with Jack and Sonia the night before she returned to France with Tom. She had spent a few days with her father, the general, and a couple of days with a girl friend in London.

Jack had wanted her to stay with them the whole time she was in London, but he sensed that Sonia did not want her. This added to his irritation.

'She doesn't want to stay here. Surely she can see her friends. She's not over often,' Sonia said reasonably.

'But you didn't make her sound welcome. I heard you on the phone. You said, "Have you somewhere to stay or do you want to come here?"'

'So,' Sonia said, 'what's wrong with that?'

'It was the way you said it. As if it would be a frightful bore to have her,' Jack said, imagining that Sonia didn't want her because she wouldn't be able to see whatever lover she had and when she came home late with these lame excuses, his mother would see straight through them.

Sonia guessed what he was thinking and, not wanting to continue down this road, kissed him, laughed and said, 'Darling, you're imagining things. Of course I want her; I love your mother. I'll sort it when she's here. She knows she's always welcome here.' And she'd swept out, saying she must see to the dinner or they wouldn't have it before midnight.

Tom was thrilled to see his grandmother. He was excited by his coming trip with her, but a little apprehensive too.

'Can I ring you, Dad?' he said anxiously. 'I mean, can you ring Australia from France?'

'Of course you can, if you get the time difference right. But ask Etienne first, it will be expensive,' Jack said, recognising Tom's feeling of insecurity.

'I expect he'll send you some exciting postcards, Tom,' Cynara said, 'and we will send him and Mummy some.'

'You will, won't you, Dad, and Mum too?' Tom said.

'Of course,' Sonia said, 'only they might not arrive before it's time for you to come home again.'

'Bring out the addresses of your friends. They might like you to send them a card too,' Cynara said enthusiastically.

'I might.' Tom went quiet again. Then he said sadly, 'I lost Miranda's address, or I could send her a card. Did I tell you about her, Grandma? She helped me make this mask, and we saw her skiing.'

'Yes, you did tell me.' Cynara made her voice sound vague.

'You can't keep bothering her, Tom,' Sonia said sharply, making Cynara look at her quickly, wondering if she was jealous. It wouldn't do any harm if she was. It might even make her behave herself.

'What's the address of the Gillard-Hardings?' Tom went on. 'I could send it to them. Address it sort of to the cottage in the garden of Chandos Hall. Do you think it would get to her then?' He looked gravely at his father, his large brown eyes staring straight into Jack's.

'I . . . I don't know.' Jack thought it was a wonderful idea. He wondered if he could suggest tactfully to Tom to ask for her proper address. He also realised that this was the first time for ages that Tom had been so animated. Of course it might be because he was pleased to see his grandmother again, but it could be thinking of Miranda that had this effect on him.

Cynara said, 'I don't know, darling. The Post Office is so hopeless now with all those computers instead of people. Without that dotty little postcode a letter takes ages to get anywhere. My letter to Gillian, where I was staying, took ten days as I didn't know her postcode. Postmen always used to know exactly where people lived, but now as they barely have the same one in the district for more than a month they know nothing.' She went on at some length about the foibles of the Post Office to steer everyone away from talking about Miranda.

Tom would not be put off. 'I'll try anyway. We saw her skiing, she came to the chalet but she left quickly. There was a horrible drunk man staying with us, Grandma.'

'Oh, nonsense, Tom,' Sonia said firmly. 'She left because she wanted to get away from us.'

'She did not,' Tom said furiously. 'She left because that Benedict came out looking for her. I was there, I saw him coming.'

'What a time you had,' Cynara said quickly. 'Now, Tom, have you everything for the journey? Things to occupy you on the plane?'

Later that night Jack went to say good night to Tom. He was leaving to visit some mines in Australia the day after. He had not asked Sonia what she would do when they had gone. He half wondered if she would bring her lovers here.

He sat on Tom's bed, relieved that the boy would be away from here, safe with his grandmother. He did not want him even to suspect that Sonia was seeing someone else. He knew sooner or later he would

65

have to confront Sonia about what would happen if Tom found out about her lovers. He was getting older now, would soon suspect, if he hadn't already, that something was going on.

He talked to him about his coming journey, answered his questions again about him telephoning him. 'I've given you my numbers, but we'll soon all be together again. You'll have such a good time with Grandma that time will whizz past.'

Tom said solemnly, 'Dad, if I do write to Miranda, do you think the letter will reach her if I address it like I said?'

Jack said nothing for a moment. He knew he should gently dissuade Tom from writing to her. After all, she may well be bored of them, left the chalet party so abruptly because she'd had enough. She might well have imagined that Benedict was a great friend of his, instead of just an extra person squeezed in by the travel company at the last minute, and not wanted to be part of them. If she'd wanted to keep in touch she could easily have written again to Tom at Pilgrim's Court.

Instead he heard himself saying, 'You could always try, though don't be disappointed if it doesn't reach her. But if you do write, ask her for her proper address. Then if you want to write to her again, you'll know for certain that it will get there.'

'I'll do that,' Tom said, smiling. 'Do you think I ought to describe the cottage. I mean there was more than one, wasn't there? Should I say the sort of pinky cottage on the Chandos Hall estate, not the white one on the other side?'

'The name of her friends is Gardiner,' Jack said. 'You put Miranda's name on the envelope and underneath "Care of Mrs Simon Gardiner", then Chandos Hall, the village and the county. It might get to her then.'

Tom jumped out of bed and riffled through his rucksack. He thrust a small diary at Jack. 'Write it in there for me, Dad,' he said, 'just how it goes on the envelope.'

They heard a step on the stairs and Jack put the book quickly in his pocket. 'I'll find a pen and do it,' he said hurriedly. Sonia came in.

'All set for tomorrow?' she said. 'What fun you'll have with Grandma in France, darling. Now hurry into bed.' She helped him in and kissed him, holding him to her for a second.

Jack felt terribly guilty, as if she had found him in bed with Miranda. He prayed Tom wouldn't say anything about her and to his relief he did not.

When Sonia had gone he went to kiss him too. Tom said, his dark eyes on his face, 'There's a pen in my bag, in that pocket in front. Please write her address for me, like you said.'

Jack did it, but the pleasure and hope that Tom might find her had gone, replaced by guilt. He knew he wanted to see Miranda again for something far more intimate and lasting than just talking over Tom's welfare.

Chapter Nine

Miranda and David March crossed the New King's Road on their way to work by tube.

'I'll ring you when I get back. Should be about Sunday, all being well,' David said.

'Fine,' she smiled at him, relieved, though not showing it, that she had a few days without him.

Their affair had started when they had returned from Verbier. After the drinks party at Jack's chalet she had felt very depressed. She had felt drawn to Jack, felt a closeness to him as if they had known each other well somewhere before. She had gone over those few minutes when they had been together on the veranda a hundred, a thousand times. But she knew she was being foolish, that whatever she felt or imagined she felt for him had to be swiftly quashed. He was married, the father of a child, and although she knew through James Darby that his wife had affairs she had no right to him.

Most probably he'd be horrified if he knew that she thought of him in a romantic way. Just because a man is nice to a girl it doesn't mean he's in love with her, or wants to be in love with her, she told herself endlessly. No doubt he needed someone sympathetic to listen to his problems with Tom. That was all there was to it.

She did not want to get involved with it all. She had a strong sense of self-preservation and she did not want to risk falling in love with a man who only wanted to talk about his worries over his child with her. Or maybe he too had affairs and thought she would do as a diversion when his wife was busy with her latest lover. She most certainly did not want to be used like this, be his plaything when it suited him. If he was divorced and free that would be quite a different matter, but while he was married to Sonia, however unsatisfactorily, she would keep away.

She had spent the rest of the holiday outwardly enjoying herself though inwardly suffering. She had tried not to look for Jack among the flocks of skiers that poured down every slope. She half hoped that he would be on the same plane returning home but when he was not, she told herself firmly it was over, what had never begun. She found solace with David who had taken her out to dinner a couple of times before slipping into her bed.

He was a pleasant lover, undemanding, easy to get on with. He was often away on business and often working long hours so they didn't see each other all that much. Neither was in love but each, she supposed, filled a need in the other. She did not tell her mother about him.

When Miranda met Davina later that day for lunch in a wine bar, Davina said, 'So David's away, do you miss him?'

'Not really,' she said, 'not like you miss Piers.'

'But he's so nice. You know, Miranda, you ought to settle with someone like him. You'd make a super mother. Remember how kind you were to that boy . . . Tom, wasn't it?'

The unexpected mention of Tom's name, bringing Jack back at once into her mind, made Miranda blush and stammer.

Davina, watching her, said, 'So there is something between you and his father. I did notice at that party how he looked at you with admiration in his eyes. I know you were stuck with that odious Benedict, and you left so suddenly but it wasn't just because Benedict was after you, was it? You're quite able to deal with men like that.'

Miranda had herself firmly in control now. 'Oh, Davina, you have the same ideas as my mother. Get married at all costs – as long as he's suitable, of course. David and I are today's kind of couple, both keen on our jobs, both valuing our independence, but in need of a little love and comfort from time to time. Not marriage and babies.'

'I think that's very sad,' Davina, who was getting married in the autumn, said. 'But tell me about Jack. Would you marry *him* if he was free?' She gave her a searching look and Miranda, who had known her since they were eleven and in the same dormitory at school, knew she couldn't fob her off with excuses.

'I like him very much. I'm attracted to him too.' She laughed. 'My heart did a double flip when I first met him. It doesn't do that very often. But that's where it ends. I don't want to be a married man's bit on the side. Whether he cares for me or is paying me attention only to spite his wife, or finds me a kind listener to his troubles with Tom, I don't know. Nor will I hang about to find out. Remember the agonies Laura suffered when Roger kept going off? An affair with a married man is bound to be full of pain. It's just not on for me.' She took a long drink of her Perrier water and checked her watch.

'I must go. I've a whole lot of stuff to sort through for Thursday's shoot. I'll ring you.' She opened her wallet and took out some money. 'This should cover it, but let me know if it's not enough.'

Davina sighed heavily. 'Of course you're right to keep away. I wish I had with Ian Fern, remember that?'

'Yes, I do. But you were very young.' Miranda remembered the agonising time some years back. Davina had fallen madly in love with Ian Fern, who was ten years older than she. Having seduced her he had promised he'd divorce his wife and marry her but having strung her along for a while, he'd brutally told her it was over and had gone off on a long holiday with his wife.

'I really loved him,' Davina said, looking sad for a moment, 'but he was such a rat.'

Miranda squeezed her shoulder. 'He was,' she said, 'and perhaps it is the memory of that terrible time that is keeping me firmly away from any involvement with Jack.'

'Jack may not be like that,' Davina said.

'I shan't hang about to find out,' Miranda said, kissing her goodbye and leaving the wine bar.

She spent the afternoon going through the clothes for the large fashion shoot they were doing on Thursday.

She hung the garments up round the room, putting the accessories with each set. Some of the shoes could be used with more than one outfit and she wrote down everything meticulously. She had just finished when Stella, the fashion editor, came in.

'Everything there?'

'I hope so.'

Stella checked it, then said, 'I don't like those shoes with this. I think strappy sandals would look much better with that dress, don't you? Have we any?'

'No . . . we have these, but they are hardly light.' Miranda produced a sturdy pair of lavender suede sandals just in from Sara, a new designer.

'No. I did want to use something by Sara, but these are rather heavy for these clothes. Look, Miranda, have you time,' she glanced at her watch, sighed, 'it's too late now . . . tomorrow to pop by her shop in Covent Garden? See if there's anything better? It will be quicker than her sending some in and us not liking them.'

Miranda had a lot to do the following day but she promised she'd go to Sara's shop in her lunch hour. She packed away the clothes to be used in the feature and went home. On the way she stopped off and bought herself some supper at the delicatessen: fresh pasta and a tub of pesto sauce. She felt relieved that she had the whole evening to herself. She hadn't done any of her miniature painting for ages; David had taken up too much of her time. The evenings she had been free she'd caught up on domestic chores or gone to bed early. She smiled, feeling suddenly pleased with her freedom. Tonight she would paint, get all her paints out again and start something new, her own adaptations of those Persian miniatures in the book she'd bought on them. She'd been meaning to get down to those for ages.

Feeling happy she opened her front door and saw Colin standing in the narrow passage. He was a pale, thin man with foxy red hair. He kept himself to himself, as she'd told her mother, who had alternated between wondering if he was nice enough to marry or a sex maniac who, living in the other half of the small house with her daughter, might attack her knowing there was no one else in the house to come to her aid.

'Hello, Colin, how are you?' Miranda greeted him. They were hardly friends, but he was a courteous and quiet neighbour. He often picked up her letters from the mat and put them through her door, or put the lid back on her dustbin after the dustmen had been. But they'd hardly ever had a conversation and then it had only been about the weather or the noise of the building works opposite.

Now he looked at her with sad disapproval. He turned and opened his own door then, turning back to face her, said, 'The wages of sin are death.'

'What?' she almost laughed. What had he said? Surely she had misheard, or it was some sort of joke she'd hadn't got.

He turned round, one foot on the stairs to his flat. His face had taken on a forgiving expression as he said, 'I suggest you read the Bible. Perhaps you have forgotten its teaching.'

His remark astounded her. 'I . . . I haven't read it lately,' she mumbled. She knew he was religious. The woman she'd brought the flat from had told her so, and also that he spent much of his time at religious meetings. She had forgotten about it – indeed he had not ever said anything about it to her to remind her – until now.

He turned round on the stairs and faced her. 'I suggest you read it again. Try Romans, chapter eight, verse five. It reminds us that to be carnally minded is death. Or, if you find that difficult, remember the Ten Commandments: Thou shalt not commit adultery.' He eyed her solemnly.

She felt a blush cover her. He was no doubt objecting to David spending the night with her. He was the first man to do so since she'd moved in. She said angrily, 'I have not committed adultery. Neither of us is married.'

'Ah, but nor are you married to each other. Think on it,' Colin said, and turned away, shutting his door firmly behind him.

Miranda stood stunned in the tiny hallway but was not brave enough to batter on his door and demand to know exactly what he meant. His words made her feel sick and then afraid. She let herself into her flat and shut the door, leaning against it, looking round the familiar room expectantly as if it would comfort her, help her to laugh away her feelings of disquiet, dismiss his words as those of a mad man. But they made her feel uncomfortable. Was he spying on her, getting some sort of shameful pleasure in condemning David and her?

She unpacked her groceries, her appetite now gone. She had had a religious upbringing, going to a Catholic boarding school as her father had been rather a better Catholic then than he was now. She did not go to church very often and if she thought about it agreed that a lot of its teachings, though hard to accept, did make sense. But she did not think it wrong if two unmarried adults went to bed together of their own free will, as long as they didn't hurt anyone else.

She felt angry now. How dare Colin judge them, condemn them? There were many sins concerned with sex – the newspapers were filled with sordid, shameful stories of child abuse and MPs who cheated on their wives and children – but David and she were not sinning and she felt incensed that Colin had suggested it.

The telephone rang to distract her, and when she found it was Laura she bombarded her with Colin's accusation, the audacity of it still burning hot in her mind.

'The old pervert! I bet he's up to something – choir boys, perhaps,' Laura shrieked down the phone. 'How horrid for you, though. Do you think he thumbs through the Bible every night to find a new sin he thinks you've committed? Don't take his milk by mistake, or he'll have you for stealing.'

'He's never done anything like this before. He's hardly spoken to me. Only nice day, good morning, you know, monosyllables. I only knew till now that he's religious from the woman I bought the flat from. She told me he kept himself to himself and he went to a lot of religious meetings.'

'Meetings not church? That sounds more of a cult thing.'

'She said meetings. I suppose they are in church. I didn't think about it.'

'It's probably one of those very odd religions. I wouldn't take any notice of him. Or maybe he fancies you and is furious that you have someone else.'

'Please, Laura, don't put any more ideas into my head to frighten me,' Miranda said. 'But it's good to hear from you. I haven't for ages. How are you both?' She felt better now that Laura had made a joke of it. Colin was entitled to his own beliefs and perhaps he did disapprove of her behaviour. Perhaps he thought she was promiscuous and would bring back many different men. Well, she didn't care what he thought, she had nothing to be ashamed about. She went on talking to Laura, laughing and joking.

At last Laura said, 'I'm ringing to ask if you'd be godmother. I'm pregnant.'

'Oh, Laura, how wonderful . . . I'd love to, I really would. Thank you for asking me. When is it being born?'

'Christmas. I feel so ill, I can't tell you,' she said cheerfully.

'But you're only just pregnant.'

'Yes, I know. I hope I don't feel like this for nine months.' They chatted some more and Laura said, 'So this David, will you marry him?'

'Don't you start,' Miranda groaned. 'No. We like each other a lot, he's a great companion, but marriage is such a commitment. I like my freedom, and my job. I'd like to do really well in that, perhaps become fashion editor for *Vogue*,' she laughed. 'Travel the world seeing the collections.'

'I'm so happy with Neil, our home, the baby coming, cosy cliché I know,' Laura said, 'but it's only natural I want you to experience the same thing. But I agree it would be terrible to marry someone you didn't love, just for the sake of it. I just hope you find someone special.'

Miranda did not remind Laura of the agony of her first marriage. Laura had eventually complained that she had never been so lonely as when she'd been married to Roger. He was always out or away on business, or working late, leaving her constantly waiting with lovingly cooked, congealing meals, which he never ate. Friends, assuming she was happily occupied with her husband, let her be, or invited both of them to things and as he was always late, or didn't turn up at all, she often didn't go to them herself. So Laura, her pride hiding the truth of her loneliness, was inadvertently locked in the purdah of a misconception of a happy marriage.

When Laura rang off, Miranda felt better and cooked herself some supper. Then David rang from Geneva and she told him about Colin. He laughed and suggested that she quote back 'He that is without sin among you, let him first cast a stone at her.'

'I feel rather uncomfortable about him though,' she admitted. 'I don't like having the Bible quoted at me. It makes me feel guilty even though I know I'm not.'

'Many a person has used God to frighten people, make them feel inadequate, guilty, whatever. Be careful he doesn't ask for money to atone for your supposed sins,' David said, his voice serious.

'You don't think he will, do you?' Another fear hit her now.

'No, I shouldn't think so.' He laughed. 'A modern-day pardoner buying up people's sins so they can get to heaven. One way to make money, I suppose.'

Miranda laughed too.

David went on, 'I wish I was there, but I don't think you've anything to worry about. After all, you've nice neighbours; you can always run out into the street and bang on their doors if you're frightened.'

'Do you think I ought to be frightened?'

'No I don't. The little I've seen of Colin, I'd say he's harmless, but don't get involved. Look, I'm ringing because I've got to stay here a week or so. It looks like there's been some cockup and I must sort it out. I'm staying at the L'Angleterre. I'll give you my number should you need me, but I'll ring you in a day or so anyway.'

Miranda did not sleep well that night and the next morning, looking pale and tired, she struggled to work. She was just about to settle for lunch and a gossip with Helen, who worked in the editorial department, when she remembered with despair that she had to go to the shoe shop in Covent Garden to look for lighter sandals for the fashion shoot. She gulped down a coffee and a sandwich and fled.

Sara, who designed the shoes and owned the small shop which was fast becoming famous, showed her the few things she had which she thought would suit the feature. Her shoes were made of bright leathers and suedes, and instead of being just a pair of shoes to go with an outfit they seemed to stand out as a statement on their own.

'*Vogue* is giving me quite a spread next month,' she said with calm excitement, her green lipstick, white face and spiky blonde hair giving her the air of a fragile elf.

'I'm so pleased for you,' Miranda smiled, knowing with disappointment that her editor wouldn't allow a whole spread of Sara's shoes. 'I'll take these. Can I have the green and the yellow?' She held up two pairs of sandals of very thin leather straps, one in bright yellow, the other citrus green. They looked wonderful but she thought they'd be agony to wear, the straps being hardly thicker than a piece of string. 'I think they'll look good with black, and we've a yellow dress these will go with. Could I take that bag too?' She pointed to a tiny sandwich-shaped bag with a skinny strap in the same green.

Miranda came out into the street with the things she had chosen packed into bags. She was concentrating hard on which clothes the sandals would go best with, and anxious that Stella might hate them and ask if Sara had had nothing in cream or black. She thought that the navy silk dress would look marvellous with the green sandals and the bag tossed carelessly over one shoulder. She thought about jewellery and wondered if she had time to go to Beauchamp Place and look there for something more exciting and dramatic than the classical pieces Stella already had at the office. She decided she would ring her and find out, and stopped to find her mobile phone. She heard a voice behind her.

'Miranda.'

She turned, still half in her thoughts about the clothes, her mobile in her hand. Jack stood there looking at her, a slight smile on his mouth, apprehension in his eyes.

Chapter Ten

For a long moment Miranda stared at Jack, unable to believe that it was really him and she hadn't conjured up a mirage. He looked wonderful, slightly tanned, wearing a crisp blue shirt and a superbly cut dark grey flannel suit.

Glancing at her carrier bags, he said, 'Are you shopping? Have you time for a coffee?'

'No . . . it's for work, and no, I haven't time for coffee, I've got to get back to the office.' But as she said this she didn't move. She made no effort to pick up the bags from the pavement and leave. She just stood there staring at him. He was looking at her intently, almost yearningly, and she could feel herself being drawn to him as if his body was magnetised, slowly pulling her in to him. She took a deep breath and said, 'I must go. I've got to get this back to the office. My editor will kill me if I haven't got everything ready by tonight.'

'Haven't you five minutes?' His eyes were on her mouth, his voice caressing.

'No, I haven't, really I haven't,' she said in panic. Panic because she wanted to be with him, leave her bags in the road and go with him. With a great effort she controlled herself. She gave him a quick smile, forcing herself to be detached. She couldn't look at him any more because she knew how much she wanted him. Whatever her mind said to her, her body betrayed her. Her heart was beating faster, she felt her skin glowing, her eyes shining. Stop it, stop it, she warned herself firmly. Don't whatever you do make a fool of yourself.

'I haven't seen you for so long. I don't even know where you live, or what you do.' He glanced at the bags of shoes.

'Oh, I'm just a fashion editor – a junior one, still just learning really.' Her voice sounded hysterical. She must go, now, at once. She picked up the bags, hung them on her arms. He took a step closer to her.

'Please let me go,' she said, as if he had built a fence round her and hemmed her in.

'I just want to talk with you. I couldn't believe it when I saw you coming up the street. I've looked for you for so long and suddenly,' he laughed, 'there you are. Can't you just spare a moment, ring your editor and say you've got caught in the tube?'

'No,' she whispered, 'no, I can't.' But still she didn't move. She could quite easily have got past him, but she stood there in the street beside him, gazing beyond him, not daring to look into his eyes, but making no attempt to go.

'I'll come with you, then,' he said. 'Are you taking a taxi or the tube or, better still, is your office walkable from here?'

'What about your work?' Now she did look at him, her eyes drawn to his, locking, pulling away, locking again.

'It can wait.'

'Mine can't.'

'Then I'll come with you.'

'You can't.'

'Why not?' he laughed. 'Is it like a convent where men are not allowed?'

She smiled and he caught it and, seeing she was softening towards him, snatched up her hand and said, 'Come, let us walk. It is such a glorious spring day – the sun shining, new flowers, blue sky.' His face spilt with a smile; he looked like a happy child.

She did not move; her heart felt heavy. She blurted, 'I can't come with you because you are married.' She looked him straight in the eyes so he would have no doubt as to what she meant.

The joy in his face died. He said, 'That doesn't stop me wanting to see you, wondering where you are.'

'It must,' she said, wondering why she had mentioned his marriage. He had, after all, only asked if he could accompany her back to her office. But deep down she knew. Knew what she had tried to hide from herself all these weeks, that she was in love with him.

He dropped her hand, said after a moment, 'I know. I'm sorry, I haven't thought it through. I just knew from the first moment I saw you helping Tom that there was something special about you. I wanted to see you again but thought I was overreacting and let it go. Then meeting you skiing, it reinforced my feelings. I just wanted to know where you were. Tom had lost your address. I just . . .' He looked sad and she knew what he meant. She would like to know where he was too. Just to know he was somewhere, not too far away, though there was nothing she would do about it.

After a moment's thought, while she tried to curb her swirling emotions, she said, 'I think we're in danger of making this more than it is. We are attracted to each other, but we know nothing about each other. You are married and we can . . . will not,' she said more firmly than she felt, 'do anything about it.'

'I feel it is more than just an attraction,' he said, looking at her intently. 'People can have very deep friendships without there being any physical relationship. We could have that.'

'I don't think that sort of thing works,' she said, 'at least not between people of our age. Perhaps if one of us was ancient, or gay or ill . . .' She tried to think of any excuse to make him see that friendship would not be enough between them.

He smiled tenderly at her. 'It's better than nothing, why shouldn't we try it?'

'No,' she said. Then summoning all her strength she hailed a taxi she saw coming up the street. 'Let me go. You'll realise how sensible it is in a moment. Give my love to Tom.'

She turned away from him and busied herself with the door of the taxi. He sprang to her side and put his hand on hers. 'I promise you I won't start anything. Just tell me where you live so I can think of you.'

'Better not,' she said.

'Taxi! Taxi!' An irate man puffed down the road towards them.

'Are you getting in, love, or not?' the taxi driver said to her, watching the fat man running towards them.

'No, not yet,' Jack said.

'Yes, I am.' Miranda opened the door. 'Please, Jack,' she said, 'think of the complications, the pain.'

'There won't be any. Can't we be friends? That's all I ask, I mean it. After all, you've got a boyfriend.'

The fat man had reached them, perspiring and red in the face. 'Taxi!' he said frantically.

The driver shrugged, but Miranda said firmly to the fat man, 'I'm sorry, it's mine,' and, ignoring his wails and Jack's pleas, got in and shut the door. The taxi moved off.

'Where to, love?' the driver asked, and she muttered the address before throwing herself back in the seat in despair.

As they drove down the busy streets she tried to go over what had happened. She could not believe such a scene had taken place. She had often allowed herself to fantasise about Jack, imagining scenes of love, of passion, of just sitting and talking to him – all the time conveniently forgetting Sonia. She had begun to think she would never see him again, which she knew would be the safest thing. She had even decided to turn down the next invitation offered by the Gardiners in case she came across him there. But now, just like that, she'd seen him and instantly both had known how much they felt for each other. She had been around enough to know the difference between love and lust. She acknowledged to herself that she had never before, even with the men she'd loved best, felt so strongly. It was madness.

Despite her despair, Miranda felt a surge of elation bubble through her. She knew now they both felt the same way about each other. Love, like chicken pox, was instantly recognisable, but she and Jack could do nothing about it. She thought of Colin and his dire warnings. She and

David were free to sleep with each other, but Jack was not. She did not believe in sleeping with another woman's husband or boyfriend, however badly that woman might behave herself. She was relieved that she had not given Jack her address, for despite her noble thoughts she knew that the temptation to love him, to get close to him, would be more than she could stand.

'Here we are, love.' The taxi pulled up outside her office and she saw Stella coming out. Firmly she pushed all thoughts of Jack from her mind as she called to her to wait and see the accessories she had found.

On Friday morning a huge bunch of expensive flowers was dumped on Miranda's desk by Pat, one of the students on work experience.

'Lucky you,' Stella said admiringly, looking at Miranda over her spectacles. 'Can I ask who they are from?'

'I've no idea.' Miranda opened the small white envelope pinned to the stalks. For a moment she wondered if they were from David, or even Colin, repentant after his biblical warnings, but all the time she hoped they were from Jack. She took out the card and read:

> My sincere apologies for bombarding you on the street. I was just so pleased and surprised to see you. As the well brought up girl I know you are you'll want to thank me for these. I enclose my office number.
> Jack.

She could not stop a smile catching her mouth; she felt a glow surge through her.

Stella said, 'Someone special, no doubt.'

'No, not really.' She tried to feign indifference and put the card in her pocket.

'You can't fool me,' Stella, who was in a very happy relationship herself, laughed. 'Now put them in water and then get all these clothes back to the designers, making sure of course that you've got all the details of fabric, sizes, et cetera.'

'Of course.' Miranda scurried off to find something to stand the flowers in until she went home that night.

There was a lot to do that day, packing up the clothes, taking notes on them, checking the availability, sizes and other colours with the manufacturers, but all the time Jack's card glowed in her pocket and the scent from his flowers enveloped her and she could not stop thinking of him. She would not ring, she could not. But as she dashed out to lunch and later home, she looked for him all the while, half expecting to hear him call her name at any moment, but knowing all the time how foolish she was being.

She did not see him. Holding his flowers she approached her flat with slight trepidation in case Colin was waiting for her with another accusation from the Bible. There was surely one about receiving flowers from a married man. 'Thou shalt not covet they neighbour's husband' swam into her mind, making her giggle slightly hysterically.

'God,' she said to herself, 'I do covet him dreadfully. *I* would never be unfaithful to him, I would always be there for him.' She let herself into her flat and saw her letters scattered on the mat. Despite his disapproval, Colin had picked them up and pushed them through her door for her.

She put down the flowers and picked up the post. There was a pretty postcard of Monet's garden and wondering who she knew who was there she turned it over.

> Dear Meranda, I have lost your adress. Please send it. I am here with Granma.
> Love from Tom.

It had been sent to the Gardiners with 'Please Forwerd' written in red ink and heavily underlined on it.

After all this time never hearing from the Lamberts, never seeing them, now I am being bombarded, she thought with elation. She read Tom's card again. She didn't like to let him down, but if she told him her address he might give it to Jack and if he came to her she might not be able to turn him away.

She was relieved that she had a busy weekend seeing various friends and having a dinner party on the Saturday night. When her friends commented on the expensive flowers she laughed and said she couldn't resist them and had treated herself.

'I thought they were from David,' Carol, one of the girls who'd been in the skiing party, said.

'Oh no, he's stuck in Geneva,' Miranda said, and went on to amuse them with his descriptions of the muddle he'd found in the office there.

'So when will he be back?' someone else asked.

'I'm not sure,' she smiled, not wanting him back now. Wondering how she would make love to him when now she knew her heart was somewhere else, even though nothing would come of it.

Mid-morning on Monday the phone rang on her desk and she answered it briskly, imagining it to be a designer who'd sent in the wrong suit and with whom she'd left a message. It was Jack.

'Did you get my flowers?'

'Yes, thank you.'

'You didn't ring me?'

'No.'

'Why not?'

Miranda glanced round the partitioned-off room. It was empty for once, but it wouldn't be for long. 'You know I can't. You're married and—'

'You needn't remind me.' His voice was heavy.

'I am reminding you, Jack.' Her heart was beating so hard that surely the whole office must hear it. Her part of the office was enclosed in glass walls and she could see the other people working around her, but they couldn't hear her.

'Look, can't we meet and talk? Meet with Tom if you'd rather. He misses you. We can just be friends, you can meet Sonia too.'

'I don't want to,' she said quickly. She couldn't bear to see Sonia now. Sonia who she felt sure didn't care for him, who didn't deserve him.

'No, perhaps that was insensitive of me. What I meant was, why can't we meet on some neutral ground? Just chat. I so value your company. I promise I'm not going to suggest anything else, or interrupt your love life. But I would like to see you from time to time and if that's selfish of me, then I'm sorry, but that's how it is.'

She was about to be strong, explain that he must leave her alone, when Stella and Pat came in.

'I must go,' Miranda said.

'Meet me for lunch at the Italian restaurant on the street round the corner from your office, tomorrow at one. Luigi's, isn't it? Please, Miranda, be there, and if after that you never want to see me again I'll respect your wishes. But just do that for me, please.'

Stella was glaring at her and Miranda, knowing she wanted her to do some chore with Pat, muttered weakly, 'All right, but after that, no more. Promise.'

'Promise. See you then.' He rang off and Miranda forced herself to turn her attention to Stella.

Many a time during the day Miranda's hand hovered over the telephone to ring Jack and put him off, but it was too difficult to do as Stella was hanging over her and did not give her any opportunities to ring. The following morning she dressed extra smartly, even found herself putting on her best underwear. Not that anyone would see it, she told herself reasonably, but she liked to feel truly feminine right down to her bare skin.

The minute she arrived at the office Stella greeted her. 'Oh, Miranda, you'll have to go round to Amanda. There's been a confusion over the clothes – you know, the ones I chose. I can't go myself as I've another appointment I can't change. Don't leave there until you've got the things we need. We've got the shoot next week and we've got to get it right.'

Miranda heard this with mixed feelings. Fate had saved her from the lunch; she might not get back in time to meet Jack. With Stella hovering, in a dither because she wanted everything ready for her feature like yesterday, Miranda dared not ring his office to tell him. She did the other chores with Stella – who was now grumbling about how uneducated and halfwitted the students on work experience were these days – the mail, chasing up some information with her, checking out a new designer, before she could set off to Amanda's studio.

As the time ticked by and she sat with the designer, surrounded by clothes, swatches of material and drawings, Miranda was sure she wouldn't make it. She was half sad and half relieved. But at twenty past twelve everything was suddenly all resolved and she was free to go and meet Jack. Stella was out most of the afternoon. She knew she had at least two hours free.

She made her way slowly, determined not to arrive until after one. At exactly ten past she went into the restaurant. It was bustling with people and she looked round for Jack, but could not see him.

'Can I help you?' The proprietor came over to her, smiling broadly.

'I'm meeting someone, Ja— Mr Lambert,' she said.

'Ah yes, one minute please.' He turned from her and ran his finger down the list of names of people who had booked. His finger stopped; he turned round, frowning.

'Mr Lambert cancelled his table this morning,' he said, looking at her gravely.

Her heart stopped, but she forced herself to smile. 'You are sure?'

'Yes, I am quite sure.'

'Thank you.' With as much dignity as she could muster she smiled at him, ignoring the flash of sympathy in his eyes, and left the restaurant. No doubt Jack had come to his senses and realised that it would not be sensible for them to meet after all. She told herself firmly that she was relieved to be let off such a delicate situation so easily, but she could not stop the aching pain of disappointment spreading like lead through her heart.

Chapter Eleven

The hospital felt alien, upsetting Jack's equilibrium and fuelling his panic. One minute he sat restless and anxious in the waiting room, the next he was up and walking about as if the movement would shift the terror from his heart. It did not and he sat down again and tried to read, or look through the papers and reports in his briefcase, willing his mind to concentrate on something else.

He had just got to his office this Tuesday morning when Sonia had rung him to say his grandfather had been rushed to hospital with a heart attack. She had on her special 'caring' voice but in the first shock of the news he did not respond to it. When she'd rung off, he registered that she was upset about the news too and he had not comforted her. This caused him further pain, as he knew she would dwell on it, but he had no time to ring her back and he also felt too agitated to cope with her emotion as well.

He had rung the hospital, which had not given him much news, before ringing his mother, who was coming from France on the next plane. He was now sitting here alone in the hospital in Oxford, not knowing if the general was alive or dead.

Of course his grandfather was an old man and Jack accepted he may not have many years left; but he'd always seemed so well and strong, and this sudden attack had shocked and distressed Jack more than he could say. The old man may have been difficult with his outdated ideas, but he had taken the place of Jack's own father and he was deeply fond of him. His mother too had been very distressed at the news, which further worried him, and he wondered if she would be all right travelling here, or if her husband, Etienne, would come with her. He got up again and paced the floor. He was alone in this small whitewashed room with what he supposed were meant to be soothing pictures of sugary sweet landscapes and gardens on the walls. There were no other anxious relatives of other ill people, which made him feel even more alienated. He wished now that Sonia had come with him to help him carry this burden of pain and anxiety.

She had sounded genuinely contrite when she'd said, 'I've so much work, darling. This couldn't have come at a worse time. I know you can't plan these things but if it had been *last* week . . .' She had gone on to say how she'd do her best, her very best to come down that evening.

He'd rung off too soon, he knew it, making it appear that he was angry with her for not being there, instead of just being worried sick. Recently their emotions seemed seriously out of step, with real and imaginary slights adding to the discordance between them.

Jack thought then of Miranda and remembered the lunch they were having together. He longed suddenly to hear her voice, knew how she would offer him comfort, strength for the ordeal ahead. He rang her office and was told she was out and no one knew when she would be back.

He got his secretary to ring the restaurant and cancel the table. Then just before he left he tried once more to contact Miranda at her office, but she was not there and he did not like to leave a message. Sitting now in this waiting room he wondered if he should try her again, but he didn't dare to leave the room in case someone came needing him urgently for his grandfather. Perhaps he should write, he thought now. He took out his pen and some paper and tried. How would he start it? Darling Miranda, as he longed to?

The door opened and a nurse came in. He jerked up, searching her face for news. She smiled at him, her eyes focusing on one of the sugary landscapes.

'You can come and see your grandfather now. The doctor will have a word with you.'

'How is he?'

'He is as well as can be expected.' She glided away and he followed her, hating her words, fearful of their meaning.

The general was hardly recognisable under the tubes and machines connected to him. For one wild moment Jack thought they'd made a mistake and this was another old man fighting for life. His grandfather was still at home or down at the pub, alive and well and putting the world to rights in his indomitable way.

A young Asian doctor, his brown eyes soft with concern, came up to Jack and, putting his hand gently on his arm, led him outside.

'How is he?' Jack hardly dared ask, bracing himself for the worst.

'He has had a massive attack. We have done what we can but he is an old man, and the next few hours will be crucial.'

Jack stared almost stupidly at the doctor's sympathetic face and forced himself to ask, 'Will he live?'

'At the moment we can't say. He is an old man and it was a serious attack,' the doctor repeated. He went on to tell Jack more details about the case, but Jack could not take it all in. Part of him wanted to shout, beg this doctor to find some medicine, some treatment that would save his grandfather, while part of him with sickening reality knew he was doing all he could and that death, always inevitable, was waiting now close by, ready to snatch him.

For hours he sat next to his grandfather, sometimes holding his hand, sometimes speaking to him, willing, yet dreading his mother to come, afraid of her pain and grief. He thought of Tom and wondered how he would take his great-grandfather's death. He relived his own father's death, the bewilderment, the angry pain that death had taken *his* father, followed by the terrifying realisation that death could take anyone, any time. Afterwards he had been afraid for a long time that his mother would suddenly die, or his grandfather, and what would he, a child of eleven, do with no one to look after him? Would he be sent to some obscure relations, or to a children's home, or be adopted by some strangers? It was his grandfather who had comforted him.

'Don't let that worry you, my boy. We'll be around for a long time yet. Remember I got through the war without a scratch so I won't succumb easily to some illness. Your poor father wasn't strong, didn't look after himself properly.'

This had strangely reassured him. He thought his grandfather so strong and brave that death would not dare approach him. Nor had it, until now.

The medical staff came in and out, offering him tea and kindness, checking the machines and his grandfather, saying nothing, but smiling sympathetically. Jack, confused, disorientated in this alien world, stopped asking any questions.

In the late afternoon his mother, with Etienne following behind, arrived. At the sight of her father comatose on the bed and her son beside him, Cynara burst into tears. Jack held her, and Etienne, murmuring words of strength and sympathy to them both, produced a silver flask from his pocket and put it to her lips.

'Here, *ma chérie*, take this. Now sit down beside him, take his hand. He is still alive.' He looked at Jack, who nodded. He felt relieved suddenly at Etienne's presence. It had seemed ridiculous to have a new stepfather when he was over thirty years old, and Etienne, a tall, grey-haired, distinguished Frenchman, had obviously thought so too. At their first meeting Etienne had shaken his hand, put his other hand on his shoulder and said, 'You are too old for a new father and having a son your age makes me feel too old, so let us just be good friends.'

Now the room seemed suddenly crowded with them all there, but Jack felt better with the life they brought in. Sitting there with just machines and this inert body had made him feel dead too – had brought home to him the terror of illness. Now he felt more confident of his grandfather's recovery. He was a fighter after all.

'Have you been here all day, *mon vieux*?' Etienne said to Jack. 'You must be tired, why don't you take a walk outside, and a meal? Is Sonia coming, and Tom?'

'Sonia will try and come but Tom's at school. Do you think he should be here?' Jack asked, suddenly wondering if it would be good for Tom to hover round a deathbed.

Etienne shrugged. 'It's up to you. How far away is he?'

Jack explained and knew that Tom's anxiety would add to his dyslexic problems and he would probably get lost if he was put on a train alone. Besides, he admitted with dismay, he couldn't trust Sonia to meet him at the station on time, and Tom might wander off and that would be something else to worry about. Also Tom had only been back at school a few days and he took ages to settle in again. He didn't say all this to Etienne but he decided he would go and telephone him and explain what was happening.

He got through to the headmaster, explained the situation, and then after a while heard Tom's hesitant voice, 'Dad, is that you?'

'Yes, Tom, it's me. Look, you've got to be a brave boy. I've some sad news. Great-grandpa is very ill with a heart attack.'

There was a silence. Then Tom said, 'Will he die?'

'We don't know. The doctors are being marvellous, but he is old, Tom.'

'I want to come and see him. Even if he's dead I want to come,' Tom said desperately. 'Can you come and get me?'

'I'm in Oxford, near Grandpa's house. It's a long way from you.'

'Then I'll take a train. There must be a train,' Tom said frantically. 'I'll get the money from Mr Castle and come, unless Mum could come and fetch me of course.' His voice sounded hopeful.

Jack's heart sank, again he felt angry and let down by Sonia. He knew she wouldn't go and fetch him this evening. He now didn't know if she was working or with her latest lover and he did not want to find out.

'Mum's busy, she's got lots of meetings,' he said lamely.

'But this is an emergency. You're not at meetings,' Tom said indignantly. 'I'll get a train. Will you meet me at Oxford? I'll ring you on your mobile.'

'I've left my mobile in the office, I came here in such a rush. Look, Tom, it's a difficult journey. You have to go to London first, change stations too, I think.'

'I'll take a taxi,' Tom said.

'No, I'll come for you tomorrow,' Jack decided suddenly. If he couldn't persuade Sonia to go for him, he would drive down himself. Etienne was right, Tom should be here with them at this time. The whole day had been such a nightmare he hadn't thought things through properly.

'He might be dead by then. I want to come as soon as possible.' Tom began to sniff and Jack realised that he was crying.

'Tom, listen. I wish I was with you, but these things happen when we least expect them. Be brave for Great-grandpa. I'll be there tomorrow, early, I promise.'

'Surely Mum could come for me,' he sniffed, 'now?'

'I'll ask her when she rings me, but one of us will be with you in the morning.'

'Miranda would come,' Tom said suddenly. 'If it was an emergency, she would come. I wonder if she's at the Gardiners'. Do you have the telephone number?'

Jack, taken aback by Tom's suggestion, was speechless. Why did he and Tom think of Miranda whenever they needed someone? He thought back to when he'd seen her suddenly in the street and how his heart had lifted. How quickly she had grasped the depth of their feelings for each other, how determined she had been to dissuade him.

'She'll be working, up in London,' he said, seeing with sinking heart that it was past six and she would have left the office, and he would not be able to contact her now as he did not know where she lived. 'Anyway, Tom, we can't ask her to drop everything just because we have a problem. I'll be with you tomorrow.'

'Let me come now,' Tom said again.

'It's late; soon it will be dark. You can't travel on your own at night,' Jack went on, trying to reassure him, feeling his pain and his bewilderment as he struggled to understand the anguish of having such a safe part of his life destroyed.

'It won't be the same without Great-grandpa,' Tom said sadly.

'He might get better. It's just I wanted you to know that he is very ill and might die, but he might get better too,' Jack said, knowing how hard it was to adapt when the balance of one's own little life was shattered. He could almost feel Tom's loneliness, reliving his own when his father had died. He wished he was with him to help him bear the burden. He talked some more until he felt he had comforted Tom and, promising to be there early in the morning, he rang off, his heart heavy, knowing how much his son needed to be with him.

He tried to ring Sonia at home, but all he got was his own voice on the answerphone.

He finally got her at home at ten o'clock.

'Oh, darling . . . How is he?'

'Still with us. Are you coming down?'

'Not tonight, darling. I've had a hell of a day. Poor you, you must be exhausted. Is your mother there?'

'Yes.' He told himself he'd known she wouldn't come so he shouldn't feel this stab of disappointment.

'How's she taking it?'

'She's better now. Etienne is here, giving her support,' he said firmly, suddenly wanting to make her feel guilty.

'Good, he's such a nice man, I'm glad he's there. I'm really sorry I can't be. Are you cross?' Her voice became like a little girl's.

He ignored her and told her about Tom. 'I wonder if you could fetch him tomorrow on your way here. I don't think he can manage a train alone yet, especially not when he's so upset.'

'But, darling, I can't, not tomorrow. I've got that lunch to promote that new French scent. I told you. I'll get him at the weekend. A death . . . well . . .' she gave an awkward laugh, 'when people are so ill it's no place for a child. It might upset him for life. You know how sensitive he is.'

'He wants to be here and I promised one of us would fetch him in the morning. If you had contacted me earlier you could have got him this evening instead of leaving him miserable at school.' His anxiety and exhaustion made him want to hurt her.

'I've been busy all day. I work too, you know. And you know how hopeless I am when people are ill. I'd be more of a bother to you than a help,' she said in a despairing voice as if she was afflicted with a disability she could not help. 'But I'll come tomorrow evening. I promise.'

'If you won't go to fetch Tom, then I will.' Jack put down the receiver firmly. He could not be bothered with her excuses any more. He had a lot on in the office too but had managed to come here. Sonia wasn't here because she didn't want to be, he told himself exhaustedly. No one liked these situations but they had to be faced. Families were meant to rally round, offer comfort in times like these. Self-pity gripped him and he was conscious of the swell of tears in his eyes. He felt so dreadfully alone.

The hospital was getting busy now with the evening visiting hours. He went outside into the cool air and walked up the street. He was a fool and he knew it. Hadn't his grandfather despised him for putting up with Sonia's flirtatious behaviour?

'By doing nothing you might as well condone it,' he'd said once when he'd seen Sonia eye one of his friend's nephews. 'You should put a stop to it at once. It's humiliating, a wife behaving like that in public. It will be the talk of the village.'

In the end his grandfather had said something himself. 'You may not realise it, my dear, but you are behaving like a tart. Stop eyeing that young man or you'll give him the wrong idea and we'll have him hanging round here like a dog after a bitch on heat.'

Sonia had been affronted, accused him of jumping to disgusting ideas, but he had just said, 'You know what I mean. You're a married woman and a mother, and even if you weren't you should have more self-respect than to go throwing yourself at any man who looks at you.'

She had been furious, demanded an apology that he wouldn't give her. Then she'd demanded that Jack stand up for her. Jack had refused, saying he didn't like the way she'd looked at the man either. Then his grandfather, suddenly bored of the scene, had whisked him off somewhere, saying they were late, leaving Sonia behind with Tom, who was quite small at the time and asleep.

Sonia had treated the general warily every since, often grumbling about him, telling Tom and Jack that he lived in another age, an age when men thought they owned women and a wife could hardly breathe without asking her husband's permission.

Jack was feeling very tired now and he went back to the hospital room. There was no change, and Etienne soon persuaded Cynara to come to the local hotel to eat and rest. Jack was too tired and dispirited to talk about Sonia and his mother, locked in her own anxiety, asked then accepted his brief explanation that she was tied up with her work.

'I'm going to fetch Tom in the morning. He wants to be here,' he said.

'Dear Tom,' Cynara said, 'he is so fond of Father.'

The general did not die; he hung on but his illness had changed his and his family's lives for ever. He stayed in hospital some time, but then there was the worry as to where he would go, or if he should, or could, afford someone to live in. Cynara was determined that he would not live alone, yet she could not stay over here permanently. Her life was now in France with her husband.

A lot fell on Jack. He visited his grandfather, now back in his own home, every weekend, and although the general was getting better, his attack had obviously severely shaken him and he had suddenly become a very old man.

'I don't want to be a burden,' he kept saying, but he seemed unable to make any decisions for himself.

'Darling,' Cynara said, laying her hand on Jack's arm as they had dinner in the general's house one weekend, 'you've been so marvellous in all of this that I really hate to ask you an enormous favour.'

'Of course you can, Mother. What is it?'

'I don't know what to do with Father. I don't like to sell off this place and put him in a home. I'd like to take him back to France for the summer, see how much he recovers and then make a decision. I wondered if you could drive us there? Etienne is so busy and I don't like to do it alone in case . . .' she gave a quick laugh, 'well, you know.'

'That would be a good idea. When do you want to go?' Jack said.

'As soon as possible. I don't like to leave Etienne so long.'

It had been almost two months since the general's attack and Jack had been rushed off his feet, not only with the anxiety of his grandfather's illness but also with work. He had gone on two business trips in that time and longed for some rest. He managed to wangle a few days off and now looked forward to spending them in France in the pretty château his mother lived in with Etienne. He went to Hatchards and bought some new novels, looking forward to a few days of utter peace.

Tom was still at school and Sonia, putting her arms round Jack, said, 'What a good idea, darling, and you love it there. I really can't come with you, though how I wish I could. How long will you be there?'

In desperation, he thought he would not tell her, thinking then she wouldn't know how long she could spend with whatever man she was with at the moment. 'I don't know until I get there,' he said.

As he packed he thought how life had changed these last few weeks, not least for his once fiercely independent grandfather. It was frightening to see how quickly and irrevocably events could shatter long-held habits and lifestyles.

Tidying his briefcase he came across Miranda's office number scrawled on a piece of paper. After she had left in the taxi, the day he'd seen her in the street, he had gone into the shoe shop, matching its name with her bags, and managed to get the name and number of the magazine she worked for. With all that had happened he had not tried to ring her for weeks. He had often longed to, but had known that at the moment he would be a dismal companion.

His family problems sapped most of his energy. There was too much to burden her with, for he knew she would pick up his mood at once and ask him about it. As if his grandfather's illness was not enough there was his mother's anxiety not only over her father but also over her husband, whom she hated leaving. Tom was finding it very difficult to adjust to his great-grandfather being such an invalid and though Sonia was being supportive and loving when she was with him he felt it was only because she felt guilty for working so hard, for possibly being with someone else.

There were too many emotional crises going on in his life and he couldn't cope with any more. And it was too late: Miranda would assume that he had taken her pleas to be left alone to heart and no doubt had made her own life. She was right, he thought sadly, what sort of relationship could they possibly have together?

He had seen how shaken Tom had been over his great-grandfather's illness; it would not be long before he found out about Sonia's behaviour with other men. He could not add to his son's distress by seeing a woman he admitted to himself he longed to be with all the time, even to the exclusion of his family.

In despair he threw away the paper with her number on it, although he knew he could always get the number again if he wanted to, knowing the name of the magazine. All the same he felt immensely sad, as if he had made a final decision not to see her again.

Chapter Twelve

Miranda drove down to her parents' house for the weekend. It was Friday afternoon and Stella had suggested that she leave at three thirty. She was kind like that. She expected people to work very hard, staying late if necessary, but if work was quiet she sometimes let them go home early.

Miranda didn't bother to ring her mother to tell her she'd be early and was pleased that she arrived in Hampshire before five instead of at dinner-time, after being caught up by the weekend traffic. She parked her car in the drive and saw her mother at the end of the garden working in the shrubbery.

'Mummy,' she called as she walked over the lawn to join her. 'It's me, I got away early.'

'Oh . . . darling, how nice.' Julia straightened up, rubbed her eyes roughly, looked away. Miranda saw with a shock she had been crying. Before she could say anything her mother hugged her.

'I'm just fighting with this ground elder. I don't know how it got in the border, but if you turn your back on it a moment it takes over.' She forced a smile on her face, turned back to pick up her trowel and fork. 'Let's go and have a cup of tea. I'm so glad you're early.'

It was on the tip of Miranda's tongue to ask what was the matter, but she stopped herself, thinking it better to ignore the tears unless her mother said anything. Julia, an expert at fussing over other people, hated it to be directed towards herself. Perhaps, Miranda thought, her red eyes were an allergy to ground elder.

Julia was not a crier. In fact the worse things were, the harder she fought to cope with them. Her zeal could be exhausting in her determination to cope with whatever crises had occurred. When Sally, her daughter-in-law, had had yet another miscarriage she had become an expert on the causes, both through muddled readings in the library and stories of other people's miscarriages. These she had showered on to Marcus and Sally in a misguided attempt both to comfort them and to urge them on to try again. In her opinion Roland's existence was almost entirely due to her efforts.

'Tea would be welcome, but only if you've finished here, or can I help demolish the dreaded weed?' Miranda looked down at the earth and saw that the elder had indeed taken quite a hold. It was a back-breaking job to get rid of it and she wondered aloud why her father couldn't help with it now that he had more time at home.

At the mention of her father Julia's mouth wobbled and a tear splashed from her eye.

'Mummy, what is it? Is something wrong with Daddy?'

'No,' she sniffed furiously, looking away from Miranda. 'Well, yes, I think there's something wrong with him, but of course he says it's all my fault.'

'What is wrong with him?' Miranda felt panic rise in her gullet. Images of terminal illness rose like an evil snake in her mind, with her father, in his dismissive way, choosing to ignore it and so not getting the medical help that might save him.

'It's his mind,' Julia said, picking the earth off her trowel with her fingers. 'I think he's gone dotty, quite dotty.' She wiped the tears off her face with the back of her hand, leaving a smudge of earth on her cheek.

Miranda felt sick and very frightened. She had never, apart from when her grandparents had died, seen her mother so upset. She had a feeling that if she had arrived later as planned, Julia would have packed away her problems deep inside her, like hiding muddle in a cupboard so a room would be tidy for a guest. But thinking she was alone until the evening she had taken them out and worried about them and Miranda had caught her at it before she had time to tidy them away and compose herself.

'Let's go in and have tea and talk about it,' Miranda said through her fear, telling herself firmly that if her father was mentally ill surely Marcus, who'd seen him recently, would have noticed and told her.

'He's dotty, totally mental,' Julia said again, as though now the words were unleashed she could not contain herself. 'Really someone of his age and position should know better.'

'Tell me exactly what has happened,' Miranda persisted.

'He's gone off with a girl, younger than you. It's disgusting. I never thought he was like that. He must have gone mad and needs a doctor, a psychiatrist.' Julia was shouting now, her usually calm face contorted with anger, her hair flying everywhere, a smudge of mud on her cheek. Miranda looked at her horrified.

'Gone off? Where?'

'Gone off to her sordid little room in Petersfield. Oh, he'll be back tonight, pretending nothing has happened or that such behaviour is perfectly normal in *hot-blooded males*, as he puts it.' She snorted derisively. 'Naturally he wants to see you, and I'm certain he won't mention a word of it to you.'

'Are you sure, Mummy?' Julia's words were like pointed missiles raining down on her. She knew her mother often imagined things were worse than they were but she couldn't really imagine her father going off in such an undignified way.

'Yes, he's admitted it. He says he's had enough of me and my old-fashioned ways.' The tears were streaming down her face now. 'He says he will never be old and this girl is so alive and makes him feel twenty again.'

Miranda took her mother in her arms and held her. She was horrified. She remembered the dislike she'd seen in her father's eyes at Christmas, but she never thought he'd do this.

Julia straightened up and moved away from her. Pacing up and down the lawn, she cried, 'I did everything for him: made sure the house was comfortable, good food on the table, endlessly entertained his business colleagues, and now he does this to me. He's been so difficult lately, moody, irritable. I've tried to help him. I know it's difficult retiring from work.'

'But he works two days a week,' Miranda bleated helplessly, flaying round for some hope, like a person suddenly out of her depth in deep water. She felt as if she'd walked into a nightmare. This couldn't be happening, not to *her* parents.

'That is hardly work any more. He feels he is just an office boy and they are being kind to him. They've taken on some new, young people, far more dynamic than he is. Women too, and that upset him – that he's been replaced by a woman.'

'I thought he thought women today were wonderful, how they combined good careers with motherhood.' Miranda remembered his remarks when Julia had agreed with Sally on her wish to give up her career to look after Roland.

'Only if they don't disturb him,' Julia answered. She took a deep breath, then said sadly: 'You know those experiments they do with rats?'

'Rats?' Miranda said. Was it her mother who was dotty?

'They show them that if they press a red button they get an electric shock, and if they press the green one they get some food. They learn pretty quickly, I believe, but I,' she sniffed again, 'I'm not as clever as a rat. I seem to have been keeping pressing the red button and making him more angry every time.'

'Oh, Mummy, of course you're not stupid.' Miranda didn't know what to say in the face of her mother's distress – her mother, who had never before revealed so much of herself, who had always been in control of every situation so that Miranda had always seen her, and indeed her father, as the stable rocks in her life. Julia maddened her often with her views, but she could always be depended upon. In fact one of the reasons Miranda had come down this weekend was to talk to her about Jack. She could not get him out of her mind, though she had done nothing about seeing him since the day he had cancelled the table at the restaurant. She had thought in her anguish that possibly her mother would put it in perspective for her in a way her girl friends would not. But now she knew she could not mention it; this was a far worse crisis.

She forced herself to say, 'Tell me about this woman. Do you mean he's . . .' the thought shocked her, she swallowed, said, 'he's having an affair with this woman or that he just likes her?'

'He's having an affair. She thinks he's wonderful, of course. She comes from a poor background and for a few favours in bed she gets taken out to restaurants she's only dreamt of, bought clothes, make-up. Oh yes,' she elaborated at Miranda's shocked gasp, 'I can quite understand it from her point of view: take what you can when you can.'

'How long has this been going on for?'

'A month . . . that I know of, anyway.'

'But why didn't you tell us? Do Marcus and Edward know?'

Julia drew herself up, fighting for control with difficulty. 'I didn't like to tell them. The fact is,' she licked her lips, burst out, 'I'm ashamed of Richard, humiliated. When everyone in the village knows, if they don't already, they'll laugh at me, and at him. If he'd gone off with someone our age, fallen in love,' she shrugged, 'well, there's not always much you can do then. But to go with a woman young enough to be his daughter, I just find that very demeaning. I mean, people might not think he's safe with their young daughters.'

'I can see that,' Miranda said, feeling quite dizzy with horror. She thought herself quite broad-minded, thought as long as people didn't hurt each other they could love whom they wished. Age, race, class, religion – if you loved each other what business was it of anyone else's? Old men had always loved young women. Stories of it abounded in mythology, in the Bible. It was supposed to rejuvenate them, revive their flagging manhood, so they could forget they were getting old and could pretend they were young again. All this she accepted and understood, but she didn't want her own father to behave like this. Could he not accept his middle age with dignity? Have fun by all means. Do more exciting things with his life which he could now he was semi-retired and had some money to spare, but not do something quite so humiliating for his family, for himself.

Suddenly she felt furious with him. She knew what the people in the village were like, what people everywhere were like. They would ridicule him. Some – men his age, of course – might envy him, wish they could do the same and get away with it. But Miranda felt it somehow made him more a figure of fun than of an exciting lover. For however nice a man he was, and however much she loved him, she had to admit that at sixty-one years old, with his thinning, greying hair and paunch, the slight stoop he had as if he was trying not to appear so tall, he did not correspond to the image of an ardent, attractive lover.

'Maybe it will finish very soon, is just a passing lapse,' she said desperately. She looked round the beautiful garden where she had taken her first steps as a child, played, gone for walks with boyfriends. She looked at the rosy brick house which had been her home – was, despite her flat, still her home in her mind. Would all this go? Would her father leave her mother for this woman?

'Maybe it will,' Julia said dispiritedly. 'But what am I to do in the meantime, wait quietly here while he goes through all the young girls in the district?'

'I'm sure it won't be like that.'

'Why not? She's not a pretty woman, just young. Why shouldn't he go after others? All his money will go on them, all this,' she gestured at the house and round the garden, 'will eventually have to be sold to pay for this sordid nonsense. He sees no reason, you know. That's why I think he's gone mad, had some sort of breakdown.'

'We must tell the boys, get them to talk to him,' Miranda said firmly, not able to bear all this herself. 'Were you going to tell me about it this weekend?'

'No,' Julia admitted. 'I keep hoping it will all come to an end and no harm, at least not to all of you, would come of it. Marcus is worried sick about his business. They may have to do bed and breakfast now that Sally has stopped work. Roland, as you know, is often ill – just colds and tummy bugs but they could so easily develop into something worse.'

'But you must tell us. We're not babies any more, we can't be protected for ever,' Miranda said kindly. 'We must know it all. Would Daddy have said anything to me? I mean, what excuse would he give for not staying here this weekend?'

'Oh, he's staying here while you're here. He often stays, sleeps in the spare room. He wants to have his cake and eat it. He loves this house, as you know, and though he may mock it, his place in the village. He thinks he can come back as and when he chooses.'

'But that's so selfish, despicable. I can't believe it of him, not Daddy,' Miranda cried. Her father had always been so kind, so honest, never someone who behaved like this.

'That's why I think he's gone mad. His behaviour is quite out of character. I think he's suffering from some deep complex about getting older, can't face up to it, and thinks he can solve it this way.'

'Then he needs help, serious help.'

Julia laughed bitterly. 'You try telling him that. He thinks there's nothing wrong with *him* at all, that it's not his fault. That I have driven him to seek understanding from another woman. "Understanding?" I said.' She gave a bitter laugh. 'The only thing that young woman will understand is his bank balance and once she's got through that she'll be off, looking for the next old fool.'

'What about if she gets pregnant?' Miranda said in horror, jealousy now eating into her. She didn't want a new sibling thrust upon her. That indeed would destroy everything.

'I warned him about that,' she sighed. 'He promises me he doesn't want any more children. He doesn't want the commitment, you see, only the fun,' she said derisively. 'He says he's had commitments and responsibilities all his life and he's had enough.' She snorted. 'We could all say that.'

'But the girl might trap him with a child.' Miranda felt more and more bewildered. Her father, like many a British man, had never talked much about his emotions. He had urged them all to do their best in life, at school, helped them with their school work, encouraged them, played with them, listened to their troubles. But he had never mentioned he had any of his own. She felt very lost, like a small child again; terrified as she envisaged what she'd always thought of as a secure and happy family being ripped open, exposing a rotten core.

She forced herself to take charge, face up to the situation, however difficult. She took her mother indoors and made her some tea. She listened some more, feeling increasingly unhappy every moment, then not able to bear it any longer on her own, she rang Marcus.

He sounded tired and she felt mean telling him about their parents' problems.

'Can you come over tomorrow? There's a serious problem here and—'

'It will be very difficult. Tell me what it is.'

'It sounds so stupid, so unlike him, but Daddy's gone off with a younger woman,' she blurted.

Marcus sighed. 'So it's true?'

'You knew about it?' She was incredulous. 'Does everyone, everyone but me that is, know about it?'

'I don't know, but Nigel Ridway thought it as well to mention it to me last time I was there.'

'When? What did you do?'

'Oh, last week, or the week before. We came over, I was in the pub having a drink and he came up to me. "A word in your ear", you know the sort of thing.' Marcus sounded even wearier.

'So what did you do? Confront Daddy at once?'

'No, Miranda, I didn't. He was there for the weekend, everything seemed as it always has been, so I thought better to leave it well alone. I figured if he was really keen on this woman he'd move in with her permanently. He hasn't so I think he'll get over it.'

'Do you? And what about Mummy and her feelings? She's shattered and it's so humiliating.' Miranda felt furious with him. She adored her brothers, but how like them not to want to get emotionally involved.

'I know it's a difficult time for her, but she's strong, and understanding. She knows in her heart that it means nothing,' Marcus said.

'That's what you want her to feel,' Miranda cried. 'What if this girl spends all Daddy's money and Mummy is out in the street and the house and garden go? Or she gets pregnant and all his money goes on supporting another child, or even children?' She was beside herself with anger.

'It won't come to that. Dad's no fool.'

'No? He sounds like one to me. I suppose Edward thinks the same?'

'I don't know, I haven't asked him. Look, Miranda, I've just had so much on this end. The business is not going well, and without Sally's salary things are quite tough. We've decided to do bed and breakfasts, but need to redecorate the rooms first and it's all quite a strain. I'll come over when I can and talk to Dad, I promise.'

She could feel he wanted to escape, could not take on any more problems just now. She felt impatient with him. Men, she thought with irritation, are nothing but trouble and when they cause it they shrug it off as if it's not their business.

When she'd rung off she joined her mother again in the kitchen. Julia looked better now, having brushed her hair and washed her face. She gave Miranda a wan smile.

'Darling,' she said, 'don't bother the boys too much with this. I don't want to be a burden on them.'

'You're not a burden,' Miranda retorted. 'We must all support you over this.'

'I'm not old, or infirm, I'll cope if I have to,' she said with spirit. 'I just,' her voice wobbled for a moment, then came out strongly, 'I just don't want to lose this house. It means everything to me.' She smiled. 'I know it sounds stupid. After all, the phrase "only a housewife" is so ridiculed these days. But this house represents the centre of my life. When we bought it soon after we were married it was derelict. We couldn't have afforded it otherwise. We, but mostly me, as your father was working to pay for it, restored what we could ourselves, only having builders in for what we couldn't do. We lived without water, electricity for weeks, but we coped.'

'It must have been dreadful. I still find it difficult to believe when I see the before and after photographs,' Miranda said.

'It was hell, especially in the winter months, but we were young and it was like shaping our lives really. We finished it over the years, had you children and it was a happy home, wasn't it?'

'The best,' Miranda said, taking her hand.

'And now it is home to grandchildren. You know how Edward's

children love it, and little Roland will as he gets older. That is why I want to keep it,' she said fiercely. 'Not just for myself and for all the work I've put in to the house, and in making the garden from an overgrown wilderness, but for your children, and even,' she smiled, 'our great-grandchildren.'

'I want it too,' Miranda said, realising what she'd always known but taken for granted: that it was a haven from the troubles of the world. Wasn't that partly why she had come down this weekend, to lay out her feelings about Jack? To examine them carefully and to try to make sense of them in the place she loved and felt the most secure in? Her mother was in her late fifties, still young and healthy. She should be able to live here for years, giving happiness to all the grandchildren, and not have it snatched away by her father's selfish stupidity.

'I don't want,' Julia said slowly, 'the boys to, well, stop coming here because they are afraid of having to cope with this. I know they will feel very strongly, will stand by me, but also that neither of them, like your father, is much good at confronting an emotional problem unless they have to.'

'Well, they do have to,' Miranda said firmly. She understood suddenly that her mother was afraid of losing them too, if she made too much fuss and became a helpless victim. They, not wanting to admit their picture of her as capable, coping, firmly in charge was being eroded, might well keep away. What a muddle it was, she thought. What we all do, or put up with, to be loved. How selfish we become to avoid our illusions being shattered.

Her father had gone off with this young woman who was giving him the illusion of youth. Her mother would have hidden her anguish from all of them just to keep their love. How terrible that she had to feel like that. Surely their love for their mother was stronger than that? Miranda knew that it was, but that much might be lost before they realised it. She thought how much she wanted Jack to love her, even though nothing could come of it, and how she had written back to Tom enclosing her address. She had told herself she was only doing it so as not to let him down, but she knew in her heart she wanted Jack to know where she was.

Not that she'd heard anything from either of them. She'd sent the letter to his school two weeks ago and he'd probably lost it. Jack had been wise, she thought, to cancel the table. He had recognised as she had that they could never just be friends. But how like a man, she thought now, to do it without any explanation. No doubt he wanted to avoid an emotional confrontation. Perhaps Sonia had found out and he had decided to sever all contact with her quickly and cleanly. She wondered if he knew that Tom had written to her. Perhaps Jack had put a stop to his son's friendship with her too.

All this she had wanted to mull over here, perhaps discuss with her mother – or even her father, who would at least listen to her love problems, though he had never thought any of her boyfriends good enough for her. But now she must forget her own worries and concentrate on this new one.

They heard the crunch of a car on the drive, the slam of its door. The women looked apprehensively at each other.

Julia said, 'I'll just pop upstairs for a minute, change out of my gardening clothes.' She laid her hand on Miranda's shoulder a moment before leaving the room.

Watching her go Miranda felt sad yet proud of her. She knew she was going to doll herself up to show her husband what he was discarding. She was, after all, still a beautiful woman.

'Hello, my darling. Where are you?' she heard her father call, and knew his greeting was for her, not her mother.

Slowly, with anguish in her heart, she went out into the hall. She stood at the door and watched him. He smiled, put out his arms to her. 'There you are, darling. How good to see you. How are you?'

She had to admit he had a boyish vigour about him. At Christmas and the last time she'd seen him, he'd been tired, pale and listless. No doubt this girl had rejuvenated him. She didn't move from her place in the doorway and he hesitated, his smile wavering.

'No kiss for your old dad then?' he said.

She took a deep breath, leant against the door as if to draw strength from the house she felt was part of her and said, 'No, Daddy. I understand that you're behaving despicably. I never thought someone like you would sink so low.'

'Steady on.' He looked annoyed. 'What's your mother been saying?'

'I came here early, just after five. I found her crying. If I hadn't she wouldn't have told me and I don't suppose you would.'

'I don't know what you mean,' he said defensively.

'You do. This girl, younger than me apparently, though I agree I'm not that young. But surely you can see she's making a fool of you, is after your money?'

He went red, clenched his fists by his sides. 'I won't be spoken to like this by my own daughter. Your mother's put you up to it, I suppose. She knows nothing about it. Linda's not like that at all.'

'So you admit it?' Miranda felt her anger rising. Now the girl had a name the whole thing became frighteningly real.

'It's none of your business.'

'Yes it is, if your actions are going to jeopardise our home, the house we all love and that Mummy has made her life.'

'That's the trouble with your mother. She should have made me her life,' her father blurted out. Then, looking awkward, said, 'She lost interest in me. I felt just like a meal ticket at times. It was always the house, the garden.'

'We came first a great deal of the time,' Miranda said.

'Yes, of course, but when you all left home and I thought we'd do more together, she wanted to do up the house, remodel the garden.'

'Didn't you ask her to do things with you?' Miranda felt impatient with them both suddenly. No doubt they lived in silence, seething underneath their calm exteriors, never sitting down and talking about the things that irritated each about the other.

'I did,' her father said defiantly, 'but she was always busy here or in the village.'

'You must give up this Linda,' Miranda said firmly. 'Try and sort things out with Mummy before you lose everything.'

'Give her up!' Richard laughed sourly. 'You don't know what she means to me. She's given me new life, understands me.' He looked embarrassed. 'I don't want to talk about it. Let's leave it.'

'If you are ashamed about it then it is wrong,' Miranda said firmly. She turned from him and walked away, going upstairs to her old bedroom to hunt for a memory of her secure childhood before she confronted him again.

As she went she wondered if he would leave and go back to this Linda, but she heard him go into the drawing room and help himself to a drink.

As she sat in her room, looking out over the garden, she thought of how buoyant her father looked. How invigorating love – or lust – was, but also how destructive. She thought of Jack and how much she had wanted him, how she was so certain she would be better for him than Sonia, would love and care for him more, but she saw now with sickening clarity the devastation their love for each other would cause for his child, his family.

However nice Linda was, and maybe she was, however much her father, through his marital misunderstandings, felt he deserved her, their union would cause untold havoc with the rest of his family's lives.

She had come here to think out her feelings for Jack. Over the weeks since he had cancelled lunch she had harboured dreams of how she could contact him. He had been there in her mind, sometimes even at the most intimate moments with David, so that David had wondered if she was bored with him. She knew she must make a decision, either to see Jack, get him out of her system, see that her illusions of him were greatly exaggerated; or forget about him altogether.

She had almost convinced herself before coming here this weekend that she could see him without causing harm to his child and his marriage. Now falling into this drama with her own parents she saw that it would be impossible.

Chapter Thirteen

'So, there it is. I don't suppose you'll come with me?' David asked Miranda, only half hopefully, a wry smile on his lips.

She matched his smile though inside she felt a turmoil of emotions. 'I can't leave my job, you know I can't,' she said regretfully.

'I didn't think you could,' he said bravely, then sighed. 'Life is so difficult for us these days. I want to go and live in Geneva. I'm flattered the firm has chosen me. It's a good step forward. It would be considered very bad form if I refused. But what would have happened if we'd been married?' He looked at her quizzically.

She laughed, assuming he was joking. 'But we're not. Neither of us wants that sort of commitment.' She hoped she sounded light-hearted and that he wasn't going to come over heavy and ask her to marry him.

'I agree. But your career is as important to you as mine is to me, and I quite understand that you couldn't suddenly leave it and move to Geneva. I don't even know if there are any fashion magazines out there, where you could work. So, had we been married, which of us would have sacrificed his or her career prospects, do you think?' He looked at her intently, stretching out his long legs and leaning back in his chair as though settling in for a debate.

'It is difficult. I suppose we could both have kept our jobs and commuted back and forth.' She hoped he was not going to get intense about their relationship. She would miss him dreadfully. It did upset her that he was going, and so soon. There had been a crisis in the office in Geneva resulting in some key person there having a nervous breakdown and David was to be sent out at once to take his place and pull the office together.

She enjoyed being with him, he was easy, undemanding. He had been very understanding over the drama with her parents. She had arrived back that Sunday night, fraught and unhappy after a nightmare weekend. She had managed to get some of the neighbours in for a drink on Saturday, and one couple had asked them all for supper, then another had invited them to a barbecue if the weather held on the Sunday. This had kept the lid on everything and outwardly no one would have guessed that Julia and Richard were going through a major crisis. Miranda had managed one more go with her father, insisting that he give up this woman and make an effort with his marriage. This had not gone down well.

'You don't understand,' he'd said defiantly. 'You only get one chance in this life, Miranda, and when I met Linda, she made me feel so alive, I wasn't going to turn it down.'

'What would you have thought if Mummy had brought home some toy boy that made her feel alive?' Miranda had said impatiently.

'That's not the same, you know it isn't,' he'd replied crossly.

'It is these days, Daddy. What's sauce for the goose. She's still beautiful and it would serve you right if she met someone else,' Miranda said with more conviction than she felt. She couldn't imagine how she'd feel if her mother followed the same course as her father. In fact she was very unhappy and insecure indeed about it all and was relieved to return to London.

She had gone round to David's flat and poured it all out at him, quite disregarding the fact that he had a report to write before the morning. He had been wonderful, told her that his father had once gone off but had come back again, and he'd made her feel that she wasn't the only person whose middle-aged parents had gone astray.

'Emotional drama makes one feel so isolated and selfish,' she'd said at last, feeling stronger with his sympathy and encouragement. But now, two weeks on, he was going to Geneva and though she could telephone and visit him, she would miss him dreadfully.

It would be so easy, she thought now, seeing him comfortably stretched out in her chair, a glass of wine in his hand, to drift into marriage with him. They would be good companions, they would make a good home together, both enjoying fine wine and good food. They had similar tastes in music, art, films. They'd get on well. Did one really need great passion? she wondered. Wouldn't it be rather restful and uncomplicated not to have it?

He caught her gaze and for a moment she thought he felt the same way. Hastily she pushed the idea from her mind. She didn't want to marry, it wasn't easy and safe, and if it was one would probably get bored out of one's mind. She didn't want to give up her job, not now that Stella was giving her more and more to do.

She said quickly, 'Colin will be pleased. He'll be able to stop poring through the Bible for suitable reprimands.'

David laughed. 'Is he still bothering you? Perhaps I ought to say something.' He sat up as if he was going to go upstairs at once and deal with it.

'Oh, no. Don't bother. Since I've stayed with you in your flat he's had nothing to say. But if you stay tonight—'

'I hope I'm staying tonight,' he interrupted her with a warm smile, 'or will you be bombarded with texts against licentiousness and depravity?' He laughed and she did too. Then he said more seriously, 'I shall miss our nights. You will come and visit, won't you?'

'Of course,' she said, and leant her arms on his knees and smiled up at him. She would be lonely, she thought as he stroked her hair. She had many friends – she was lucky in that and also in having her painting – but a man, like a friendly dog, was good to have around. She smiled, thinking of that, and when he asked her what had made her smile she felt that comparing him to a friendly dog might sound rather unkind, so she said, 'Oh, just Colin. What an extraordinarily empty life he must lead to be so bothered about our sins. I mean, we're so quiet, hardly having orgies every night – any night,' she laughed.

'I think it's rather sinister,' David said. 'I hope he's not some pervert who's going to make himself unpleasant. You will be careful, won't you, Miranda?'

'Oh, don't frighten me,' she said, feeling a prickle of fear run up her spine. The newspapers were full of stories of weird men stalking women, attacking them because some voice or force had told them to.

'I don't mean to, but don't let him in here when you're alone, will you?'

'Of course not. He's never shown the slightest sign of wanting to be near me. In fact, I think I disgust him, with my sinful behaviour,' she laughed, trying to dispel the fear David's remarks had germinated. 'My brother Marcus stayed a couple of nights last week, as you know. Colin didn't say anything, just glared, but I think he thought he was another of my lovers.'

'Take care, that's all,' he said, and kissed her.

He left for Geneva at the end of the week and on the Friday night Tessa rang her.

'I know I'm the most selfish woman in the world, Miranda, but if you're doing nothing you wouldn't like to come here for the weekend? Simon's just rung to say he's got to stay in New York until Tuesday, and I don't think I can bear another minute alone with the children and no adult to speak to.' She sounded desperate.

Miranda laughed. 'What about the – oh, I don't remember their names, the ones in the big house?'

'Gillard-Hardings. I hardly ever see them, let alone speak to them. Oh, Miranda, I know I'm selfish and I truly have been meaning to ask you for ages. In fact I remember I did ask you and you put over some lame excuse as to why you couldn't come to stay. So can you, or for the day even?' She prattled on, pouring out her feelings of frustration, boredom and disappointment that Simon wasn't coming home for a few more days.

'I'd love to,' Miranda said laughing. It would do her good too to get away from thinking about her parents, missing David. Tessa was a childhood friend and they'd have a good laugh. Also they'd recently had their new baby, Luke, whom she had not yet seen. Although she liked Simon, without him they could really gossip. She promised Tessa she'd leave early in the morning.

When she put the phone down she thought suddenly of Jack. She hadn't been back to Chandos Hall since that weekend she'd first met him. But why should he be there? Even if Tom was still at Pilgrim's Court they didn't take him out every weekend. Anyway, she told herself firmly, she was being so stupid about him. She was letting him take over her life when he had shown, by cancelling the lunch without an explanation, that he was not interested in her. It was foolish of her to put off visiting one of her oldest friends in case she ran into him. Tessa had said she never saw the Gillard-Hardings and as long as she didn't walk near their house, even if Jack was there, she wouldn't see him.

All the same she washed her hair and packed a pretty dress she'd bought at Monsoon. She told herself that the weather might be too hot for jeans.

Tessa was thrilled to see her and Miranda soon saw why. Luke never stopped whingeing and crying, and Henry seemed to be permanently clamped to her leg.

'Luke demands so much attention and Henry's so jealous. He's fine when Simon is here because they go off and do masculine things together, but when I'm on my own, it's murder,' she complained. 'I'm sorry, it will be such a boring weekend for you. You are good to come.'

'It's great to get away,' Miranda said, thinking how trapped poor Tessa had become. She was sure she wouldn't have the patience to be holed up with two crying babies, however pretty the cottage and luscious the landscape. It may be lovely to be isolated in the country if you could read and paint or be alone with a lover, but to be stuck with crying babies would be sheer hell, she thought.

They spent the weekend in the cottage and its garden, going out to the village on Sunday morning. They saw only a few people who lived in the village and Mrs Peabody in the shop.

When they came into the shop, Henry leaving go of Tessa's hand to peer into the ice-cream cabinet, Mrs Peabody's face lit up. She immediately said in a loud voice, looking furtively round all the time as if spies were lurking in every corner, 'She's back. I never thought she would come back, but she is. The old man made her come back, I'm sure of it.'

Miranda was about to ask who, when Tessa said, 'You mean Bunny, Ralph's wife?'

'That's it. Came back last week. I haven't seen you for days. It's quite stale news by now.' She closed her mouth tight shut, gloating at her news as if to remind Tessa that if she insisted on struggling to

Sainsbury's to do most of her shopping, she would miss out on the important news of the village.

'I've been stuck at home with the children,' Tessa said lamely.

Mrs Peabody looked unconvinced, but her longing to pass on the news yet again overcame her. She said, 'It's funny you not knowing, being on the estate and all.' Her small eyes darted over Tessa's face as if gleaning any titbits of gossip she might have heard of the matter.

'They are quite some way from us, and as we don't share a drive I never know who is there or not. Anyway, since Luke was born I've had my hands full.' Luke, whose pram was taking up most of the shop, was obvious evidence of this.

Mrs Peabody digested this. 'Well, she's back and there's talk,' she paused, looking from Miranda to Tessa, 'that she's to have a child, an heir, even if,' she lowered her voice, leant towards them and said in shocked delight, 'she has to go to one of them fertility clinics, perhaps even have "donor sperm".' She mouthed the last two words, her eyes on Henry, who was engrossed with the board of bright pictures of ice creams.

'What!' Tessa was amazed. 'That can't be true. They've got a child already, surely they can have another. Anyway, if it's not his child it can't inherit, can it?' She looked at Miranda.

'I don't know. Maybe if it's adopted it can.'

'Well, that's what I heard,' Mrs Peabody said triumphantly. 'There have been all sorts of people in and out of that house all week. The old man is determined to get an heir.'

'I want that chocolate one.' Henry pulled at his mother, pointing to a picture of a cornet smothered in chocolate and nuts.

'What . . . ? Oh, OK, Henry.' Tessa was too distracted by Mrs Peabody's news to insist on her rule of no snacks before meals.

When at last they left the shop she said to Miranda, 'I'd take most of what she says with a pinch of salt. She hears a few things then elaborates on them until neither she or anyone else knows the truth.'

'What does she mean, all sorts of people in and out of the house?' Miranda asked, wondering if Jack was one of them.

'I've no idea,' Tessa laughed. 'Perhaps she means potential sperm donors, or doctors and lawyers to force poor Ralph to perform. Honestly, I do feel sorry for him. Some old aristocratic families probably do deserve to die out.'

'But you never know who is there, or what's going on?' Miranda pursued, pretending to herself that she was fascinated by the plot to produce an heir but really knowing that all she cared about was whether or not Jack was there.

'Not unless I walk right down over the fields and peer in from the other side. Or meet one of the men on the estate who'll gossip to me, or see Mrs Peabody.' Tessa unwrapped Henry's ice cream for him as he jumped frantically round her in his frustration at not being able to get into it himself. 'Henry, do stop for a minute or it will drop on the ground and you won't have it.' She handed it to him. 'Since they've opened the main part of the Hall to the public we're even more cut off, thank goodness. They've fenced that off so the Gillard-Hardings won't be disturbed in their wing.'

'I wondered why we didn't see coachloads of tourists photographing your washing line,' Miranda joked. 'So it's like living on an island?'

'I do hear everything eventually, of course, but this last fortnight's been frantic with the children. Luke's had a cold so I haven't been around in the village much.'

As they wandered up the lane to the cottage, Miranda saw that because of a curve in the land it was possible to see only the tops of the chimneys of Chandos Hall from Tessa's cottage. The front of the house and the drive weren't visible at all. There was no way Tessa would know who was there.

'Did you ever see that child again? The one you helped with the mask?' Tessa said suddenly, the unexpectedness of her question making Miranda blush. Seeing it, she said quickly with a teasing smile, 'I know he has an attractive father. He came here that time and I've seen him at church.'

'Have you?' Miranda felt the blood rush to her face again.

'Yes, two or three times, with the boy. Simon thought it a good idea to introduce Henry to church.' She laughed. 'It didn't last long. Henry kept filling in the quiet bits with songs from his nursery school, but we saw the man about twice and his son.'

'And his wife? Remember we saw her that time in the shop?'

'Yes, she's beautiful, but standoffish.' Tessa pulled at her sweat shirt. 'Oh, to dress elegantly again, to know that everything one wears hasn't a line of baby sick running from shoulder to hem. At the moment it's only worth wearing stuff that can be constantly flung in the washing machine. I don't mind telling you, I feel quite jealous sometimes of women like her – like you too, Miranda – who have the time and money too, I suppose, to look good,' she said cheerfully.

'You can look marvellous if you have to,' Miranda said, not wanting to admit that she felt jealous of Sonia too, but for a different reason. 'You won't always be feeding and washing babies.'

She'd been amazed at how much work Luke and Henry were. Tessa never seemed to have a moment to herself. Luke cried a great deal of the night too. Miranda was sure she wouldn't have the patience to be a mother herself.

She wanted to find out more about Jack, but Tessa knew her so well and would soon guess at her feelings. She wanted no one, especially someone who knew Jack, or could get to know him, to have a single suspicion.

'I suppose I won't,' Tessa said and then went on to say how without Simon she was sure she'd soon sink to the extreme dregs of scruffiness. 'The thing is,' she said, 'I used to long to know all the gossip, like Mrs P. telling us about Bunny coming back, but now I can't really be bothered with it. I mean, I'll listen and speculate like everyone else, but I can't be bothered to go out of my way to ferret it out for myself. I'm just too tired at the moment, trying to keep this show on the road.' She gestured towards the baby, who was now sleeping peacefully in his pram, and Henry, who she suddenly grabbed, scrubbing at his face, which was covered with most of the ice cream, now also dripping down over his shirt.

'I try also,' she said, wiping at her own now sticky fingers with the remnant of a Kleenex, 'to be vaguely attractive and interested in Simon. I noticed that chap's wife eyeing him up during Communion.'

'Oh, Sonia – she's often having affairs, apparently. She had one with James Darby,' Miranda said, pleased the conversation had come back to Jack again.

'Haven't seen him for ages. Haven't seen anyone for ages, for that matter. But he had an affair with her? Are you sure?'

'Yes. I don't know why she has affairs when she has such an attractive husband,' Miranda said as lightly as she could.

'Maybe there's something wrong with him. Maybe he's gay,' Tessa sighed. 'Often the most good-looking men are. Such a waste, I always think. Not that I'm on the lookout,' she laughed. 'But other people's marriages are a puzzle. Who knows what he's like at home?'

Miranda did not like the way the conversation was going. There was nothing wrong with Jack, she was sure of it. It was Sonia who was at fault.

After they'd had lunch Miranda thought how tired Tessa looked. There was a pile of unread Sunday papers and a novel among a pile of children's books recently taken from the library.

Miranda heard herself saying, 'Would you like me to take the children out for a little while? Give you time for a read?' She glanced at the papers and the novel.

'Oh, no, you don't want to do that,' Tessa said in a voice that barely hid her yearning to have a few minutes to herself.

'I'd like another walk, more fresh air before I set off for London,' Miranda said firmly. 'I'll take Luke in that bag thing on my front. You can give me a bottle to take too. We'll go over the fields so we won't have to cross any roads.' What had started off as an impromptu kind gesture now became a necessity. She had a sudden urge to see Chandos Hall again and if she walked through the yard by the outhouses where she'd found Tom and up the side of the fields, she'd be able to see it.

Henry protested a moment, clinging to Tessa, but when he was told he could take his kite and that Mummy was going to wash her hair and would be there when he came back, he consented.

'Besides,' Miranda said, 'I don't know the way. I need you with me in case Luke and I get lost.'

'You needn't go then,' Henry said, but he put his boots and jacket on and clutching his kite in one hand, he set off with her.

They passed through the yard and it was deserted. Henry wanted to stop to fly his kite, but Miranda urged him on to the fields.

'We'll be higher there,' she said. 'It should fly better.'

She walked briskly up the side of the field, Luke close to her chest in his sling. She rather liked the feel of him, warm and snuffing against her, like a tiny puppy. Henry strutted up behind them flapping his kite. They came to the edge of the field bordered by a straggle of woodland. Turning and standing with her back to the trees, Miranda looked down at Chandos Hall.

It was a beautiful house flanked with trees and lawns, the old brick of the walls a warm red in the afternoon sun; its massive front door with its huge porch held up by pillars, the long windows catching the sun. She stood there a long time looking at it, hearing Henry coming up behind her, singing one of his songs.

Then she heard a man's voice, 'Hello, old chap, are you lost?' She whipped round, seeing a tall, willowy man coming out of the trees and addressing Henry. She felt a sudden shame: perhaps she was trespassing, or they'd think she was a tourist who'd got lost. She went down to them, calling, 'It's all right, he's with me. I hope we're not trespassing. I'm staying with the Gardiners, you see, and . . .'

'Not at all. I recognise this young man.' Ralph smiled at them both. 'It's a nice day for a walk.'

'Lovely,' she said, guessing who he was.

While she was speaking, Henry ran, pulling his kite, twisting his body round to watch it. He caught his foot and fell flat on the hard earth and screamed. Miranda, running to him, disturbed Luke, who began to scream too. The old Labrador, Troy, lurched out of the wood towards the scene and Jack followed him.

Miranda stopped, trying to register that she had really seen him but Henry's screams drove her on to pick him up from the ground. The sound of his screaming and Luke's made her feel faint. Through it all she heard his voice: 'Miranda, I can't believe it. Miranda.'

Ralph said to Henry, 'Are you hurt?'

Henry bawled louder. Luke's voice rose in sympathy.

'Miranda.' Jack was with her now, his hand on her arm. 'What are you doing here with all these babies?'

'I . . . I don't know,' she said, meaning that she didn't know what she was meant to do with all this noise.

Troy barked as if he felt he must put his own mark on the situation. Ralph said, 'Don't you start . . . Look,' he said to Miranda, 'why don't you come to the house and sort out the children? I don't think he's hurt,' he looked at Henry, 'but he could do with a wash.'

'Yes, that's a good idea,' Jack said, picking up the screaming Henry and his kite and taking her arm. 'I can't hear myself think with all this noise and I do want to talk to you. I've so much to say.'

'Do you know her?' Ralph said, looking at them both. 'She doesn't live at the cottage.'

'I'm staying with the Gardiners,' Miranda repeated weakly, thinking that she was probably hallucinating with all this screaming and she'd conjured up Jack from her imagination.

'Right,' Ralph said, 'but you know Jack. You should have said, Jack, asked her to dinner.'

'I didn't know she was here,' he said, then introduced them. He then went on, 'It's a long, complicated story, but I first met her here. She helped Tom with that mask.'

'What story to do with this place isn't complicated?' Ralph gave a sour laugh. 'But come and have some tea, Miranda, and tell us about it.'

'I must ring Tessa. I mustn't be too long, she's expecting us back,' Miranda said, wondering if Henry was hurt or just couldn't stop screaming.

'You are not to rush off now that we've met again,' Jack said insistently in her ear. 'I'm here quite by chance. I came last night, so if you believe in fate, our meeting is just that. You will not go until we've had a long talk. Agreed?' He pulled her a little towards him, his gait cumbersome with Henry, still screaming, clinging to him.

'Yes,' she said weakly, thinking she'd go anywhere to get away from this noise.

She stroked Luke's back. 'Shh,' she said, 'please, Luke. It's all right.'

They arrived, muddy and screaming, at the west wing. Ralph opened the door and ushered them in.

'Please, Henry, stop now,' she said to him desperately, imagining the beautiful, elegant Sonia coming upon them and looking at her as if she was dirt.

A small girl ran out of a room and stared at them.

'Run and find Nanny or Mummy, darling. This little boy's hurt,' Ralph said.

Almost immediately they heard the child running back along the corridor and a woman's voice saying, 'Calm down, Amelia. There's enough caterwauling without you adding to it.' She came upon the unhappy, bedraggled bunch, a woman in her seventies, brisk, grey-haired and evidently capable.

109

'Now, what's all this?' she said, going at once to Henry. 'Let's clean you up, young man, and see if there's any wounds worth making this noise over.'

Ralph explained what had happened and Henry, to Miranda's surprise, gulped, stopped screaming and let Nanny take his hand.

'And this little one hanging there like a stuffed chicken,' Nanny clucked disapprovingly at Luke. 'No wonder he's screaming. It's enough to put his back out of shape for life.' Jack undid the strings that attached him to Miranda and Nanny cuddled him to her. He stopped crying at once.

Miranda felt inadequate, bedraggled and awkward under Nanny's piercing gaze.

Jack, behind her, stood very close to her and whispered into her hair: 'Don't worry, Nanny knows best.'

'Thank you, Nanny. We'll be having tea in the drawing room, if you'd like to bring the children back later,' Ralph said, leading them into a room. Nanny, Amelia and the boys went in the other direction.

Ralph laughed when they closed the door. 'Don't mind Nanny,' he said to Miranda. 'In her day mothers didn't hang their babies round their necks in slings, or do half the labour-saving things we have to do today. She's always telling my wife, Bunny, off for something she's doing wrong.'

'I don't know anything about babies at all. They don't belong to me,' Miranda said, liking him and wondering if half the stories she'd heard of him were true. 'Was she your nanny?'

'She came when I was about four, when my sister was born. She's worked for some very grand families. When she retired we bought her a house in Salisbury with her sister. She comes here sometimes to help with Amelia, but my daughter's getting too big for her now. Besides,' he sighed, 'she makes Bunny feel inadequate.'

'I can understand that,' Miranda said.

All the time they were talking she was aware of Jack. Just his touch made her heart race, and she was trying so hard to remain calm, in control. To brace herself for Sonia's entrance.

Tea was brought in and then she telephoned Tessa, who gasped, 'Oh God, and Henry's in his oldest dungarees.'

When Miranda had finished speaking to Tessa, Jack sat next to her on the sofa. 'How long are you here?' he asked.

'I go back this evening.'

'So do I,' he said, fixing her with his eyes. 'Let's arrange to spend the evening together.'

'I couldn't possibly,' she said before she could stop herself.

He gave her a slow, amused smile. 'Just one evening, you can't begrudge me that,' he said.

Chapter Fourteen

Miranda felt in a complete daze. She wished that she could leave this place. She found it difficult to believe that she was sitting here, in Chandos Hall in this chilly room of faded grandeur, beside Jack. She felt edgy, a little guilty that she had let the children get in such a state, and dreaded Nanny returning with her disapproval. She also felt rather apprehensive at meeting Sir Quentin in case he accused her of trespassing and took it out on Tessa for inviting such an undisciplined friend to stay at the cottage. But worst of all she dreaded meeting Sonia.

Ralph lolled opposite them, eating a large piece of fruit cake. The dog lay at his feet. Previously he had been talking to Jack about the Hall being open to the public. He continued now with this conversation, which the screaming babies had interrupted. Every so often he glanced over in Miranda's direction as if to include her and show he was not ignoring her. But Miranda could think of nothing whatever to say that would contribute to their conversation.

Jack was not touching her but she could feel him as if his body was generating heat. She folded herself as small as she could and sat stiffly away from him like a spinster terrified of contact with the opposite sex. There were four more cups and saucers on the tea tray and any moment she expected Sonia to come in.

After ten agonising minutes she couldn't bear any more. In a lull in Ralph's discourse, she put down her cup, smiled and said, 'Thank you so much for rescuing us. I must take the boys home now, not disturb you any more.'

'Don't go yet.' Jack dropped his hand casually on her shoulder. His touch made her body glow. She glanced guilitily at the door, expecting Sonia to come in. To her horror as she watched it, the door opened. She flung off his arm and sprang up ready to leave the room. A tall, fresh-faced woman came in, her blonde hair tied back. She wore tan trousers, a cream shirt and a camel-coloured long cardigan.

'Bunny,' Ralph half rose then sank back in his chair, 'meet Miranda. She's staying at the cottage.'

'I've heard all about it from the children,' Bunny said with a slight American drawl. She smiled at Miranda and held out her hand.

Miranda took it. 'I'll take them away,' she said. 'I'm sure it's bedtime.'

'Please don't on my account, they're keeping Nanny busy,' Bunny said, with a look that implied that they were keeping Nanny out of her hair too. She gestured for Miranda to sit down again. She offered more tea, then poured herself some, picking up the cup and hunching herself in a chair, holding the cup in a nest of her hands as if she needed its warmth.

'You cannot go just yet,' Jack said, leaning closer to Miranda. 'I really do want to talk to you.'

She saw Ralph look curiously at them, then away, and was embarrassed. Already she felt the awkwardness that their situation would provoke, even though nothing untoward had happened. Ralph – surely all of them – could feel the surging tumult in her heart, her senses. She longed to lean back against Jack, to feel his arms round her, smell the scent of him as he whispered in her ear. She shut her eyes. Why, she thought, are some people so intoxicating? Why do I feel as if I belong to him, as if I know him as well as I know myself, when in reality I cannot have him and I do not know him at all?

Bunny said, 'When is Quentin back?'

'For dinner,' Ralph said, not looking at her.

'We must sort things out,' Bunny said to him. 'Amelia needs to be settled.'

'I know,' Ralph said, his hand tugging at Troy's ears, his eyes still away from her.

'Did you come down here in a car or can I give you a lift?' Jack said to Miranda, who now felt relief that Sir Quentin was away. Ralph and Bunny continued their personal conversation and Miranda was glad of the distraction.

'I came in a car,' she said, not daring to turn round and look at him. She wished she had something to do with her hands to stop them pulling restlessly at each other. She got up to put her cup on the tray, then sat down again, on a chair instead of the sofa, so that Jack would not be beside her. Feeling out of place, she wondered if she should ask for another cup of tea or take a piece of that dry-looking fruit cake.

'Do you know that huge hotel with the clock tower standing back off the road, just before the motorway, about half an hour from here?' Jack asked her, leaning forward on the sofa and turning towards her.

'I think so.'

'We could meet there, have dinner.'

She wanted to say, 'What about Sonia?' and wondered for the first time if perhaps she was not here.

'How's Tom?' she said, thinking she'd find out that way.

'Not too good, not doing well at school,' he sighed. 'Will that suit you? Dinner at that hotel?'

If I ask if Sonia's here and she is I don't want to go, she thought, but if she isn't and I do go it will be because I want to be alone with him and I should not be. We may sit down as friends but I'm certain we'll end up as lovers.

Dimly she heard Ralph and Bunny talking to each other in polite, brittle words.

Then Jack leant still closer to her. 'Have you another date for tonight or will you have dinner with me? Sonia's away. I'll be having it on my own otherwise.'

She could feel the whisper of his breath on her face, sense the scent of him and she knew she should say no.

'No, I can't, I'm sorry,' she said, but she would not look at him.

'Are you sure?' His voice was quiet.

She looked round the well-proportioned room with its beautiful furniture. The heavy silk curtains now faded and fraying, the huge fireplace with logs neatly stacked in the iron grate, two large wicker baskets filled with more logs at the side. She felt that Ralph and Bunny too were watching them while they bombarded each other with their tight, precise barbs.

'No,' she said again. 'Really I cannot.'

Before he could say any more the door opened and Nanny and the children came in. Henry, his face washed, his hair slicked down, came over to her, relief to see her on his face. She took him on her knee, thankful he had come to distract her from Jack.

Nanny came over with the baby. Luke's hair stood in a long curl on the top of his head. He too looked rather cleaner than before.

'I've cleaned them up as best I could,' Nanny said disapprovingly to her as if certain these children had never been washed in their lives.

'Thank you,' Miranda said, and put out her arms to take the baby.

Nanny glared at her and clutched him to her. 'Poor little mite,' she said, 'he shouldn't be out with a cold.'

Feeling chastened and remembering her own nanny and indeed various teachers that seemed to delight in finding fault with her, Miranda swallowed her excuses. Even if she'd known what to say, Nanny would have disagreed with her.

She noticed that Amelia was squeezed into the chair with her mother. She was a pale child with wispy hair and large blue eyes. Miranda thought she looked quite sickly compared with Henry and Luke's rosy, plump faces. Tessa might be chaotic and Nanny would no doubt be horrified about her standards of childcare but her children looked far happier and healthier than that unfortunate little girl.

'I should think it is getting on for this baby's bedtime,' Nanny said, giving Luke, who was lying placidly in her arms, a sympathetic look.

'You're right.' Miranda gently pushed Henry off her knee and sprang up. 'We must go. Thank you so much again for rescuing us and for tea. Henry, say thank you.'

'Thank you,' Henry said to the room.

'I'll come with you, walk you back. Or would you rather I drove you?' Jack said, getting up too.

'Please don't bother, I'm fine . . . thank you,' Miranda said.

'I'm sure that baby shouldn't be out in the evening air, should he, Nanny?' Jack said mischievously.

'I should think not. He'll get pneumonia, poor little mite,' Nanny said, gazing mournfully into Luke's pink, chubby face.

'It's only a short walk,' Miranda said, but Jack, taking her arm, scooped up the baby from Nanny and shepherded them out.

'You know he won't get pneumonia,' Miranda hissed at him as they put on their coats.

'Nanny might will it on him,' he laughed at her. There was a gaiety about him that she found infectious, an excitement as if they were playing truant, had escaped for a few moments of heady freedom.

'I'd rather walk.' She tried once more to escape from him.

'So would I,' he smiled. He gave her Luke and, picking up the baby sling, tied it tenderly round her, his hands caressing her gently as they smoothed down the straps. She wanted to tell him to stop, yet she could not. She could not beat him off with her hands as she held Luke, and yet she could not bear for him to take his hands away from her.

They set off through the back door and down past the outhouses to the cottage. She noticed that Henry had his boots on the wrong feet, and said so.

'Never mind,' Jack said, pulling her arm through his and taking Henry's hand in his other one. Henry jumped happily beside him, dragging his muddy kite behind him.

'So,' Jack continued, 'you have another date tonight.'

'No,' she was caught off guard, 'I mean I . . .'

'Why won't you come and have dinner with me?' His voice was soft.

'I can't.'

'You must tell me why.'

'You know why. You knew when you cancelled that table for lunch. It was the only sensible thing to do in the circumstances.'

'Oh, that.' He whirled round to face her. 'That was terrible. My grandfather had a heart attack that day. I tried to ring you, but you weren't there.' His voice held a note of pain, remembering the agony of those weeks.

'I'm so sorry,' she said, standing still, looking at him with sympathy. 'Did he . . . did he get better?'

'I suppose he did, but he'll never be the same again,' he sighed. 'I think now he'd rather he had died.'

'I'm sorry,' she said again, fighting to rearrange her thoughts. Jack hadn't cancelled the lunch because he'd thought better of it. He had *had* to cancel it.

'You said you'd come then, so we've just postponed it. Why can't you come tonight?'

'Jack, you know why. Because you're married.'

'I was married then as well.' He looked at her intently.

Henry began to sing one of his songs. '"The wheels on the bus go round and round, round and round, round and round",' he repeated like a stuck record.

She said, 'I know these days anything goes, but I've never been out with a married man. It's something I don't agree with. Besides, lunch is somehow . . .'

'Safer?' he laughed. 'Were you brought up to think that nothing was safe after dark?'

She smiled. 'You do know exactly what I mean. I did accept lunch, but after you'd cancelled it without saying anything I thought that you had realised that we can't meet. And I agreed with your decision. I think it's best we keep to that.'

'Let's talk about it this evening. We're in separate cars, I won't stop you driving home, and I won't follow you.'

'"The wheels on the bus . . ."' Henry sang.

She knew she should refuse, but the day had been long and exhausting with the children. They were upon the cottage now and Henry had run forward, calling for Tessa. She suddenly knew she didn't want Tessa to see Jack. Tessa would guess her feelings at once and do her best to dissuade her. She would see him just this time and get things cleared up once and for all.

'OK,' she said quickly, 'I'll meet you there about,' she looked at her watch, 'eight o'clock.'

As if he guessed her anxiety, he pressed her arm and said, 'Eight it is.'

He walked away and Tessa came out.

'There you are,' she said. 'How shaming, their nanny seeing these two at their worst. Who was that?' She'd caught sight of Jack's back disappearing round the corner.

'Oh, just someone staying who walked us back. Yes, you're right, the nanny was pretty disapproving.' She laughed, feeling a surge of happiness rise in her. She handed over Luke and told Tessa, amid shrieks of giggles from both of them, all about it.

Miranda left Tessa at half-past seven. She had bathed, washed her hair and put on her Monsoon dress.

'Wow, who's the lucky man?' Tessa said.

'Oh, I might just go out when I get back,' Miranda said vaguely.

'So you dress up just in case you go out. Now that's something I've not done since I was seventeen,' Tessa said. She sighed. 'I'd love to go out tonight.'

'Simon will be back soon,' Miranda said, hugging her goodbye.

'I know. I can hardly wait.'

Miranda drove carefully down the winding lanes, wondering if Jack was behind or in front of her. As she drove she felt the butterflies of anticipation, excitement, fear of the pain of not being able to have him, flutter through her. They played havoc with her emotions, making her feel she could never eat again. Too soon she saw the hotel. For a sudden decisive moment she thought she ought to drive on, go on to the motorway where there was small chance of getting back here again before it was too late. But she drove in through the gates and parked on the gravel beside the vast archway that horse-drawn carriages used to drive through in earlier days.

She sat for a moment in the car, then, taking a deep breath, got out and walked to the hotel. She found the bar, but Jack was not there. She felt a wave of panic, seeing the few men there eye her up appreciatively. She decided to go the ladies', wait a while there.

'Miranda.' He came in just at that moment. 'I thought I'd never get away. There are so many dramas at Chandos Hall, you'd never believe.' He smiled into her face. 'Come on,' he said, 'let's find somewhere quiet.'

She supposed they ate and drank; they certainly talked. They found they had so much in common, enjoyed the same things, each exclaiming with delight as the other mentioned a writer, a film, a play they had both enjoyed. Later Jack told her how Ralph had suddenly telephoned him and asked him to come to Chandos Hall as his father was away.

'We've become closer since I've stayed there and besides, as I'm family of sorts, he felt I was an ideal person to offload some of the family's problems on to.'

They went on to talk of David, of her parents and his grandfather, and of Tom, but not of Sonia. It was as if she stood before them like a huge land mine they had to juggle round and not touch.

It was half-past eleven before they realised the time.

'I must get back,' she said, dreading the drive home alone.

'We must meet again,' he said, his eyes lingering on her face, his mouth heavy with unspoken desire. 'If only we didn't have to leave. It will be a lonely drive back.'

The invitation was there, laid out between them, ready to take up. She yearned for him, imagined a cosy room upstairs and lying between linen sheets with him beside her. What was one night in a lifetime? A magic night that would stay with them for ever but not destroy their lives.

Looking into his eyes she saw he felt the same. Then she remembered his telling her about Tom. Tom, who was unhappy and confused at school; so bewildered by his grandfather's sudden illness and now dependence on him, on of all them, when before he was the one who ruled them all. One night . . . It would not stop at one night.

'Jack,' her voice was a whisper of regret, 'I must go back and so must you. You have a child; he must not be hurt.'

He took her hand, smiled sadly, laid it against his lips and then held it against his cheek. 'You are so special,' he said, 'and so strong. Let me follow you back to see you get home safely. I promise you I will not come in.'

'Thank you,' she said, knowing that if he did she would not be able to stop him, nor would she want to.

'Is it too selfish to ask if we can keep in touch?' he said. 'I cannot bear to lose you again.'

'I think we can,' she said, knowing she too could not bear to lose him. But he is not yours, her conscience told her as she went to the ladies' room. You are furious with your father for breaking his marriage vows, you can see at first-hand what anguish that can cause to you, a grown-up and mature child. Think of the devastation to a child like Tom.

But Tom, she thought, he and I get on so well. I might even be able to help him.

But she forced herself to stop thinking like this, for that way danger lay.

Jack held her in his arms a moment before kissing her on her cheek, holding his face against hers.

'I hate to let you go,' he said.

'But you must,' she said with more strength than she felt, and left his arms and went outside into the cold and darkness to the car.

Chapter Fifteen

'So, darling, we'll have a nice little dinner, just the two of us,' Sonia said, snuggling up to Jack on the sofa.

He was busy writing a report and looked up at her distractedly. 'In about an hour, if that's all right. I must finish this.' He did not return her look of flirtation.

'You've been working on that for ages, and I'm getting hungry.' She nibbled his ear.

If Jack had not been thinking about Miranda he would have finished the report ages ago. He moved a little away from Sonia, saying, 'I'll finish this as quickly as I can. Why don't you start cooking the dinner?'

'I thought we'd have a little aperitif,' she whispered, licking his ear and slipping her hand on to his thigh.

'Later,' he said firmly, impatiently jerking his leg away as if her hand was an annoying insect. He did not want to be seduced by her. He guessed she was only like this because she felt guilty about her latest affair. He realised suddenly that he didn't care whether she was having an affair or not. Since meeting up with Miranda again and keeping in touch with her by telephone he found he was not so anxious about Sonia's behaviour.

He'd thought lately that falling in love with Sonia had been a kind of sudden virus. They had married six months after they'd first met. He had been foolishly flattered and naturally inflamed by Sonia's passionate overtures. She could have chosen any man and, indeed, they hovered round her like love-sick moths. He suspected also that he had been guilty of a touch of male arrogance, showing off to them that it was he who had won the prize. But he and Sonia had loved each other with a passion that was intoxicating, and he thought that in spite of everything there was love between them.

But since meeting Miranda he found he was becoming less tolerant of Sonia's weaknesses, more irritated by her continually demanding behaviour. What had intrigued and enchanted him in the early days of their love was now becoming its destruction.

Then out of the blue Ralph had rung him and hesitantly asked if he could bear to come to Chandos Hall for the weekend as he had various family problems. Sir Quentin, after much grumbling and deliberating, had decided to go to Scotland for the funeral of an old friend, so they could talk freely. Sonia had refused to go, complaining of the discomfort and cold of the place. Jack, feeling sorry for Ralph, hadn't been able to get there until the Saturday night. He had been subject to Ralph's long and sorry tale of how Sir Quentin was bullying him and Bunny to have a son.

'Even if you have to go to one of those clinics and have artificial insemination, you must do your duty and have an heir. This property has been in our family for over four hundred years, and surely you don't want to be the one who lost it,' his father had thundered at him.

All this Jack had told Miranda as they dined together that Sunday night. He felt so happy and relaxed with her. She was such a straightforward girl with no destructive, demanding traits as far as he could see. She was so caring and kind as well as being so very attractive. It was ironic, he thought, looking up again from his report – Sonia having left rather grumpily to cook the dinner – that another thing, apart from her extraordinary beauty, that had attracted him to Sonia was her air of mystery. A feeling that he could never quite know her, that often he got tantalisingly near, felt in the intimacy of lovemaking that he had possessed her, only to find a moment later that she was as elusive as ever.

This elusiveness had now turned into mistrust. He was certain she was having affairs – her long and sometimes obscure working hours did not ring true to him, despite her assurances. Miranda's direct honesty appealed to him. She had said straight out that she did not want to see him because he was married. She knew at once how easy it would be to slip into an affair. She had made it clear that if things were different and he was free, she would welcome it. He admired her moral standing, especially today when so many married people saw no wrong in having a quick fling elsewhere; felt that any pleasure that came their way should be grabbed and enjoyed despite the pain and destruction it might cause in the family.

After dinner they had driven back to London in their own cars. He had stopped outside her house and again kissed her good night. This time she had not let him hold her and had run quickly inside, calling good night to him over her shoulder.

It was, he'd thought wryly, a good thing she'd been so strong for despite his assurances that he would not come in, the temptation to follow her had been almost overwhelming.

He had her home number now, and for the last three weeks they had telephoned each other. She had told him she felt it best not to meet again for a while. He had to go away on business quite a lot so it was easy to keep to her suggestion. But when he was away, in the evening, alone in his hotel bedroom, he had lain on the bed for hours talking to her. There was something about the intimacy of a telephone, just the voice of the other person with no distraction of having them sitting opposite one in the room, that had unleashed so many private thoughts. Intimacy, he thought, is not just physical; mental intimacy is just as precious, perhaps more lasting. And yet, he thought, sitting there in his smartly decorated drawing room, he wanted physical intimacy with her too.

'I can't see you this week and I'm going to France to see my brother and his family at the weekend,' she'd said last night when he had suggested that they lunch together.

'Talking to you is not enough,' he'd said, and she had answered, 'I know, but we cannot have any more. You know that. Think of Tom.'

She never said 'think of Sonia', he realised now. He had told her about Sonia's insecurities, made excuses for her because of her childhood, her parents had died, she never saw the brother she adored.

Miranda had just said tartly, 'Why do people who have had unhappy childhoods always do their best to ruin their own families, when they could find the happiness and security they crave with them?'

He wanted suddenly to hear her voice again, to hear her laugh. He listened to Sonia in the kitchen. She had a CD on and he could hear the rich voice of José Carreras singing to her while she cooked. He put his hand out to the telephone. He knew he shouldn't ring Miranda now, from home, but he would only be a second.

He dialled quickly, almost desperately. It rang, two, three, four times. He wondered where she was: in the bath; out with another man?

She answered, 'Hello.'

'Miranda, I can't talk long. How are you?'

'Fine,' she laughed. 'We only talked yesterday. Nothing has happened to change me since then. Where are you?'

They'd made a rule never to ring from or to his home. She had made it, saying she knew it sounded hypocritical, but she didn't want to talk to him while he was with his family.

He said, 'I just longed to hear your voice.'

There was a long silence. Then he heard the unmistakable voice of a man in the background. 'Does this rice need more water, Miranda? It looks as if it's sticking.'

'Yes, oh help, I forgot it. Take it off the top, please, David.'

Jack's heart pounded, jealousy surging through him. He wanted to throw down the telephone receiver and rush round to her flat at once. Terrible images of David filled his mind. Would she give

David the sort of kisses that she had denied him? Would she let him stay the night, love David as he wished she would love him? Anger, pain surged through him, then despair flooded over the lot. He, as she had repeatedly reminded him, was married with a child and she did not want to destroy that. She knew that their affair would not be a quick, one-night fling that meant nothing but a few hours of physical pleasure. She knew that they would love each other and that their love might push away everything else in its path.

As if guessing at his anguish and pain she said gently, 'David is an old friend, you know he is. He's back from Geneva for a couple of days.'

'I know,' he said miserably. He was then suddenly aware that Sonia was standing at the door. 'That's fine, thank you. I'll keep in touch. Goodbye,' he said, forcing his voice to sound noncommittal.

'Goodbye.' Miranda's reply lingered in his mind and he felt immeasurably sad. What future was there for them without destroying his family?

'Who's that?' Sonia said briskly, coming in, a glass of white wine in her hand.

'Oh, just a colleague I needed to ask about this.' He indicated his report. He did not look at her. He felt terrible as he realised how easily he had lied. It was the first direct lie he had told her concerning Miranda and he felt uncomfortable about it.

'Well, dinner's ready, *if* you want it,' she said archly. He wondered how long she'd been standing in the doorway.

'I do want it,' he said, putting away his report and getting up. 'I could do with a glass of wine too.' He watched her covertly. She did not look at him but began to tidy the room, punching the cushions on the sofa back into shape with a vigour that could be anger or just her normal energetic agitation at keeping a spotless house.

If I behave completely normally, go through the motions of a typical evening at home, this pain and doubt will go, he told himself. Then he wondered how he could be 'normal' when he was suffering such torment. He knew that his feeling of jealousy of Miranda and David, his utter pain that David was free and so they could meet, make love to each other, go out and about together hand in hand in London without restraint, far outweighed any feeling of guilt and shame he had for cheating on Sonia.

The telephone rang and for one wild moment he thought it must be Miranda wanting to reassure him, reassure herself about their relationship. The relationship that was conducted on a telephone, he thought sourly. Sonia had snatched it up before him. He feigned nonchalance and went into the kitchen to pour himself some wine, all the time straining to hear who it was. He still didn't know if she, the practised deceiver, had seen through his feeble attempt to calm his surging emotions and pretend he had been speaking only to a colleague. Or was it, he thought ironically, one of her lovers?

'Oh dear, well, it is so near the end of term, only four days. Couldn't he hang on until then? I'll speak to him,' Jack heard as he came back into the room. His heart went cold.

He went up to her and said anxiously, 'What's happened?'

She frowned, said into the phone, 'He's in bed already? But it's only half-past eight.'

All the agitations of the evening coursed through him, increasing his concern over his son. 'Let me deal with it,' he said, and took the receiver from Sonia.

'I'm so busy this week,' she said urgently to him. 'Surely he can stay there just a few more days? I'll go and visit him tomorrow.'

The voice of the headmaster was calm. 'I think Tom should come home early,' he said. 'He's not happy, we've had a lot of tearful scenes. I just think he's got overtired, worried about his grandfather. Things like that have just got on top of him.'

'What's happened to him?' Jack felt a bolt of fear shoot into his stomach.

'He just can't cope for the moment. I don't think it's serious. A few days' rest and good food at home will soon perk him up again,' the headmaster said cheerfully. 'It's all this talk of Common Entrance – well, it sometimes upsets the less able ones, especially if they suffer from lack of confidence.'

'Are you telling me he's having a breakdown?' Jack said, impatient in his fear.

'Oh, no,' the headmaster said quickly. 'But as I said, he's overtired. We've just had end-of-year exams and he found them very difficult. It doesn't help that he's upset about his grandfather and so as it is so near the end of term I think it would benefit him to come home early.'

'I'll come and get him at once,' Jack decided suddenly. He couldn't bear to think of Tom miserable for a moment longer than was necessary.

'I didn't mean as soon as that. He's in bed now and probably asleep. Tomorrow would do,' the headmaster went on.

In the end Jack said he would ring the headmaster back.

Sonia said, 'I don't mean to sound callous, but I've so much on at the moment. I can't look after him full time here. I'm trying to cram everything in so I have time for him in the holidays. Why is he overtired? Surely it's the school's responsibility to see they get enough sleep?'

'We'll worry about that later, this sounds crucial. Are you sure you can't work from home for a few days and be with him? What exactly have you got to do?' Jack said, his mind whirring on his commitments and wondering if he could change anything.

'I could visit him in the morning for an hour but we've got a presentation the next day and—'

'OK,' Jack said. 'But bring him home tomorrow morning – that will give me time to arrange things in the office. I might be able to take Friday off, then we've got the weekend. Oh God,' he put his head in his hands, 'do you think there's more to it than just tiredness?'

The rest of the evening was spent worrying about Tom, the call to Miranda forgotten. Cynara rang and she too was dragged into the discussion.

'Send him here, darling,' she said to Jack. 'It's quite lovely at this time of the year and he can be outside. That's all he needs, I'm sure, fresh air, good food and rest.'

'But you have Grandfather and . . .'

'He can help with him, fetch and carry. I could do with another pair of hands. Yes, do that, put him on a plane any time, and I'll take him off. He can stay here as long as he likes.'

'She's a brick. He'll have a much better time with her, and she's got step-grandchildren, hasn't she? Other children for him to play with,' Sonia said, looking relieved at the new situation.

Jack didn't say anything. It would solve a lot of practical problems if Tom went to his mother at her château in France, but he felt he wanted to be with Tom himself, find out what was really bothering him, try and help him. He said this to Sonia.

'But, darling, your mother is so good with him, and you could stay a few days too. Couldn't you?'

'It's not so long since I was over there with my grandfather. Etienne is the nicest man, but does he really want the whole of his wife's family taking up his space?'

'I'm sure he doesn't mind. He adores her and you know how family-minded the French are,' Sonia said airily.

'We'll have Tom home with us for a few days and see how he really is. Then if he wants to go to France he can, but I'm not sending him if he's the slightest bit . . .' He paused, wondering what word to use.

'Depressed, you mean?' Sonia said.

'Yes, or . . . well, if he's at all overstressed. Mother cannot be expected to take on any more invalids,' he said firmly, knowing his mother would not believe that her grandson had any mental problems, only needed country air and good food. He worried that Tom might be severely depressed. Stories he'd read in the newspaper of school children killing themselves loomed up to frighten him so he quickly dismissed it. Guiltily he found himself wondering what Miranda would do in the circumstances, but she worked too. That was the trouble these days – people were locked into their work and couldn't always just drop things to cope with family dramas. He knew it wasn't Sonia's fault. She had work commitments too, but his anxiety made him irritated with her. He longed for Miranda, but he knew with painful jealousy that she was busy with David. He would not dare ring her now in case from her manner he knew he had disturbed their lovemaking.

He scrunched his eyes shut and put his head in his hands. He could not bear the thoughts, the images of her entwined with David that loomed in his mind.

'It can't be that bad. I mean, they'd have called a doctor if he'd been that ill,' Sonia said, seeing his distress, putting her arm round him.

'I shan't be happy until I see him for myself,' Jack said, torture of imagining Miranda and David together coupled with anxiety about Tom.

He did not sleep well and it was not until the dawn streaked across the dark sky that he remembered that Miranda had said she was going to France too. He wondered where in France and for how long. He wondered if there was some chance that they could go together, or if they could meet up. He felt the excitement stir deep inside himself. To be alone with her there, out of their usual environment, would be . . . well, dangerous. Away from all their commitments they would be two different people, people who might forget their responsibilities. He should not even suggest it, he knew, but he felt suddenly happy and began to plan their meeting in France in his mind.

Chapter Sixteen

Miranda longed suddenly to escape from the ratrace of London. Normally she thrived on it. The faster it went, the better she liked it, but her emotions, mostly over Jack, were weighing her down, curbing her vitality.

If only one could choose who one cared for, she thought more than once. If she could feel this way for David, how much more satisfactory it would be.

She had been pleased to see David on his fleeting visit back to London, enjoyed his lovemaking, though to her surprise she had felt a little guilty as if she should not be enjoying it when she loved Jack. But did she love Jack, or was it just lust? she wondered. Lust packaged up in the exotic guise of forbidden love?

'You seem somehow detached, in another world,' David had said on the Sunday morning. He'd watched her carefully as she sat across from him in her small garden, rather vaguely eating breakfast.

She'd smiled, found herself lying, yet not quite lying. 'I'll miss you. I wish you didn't have to go back so soon,' she said.

'Come with me?' The words like a challenge lay between them. She wondered if he meant marriage.

'I can't,' she said reluctantly. 'You know I've my job.'

'Come on holiday to Geneva, instead of going to your brother in France. I'll try and take a few days off. There's lots to do there. We've never been together . . . well, as lovers,' he smiled, 'for more than a weekend.'

'That's probably why we get on so well,' she replied. Then, seeing his look of disappointment, said, 'I will try and come and visit you but I'm committed to going to my brother now. I really do enjoy it there and I want to talk about my parents.'

'Of course, I understand.' He poured them both more orange juice, nursed the glass in his hand, studying it reflectively. 'I wish . . .' He paused, and she knew he was about to say something important. She flayed around in her mind for some way to deflect him but he went on: 'I wish we could be together more. I know everyone's meant to be so cool about their relationships these days.

All so busy working, climbing up the slippery tree of achievement, cramming one's love life into small corners, whenever one has a spare moment. I would like us to have more than that.' Then, seeing her expression, he gave a rueful laugh. 'I don't mean marriage, you staying at home having babies. But I wish we had more time for each other.' He looked at her intently, then added quietly, 'Don't you?'

She leant back in her chair and regarded him. He was such a nice person and they were so rare these days. If it wasn't for Jack she'd be happy with him. She remembered how understanding he'd been when she'd told him about her father's affair.

She said, 'I would. David, I really would. But the trouble is . . .' She let out a long sigh, bit her lip, then blurted out: 'I'm quite mad, you know. I've got myself into a mess. I seem to be attracted to a married man.' She saw the pain shaft across his eyes. 'Oh, there's nothing in it, there never will be. He has a son, and is married, as I said. It's rumoured his wife has affairs, well, I know James Darby had an affair with her,' she laughed awkwardly, keeping on talking to ward off his disappointment. 'I happen to think marriage is for keeps and that affairs are wrong.'

'But you love him?'

'No . . . I don't know.' She clawed her fingers through her hair. 'I met him when I stayed with some friends in the country.' She went on to tell him everything, ending, 'So we had dinner, but that was it. We do telephone each other from time to time, but I think in a way he uses me as a sympathetic ear to talk about his son. He'd never leave his wife for me, and I wouldn't expect him to.'

'I'm sorry,' David said. 'So what will you do? Hang about for the occasional word thrown at you when his wife or son is not listening?'

His words, said quietly, hurt her. 'Of course not,' she said sharply, but she knew that was exactly what she was doing and that would be her life, waiting for the odd crumb from Jack to come her way. It was easy to have a relationship over the telephone, to imagine things were more important than they were, in that intimate, isolated world of voices and shared secrets. Maybe Jack saw it like ringing the Samaritans. The thought chilled her.

'Well,' David said, 'you'll have to make up your mind over it.' He got up and went into the bedroom to get dressed. At the door he turned and said sadly, 'Perhaps it's a good thing I'm going back to Geneva – leave you to sort this out.'

'I wish it wasn't this way, believe me, David. I do so wish it wasn't,' she'd said, but he had given her a sad smile and a shrug and had left her soon after with some rather lame excuse about having things to do before his plane went. She'd played along with this, a little relieved but also unhappy that she had hurt him.

All this had added to her feelings of wanting to leave London. Of wanting to be with Edward and Nicole and their four children in their pretty holiday house in Normandy. It was quite a different life to what she was used to. There was so much going on and new people to meet, rather intellectual French people, who talked half the night of politics, the arts, philosophy. Edward, who had studied international law and worked in Paris, where they lived most of the year, was surrounded by this sort of people. Miranda wished her spoken French was better. She understood most of what was said, but found it difficult to say what she really felt about a subject in the language. She liked the mental stimulation their conversations gave her.

She rang Edward to confirm her arrival. 'I'll drive out, be with you late Saturday.'

'And stay at least a week, I hope,' Edward said.

'I'd love to. I need to get away.' She didn't say she had two weeks' holiday. She knew she could stay on with her brother if she wanted to, but after stopping a few days with them she felt as if she was intruding and that Nicole wanted him to herself again. She could always go on somewhere in France by herself, or visit a school friend who lived in Paris. She did not feel like making plans; she would see how things went.

She tied up her jewellery feature in the office by Friday evening, wrote up her captions and gave them to the copy editor. The editor had already made her choice of the photographs. She was just about to leave when the phone rang. It was Jack.

'I'm glad I've caught you. When are you off?' His voice was rich and warm and she felt it ooze into her, quite killing all her resolve, since telling David about him, to put him from her mind.

'Tomorrow.'

'How are you going? Eurostar?'

'No, I might not get on. I'm booked on the ferry.'

'Tell me where you'll be.' His voice was so persuasive. Why should it matter if he knew where she was? she thought. She would be in France and he was here.

She told him where she was going, sure he wouldn't know it, but when she said near Les Andelys in Normandy, she heard him laugh.

'Why are you laughing?'

'Because you will be staying quite near my mother – well, about thirty miles away – and I'm bringing Tom out to stay with her in the middle of next week.'

She hardly heard his explanation about how Tom was so stressed out from his term. She felt the blood rush to her head, felt a feeling of elation, of dread. Jack would be in France the same time that she was, and so near. She took a deep breath, forced herself to think calmly. Sonia would no doubt be going too; there could be no way of meeting him.

As if he could read her thoughts he said, 'Just Tom and I are coming, Sonia's too busy, She's had to move her work around a bit to look after Tom this week. I'm able to tie in a few meetings in Paris. How long are you going to be there?'

'I don't know,' she blurted out, feeling as if she was being hurtled along out of control, her resolve and common sense being swept away by the speed of events.

'Miranda,' his voice was calm, 'we must meet. Please. It's too much of a coincidence that we are both going to France and being so close to each other. My mother would love to meet you,' he added hastily.

'I don't think that's a good idea,' she said quickly, feeling that once one met men's mothers it meant a sort of seal was being set on the relationship.

Jack tried a different tack. 'Tom would simply love to see you. He's rather down at the moment, and seeing you would cheer him up, I know it would.'

'What do you mean, down?' she asked, really to get away from his pushing her further into a meeting. She thought back to what she'd said to him. She hadn't given him her exact address. Would he think to find her brother's address in the phone book? She wanted him, how she wanted him, but it could not be. Since telling David, her resolve not to get further involved with Jack had hardened. She may not care for David in the same way that she cared for Jack, but she knew any relationship between her and a married man was doomed. Better to stop it now before it got out of hand. Above all, she must not see him in France, away from their families and friends, for she knew that then they may not be able to stop themselves and the damage their feelings for each other might cause would be devastating.

'He's just depressed, exhausted, about school. He found the end-of-year exams really hard. You are so good with him, make him see the best in himself. I hate to see him like this.' Jack sounded despairing. 'I'm not sure parents are always the best people to deal with this sort of thing. Perhaps we're too close. Too emotionally involved. I'm sure seeing you will do him an enormous amount of good.'

Miranda could feel the pain in Jack's voice. Knew how he hated Tom to suffer, knew how difficult he found it – his only child plagued by this dyslexia. Briefly she wondered if Jack was playing this card to arouse her sympathy, make her overcome her reluctance to meet him away from home.

'Please,' he said again. 'I quite understand if you don't want to see me alone.' He laughed hoarsely. 'I know it will be difficult for both of us. I give you my word that I won't embarrass you, or pressurise you to see me, but if you could see Tom? Come over for the day with my mother, grandfather and stepfather there. You'll be safe then.'

'I'll think about it,' she said lamely, wondering if she was strong enough to ring off before he asked for her address. She was not and found herself repeating Edward's address and telephone number like a robot.

'I'll be in touch. Safe journey.' His voice sang in her head for the whole evening.

'I think your father is being very selfish,' Nicole said, giving Edward a stern look as if to dispel any ideas he might have of going off with a younger woman.

'I thought you French were more understanding of such things,' Edward teased her, making her frown.

Miranda said, 'I do think he is being silly. It's rather shaming really, going off with someone ten years younger than me. You know how the village gossips. Before we know it they'll be locking up their daughters when he's about.'

'Older men have always gone for younger women. Biologically, while they can still reproduce they are attracted to women who are still fertile,' Edward said.

Nicole let out a whoop of laughter. 'Oh, *chérie*, is that your explanation for, what did that friend of yours call it, *le droop*?' She turned to Miranda, who was laughing too. 'You know, when their powers in bed have gone and they think they need young women, they make this sort of excuse.'

Edward smiled at her. 'I read about it, or saw it on television.'

'There are more than enough people on this earth without old men making more,' Nicole said. 'You have your chance when you are young with a young woman, then that should be the end of it. No more reproduction.' She got up and went over to where he sat, kissing him and ruffling his hair. 'You have done your bit for the continuation of mankind. In ten, twenty years' time, don't tell me you have to reproduce again.'

He put his arm round her, pulled her down to sit on his lap. 'I won't need to. You will never grow old.'

She laughed, kissed him again, then said seriously, 'Nor I think has your mother. She has aged well. Perhaps there are other reasons that has made your father go with this girl.'

'Male menopause,' Miranda said. 'Middle age seems to affect men worse than it does women. I've heard of other men chasing youth. Ironic really,' she grinned, 'when men often get far more attractive as they age than women do.'

'Whatever it is I just hope he pulls himself together and comes back to her,' Edward said with a sigh. 'What will she do on her own?' He looked gloomy. 'Roam round all of us, I suppose. Oh, I'm fond of her, but she can be rather tiresome with her theories and ideas of child-rearing, especially ours.'

He squeezed Nicole, who grimaced and said, 'Our children have too much school work, go to bed too late, eat too rich food . . .' She ticked the list off on her fingers. 'Yes, she can be difficult.'

Miranda, though agreeing with them, felt a wave of sympathy for her mother. She remembered the weekend when she'd gone down and found out about her father's affair and how her mother had dolled up for dinner, acted as if nothing had happened. It took a lot of courage to do that, she thought, and said so.

'Nor has she rushed to the doctor demanding Prozac, the happy drug that relieves all unwanted emotions,' she said.

'Maybe she'll meet someone else,' Nicole said. 'If I was her, I would look for someone else. Not every man wants a young woman.'

Edward looked rather shocked. 'I don't think she can do that,' he said.

'And why not? Having affairs is not just for men, you know. A woman has as much right as a man to have an affair,' Nicole said. 'If men think it is wrong for women to have affairs what do they think of the woman they are having an affair with?'

She turned to Miranda, who said, 'That's true. Men are funny about their mothers and their wives. They seem to think they should be immune to wanting love too. Edward, that's what you think, isn't it? Admit it?' she teased. 'Do you really think Mummy, and perhaps in a few years Nicole, no longer want . . .' She was about to say love, but she meant sex and said so. The word made Edward blush and Nicole hoot again with laughter.

'You English men, you think sex is not nice for your mothers and your wives.' She dug him in the ribs. 'What a pity your wife likes sex so much with you.'

Edward looked rather pleased but also rather embarrassed at this remark. 'You know what I mean,' he said lamely.

'I do,' Nicole said, 'but don't let your strange British ideas stop your mother from having a good time. She should come to France. The French men adore women, are not afraid of them as some public school men are,' she teased him.

'We're not afraid of them,' Edward retorted.

'Not you, you live in France. But others are, or use them for sport, like hunting.' She kissed him, extricating herself from his arms, and got up. 'And you, Miranda,' she said, 'have you a nice lover?'

Miranda, used to Nicole's direct questions, smiled and said, 'Sort of.'

'"Sort of"? What kind of lover is that?' Nicole said, laughing. 'I will find a French man for you.' She turned to Edward, saying excitedly, '*Voilà*, Jean-Paul. He is back. What do you think of him for your sister? He would not be a "sort of" lover.'

Edward said, 'He's had two wives already.'

'So? He has good practice. I didn't say she should marry him.'

Miranda made herself laugh. 'I don't think I can be bothered with him, Nicole. My boyfr— lover lives in Geneva at the moment. We meet when we can.'

'A new man? Anyone I know?' Edward said.

'I don't know if you know him. He's called David March. He's very nice,' she finished lamely, aware that Nicole was watching her closely.

'Might you marry him?' Edward asked again.

'I don't really feel like marriage just yet,' Miranda said, bracing herself for his insistence that she must marry and have children before she got too old.

'No good marrying unless you want to,' Nicole said. The ring of the telephone cut off anything else she was about to say on the subject. She picked up the receiver. '*Allô*.' Her eyes swung to Miranda as she listened. She said carefully, 'One moment, she is here.'

Miranda felt faint, and the colour rose up her face. She saw Nicole's knowing smile as she watched her get up slowly, robot-like, and go over to the telephone as if some unseen vibes were drawing her to it.

'It is a man called Jack, not the David. I do not think,' Nicole handed her the receiver as if it were a trophy, 'that this Jack is just a "sort of" lover.'

Chapter Seventeen

Monet's garden at Giverny was full of soft-coloured flowers like his paintings. Miranda stood on the arched bridge looking down on the water lilies. The peace and tranquillity of the garden was somewhat marred by the troop of tourists who jabbered away in their various languages, jostling with each other while they flashed their cameras at every corner. It was further spoilt by a couple of extraordinarily bad artists trying with heavy-handed ineptitude to recreate Monet's beloved lilies floating like translucent boats upon the shining water.

'I wish we had this place to ourselves,' Jack said, standing close to her on the bridge.

'We are tourists too, and yet we hate to be thought so,' Miranda said, knowing that he meant something different. Jack had invited them all over to spend the day with his mother and stepfather. As the château was quite difficult to find he had suggested that they meet at Monet's garden.

'I should adore to see it again,' Nicole had said, her eyes teasing Miranda, who knew she was longing to see who this Jack was.

'It's too much trouble for your mother,' Miranda had said down the telephone to Jack.

'No, it's not,' he'd replied. 'We will have a picnic. The weather is wonderful, and if it does rain we'll eat it in the barn.'

So it was settled. Nicole insisted on bringing half the picnic, and in the event two of the children, ten-year-old Lawrence and eight-year-old Clair, spent the day with friends, leaving the eldest daughter, Celine, and the youngest, Frederique, to come with them.

Jack was waiting for them. Tom slouched beside him, hands in pockets, head down.

'He is so good-looking,' Nicole said to Miranda. 'I can see why you chose him.'

'It's not like that at all. Please, Nicole, don't say anything embarrassing,' Miranda begged her, wishing now she hadn't come, despite the feeling of elation that had leapt up in her when she'd caught sight of Jack's tall, elegant figure waiting for them.

'It should be like that,' Nicole said, 'but don't worry, I will say nothing.' She laid her hand on Miranda's arm. 'It is bad luck that he is married, but if he was mine I wouldn't leave him to go about alone.'

Edward laughed. 'You sound like a jailer, my love.'

'But I am.' She blew him a kiss. 'You are far too attractive to be left too much on your own.'

The girls began to squabble on the back seat, and Nicole shouted at them. *'Alors, mes enfants, ça suffit!'*

Tom had looked rather horrified at the sight of the two girls, though Celine on seeing him had quietened down at once and Miranda saw her eyeing him from under her lashes.

Jack came forward and kissed her on her cheek, then greeted Nicole and Edward, introducing Tom.

'Hello, Tom. How are you?' Miranda said, unsure whether to kiss him or not, but feeling sure he would hate it, so she didn't.

'OK,' he muttered, looking at his feet.

After they had seen the garden and the house, all staying together, exchanging opinions with each other, leaving no opportunity for Jack and Miranda to be alone, they went back to the car park to go to Jack's mother.

'Why don't you go with Jack, Miranda?' Nicole said when they reached the cars. 'Give you a rest from these girls.' She smiled at Jack and said, 'My other two children are with friends today and these two always fight when they are left together. Poor Miranda will be so tired with it.'

Miranda was about to protest, but Jack smiled, took her arm. 'Fine, now follow me. It's only about five miles.'

Sitting beside him as they drove through the pretty countryside, Miranda fought to calm her tumult of feelings. Jack, his skin slightly tanned, his hair curling into his neck and his blue open-necked shirt emphasising the deep blue of his eyes, filled her with excitement and desire. She was ashamed, shocked by the strength of her feelings, sure that everyone must know of them. Already Nicole had whispered, 'This man will not be a "sort of" lover, I think. Both of you are made for each other. I can sense it.'

'He is married,' she'd said frantically, really to remind herself to hold her own feelings in check.

Nicole had shrugged. 'He cannot be happily married if he looks at you like that.'

Miranda dreaded meeting his mother. She would surely be horrified at the situation, would label her a tart, a marriage breaker. She had been mad to accept this crazy invitation. She had tried to say they were too busy, had made too many other plans that could not be changed, but Nicole, on hearing the invitation, had ignored

Miranda's whispered plea to say they could not go and jumped at the idea.

'Monet's garden, how I love it, and to meet new people. Yes, we would love to come.'

'I don't think I should be coming,' she said desperately to Jack on the journey to the château.

'Yes, you should. Shouldn't she, Tom?' Jack asked his son, who was lumped in the back of the car.

'Mmm,' he muttered.

'That doesn't sound very welcoming, Tom,' Jack said with a false note of cheerfulness in his voice. Miranda at once sensed that he was worried about Tom and her heart went out to him.

'It's so good to see you again, Tom,' she said, turning round and smiling at him. He looked terrible, she thought: pale and sort of lost. 'Have you done any more papier mâché things, or other art?'

'Nope.' He stared out at the passing countryside.

Jack sighed, shot her an anguished look. She tried again.

'Have you brought any of your work with you? I'd love to see it.'

'Nope,' he said again, still staring out of the window.

'Tom, do try and be more forthcoming,' Jack retorted.

Seeing the look of resignation passing over Tom's face, Miranda said with a cheerfulness she did not feel, 'I'm probably asking him such boring questions. I remember hating it when I was a child and relatives quizzed me all the time about my school work, as if I had no other interests.'

'I expect you were polite, though,' Jack said, turning off the road and driving down a long path between two wheat fields. He glanced in his mirror to make sure that Edward was following them.

Miranda said nothing. Her feelings of shyness and dread rose in her throat as if they would suffocate her. She wished she could jump out and run through that wheat field and away.

Jack said, 'This is the back entrance through the farm. It saves going through the village and round to the front entrance.'

They passed a small stone farmhouse, drove through a farmyard, and then she saw the château. It was beautiful, small for a château she supposed, built in dove-grey stone, a tower at each corner, the roof a dark slate.

'I'd better drive you to the front or Mother will complain,' he laughed, and she felt sicker, imagining a terrifying women who was a stickler for correct behaviour and who hated her already.

They drove round to the front of the château, he stopped the car and she sat awkwardly there wishing she was anywhere else in the world but here.

'Come on,' he said gently. 'No one will bite you.'

Tom got out and she reluctantly followed. She went straight to stand beside Edward's car as he parked it beside Jack's, remembering when she was a child and they had gone to visit relatives or her parents' friends, and she had clung to his side in her shyness.

'Wonderful place, how many hectares?' Edward said to Jack, not seeming to notice her awkwardness.

There were long, wide steps leading up to the front door, which opened suddenly and two small children hurtled out, followed by Cynara, who shooed them away before her like chickens.

Miranda knew she was Jack's mother. She had the same elegant stance, the same look about her eyes. She swallowed; her mouth was dry. She felt so awkward standing there and was relieved when Frederique crept up to her and slipped her hand in hers.

'Welcome,' Cynara said, coming down the steps slowly. She wore a green and white summer dress and her legs were bare. Behind her came a tall, grey-haired man who hovered, slightly reserved, behind her.

The introductions were made, Miranda felt her take her hand, smile at her, then move on to Nicole. In a moment they were seated on the terrace with a Kir Royale in their hands. A white-clothed table stood at the far end of the terrace, laid with flowered china plates and silver cutlery. It looked like a very smart picnic indeed.

The children, two little boys who, Miranda soon learnt, were Cynara's step-grandchildren, scooped up the girls and they all disappeared, shrieking and running over the lawn. Tom sat down on a chair beside Jack and stared into space.

'Why don't you go with the others, darling?' Cynara said to him. 'Show the girls the doves.'

'Later,' Tom said, not looking at her.

Miranda saw her turn away and noticed Jack's mouth tighten. She thought for a moment he was going to reprimand Tom, but fortunately Etienne, Cynara's husband, asked them about Monet's garden and the conversation, in a mixture of French and English, steered safely on to that.

Jack sat next to Miranda and tried to talk to her. She felt wretched. She longed to be with him and yet she knew she should not be. Fortunately there were so many of them here, and with the children running in and out it was easy to distance herself from him. An old man, rather furiously, Miranda thought, leaning on a stick, came on to the terrace.

'Bloody hot in there,' he said.

Jack and Cynara jumped up. He waved his stick at them.

'Don't fuss, just introduce me.'

When the general was introduced to Miranda and Nicole he smiled, his eyes twinkling. He took their hands in his old one, its skin like paper, and raised them to his lips. 'I like pretty women,' he said, 'and you two are corkers.'

'*Charmant*,' Nicole cried, and Miranda found herself smiling and liking him at once. He sat down beside her and began to talk to her, asking what she did and where she lived. He did not ask why she was here, and seemed not to know that Jack had asked her.

Two young women appeared with some food, a plate of chicken in aspic, a green salad, some small potatoes and baguettes.

Nicole, no doubt used to French 'picnics', had brought a *tarte aux framboises* and crème fraîche, which fitted in perfectly. They sat together at the long table – the children giggling at one end. They were offered large glasses of chilled cider made on the estate, or red wine.

Miranda accepted cider instead of wine as she assumed that it would be less alcoholic and she felt she needed to keep her wits about her. But she was wrong and realised halfway through the meal that the cider was much stronger than she'd thought and she felt quite light-headed.

She was sitting between Etienne and Tom, Jack sitting opposite her. She tried to talk to Tom and managed to get a little from him. Etienne was a courteous host and kept her busy most of the time. Jack smiled at her, pleased that she was here. But she sensed that his mother was watching them all the time while she talked to Edward and Nicole, or saw to her step-grandchildren, or her father.

Every so often, Etienne, who obviously adored her, threw Cynara a loving glance or word. Miranda felt envious in a sad way, happy for them but wishing that she too could have a relationship as contented as theirs. Edward and Nicole also exchanged loving glances, and again she felt a pang, wishing she could experience that special closeness, the trademark of a good relationship. She wondered what Jack was feeling, if he too wished that his marriage was as successful. She felt they sat alone, isolated in their unhappiness, her, the general, Jack, Tom. The other children were gabbling together in French. Tom yet again was left out.

The meal progressed and Miranda felt as if she was floating, detached from them all. They finished eating at last and got up from the table, leaving the debris, the heels of cheese rind, the crispy breadcrumbs, for the young women to clear away. Coffee in a silver coffee pot was brought to them as they sat back away from the table.

Miranda found herself next to Cynara.

'I understand you have been so kind to my grandson,' Cynara said.

'Well . . . I . . . it wasn't anything,' Miranda muttered, surprised that there was no reprimand, no warning in her voice. She was just smiling at her in a friendly way. She realised that she liked her and had been afraid that Jack's mother would be judgemental, a woman jealous of other women loving her son, distrustful of a woman who might destroy his marriage.

Cynara sighed, glanced towards Tom, who hung over the low, pillared wall at the edge of the terrace overlooking the lawn. 'Poor boy, it is so difficult to get through to him at the moment. This dyslexia is such a handicap to him. Once you leave school I believe it doesn't matter so much. After all, there is nothing wrong with these children's intelligence. It is just such agony for them at school.'

'I wish there was something I could do,' Miranda said without thinking, caught up in Cynara's concern.

Cynara smiled. 'You are a kind person and Tom likes you. But at the moment he is in a difficult mood. Also, he cannot speak French, so is a little left out with the children. Adolescence,' she sighed. 'I remember it well, such an awkward age. He needs time, that's what I tell Jack. Love and time.'

Miranda had a feeling now that she was warning her – not unkindly, but just somehow saying that if she tried to help Tom too much it would involve Jack too. She fought with the lethargy the cider had induced in her, yet it had given her courage too.

'Surely his mother helps him, supports him?' she heard herself saying.

'She's very busy. She works, you know. Promoting things, I believe – I never quite know what. Something in the cosmetics field. But she does help him when she can,' Cynara said pleasantly. Then she went on about the difficulties of modern life, when both parents worked to achieve the standard of living they'd grown used to, sometimes, in her mind, to the detriment of the family.

Miranda was aware that Jack was watching them, and so was Nicole. Then the children came again and pulled Nicole and Edward off to see the river and take them on the boat moored there. The general, who had been snoozing, woke, tried to get out of his chair, saying it was too hot, he wanted to go inside. Cynara, calling for Tom to help her, led him inside. Etienne followed them, saying he had a few telephone calls to make, and suddenly Jack and Miranda were left alone on the terrace.

'Feel like a walk, or are you too hot?' he said.

She wondered what to do – stay here near the château, the young women clearing away the lunch and the possibility of the others drifting back, or let him spirit her away somewhere in the garden.

As if he guessed her thoughts he said, 'Let's go to the river. There's a couple of rowing boats there. We can see what the children are up to.'

'Will Tom come?'

'He'll come if he wants to. He often plays chess with my grandfather at this time of day.'

'But he'll join us?' she said, looking up at Jack standing in front of her, feeling he was crowding her, yet enjoying the sweetness of his proximity.

'He'll find us if he wants us,' Jack said, and took her hands and pulled her up. They stood face to face for a second, their bodies close yet not touching, but she could feel the warmth of him against her as if his body generated heat like a fire.

'Come on then,' he said, and keeping one of her hands loosely in his he led her down the steps of the terrace and over the lawn. They did not speak and she felt her feet sink gently in the soft, springy grass. She felt she was walking on air and would float away attached to him only by their hands. She could not think what to put into that silence that enveloped them. She felt dozy with the cider and the warmth of the sun on her body and still she walked beside him, her legs automated, matching his stride.

They reached a thick clump of trees and walked through their cool shade. Their trunks were old, gnarled and twisted with time. Through them she saw the glint of the river and far away she heard the cries and laughter of the children, the rhythmic hum of some farm machinery. She stumbled on a knobbly root that pushed out from the dry earth. He caught her, his arm round her waist. She felt the tautness of his body as he held her and for a second she rested her floating head on his shoulder.

The scent of him intoxicated her. She told herself to move away, run out into the sunlight to the children, but she could not move. She felt him groan, deep inside himself as if his very soul was in torment. She lifted her head and his lips caught hers. She could not pull away. His hands were on her and then he pulled her down on to some long grass. She felt the damp coolness of it against her bare skin, and then only the tumult, the passion that rose in both of them, the searing heat of mutual desire. There was no one in the world but them, no wives, no children, no commitments.

At last they were sated. He smiled, traced her eyes with his finger. 'Oh, Miranda, darling Miranda.'

As the passion left her she felt a great melancholy envelop her. She pulled her clothes about her. 'We shouldn't have done this,' she said, afraid suddenly that the children would come upon them, or worst of all, Tom. Now, with the heat of passion spent, she felt embarrassed. How could they have been so foolish to make love with such abandon here, where anyone could have seen them?

'Hush,' he said, 'no one comes this way. The little ones are frightened after a book they read about a dark wood. Tom will not come either.'

'I'm sorry,' she said. 'I didn't mean it to happen. I should have stopped it, but the cider, the heat . . .'

He put his fingers on her mouth to silence her. 'It was bound to happen, one way or another. And I'm so glad it has, though it's true I would rather we had been far away, utterly alone with endless time to be together. To make love again,' he smiled. 'It was glorious, wasn't it? Are we not made for each other?'

'Please don't make it worse. I—'

'Miranda, be honest with yourself. You enjoyed it as much as I did, wanted it. Didn't you?' He regarded her intently with his blue eyes.

'Yes. I did. But that doesn't make it right.'

Tenderly he did up the buttons on her shirt, kissed her in the hollow of her breasts. 'I want us to be together just a few days, alone. Can you come away somewhere? I can make an excuse and we can slip away somewhere in France. That's all I ask you. Please.'

'I can't,' she said. 'You know I can't . . . We can't.' And yet even as she said it she knew she could. She felt a kind of recklessness, brought on no doubt by the heady cider, the hot sun and their sudden abandoned lovemaking. She thought, why shouldn't I? His wife doesn't care enough for him – why shouldn't we snatch these few moments out of a lifetime? Deep inside she felt the echo of sadness, the knowledge that she would be the loser in the end. But why think only of the loss in life? Why not live these next few days as if they were the only days one had? Think of them as a bonus, a special gift that would be treasured and looked upon for the rest of her life? She would not jeopardise his marriage, would not demand he leave his wife for her.

As if he could read her thoughts, he said, 'I'll arrange it all, and ring you.'

They finished dressing silently. Jack gave her one more kiss and they walked quickly through the gloom of the trees to the sun. 'I love you,' he said to her.

Seeing the children ahead jumping out of the boats, Edward and Nicole with them, turning to wave, she did not answer. She was determined now to act as if nothing had happened, not wanting any of them to know how her body and her heart sang, bursting with the joy of loving Jack. She refused to allow the niggling feelings of guilt and fear for the future to intrude on her elation. There would be plenty of time for that later.

Chapter Eighteen

The sun shone again the following day although rain had been forecast. Nicole and Miranda cleared up the kitchen – the meal from the night before and the breakfast. The children – except for Lawrence, who sat at a desk in the corner of the room, doing some school work – played outside. Miranda could hear them calling out to each other and laughing. She admired Lawrence's stoicism at sticking to his studies.

Nicole had said nothing about Jack, but Miranda was sure she had guessed at their feelings. On the way home they had discussed the day, all having enjoyed it. They reminded each other who fitted in with who there, but it was as if there was a tacit agreement not to mention Jack's name at all.

Miranda, who longed to sing his name out loud, make a litany of it in her joy, forced herself to keep quiet. She knew Edward, who had gone to play tennis for the day, was not a great one for noticing such things. It probably hadn't occurred to him that she'd have an affair with this 'friend', who'd invited them over, she thought with relief, but Nicole was more perceptive.

Miranda felt strangely calm about it, as if whatever happened now was inevitable. She felt detached from his marriage, only able to think ahead to their next meeting. She did not know Sonia, and Tom had retreated deep into his shell so she felt she did not know him any more either. Adolescents – and he was probably just embarking on that stage with its dark and bewildering moods – often cast off adults they felt superfluous. She accepted that, remembering herself how she dreaded the adults who questioned her on her life, expecting her to have it all sorted out and be achieving great things, when by and large most of her inquisitors led such mediocre lives themselves.

'How long will you stay here, do you think?' Nicole asked her nonchalantly, taking up the cloth from the breakfast table and going to the open door to shake out the crumbs in the garden.

Miranda knew she meant how long before you and Jack go off together. They had left the château soon after she and Jack had joined them at the river. Goodbyes were said and, apart from Jack whispering, 'I'll ring you,' they'd behaved as if they were just friends, not new lovers.

'I don't know. Perhaps a day or two. Is that all right?'

'Of course, stay as long as you like.' Nicole glanced at Lawrence, who was sucking his pencil and staring into space.

'*Ca va, chéri? Ce n'est pas trop difficile pour toi?*' She went over to him, ruffling his hair.

'*Non, j'ai presque fini.*' He wrote something down, closed his book with a flourish and jumped up. Nicole kissed him, gave him a piece of chocolate and he ran outside to join the others.

'You know you are playing with fire with that man?' Nicole poured them both some more coffee and sat down at the table, looking at Miranda intently. 'He's still married, isn't he, and you are in love with each other?'

'Yes.' Miranda sat down opposite her, blushing at her directness. She prayed no one else had noticed. 'I've always thought it wrong to go out with a married man. I've seen the devastation it can do to families. After all, I feel terrible about my father going off like he has, and I'm grown up with a life of my own, yet here am I about to do the same.'

'You don't have to. You can go home tomorrow, or will he follow you?' Nicole said, sipping her coffee, watching her over the rim of her cup.

'I know I should go home, but I can't. I know nothing will come of it, just a few days together somewhere in France. I won't ask him to leave his family for me. I can't think of his family now, only him. I feel,' she paused, thought a moment, then gave an awkward laugh, 'I feel as if there was only him and me, and no one and nothing matters just for the moment. It will be something outside our normal lives, a precious gift, which will not affect anyone else.'

'I think you'll be hurt,' Nicole said. 'I may tease you about your lovers but this is serious. When you both go home, you will want to see him again. How will you cope if he is always with his wife, only able to see you in secret and then for just a minute or two?'

'I'll cope with that when it happens. Just now I want to live for these next few days. No one can tell the future.' She felt buoyant. If she had thought sensibly about it she might have heeded Nicole's advice. But she had tasted the joys of Jack's lovemaking and she wanted more. She was past acting sensibly, and pushed away any unpleasant thoughts of the consequences. She knew she could handle it – just a few days alone with him, that was all she would ask. It would be worth any pain.

There was a scream and a child ran in with a grazed knee. Miranda was relieved for the diversion but she knew that nothing anyone said would change her decision to spend this time with Jack.

'Don't say anything about it to anyone, will you? Even Edward,' she said in English, as Nicole washed Frederique's grubby little knee, and covered the wound with bright red antiseptic.

'No. You are over twenty-one, and I understand. You both love each other, that is obvious. It is unfortunate that he is married.' She hugged her child to her, giving her a few quick words of comfort. 'You say his wife is already unfaithful – then you have not broken the marriage – but only expect the crumbs of his love,' she warned, setting the child down before being swamped by the others, who ran in demanding drinks as it was so hot.

Jack rang in the late afternoon. Nicole just handed Miranda the telephone with a faint smile.

'Can you leave tomorrow? Meet me in Evreux, stay for the rest of the week?' His voice was quiet, urgent and Miranda suspected that he was afraid one of his family was listening.

'Yes. Tell me exactly where. Wait while I get a pencil to write it down.' Carefully she wrote down his directions, and they arranged to be there the next afternoon. She did not ask how Tom was, not wanting to think about anyone but Jack.

That evening at supper she told Nicole and Edward she was moving on. 'I'm meeting a friend,' she said, not meeting Nicole's eye, 'then going home.'

Edward, deep in conversation with Lawrence about the Russian spaceship, said, 'Is it that chap in Geneva? Why doesn't he come here?'

'*Chéri*, you are a spoilsport. Why should he come here so you can look him over?' Nicole teased him. 'Let Miranda meet him on her own.'

He laughed. 'I'd just like to see who my sister is going out with.'

'Leave that until your daughters bring home boyfriends,' Nicole said.

Miranda threw her a look of gratitude and quickly, in her inadequate French, joined in the conversation about the space vehicle.

Evreux was about twenty miles from her brother's house. She kissed them all goodbye and gave Nicole an extra hug.

'Don't get hurt, though it might be worth it,' Nicole said quietly in her ear as she said goodbye, standing on the front doorstep, the children round her.

Edward hugged her. 'Keep in touch.'

'I will,' she said, but she felt she had left them already. Had left everyone but Jack.

He was already waiting for her at the small garage where they'd arranged to meet. He opened her car door and pulled her out and into his arms.

'I can't believe it,' he said, kissing her, 'I can't believe you've really come.'

'I couldn't stop myself,' she said, returning his kisses, feeling intoxicated by the feel of him, the scent of him. All feelings of guilt and apprehension masked by these overwhelming emotions.

'I've found a marvellous hotel about fifty miles away. I've arranged for you to leave your car here, then we'll go on. Is that all right?'

'Fine.'

A short, stocky man, with hair *en brosse* and a moustache, swaggered up to them. In impeccable French Jack told him this was the car he wanted to leave with him and, ignoring the smirk in his eyes, took out Miranda's cases, handed him the keys and walked with her to his own car.

For the first few miles they drove almost in silence, just basking in the joy of being together. Miranda did not want to talk about his family and he seemed to understand this. They just wanted to absorb as much of each other as they could. Then they did talk – about France, about good food and wines, about life, love, each enjoying the sound of the other's voice, each marvelling at the way they thought alike, how perfectly their opinions matched.

The hotel was built of grey stone with a modern piece tucked on to the end. It stood in a pretty garden with a water wheel turning gently in the stream, picking up and tipping out the water which sparkled in the evening sun.

'I hope our room is in the old part. That new bit rather spoils it. It doesn't look at all romantic, too much like a soulless motel,' Jack said as they checked in.

She smiled. They stood apart, not touching, and yet she could feel his presence right through to the core of her. The girl behind the desk was friendly, made remarks about the weather, the sights to see in the area, the times of dinner. All this Miranda heard but did not take in. The girl's voice was just a background like the sound of the water wheel and the soft faraway hum of farm machinery. All Miranda's senses were focused on Jack; nothing else mattered.

When at last they were alone in their room they just stood there looking at each other with wonder, as if they had just discovered each other and were amazed at the discovery.

Tenderly, almost reverently, he took her in his arms and kissed her, first gently then, feeling her desire, with increasing passion until, unable to control their raging emotions, they fell on to the bed.

The next time they made love it was slower, languid, with gentle caresses and laughter.

'I never want to leave this room, this bed,' he said. 'It has all I want in the world in it.'

'Let us never leave it then,' she said, close in his arms. 'Be found here centuries in the future, covered in cobwebs.' She laughed at the absurdity of it, then felt a fleeting pang of tears as she knew it would never be.

He caught her look and said, 'Don't think, just live for now,' and kissed her again – her mouth, her ears, her eyes – tasting the one salt tear that had escaped from the corner.

'I will only think of now, of you, of us,' she said, holding him to her, determined not to let sad thoughts intrude on this magic.

Hunger and the aroma of delicious food finally drove them downstairs. They sat opposite each other in the light dining room, with its pink-clothed tables. There was a huge trolley laden with a glistening *tarte aux fraises*, raspberries on meringue dusted with icing sugar, chocolate and fruit mousses. The pungent smell of the wide array of cheeses arranged on a bed of straw added to their feeling of sensuality.

'Making love, a good wine and good food – surely they are the best pleasures of life,' Jack said, taking her hands in his and kissing her fingertips.

For four days they loved each other. Sometimes they did go out to explore the countryside, always holding hands, touching each other as if they could not function without the physical contact of the other. They gorged off each other, senses, scents, words, feelings, quite oblivious to anyone else, absorbing the beauty of the countryside, the wonderful food as part of their love, their time together.

On the fourth day they came back to the hotel after a long walk. They were pleasantly tired and Miranda looked forward to getting to their room, to their sleepy lovemaking before a rest and then dinner. But as they approached the hotel she was assaulted by the coldness of sudden departure; the realisation, which she had tried so hard to ignore and had, until now, successfully achieved, that this magic time would end. They had sworn not to talk of it, but she knew with painful certainty that the time had now come.

Jack guessed her mood, the sadness hitting him too. He stopped, took her in his arms. 'We love each other, nothing will ever change that. We'll keep in touch, see each other when we can.'

The sorrow in her bit hard. She felt the tears that she'd sworn she would not shed rise in her throat. She heard the words she had promised herself she would not say pour from her mouth.

'How often can we meet? How can we see each other?'

His mouth was grim. 'We will, I promise you we will. We have too much to just leave each other now. Be patient, darling, something will work out.'

She forced herself to smile, not to nag nor beg him to stay here with her. There was always a price to pay with love and she'd known it. She'd gone into this affair with both eyes open. She could not now stamp her foot and scream that it wasn't fair. She had known it would be like this, but even in her worst imaginings, she had not known it would hurt so much.

They went into the hotel, arms round each other as if each supporting the other one's grief.

When they got inside and got their key, he said, 'I'll be up in a minute. I just feel I ought to ring Tom. I said I would.'

'Of course,' she said dutifully, feeling that she was losing him already. She was glad he was not ringing him from their room. Somehow that room seemed sacrosanct, their secret place away from the world and intruders. She went upstairs, scolding herself for her feelings of despair. They loved each other, it had not been a hasty affair, a greedy snatching of sexual pleasure. They would, she thought, manage a sort of life together. It was good that she was free and could travel anywhere at any time – well, for weekends anyway. She had her own flat, that made it easy, though Colin no doubt would wear out his eyes finding warnings about adultery in the Bible to quote at her. She smiled at the thought.

She began to feel better, more positive, remembering countless stories of married people who had had lovers for years. If she could put up with sharing him, then it would work without hurting anyone. Perhaps, her mind began to fantasise, Sonia would go off with one of her lovers, leave the coast clear for them. Or maybe when Tom was older, in six or eight years, Jack could leave Sonia and come to her for good. She would have to be patient. She lay back on the bed waiting for him, savouring the wonder of their love, longing to hold him again.

She heard his steps coming along the passage, her body restless with anticipation at his every step. He walked fast and she smiled, thinking of his desire. He opened the door and she turned eagerly to him. His face was ashen, his voice a sob.

'What is it?' Icy lead hit her warm feelings, killing them dead.

'It's Tom. He . . . Oh God.' He sank down on the bed, put his head in his hands.

She held him, feeling his body trembling against hers. 'What?' she said, terror, pain, guilt rushing through her.

'He tried to . . . to kill himself. He took some of my grandfather's sleeping pills.'

'But he's . . . not . . .' she could hardly bear to say the word, 'dead?'

'He's very ill. Something made me ring.' He looked bewildered. 'Thank God I did, and not tomorrow like I thought I would. I must go to him at once, darling. Will you come?'

'But . . .' It is not my place to come, she thought. It should be Sonia.

He looked at her, reading her thoughts. 'My mother cannot contact Sonia. She has gone away. It has only just happened. I rang the château and spoke to my grandfather, then my mother at the hospital. They all feel . . .' he gulped, tears shone in his eyes, 'shattered, upset they couldn't contact us. Thank God something made me ring now.'

She held him a moment longer, then with a heavy heart helped him pack. Nothing, she thought, lasts for ever, but everything leaves its own mark. Would Tom's act tarnish the love they had felt for each other these last few days? Be its death knell?

Chapter Nineteen

The long, slow drive to the hospital was agony. Miranda kept her hand on Jack's thigh, needing to touch him for reassurance, wanting to take away some of his pain and the guilt she knew they were both feeling.

She experienced a mixture of emotions, pain for Jack, anger that she felt guilty. The primitive fear that this was a punishment for their stolen happiness and that Tom was suffering because of it. Colin, she thought mirthlessly, would no doubt be triumphant if he knew. Would find passages in the Bible to convince her that they had to pay for their sin.

'I don't know if this helps,' she started, unable to bear the silence and the torture of her thoughts, 'but when I was at university and a student, not someone I knew actually, took an overdose, we were told that some young people can't understand the concept of the finality of death. They do it, as a cry for help, whatever, thinking it will be over by after the weekend, that they will then be able to carry on just as before, only things will be better.'

'I can see that,' Jack said. 'I know I should have rung him before. But he seemed contented enough about being left with my mother. I know he's not been very happy lately, but he loves it there, being in the country, helping on the farm. I thought it would make him feel better about himself. He knew I had to go for a few days, what he didn't know was that I was with you, instead of going back to the office.'

'Perhaps he tried to ring you at home and you weren't there,' she said, feeling sick at the thought. 'But where was Sonia?' Her pain made her cry out, then she bit her tongue. 'I'm sorry, I shouldn't have said that. It's none of my business.'

'I don't know where she is. I rang her before I left with you.' He swallowed, looked strained. 'I said I had a few things to see to in Paris, I'd ring her. I didn't.' He paused and before she could jump in with anything he continued, 'She sounded as if she didn't care, was pleased about it, in fact. "Stay as long as you like," she said, "I've so much to do here, and I don't have to cook if you're away."'

'Do you think she guessed? About us?'

'I don't think so. Why should she? I think she was relieved that she could go off with whichever man she has in tow at the moment. I must say, it's a hell of a mess. She . . .' He paused then blurted out, 'You may find this difficult to believe but she's very insecure. I realised recently that when anything goes wrong with Tom, or if I have to go on a long trip, she seems to have an affair.'

'What do you mean?' Miranda looked at him incredulously, feeling that if this was Sonia's excuse for hurting him, for hurting Tom, it was a pretty poor one. 'Surely she should be supporting him, not having affairs? Oh, darling, what psychological mumbo jumbo has she fed you?' Seeing his face, she immediately felt contrite at her outburst. It made her angry, this new idea of finding a psychological excuse for self-gratification or wrongdoing.

'I'm sorry, this is not the time to argue about Sonia's ex—' she was going to say excuses but changed it quickly to, 'reasons for having affairs.' Seeing his face so taut with pain and anxiety she went on, feeling rather desperate with it all, 'I thought there'd be no harm in us having a few days together, probably because I wanted it so much. I convinced myself it would be all right. But I was wrong, I fully admit it. I should have been stronger, kept to my original convictions, hard though they were.'

'Nonsense,' he said, taking his eyes off the road to look at her, swerving, then shooting his eyes back to the road again, his hands clenching on the wheel. 'Tom was fine when I left, well, as fine as he's ever been lately. There were various outings planned and he loves being there, outdoors. Something must have upset him, made him do it. A sort of impulse. My mother can't think of anything at the moment, but she's so shocked.' His voice trembled. 'But where is Sonia? She said she'd be at home,' he cried out, banging his hands on the wheel.

Miranda didn't say anything. She was now terrified that Sonia would suddenly turn up, be there at the hospital when they arrived. Then what would she do? How would she explain herself? Though, she thought defiantly, why should she when Sonia behaved as she did?

Jack said, 'I can't tell you how much it means to me having you here. Other women might have turned tail and run, not wanting to get involved. I'm really sorry to have put you through this, my darling.'

'It's not your fault, you mustn't think that. These things . . . people trying to take their own lives, always make everyone feel they could have stopped it. If someone is determined enough to do it . . .' She let her voice run off, feeling that perhaps she'd gone too far. Tom was a child, he surely didn't mean to do it, not like a depressed adult who could not cope with life.

'It's such a nightmare. I can't really believe it.' Jack looked grimly ahead. They'd arrived in the town and after a few yards they saw the hospital. Miranda felt faint with dread. She longed to get out and run away. Instead she put her arm round his shoulder to offer him and herself support.

He parked the car and sat a moment, staring in front of him, as if gathering strength for the ordeal ahead. Miranda guessed he was afraid that he would hear that Tom was dead.

She said, 'Don't think anything until you know for sure, darling . . .'

'You're right.' He turned to her, stroked her cheek. 'Thank you for being here. For being you.'

Then he was out of the car and they walked without speaking across the car park to the hospital. Cynara and Etienne were waiting for them. Cynara came running up and took Jack's hand.

'They think he's out of danger.'

'Thank God.' Jack looked as if he might cry. He steadied himself. 'May I see him?'

'I'll show you where he is. Then you must see the doctor. He wants to talk to you.'

Jack touched Miranda's arm and was gone. She felt isolated, alone without him. She wondered if she should leave, but she felt drained, too exhausted suddenly to do anything. She sank down on one of the grey, gloomy chairs in the corridor.

Etienne said, 'A terrible business and we can't find his mother. Let me get you a coffee. I don't think there is anything stronger.'

'No thank you.' She managed a small smile. She felt so agitated, wondering what would happen if Sonia suddenly appeared and saw her sitting here, what further pain she would inflict on Jack. She ought to leave, she decided. Go to a nearby hotel, leave word for Jack where she was.

Cynara came back alone. Miranda felt sick, wondering what she would say to her, but she smiled, sat down beside her.

'The doctor thinks he will be all right.'

'I'm so glad,' Miranda muttered, feeling suddenly rather tearful.

Cynara took her hand. 'You must not blame yourself. None of us knew this might happen.' When Miranda, too overcome to trust herself to speak, stayed silent, she went on: 'I know my son has a difficult marriage. I have never interfered and I don't want to now. But for the moment I'm sure you'll agree that Tom must come first.'

'Of course. I'm not going to break up his marriage, you needn't be afraid of that,' Miranda burst out, a tear running down her face.

Etienne got up and wandered over to the window.

Cynara said firmly, 'I'm sure you're not.' She let go of her hand, sighed and said, 'We must find out why Tom did this. At the moment he's not speaking about it. But we must make sure it never happens again.'

'Of course.' Miranda sat there too emotionally exhausted to move. She wondered how Jack was coping and longed to be with him. She wondered again what would happen if Sonia, having got their message, should appear here. She imagined her rushing in, her elegance in disarray in her anxiety, seeing her here, and demanding that she leave. She half rose, trying to work out how she could fetch her car, find a hotel before starting home.

She said, 'Perhaps I ought to go and stay nearby. I don't think it right that Sonia finds me here.'

Cynara's face tightened. She said, 'I don't think she knows about this yet. I rang my home just before you came and she still hadn't rung us. We'd left a message saying Tom was ill and to contact us at once.' She paused, gave Miranda a quick glance. 'I didn't like to say he'd taken an overdose, but also . . .' Her eyes filled with tears and her voice trembled, making Etienne come back from the window and put his arm round her. 'I didn't know if he would die.'

'It must have been awful for you,' Miranda said. 'When exactly did it happen?'

'Just before lunch. Yesterday we went out for the day to some friends with ponies, tennis and things. We had a wonderful day but we got back quite late. He was listless this morning, but I thought he was just tired from all the things he'd done the day before.' She gave a deep sigh.

Etienne said, 'It was lucky I went into the barn to look at the lawn mower – we are thinking of buying a new one. Tom was lying on some straw in the corner. It was just luck I saw him,' he repeated, stroking Cynara's shoulder.

'And you've no idea why he did it?' Miranda asked.

'Not yet.' Cynara looked grave. 'I suppose it will mean psychiatrists, all that.'

After a while Etienne rang home again but there was still no news from Sonia.

'Miranda, you must stay with us tonight,' Cynara said suddenly, as if she had been wrestling with herself over her decision. 'As his wife is not here, Jack needs all the support he can get.'

'What happens if Sonia comes?' Miranda was sure staying in the château would be a bad idea. 'I think it's better if I stay at a hotel nearby.'

'As you like,' Cynara said, 'but we have plenty of room.'

Miranda didn't know what to do. She sat there awkwardly, feeling that she didn't want to leave until she'd seen Jack again, heard from him how Tom was. She didn't want to go on bothering Cynara and Etienne, who were obviously in shock. Then Jack appeared, looking so tired and drawn that Miranda could not stop herself going to him and taking him in her arms.

He held her to him a moment, then he said, 'I'd rather stay with him, for the night. My mother and Etienne will look after you. Go back with them and rest.' He looked at them as if he were asking them to look after her.

'I'll stay here if you want me to,' she said, feeling that even if she didn't see him again this night, she'd rather stay here near him.

He smiled, kissed her. 'No point in us all getting tired. Come back tomorrow. I'll ring you later.'

'All right. Take care. Give him my love,' she said, wondering if perhaps he too was afraid that Sonia would suddenly appear and see her there.

Etienne and Cynara hardly spoke on the drive back to the château. Miranda sat in the back of the car, looking out at the night, feeling as displaced as a refugee thrown into an alien country. They were greeted by the general, who hovered anxiously in the doorway.

'Well?' he said brusquely, as if waiting for the list of casualties after a battle.

'He's going to be all right as I told you when I rang before. Jack is staying with him,' Cynara said. 'You remember Miranda.' She gestured towards Miranda, who smiled politely at him, wondering how on earth she was going to explain her presence.

'You came the other day,' General Callendar said, looking at her sharply. 'Where do you fit in, in all of this?'

Miranda swallowed, threw a look at Cynara, wondering what on earth to say.

Cynara took the general's arm to lead him back inside. 'She knows Tom, has helped him with his school work.'

'Was it this dyslexia business that made him do it?' he demanded of her.

'No . . . I'm sure not,' Miranda said. 'We don't know what it was.'

'Come on, Father. Have you had your supper yet?' Cynara urged him on. One of the young women Miranda had seen serving the lunch appeared, saying that she'd left a light meal in the dining room.

'*Merci, Yvette.*' Cynara then asked her to show Miranda to her room, explaining that she was staying for the night.

'I must say you're pretty for a teacher,' General Callendar said to her from the chair Cynara had parked him in. 'Big improvement on my day, but I don't like your methods. Hard work and discipline is what children need, none of these excuses for shoddy work under fancy names.'

'Now, Father, I'm sure Miranda doesn't want to discuss education tonight,' Cynara said firmly. 'It's been a horrendous day and we're all tired. Now, Miranda, let Yvette show you to your room.'

She was shown to a large room overlooking the front drive. Relieved to be alone, Miranda sat down on a chair by the window and stared out at the gathering dusk. A few hours ago she and Jack had been in each other's arms, delirious with love. Now she was here, feeling like an unwanted guest, living through the tragedy of his only child trying to kill himself. She wished she could go to him, share his pain with him. But it was not her place, she thought with sadness. Sonia should be there.

She was too tired to leave tonight, but she must go tomorrow. Slip away and not add to Jack's problems. Keep away until he contacted her again.

There was a knock on her door and Yvette stood there with a tray of supper. She explained that Madame had thought she might like to eat in her room. Miranda thanked her and wondered if Cynara had done this to spare her any more questions from the general or if she did not want to eat with her, her son's mistress. After all, she thought, when Sonia comes and finds that I have been here it's bound to make things worse.

She barely slept. Her body, her soul, yearned for Jack. She wondered how he was coping and if he was looking out at the same dark sky, yearning for her. She felt she had just fallen asleep when Yvette knocked on her door and said she was wanted on the telephone.

Drugged with sleep, her mind racing as to who it was and praying it was Jack, she pulled on her dressing gown and followed Yvette downstairs to the telephone in the drawing room. She picked up the receiver.

'Miranda.' To her great relief it was Jack. 'Can you come? Tom wants to see you,' he said at once.

'Well . . . but Sonia, what about her?'

'There's still no word. Please, Miranda, if it's not too much to ask. He didn't take as many pills as they first thought, thank goodness. He's quite bright today. But he won't talk . . . about what happened, and the doctor and I think as he's asking for you, if you could bear to—'

'Of course I will, but . . .' Sleepily her mind turned over his words. Surely Tom should have his mother with him, not her. She felt a tightness of anger in her. If Tom really wanted her, she would go. Perhaps he wanted to talk to someone outside the family. She looked up and saw Cynara watching her from the doorway.

'If that's what he wants I'll come. I'll get a taxi,' she said, longing to say more, to ask how he was, to say she loved him, but she was afraid to show her feelings with his mother standing there.

'Have breakfast first. I'm going to have a shower. Thank goodness I've got my suitcase here,' he said.

'I'll be there,' she said. ''Bye . . . Oh, wait, do you want to talk to your mother?'

'I already have. See you, darling.' Hearing his endearment she glanced guilty up at Cynara in case she'd heard it too and disapproved.

Cynara said, 'I'll run you there. I want to see how things are.'

'Of course you do, but are you sure that won't be a bother?' Miranda asked her.

'No, I'd like to see him, see both of them if I can,' she said. She looked defeated, pale. Miranda supposed that she hadn't slept either. 'Would you like breakfast in your room?' Cynara asked her. 'We could leave about nine thirty.'

'Whatever's easiest,' Miranda said, not knowing if Cynara wanted to sit opposite her at the breakfast table.

'I've had mine, it's as you like. It's laid up in the dining room. Left at the bottom of the stairs,' Cynara said, leaving her.

'Thank you. I'll dress and come down.' Miranda went back to her room to get ready.

She ate alone in the pale grey and blue dining room. The table was laid with pretty china, white with blue flowers to match the walls. There was a basket of croissants wrapped in a napkin to keep them warm; home-made preserves in glass pots with silver lids; coffee and hot milk in silver pots on the sideboard. Miranda drank a lot of coffee and nibbled at a croissant. She dreaded today, for surely Sonia would come and she would have to escape, leave Jack behind.

It was Friday and she'd have to return anyway for work on Monday. Stella was taking her holiday that week and she had to get back. It would be a relief, she thought, that she had something to get back to.

On the way to the hospital – Cynara driving with exaggerated care – Miranda said, 'I have to be back at work on Monday. I'd better leave after lunch. Fetch my car and go.'

'Where is your car?'

'In a garage outside Evreux. I think I can find it.'

Cynara said nothing for a moment. Then, her eyes firmly on the road ahead, she began, 'It must have been so difficult for you, being sort of thrown into a situation like this. I don't know, nor is it my business to ask, about you and my son, but I can see he is very fond of you—'

'I'm very fond of him,' Miranda broke in.

'I know. That's what makes it worse in a way. Had you both, well, just had a quick fling, it probably wouldn't have mattered. But at the moment . . .' They stopped at a traffic light and Cynara turned to her and said gently, looking her straight in the eyes, 'My dear, however happy you and Jack are together, Tom must not suffer any upheavals. There can be no question of you taking Sonia's place.'

'But I don't want to . . .'

Cynara ignored her remark, pressed on: 'Tom wants to see you. That is fine, just this once. Then you must go, leave the family to sort this out alone.'

'I understand,' Miranda said miserably, knowing that she had made that decision herself but saddened that Cynara had put it into words, and ashamed that she might think her too insensitive not to have realised it herself.

'You must not on any account make Jack think you need him,' Cynara said. 'Believe me, my dear, I know it will be hard, but until all this is resolved and Tom is completely well again, you must keep out of the way so that they can work things out themselves.'

Miranda felt terrible. She resented Cynara's words. She and Jack were adults; she wanted to do what he wanted her to do. If he told her it was over, that it was impossible for them to see each other again in the circumstances, then she'd abide by it. But his mother telling her, making her feel that she was a manipulative woman, who with tears and tantrums would make Jack feel that he must continue to see her, adding to his grief, was absurd. She felt like getting out of the car and continuing on her way alone, but she did nothing but sit there seething.

'I know you think I'm a nosy old bag,' Cynara said lightly. 'I don't blame you. For what it's worth I like you. I like you because I can see you make Jack happy, and he deserves it. But all that is a luxury at the moment, you must understand that.'

'I do, it's just I . . .'

'I know, believe me I know. But don't make Jack take any decisions now. See Tom, then say goodbye. A quick one, no lingering. Say you must get back to work. When Sonia comes Jack will see the sense of it, keep the family intact for Tom. One day things may change.'

They had arrived now. Cynara parked the car.

'What if Sonia never comes? Has gone away for good with someone? Perhaps she left a note at home.'

'She'll come. I know she behaves badly, she's one of those women who seek attention, need men to fall at their feet. She probably goes to bed with them to prove her attraction, her power. I don't think it means much to her,' Cynara said, looking gravely at Miranda. 'But you see, she loves Jack and Tom. They are her base. She'll never leave them, I'm sure of it. But Jack,' she paused, 'he might get bored of her behaviour, want something better.'

'Why shouldn't he?' Miranda felt irritated now, irritated with Cynara and Jack for making excuses for Sonia. Why should Sonia sleep with men when it meant nothing to her but to exercise her power over them? Why was she not here with her son when he needed her? She did not deserve Jack or Tom. Jack, even in the midst of loving her, had thought to ring his son. Sonia was a spoilt child who expected to have her own way and to have everyone put up with it.

'I'm not saying it is right, Miranda. It's just how it is and for the moment Tom needs his parents to stay together. To my mind Sonia doesn't give her child enough time, but I've seen them together and she does love him. This . . . this thing with him will give her a shock. It may make her see sense, organise her life to stay at home with him more.'

Miranda got out of the car. She couldn't breathe, she needed fresh air. It was so unfair that Sonia would get away with this, that Tom's action might well save their marriage, make even the most innocent contact with Jack forbidden. She'd be happy to share Jack, see him only when he was free, but Cynara was asking the impossible – for her to stay away and give Sonia, unfaithful, selfish Sonia, the chance to become a faithful, good wife, which she should have been all along.

Cynara came up and touched her arm. 'It is as Tom's parents that we must think of them, Miranda,' she said gently. 'Not as my son or your lover, but as Tom's parents, whom he loves and needs.'

'I know,' Miranda said with an enormous effort. In a few moments, when she'd mastered her feelings, she went into the hospital with Cynara.

Jack, looking tired but happier, kissed them both. He took Cynara in to Tom first and then after a little while came out with her.

'I'll be back later this afternoon to help you bring him back,' she said. 'I'm so relieved that he's coming home.'

'Goodbye.' She held out her hand to Miranda, who took it. 'I do hope I see you again,' she added with a smile before leaving.

'Darling.' Jack waited until his mother was out of sight, then took Miranda in his arms. 'How I longed for you. It was such a lonely night. How are you?'

'I'm fine. Tell me about Tom.' She held on to him, determined to get as much of him as she could before she had to leave.

'Better. He won't talk . . . about what's happened. But this morning he suddenly asked about you coming over to the château that day. Said if you were still in France he wanted to see you. I hope you don't mind.'

'Of course not. Shall I go to him now?'

'In a second. I just want to be with you a moment longer.' He held her again. 'Listen, he's coming out later this afternoon. I'll stay here with him until he's strong enough, then probably bring him home. I must wait for Sonia,' his mouth went hard, 'if she deigns to get in touch.'

'I must go back for work,' Miranda said.

'I know, and if Sonia comes it will be difficult. I can't bear you to go, but—'

'I shall go today. Tell me where my car is and I'll set off.'

'I'll take you there to fetch it. Will you be all right?'

'Don't be silly. I was going to drive back on my own anyway.'

'I didn't mean that.' He looked serious.

'Let me see Tom,' she said. 'We can't keep him waiting.'

She felt nervous as they approached his door, not knowing what she would find. Jack came in with her and to her surprise and relief she saw Tom sitting on the edge of the bed watching television. He looked pale but otherwise fine.

'Hello, Tom,' she said.

'Hello, Miranda.' He glanced at her, then at Jack. 'I want to say something private. Do you mind, Dad?'

Jack looked a little hurt, she thought. 'N-no . . . I'll come back in half an hour.'

'OK.' Tom stared back at the television screen.

Jack left and Miranda sat down on a chair beside his bed. Tom continued to stare at the screen.

At last she said, 'What do you want to tell me, Tom?'

He glanced at his bare feet, at her, then at his feet again, swinging them listlessly over the bed.

'Only tell me if you want to,' she said.

He bit his lip, avoided eye contact with her as if he was ashamed of something. 'Some of the people . . . at school. They . . . well, there's this boy, two of them really. They say they're going to kill me, cut bits off me.'

'Oh, Tom . . .' She was horrified.

'At school they come for me. One has a knife, the other a compass. They put a bird's leg in my desk, to remind me.' His eyes were round with terror.

She sat down beside him and held him. She felt numb with horror. 'But the teachers, surely they—'

'They made me promise not to tell anyone. Then they put a dead frog in my bed.' He shuddered. She held him tighter. 'I screamed, and the headmaster came. I tried to tell him about it, but he laughed, said it was just a bit of fun, he'd speak to them, but he said that there was no bullying going on in his school.'

'Tom, I can't bear it. Couldn't you tell your parents?'

'No. They like me going there. They want me to go to a good public school and I need help with my dyslexia. Dad likes going to Chandos Hall, so do I,' he added loyally. 'If I do well and pass my Common Entrance I'll get away,' he said desperately.

Miranda kept her arm round him. She felt stunned with horror and pain at what he'd told her. 'You must tell them, Tom. They'll understand. You cannot keep this to yourself. Or tell the doctor,' she said.

'He's French,' Tom said reasonably.

'But someone will translate for you. Your father's pretty good, or Etienne, or, well, someone in the town,' she said desperately, not knowing how to handle this.

'They sent me a parcel,' Tom said, staring ahead. 'They sent it home, but Mum posted it on to me at Grandma's.'

'What was it?' She could hardly bear it.

'A whole dead bird,' he said shuddering. 'A blackbird.'

'Oh, Tom. Didn't your grandmother or someone see it?'

'No. I was playing outside when the postman came. He gave me the post. I thought the parcel was some comics and sweets from Mum – she said she'd send me some. I left the letters on the table and opened . . .' He shuddered again. 'They are coming to get me, I know it. There was no letter, but I know it.' His voice was flat, resigned.

'No, they're not,' she said firmly. 'They are sick, horrible boys, but they won't hurt you. I promise you that. But why did you . . . take the pills and where did you find them?'

'Great-grandpa had them in his sponge bag. He showed them to me, said he'd been given enough sleeping pills to put a whole army to sleep and that it was no wonder the Health Service is losing money if they dish out so many pills at a time.'

Miranda could imagine him saying that. 'But, Tom, why did you take them?'

'I only took a few. I thought – well, I thought if I went to sleep for a long time they couldn't send me back. I think,' he shivered, looked terrified, 'that they'll be waiting in London at my house. Mum and Dad are often out and I'm alone.'

'Oh, Tom.' She could not bear his anguish. 'You know you could have died.'

'Then I wouldn't have been able to go back to school, would I?' His eyes looked directly into hers.

'Tom, you must tell your father everything you've told me. Then we can stop it.'

'I can't. He'll be disappointed, so will Great-grandpa, if I don't go to a good public school. Pilgrim's Court is my only hope. That's what Mr Castle, the headmaster, said.'

'Oh, Tom.' She hugged him. 'That's not true. Your father will be horrified when he finds out. He loves you. He'd never let you suffer like this. You must tell him. Please, I know he'll understand.' She almost said that it was wrong of him to have caused his family so much pain by taking the pills, but she thought that might make him feel worse. Instead she said, 'If you don't tell your problems to the people who love you, how can they help you?'

Tom looked pensive for a moment. 'Will you tell him?' he said at last. 'I'd rather you did.'

'If that's what you want,' she said, thinking: yet again another strand to bind me tighter to this family. 'But it will be all right, Tom, I promise you. But you must never take pills again. You promise me.'

She thought he looked relieved, a little ashamed. She could imagine the general scolding him for his weakness. 'Shall I fetch him and tell him with you, or on his own?' she said gently.

'Tell him on his own.'

To her relief a nurse came in. She realised that she'd been afraid to leave him alone even for a moment after hearing his ghastly story. She could not bear to think of this cruelty, his fear and the headmaster's dismissal of his plea.

'I'll go and tell him now,' she said, adding in French to the nurse where she was going.

The nurse smiled and said in perfect English, 'I will stay a minute. I have his temperature to take.'

Miranda saw Jack idly reading the paper further down the corridor. He jumped up as soon as he saw her. Then, seeing her expression, the tears she'd kept from Tom coursing down her cheeks, he cried out, 'What is it? He's not worse?'

'No, no.' She held on to him, putting her head on his shoulder, feeling the sobs rising in her as if they would choke her.

He held her tight. 'Tell me what it is. Shall I go to him?'

She struggled to control herself, took a deep breath. 'Wait, I'll tell you. It's so horrible.'

'What is?' She saw he was fighting to remain calm. He threw an agonised look in the direction of Tom's room, as if he didn't know who needed him most.

She sank down on a chair, still holding on to him. Then still crying, but as clearly as she could, she told him about the dead animals, the sick boys.

'My God, if only I had known. The bastards.' He looked distraught. 'Of course he must leave the school, or those boys must. I'll ring that headmaster at once. I must go to Tom.'

'In a minute. Try and compose yourself,' she said, still clinging on to him.

'So that's why he did it. He thought they were coming after him?'

She nodded. 'Would be waiting at home when you and Sonia were out. The pills were easy for him to take. They were just left in the bathroom for anyone to help themselves, apparently.'

'I'm amazed Mother never thought to move them. The little children could have taken them, thought they were sweets.' He sighed heavily, ground his hands together. 'If only I'd been there, if only someone – Yvette, Mother, someone – had seen the parcel, been there when he opened it.'

'But nobody could have known what was in it,' she said.

They saw the doctor coming down the corridor, a tall, dark-haired man with a preoccupied air.

'I must tell him, see what we can do. Will you go back to Tom? Tell him I'm with the doctor and will come soon. Tell him not to worry.' He looked bewildered, devastated.

'Of course.' She kissed him, holding him to her for a second, not caring what the doctor thought of her action.

Tom looked very small when she returned. He threw her a frightened look. She sat down beside him and put her arm round him.

'Daddy's coming in a minute, but the doctor came past and they're talking. He's very pleased you told me, thinks you're very brave,' she said, not knowing what else to say. 'He's going to deal with it.'

'They'll come and get me,' he said again, his voice sounding resigned.

'Oh no they won't. They were just bullying you. They wouldn't dare, and now that your father knows, everything will be all right.'

'And I won't have to go back to Pilgrim's Court?'

'We didn't talk about that. But don't worry any more, Daddy is going to cope with it,' she said with as much fervour as she could.

He stared at her. 'Your eyes look as if they've been crying.'

'Oh, it's my mascara, it has little bits in that get into my eyes,' she said quickly.

'I wouldn't use it then,' he said, looking back at the television.

Jack and the doctor came back into the room. The doctor smiled cheerfully at Tom. Jack sat on the other side of him, put his arm round him.

'Everything is going to be all right, Tom,' he said. 'You're not to worry any more. Promise.'

Tom nodded, pushing himself against Jack. Miranda got up. 'I'm just going to find a coffee,' she said to Tom, knowing they wanted to be alone with him.

'Come back,' Tom said.

'I will.' She left the room. She waited over an hour and then Jack found her. He looked calmer.

'Thank you,' he said, taking her in his arms. 'Thank you for finding out what made him do it.'

'I hardly did that. He just told me.'

'He trusts you. Oh, darling, if only things were different.' She knew what she meant, he wanted her instead of Sonia, but she said nothing.

She remembered Cynara's words and said, 'Tell me where my car is, I must start for home. I'll ring you when I get there.'

'Go tomorrow,' he said. 'I want to spend tonight with you.'

'So this is what you're up to, Jack.' Sonia's voice hit them like a rain of bullets. 'My son is dying and you are cavorting with this woman.'

Miranda sprang from his arms. Sonia and Cynara stood there in the corridor, staring at them.

Chapter Twenty

'But you could not be contacted,' Jack said, furious with his wife – with himself for putting Miranda in this position.

'So you call in Miss Goody Two-Shoes, Mother Theresa, the woman with nothing better to do with her life but interfere with other people's children, instead!' Sonia raged back at him. 'Or, perhaps,' her eyes flashed, 'she's not so good at all and you are having an affair with her.'

Jack turned away, struggling to keep his emotions in check. He was exhausted by Tom's overdose, not being able to get hold of Sonia, his love for Miranda and their being seen by Sonia; the terrible scene that he would have done anything to spare Miranda. He remembered her face as she saw his mother and Sonia glaring at them, his mother more in sorrow than anger. Sonia's cutting voice asking why Miranda felt she had to take out her obvious insecurity, her lack of love in her life, with a married man, throwing herself in such a vulgar way at him. It was all done with such arrogance.

Miranda had said nothing, barely looked at Sonia. Jack had stretched out his hand to takes hers but she had moved out of his reach, holding her head high, but not looking at him.

Cynara had done what she could to salvage the scene.

'Miranda, I'll take you to your car,' she'd said firmly. 'Where is it exactly?'

Jack had broken in quickly as she hesitated. 'It's at the garage just as you go into Evreux.' He'd said it quickly, hoping Sonia wouldn't connect, start putting two and two together.

'I know it,' his mother had confirmed, and Miranda, still not looking at him, at anyone, had just said, 'Goodbye. Love to Tom,' and walked away from him.

He had to turn away so Sonia wouldn't see the pain on his face. His whole body longed to run after her, take her in his arms and beg her to stay – well, not to stay for that would be impossible for her, but he wanted to go with her. But he did not move, willing himself to appear calm, to overcome the terrible feeling of being torn apart, knowing he could not leave Tom.

Sonia then moved in on him, her face tragic, furious. 'Where is Tom, my son? How can you leave him, be with this woman when he is dying?' she said dramatically. Jack sighed heavily. He knew this selfish mood of hers, the 'why should fate be so unkind as to do this to me?' mood.

'He is *not* dying,' he said curtly. 'Come to him, he's longing to see you. He has needed you badly.'

She had the grace then to look contrite. She followed him, saying, 'How could he get hold of these pills? And how could you leave him if he was so unhappy?'

'He wasn't unhappy when I left him,' he said, realising with sinking heart that he'd have to elaborate on the 'business meetings' he'd told her had held up his return from France. 'Wait, I'd better tell you all about this wretched pill business before you see him. How much do you know?'

He told her everything about the bullying, the parcel, but he didn't tell her that Tom had opened his heart to Miranda. He supposed that would come out and wondered what poison Sonia would put in Tom's mind about her. But there was nothing he could do about it now. Tom would want to see his mother as soon as possible.

He left them together, went outside and waited for Cynara to come back from dropping Miranda.

When she did she said immediately, putting her hand on his arm, 'We won't talk of it again, Jack. We picked up her luggage on the way and she's gone back to England. Just think of Tom. He needs you both now.'

Later they took Tom back to the château, Cynara and Sonia with him in one car, Jack alone in his. They all stayed together for the rest of the day, Sonia spending her time with Tom, who apart from being tired seemed pleased to be back. But now that most of the household had gone to bed and they were alone in their room, the showdown had begun.

'Tell me exactly what is going on between that woman and you,' Sonia said, confronting him full on, her eyes like searchlights on his face.

He felt empty. He longed to tell her that Miranda had changed his life, that the love they had shared over these last few days had been greater than anything he had shared with her. It had been deeper, more honest. He felt he could depend on her, trust her implicitly. Miranda didn't suffer from the insecurities that turned Sonia into a spoilt child when the going got tough. But he thought of Tom, white-faced, still shaken from his ordeal, clinging to his mother saying 'Where were you, Mum? Why didn't you come?' and Sonia's answer, as soothing as she was with him when she had been unfaithful: 'I was working, my darling, but I'm here now and I'll be here always for you.'

Although Jack felt angry at her betrayal, he knew she loved Tom, in her way. No doubt she felt guilty at not being there, though she would pretend it was not her fault, weave some plausible story of how she was tied up with some tiresome client, couldn't get away, until she had convinced herself, and everyone else, of its truth.

He turned to face her. She was sitting on the bed half undressed, wearing her pants, her shirt undone, her voluptuous breasts rising and falling furiously with her agitation. For the first time in their relationship he felt no desire for her at all. He supposed she was sitting like that hoping to seduce him when he started asking questions about her whereabouts

'I'm waiting for your answer,' she said.

'Until you tell me what you were doing these last two days, why you weren't at home even late at night, I will tell you nothing,' he said. 'Our son could have died and no one could find you.' He felt guilty that he too had left no telephone number where he could be reached. He had rung – something had made him ring here just after it had happened – but he knew, wretchedly, that that had been more by luck than design.

'I was working,' she said defiantly. 'I had to take these clients out to dinner, then on to Tramps.'

'Then bed, I suppose,' he said. 'What are you? A high-class tart that sleeps with clients who sign your deals?'

'How dare you?' she said, shaking with fury. 'Don't think you can justify your actions with insulting me. That girl is a tart if ever I saw one, intent on breaking up our marriage.'

'If anyone is breaking our marriage it is you,' he said. 'You and your lovers.' He saw her flinch, open her mouth to deny it, but he pressed on before she could speak, determined to have everything out in the open now. The anger, the resentment, the emotional trauma of the last few days simmered, then burst from him.

'How dare you criticise Miranda when you have never been faithful to me? I know what you've been up to, though like all poor fools I was probably the last to know.'

'You were always away on business trips, you know I hate being alone,' she shouted back at him, as if her infidelity was his fault.

'So are countless men, and *their* wives don't need to jump into other men's beds the moment their husbands' backs are turned.' He felt his whole body tighten with fury. He clenched his hands hard by his sides, afraid suddenly that he would hit her. 'I didn't want to think about what you were doing, so I let it go,' he said, controlling his voice with effort. 'I should have kicked you out at once instead of pretending it wasn't happening, then when I knew it was, I made silly excuses about you not being able to help it.'

'You make me sound like an imbecile.'

'You're spoilt, you think of yourself too much and the pleasure you can get, regardless of if it hurts anyone else or not,' he cried. Then, seeing the shaft of pain in her eyes at his words, he said, still angry, 'It was your father's fault, and your brother's for giving you everything you asked for and more. But now,' the pain of Tom's suffering, the fear of nearly losing him wound as tight as a wire inside him, 'my only concern is Tom.' He stood over her, tall and defiant. 'You have no right to question my behaviour while yours is so despicable.'

He saw fear in her eyes, surprise too. He felt strangely elated. 'If it came to it I could name some of your lovers,' he said recklessly. 'Tom has suffered enough. He needs us both at the moment, but you, his mother, especially. You can give up your work. You know I earn more than enough to support us all until he is over this. Until he is happy and confident again. We must speak to the headmaster at Pilgrim's Court and Tom probably will leave there, unless those bullies do, of course, or he wants to go back. But he may have to stay at home with a tutor until we find somewhere better.' All these thoughts shot into his mind as he spoke.

She sat on the bed in silence, head bowed like a child receiving a reprimand. To his surprise he felt a sudden pang of sympathy for her. Tom's overdose had given her a serious shock.

But he went on, 'I will do everything I can to help him, be there as much as I can for him, but I can't take much more time off work, especially as we're going away to Spain in a couple of weeks. It will be up to you to give him the most support, so I suggest you put your work,' he almost added 'and your lovers' but he knew that was perhaps unkind, though he could see she had read his thought, 'on hold until he is completely over this. It may take some time. Will you promise me you'll do that?'

'I am his mother,' she said, her face tight. 'Are you telling me I'm a bad mother?'

'Love is having time for people,' he said, then turned away, a wave of tiredness hitting him. He thought longingly of Miranda. Their few days together seemed like a lifetime away. She would be a better mother for Tom. Loving a child was not enough, you must be there for them too, even when it may be inconvenient, he thought dully. He knew he must give Sonia a chance to look after Tom. This tragedy might be a turning point for her, might make her mature, become a selfless mother. He had to give her the chance, put Miranda aside. But he had a terrible feeling that it might be for ever and some other man would snatch her up and take her from him. In his tiredness, he felt despair. Miranda had loved him, did still love him, but she wouldn't want to be caught up in this drama. He knew she had the decency and tact to keep away for Tom's sake. She might so easily turn back to this David, feel life would be easier with him.

'You haven't answered me, Jack,' Sonia said, taking off her shirt and then her bra, watching him from under her eyelashes.

'You are not a bad mother when you are there,' he said, going into the bathroom and shutting the door firmly behind him. He ran the cold tap and splashed some water on his face. He felt defeated, envisaging an empty marriage ahead, for he could see it now in its true colours after his days with Miranda. Also there would be constant worry about Tom's state of mind. Jack didn't want to live without Miranda. He wondered if he could still see her, if once they were settled back home he could take up with her again.

He stared out of the window into the dark night and wondered where she was. Had she driven straight home, or stayed somewhere on the way, perhaps with her brother? He had an overwhelming urge to ring her, to find out that she was safe. He made a move towards the door, planning to go downstairs and telephone Edward. Then he looked at his watch. It was past eleven; he couldn't disturb them now.

Perhaps she had gone straight home. He calculated the time she could have caught the ferry, driven back to London. Then he remembered it was an hour behind in London. She might not be back until midnight. He would give her another hour, then ring her.

He felt happier now. It would work out, he was sure of it. He didn't quite know what would work out, but it was pointless to speculate. He wanted to tell her he loved her, to apologise about the scene at the hospital, tell that he longed to see her again.

He finished in the bathroom and went back to the bedroom. Sonia was sitting naked at the dressing table, brushing her long dark hair. It gleamed in the soft light. She caught his eye in the mirror and gave him a slight smile.

'Jack,' she said, 'we must not quarrel. We must think only of our Tom.'

'You're right,' he said, barely looking at her. 'I'm just going to check on him. Go to sleep, you must be tired.'

He left the room hearing her call, 'Don't be long.'

At his request they had left Tom's bedroom door open. Jack crept inside. He heard Tom say, 'I'm not asleep, Dad.'

He went over to the bed and sat down on it, suddenly feeling guilty that he might have heard their quarrel. 'Can't you sleep? It's so late. Shall I read to you?' he said, thinking if he stayed, Tom might tell him and he could comfort him.

'No. I did sleep, then I woke up again. It's good Mum came, isn't it?'

'Yes. I knew she would. We just couldn't contact her quicker,' he said, not wanting Tom to suspect that she hadn't been at home.

'When will we go home?' Tom asked.

'When do you want to go? You can stay here a little longer, then we're going to Spain for a fortnight at the end of August.'

'I'll stay here till then. Will you and Mummy stay?' His face was eager.

Jack stroked his hair. 'Mummy will, and I'll come out every weekend, but I have got to work.'

'OK.'

'Try and sleep.' He kissed him, relieved that he didn't seem to have heard them rowing. Tom must have been too deeply asleep.

'I will.'

Jack got up, went to the door.

'Dad?'

'Yes.'

'I didn't tell Mum that I told Miranda about . . . well, you know, the bird.'

'Tom,' Jack went back and sat down beside him, 'I know some things are difficult to talk about with those close to you, especially your parents. I quite understand why you found it easier to tell Miranda about it.'

'I don't think Mum would like it, though,' he said, his large dark eyes looking into Jack's.

'Perhaps you're right.' He kissed him again. 'I told you, didn't I, that Miranda's gone home, she's got to get back to work. She said goodbye, sent her love,' he said. He wanted to say her name, wanted to think of her. He thought suddenly that Tom was the only person he could talk to about her, but that even with him, especially with him, he could not say what he longed to say about her: how much he wanted and loved her.

Tom said, 'What about Mum's work?'

'She'll have a rest from it for a while, take it up again later,' he said. 'She'll stay here with you.'

When he'd finally left Tom's room he went downstairs. It was dark but the moonlight lit his way down the staircase. He did not put on the lights but felt his way down the passage to the kitchen and the small scullery beyond where Etienne had installed a telephone to make it easy for the staff to answer if they were away from the main body of the château or in the garden. He dialled Miranda's number in her flat, yearning to hear her voice, knowing that even if he only heard her on the answerphone it would be better than nothing. Then he could leave a message so she would know he was thinking of her.

It rang four times then he heard the answerphone kick in. A man's voice said, 'We're sorry we cannot take your call at the moment. Please leave your message after the bleep.'

Jealousy, pain, tears of disappointment surged through him. Then he remembered she had told him that she'd thought it safer if one was a woman living alone to have a man's voice on the answerphone.

He was sure the man was David and he felt torn with jealousy, hating the word 'we' as if he was part of her life, lived with her. Then he was hit by anxiety. Where was she? Was she safe, or had she in her agitation after the scene at the hospital had an accident? He felt the iciness of loneliness, the terror of helplessness. Having been so close to her these last few days he'd been wrenched away from her before they'd had time to make plans, even to say goodbye. He wondered if he would ever see her again.

Chapter Twenty-One

Miranda heard the telephone ringing from the street as she opened the front door. Knowing the answerphone would pick up the message she didn't rush to answer it. She couldn't anyway, she felt too exhausted. She did wonder if it was Jack, but the thought of hearing him but not touching him, of him perhaps telling her that their situation was hopeless, as indeed she knew it was, was more than she could stand just now.

It was a good thing that Cynara had taken her away from that dreadful scene. She'd felt like a rabbit mesmerised by headlights, standing stupidly there, quite unable to make any sensible decision for herself. Apart from suggesting that they pick up her suitcase from the château on the way to fetch her car, the two women had not spoken. Miranda, fighting tears, had stared resolutely out of the window at the passing scenery, forcing herself to do a running commentary in French on the passing scene in her mind, to stop herself thinking and blubbing.

When she'd got her car – the man she'd seen before, with his hair like a black loo brush, smirking at her – she stood by it rather awkwardly, not knowing what to say to Cynara.

But Cynara gave her a brisk smile, a squeeze on the arm, and said, 'Goodbye, Miranda. Safe journey, and . . .' for a split second her guard dropped and Miranda saw the compassion in her eyes, 'get on with your life, Miranda, you have so much to give.' And she turned and left her as if afraid to say more.

Miranda longed to get home, away from France, from them all. She'd driven fast, too fast, to get to the first ferry she could. She longed to get back to her flat, to hide among her familiar treasures.

She put her arms round herself now, standing alone in her sitting room, feeling empty and wretched. Was it a dream that Jack had loved her so? That their very souls had seemed to have become entwined with their bodies? She looked out at the silent, dimly lit street. There was the slight drone of passing cars, the cry of a cat. Today, she thought, the emphasis is on the quality and the quantity of sex, people boasting about their prowess in bed, teenage magazines extolling the techniques of better lovemaking. They no longer wrote of the sweet agony of real love.

All some people were left with, she thought, was the cheap tackiness of instant gratification. Perhaps that was why there was so much misery about, as they sensed they had been short-changed. At least she'd been left with much more than that, even though the pain of parting was so intense.

She took down a book of love poems and curled up in a chair to search for words to soothe her anguished heart. From the beginning of time, she thought, people have tried to come to terms with love, rejoiced when it was good, suffered when it hurt.

But just as suddenly she put down the book. She could not bear to read of other people's pain, to know that the suffering of tragic lovers had gone on too, since time began. She got up, went to her room to undress and go to bed. A thump from upstairs made her jump. What was Colin was up to now? Perhaps he had dropped his Bible while looking up something unpleasant to read to her, she thought wryly.

There came another thump, then another. She wondered if she should go up to him. Was he banging because he'd had an accident or something, and needed help? Then there was silence. She got into bed. She felt too drained to deal with anyone else's dramas. Anyway, it was probably nothing. He might misinterpret it if she appeared at his door at this time of night. She had never been up to his flat and she had never asked him into hers. She tried to speculate on what he was doing but Jack came back into her mind forcefully, pushing himself in, chasing away all other thoughts.

The morning found her agitated and headachy. The thought of two days alone frightened her. She needed people, longed for their cheerful, supportive company and yet she longed to hide away and nurse her misery on her own. Perhaps she should go home, but she knew guiltily that her mother's pain, for her father was still behaving badly, would only reinforce her own.

Impatient with her misery she rang Tessa, who at once sensed her unhappiness and on hearing what was wrong said at once, 'Come here. You can't sit moping alone. I know it's noisy and desperate with the children but come anyway. And,' she giggled, 'we've been invited to the Hall for a drinks party. You must come for that.'

'I don't know if I could face it, but I'd love to see you. Thanks, Tessa. I'll be there early afternoon. I must get sorted out for work on Monday.'

As she fiddled around her flat, re-packing for the weekend, doing the washing, Miranda felt a wave of longing for Jack, thinking of the last time she'd seen him at Chandos Hall. She knew also that she was hoping that Jack would ring her. But the telephone remained obstinately silent.

As she drove over Putney Bridge she remembered the thumps from Colin's flat. She had not heard him this morning, which was strange as he normally got up early and went out to buy the newspapers. She wondered if he was ill, or someone was up there with him. Where, she wondered, did concern for people overstep the mark into intrusion? Since his Bible quoting she'd become irritated with him, kept out of his way. She knew none of his friends, even the name of the church or religious group he was supposed to attend. Well, she thought, there was nothing she could do at the moment.

When she arrived at Tessa's Miranda found that Simon had taken the boys out and Tessa was waiting for her alone.

'They are so noisy, so Simon's taken them to the gunsmith to collect his guns. That will take a bit of time, give us some peace together,' Tessa said after hugging Miranda and pulling her inside. 'Coffee, Pimm's, white wine? Let's sit outside, it's so hot.'

They settled down on an old wooden bench, a bottle of wine between them.

'So,' Tessa said, eyeing her intently, 'do you want to tell me about it, or shall I talk of something else, the goings-on at the Hall?'

Miranda smiled in spite of her pain. 'There's no answer to it, or rather there is but I don't like it.' She then proceeded, sometimes with tears, to tell her all about her affair with Jack.

'Sonia doesn't deserve him. They didn't like her round here, you know. Found her far too snooty,' Tessa said, when Miranda had finished, as if knowing of Sonia's unpopularity would make it easier for her to bear. It did not.

Miranda, weary of all this misery, said, 'Tell me about the Hall then. I'm sure I can't just turn up with you tonight. I'll baby-sit.' She sat back, letting the sun caress her face.

'I've got a baby-sitter. A girl from the village, a godsend I can tell you, gives me time to be myself again occasionally. I rang the Hall this morning, explained you were visiting. I got on to Ralph, he said you must come.'

'How is he? The heir on the way yet?'

'I don't know,' Tessa giggled. 'Sir Quentin sent Ralph and Bunny away on holiday to some remote cottage on the west coast of Scotland. Probably far too cold to take their clothes off,' she laughed. 'Anyway, he just about said don't come back until you're pregnant and they came back last week. We're all speculating like mad, of course. Mrs Peabody swears she saw Bunny come out of the doctor's surgery a couple of days ago.'

'That doesn't mean she's pregnant,' Miranda said.

'Of course it doesn't, but it just shows how little we have to think of down here.' She grinned. 'Our own soap opera on our own doorstep. Life is all a soap opera really, though so many people forget that and watch it on the television. Remember that description in Proust when all the servants took their chairs into the village street and sat there watching the world go by?'

'Yes, and how the ill aunt watched the church to see who got into Mass on time, before the elevation of the host?'

They both laughed and Tessa said, 'How I long to use my brain again. If Tracy, this baby-sitter, works out, I thought I might do some obscure course at the Open University. Medieval folklore or Elizabethan love affairs or something.'

'I'm sure they don't offer anything as interesting as that,' Miranda said. 'More like subjects like psychology of ethnic minorities, or political correctness in Western society.' As she joked and they laughed together Miranda felt better.

Henry suddenly appeared like a rocket through the door, emitting a noise like a police siren. Simon followed him carrying Luke.

'Peace shattered,' Tessa said happily, putting her arms out to catch Henry to hug him.

Tracy, the baby-sitter, was a large, placid-looking girl. Henry wouldn't look at her and hid behind the sofa.

'Henry, be friendly,' Tessa said, putting on her earrings as she came into the room.

'Shan't,' Henry said mildly.

'Henry, come out at once and say good evening to Tracy,' Simon thundered.

Henry burst into tears.

Tessa said anxiously, 'Oh, Simon, don't go on at him, or we'll never get out.'

'He must learn good manners,' Simon said, pulling him out and standing Henry in front of him. 'Henry, when people come into our house you are polite to them. Tracy has come to look after you. It's very kind of her.'

'Leave him with me,' Tracy said, unperturbed by the scene.

'He must say good evening,' Simon said, his voice firm.

'He will in a minute. Let's go,' Tessa said, looking agitated.

Miranda watched them, guessing that now Tessa didn't want to go to the party. A few minutes ago she'd been looking forward to it, speculating with Miranda on who would be there and if perhaps there would be an announcement on a coming birth. Now seeing her child upset, upset she had to admit by Simon's insistence on good manners, she didn't want to go. Children, Miranda thought, thinking of Tom, have such a hold on your emotions.

Finally they set off for the Hall, Simon and Tessa arguing about discipline, Miranda feeling the pangs of nostalgic pain, sharp as arrows, as they passed the outhouse where she'd helped Tom with his mask and she'd first met Jack. They passed the trees and the path they'd walked down together that evening he'd brought her back to the cottage.

They arrived at the Hall and were ushered by an elderly retainer into the drawing room where Miranda had had tea. She was introduced to Sir Quentin, who was courteous but cold, and to Bunny again and Ralph.

'How nice to see you,' Ralph said. 'How is Jack? Have you seen him recently?'

His remark, made no doubt as polite conversation, took her breath away. She gulped, stammered, but he didn't seem to notice.

'Have a drink,' he said, gesturing towards a loaded silver salver being held by a very good-looking youth, who approached them.

Taking a glass of wine Miranda couldn't help noticing how the youth looked at Ralph with a sort of familiarity, an arrogance as if he was above waiting at parties.

'He's a good chap, Jack,' Ralph went on. Miranda, fighting not to be overcome by his continual mentions of Jack, could not help feeling a frisson spark between the two men. Ralph's eyes lingered on his face and the young man stared boldly back, a smile of amusement on his mouth. Ralph, realising she was looking at them both with surprise, said hurriedly, 'Now let me introduce you to Colonel and Mrs Stackford.' He led her over to a burly man and a little faded woman in a flowered dress.

Miranda smiled and talked and listened to the other people in the room like a robot. We are all playing a game, she thought, watching everyone on their best behaviour talking politely to each other, wondering what seething thoughts simmered underneath this courtesy. People living so closely together in this village, like her village at home probably, could not afford to fall out with each other. She wondered how often they acted out this charade.

Bunny came up to her. 'Those little boys all right?' she said. 'Nanny kept on that that baby would get pneumonia.'

'I think they're fine,' Miranda said. 'You can ask Tessa.'

'I will,' Bunny said, but she didn't move. She said, 'I still can't get close to these people, yet I see them most days. They keep themselves buttoned up so. You never know what they are really thinking.'

'We do tend to keep our feelings to ourselves.' Miranda was about to add, 'Some Americans tell you their whole life story within five minutes of your meeting them,' then thought perhaps Bunny might find that offensive.

Bunny burst out, 'I hope you don't mind me confiding, but there are so few women my age around here, but I think I'm pregnant. I feel so sick.'

'Oh . . . congratulations,' Miranda said, thinking that's something to add to the soap opera, nine months of wondering what sex the baby would be unless Sir Quentin made them find out before.

'The old man wants me to have a boy. Ralph and I are not compatible . . . Well,' she raised her eyes to the ceiling. Miranda wished Tessa was listening to this, 'Quentin insisted that I did my duty, be the mother of the heir to one of the oldest families in Britain.' She paused, took a sip of the glass of water she held in her hand. 'I feel like Princess Diana, just there for sons. Do you think she felt used?' Bunny went on.

'I really don't know,' Miranda said. 'I mean she knew – they both knew – they had to try for an heir, but I expect they wanted children too. Most married people do,' she finished lamely.

'I do, but . . . well, I suppose you're used to it, being British, but British men do seem to prefer their own sex, don't they? They're sort of frightened of women, aren't they?'

'They are not all like that,' Miranda said, thinking of Jack, yearning for him.

'Not all, I suppose but it must be something to do with going away to boarding school with just boys. I mean, they can't relate to women, can they? Look how they all like shooting and hunting together.'

Before Miranda could comment on this Bunny went on, 'When I've had this child I shall go back to the US, take the children with me. They can come here for the holidays to be with their father.'

'Does Ralph know about your plan?' Miranda asked her, feeling rather sorry for her, thinking that now she had started talking about her problems she seemingly couldn't stop.

'I told his father that was part of the deal. I'd have another child then go and live near my parents back home. Ralph can visit and the children can visit here. But I want them to be American.'

'Did they agree?'

'Yes,' Bunny said, her mouth hard. 'But if the old man goes back on his word I'll sue him.'

Miranda didn't say anything, wondering what a court would say. She saw Ralph coming towards them and quickly tried to think of something to change the subject. He came straight up to her and said, 'You'll never guess, Miranda, but Jack has just rung here. Seems he's had some problem with his son and wants to come and stay for a night next week to see the headmaster of Pilgrim's Court. I told him you were here.' He smiled, took a sip from his glass.

Miranda thought she'd faint. She glanced towards the door as if she expected to see Jack coming in at that moment.

'He didn't say anything. Funny that, as he seemed rather keen on you that time you were here.' Ralph said it in a friendly voice as if making fun of Jack. 'Perhaps he didn't hear me. He's in France, you know, and there have been storms. Maybe the line was impaired. Anyway, at the mention of your name there was complete silence.'

When Miranda still said nothing he went on, 'Are you a friend of Sonia's?'

Miranda gave him a sharp look, wondering if he was being bitchy or just polite. 'No,' she said, 'I'm not. Now if you'll excuse me . . .' She walked away from them, her heart aching. Jack was everywhere, but so was his family and she was the outsider.

'His wife was probably there, breathing down his neck,' Tessa said much later when Miranda told her about the telephone call from Jack. 'He no doubt feels guilty and they are all milking that for all they're worth.'

'I know.' Miranda tried to smile. Then she said, 'I'm sorry, Tess. I feel such a wet weed. I think unhappiness makes one awfully selfish and insular. I can just hear old Rat Bag Jenkins telling us to pull ourselves together and offer up our troubles to the Holy Souls.' She spoke of their headmistress, a terrifying spinster who relished suffering and accused her girls of self-indulgence if they allowed themselves to succumb to it.

'Heavens, yes,' Tessa shrieked. She mimicked the Principal's voice: 'There will be wailing and gnashing of teeth. It's all in the Bible, which I suggest you read and write an essay on it.' She laughed. 'God, all those essays. Do you remember them as punishment for petty things like talking after lights out? How did we stand it?'

'It put us off religion for a start,' Miranda said. 'But talking of Bibles . . .' She remembered the odd thumps from Colin's flat in the night and told Tessa about them.

'Bet he had someone there, or perhaps he was performing some sinister devil worship . . . Well, not devil because he wouldn't read the Bible then, would he?'

Simon came in and, catching the tail end of their conversation, asked them what they were talking about.

They told him, Tessa finishing, 'And there he is having the audacity to quote passages about the sin of lust to Miranda when David stays the night.'

'Jealous, I'd say. Can't do it, so doesn't see why anyone else should,' Simon said, sitting down beside Tessa.

'Maybe. Well, he needn't be jealous any more. I'll be living like a nun from now on,' Miranda said sadly.

'Don't despair,' Tessa said.

Simon, who'd been told about Miranda and Jack, said, 'I'm so sorry, Miranda, but you know it's better it's over, agony though it is. My sister's been in love with a married man for years. She has a hell of a life waiting for him to get away and see her. She's always waiting, it seems to me. Missing other fun things just in case he can come to her.' He sighed. 'She wants his child, but he's got three to see through school and she's afraid to lose him if she just goes ahead and has one.'

'Jack's not like that, and . . .' Did she want his child? Miranda realised she hadn't really thought about it. Then she reminded herself sternly that she'd justified her decision to spend those days with him knowing that she would leave him to his family afterwards. She would expect nothing more from him. They had had such a magic, wonderful time, she had no right to complain of the pain now.

'Just don't waste your life, love,' Simon smiled at her. 'You only have one shot at it.'

'I know.' She tried to smile. Then, to get away from the pain of it all, said, 'Did Bunny tell you she's pregnant?'

'I knew it,' Tessa said triumphantly. 'Sir Quentin has got his way. You know,' she lowered her voice as if the Gillard-Hardings had spies behind the curtains, 'some say he was so determined to have an heir he'd have impregnated Bunny himself.' Her eyes shone with delighted shock.

'Oh, really, darling. I bet that's old Busybody from the shop,' Simon said in exasperation. 'You know that's not true.'

'I hope her being pregnant is true and it's a boy, or the line will die out,' Tessa said.

'The Gillard-Hardings have probably outlived their usefulness,' Simon said.

'Aren't there distant cousins somewhere?' Miranda asked.

'There were.' Simon leant back, folded his arms across his chest, said to Miranda, 'I had my family tree looked into a few weeks ago. A friend of my mother's is a retired researcher. When she heard we were living here she asked if I wanted to know about the Gillard-Hardings too. It amused her to look it all up.'

'You never told me. What did she find?' Tessa said.

'I'm sure I told you. You probably weren't listening, bogged down with babies,' Simon said, tweaking her hair playfully.

'So tell us,' Tessa said.

Simon thought a moment. 'After Ralph there were two male cousins. One went to Australia and died childless last year, and the other is in a mental institution and will remain there for life.'

'So this is their last chance?' Miranda said.

'There is a possibility, though I don't know the legal ins and outs, but there's another branch to the family,' Simon said, flashing Miranda an intent look. 'They had a row, changed their name, three or four generations ago.'

'Are they the same blood?'

'Yes.'

'Who are they? Don't tell me,' Tessa shrieked, 'that somehow you are related to them and that we,' she put on a dramatic voice, 'the poor distant relations, living in a hovel in the grounds of the estate, stand to inherit that huge pile.'

Simon laughed. 'No, not us, I'm afraid. All we'll get is my father's potting shed if we're lucky.'

'So who is it? Do we know them?' Tessa went on.

Simon looked again at Miranda, then said quietly, 'The name is Lambert.'

'Jack?' Miranda whispered.

'You mean that Jack Lambert will be the heir to Chandos Hall if Ralph does not have a son?' Tessa seized on the idea like a terrier with a stick.

Simon shrugged. 'They are the next blood relations. But there may be some legal reason against his inheriting it.'

'Does Jack know? And that wife?' Tessa asked Miranda.

'I don't know. He never said anything,' Miranda said, thinking of Jack living at Chandos Hall. Her heart and body felt sore with wanting him. She wouldn't care where he lived, if only they could live together.

Chapter Twenty-Two

Miranda got back to London quite late on Sunday after staying for supper with Tessa and Simon. She was about to undress and have a bath when she heard a furtive tapping on her front door.

She felt a frisson of fear; it was almost midnight. For a second she wondered if she hadn't shut the main door properly and someone had got in from the street. The tapping came again, slightly more insistent this time. Perhaps it was Colin, she thought with impatience, though he had never disturbed her before.

'Who is it?' she called through the door, before putting on the chain.

There was silence, but she could hear breathing. She called out again, this time with a sharper tone. Sensing that the person was still there, she picked up her mobile phone ready to dial the police if necessary and cautiously opened the door, peering out over the chain. It was Colin.

'Oh, Colin, how you scared me. Why didn't you say it was you?' she said, her fear making her cross. She still kept the chain on the door and asked, 'What is it? Is anything wrong?'

'You have had a caller,' he said in a voice of doom.

'A caller? What do you mean?'

'A man came . . .'

'A man?' She thought instantly of Jack. Had he come, unable to keep away? Had he come to her?

'Your soul is in mortal danger,' Colin went on, his pale eyes staring reproachfully at her through the chink in the door.

'Who was it? Did he leave a message?' Her emotions swooped from elation to impatience. 'When did he come?'

'I told him it was wrong what he was doing. It was against the will of God. I told him he must save himself, save you from damnation.'

'You leave my soul to me, Colin, it is none of your business. Now tell me, did he leave a message?' She almost took off the chain the better to confront him but something about his staring eyes unnerved her. She looked quickly on the floor to see if the caller had pushed through a note, but saw nothing.

'The wages of sin—' he began.

'Colin, stop this nonsense at once and tell me when he came,' she demanded again, feeling she was in a losing battle. It was like talking to a mad person, someone who couldn't understand a plain question. It couldn't be Jack, she thought, surely not so soon. Or perhaps no one had come at all and he was imagining it.

'Was he tall with brown hair?' she tried again. Jack might have come straight from the ferry. He might have to be back at work tomorrow.

'I told him not to come back. This is not a house of vice,' Colin intoned.

'How dare you?' she screamed at him. 'Poking your nose in other people's business.' She slammed the door and stood against it, her body quivering with anger and despair. Then the phone rang and, running to it, certain it was Jack, she snatched it up.

'Jack?'

'Miranda, it's David.'

'David.' She could not keep the disappointment from her voice.

'I've just been attacked verbally by your religious maniac upstairs,' he said. 'I did ring you, left a message on your answerphone to ring me back.'

'I'm sorry . . . I was away for the weekend with friends.'

'I flew in tonight. I've a couple of meetings here tomorrow. I hoped to see you. I rang again but knowing you often leave on the answerphone when you paint I came round on the off chance, just to be preached to,' he laughed. 'Really, he's a nutter. You should watch him.'

'I know. I've just had him banging on my door, telling me I'd had a caller.' She explained quickly what had gone on between them.

'I'll come round. I'm only at a wine bar round the corner. I thought I'd wait a little, ring again.'

She didn't want him to come. She knew he would expect to make love to her and she couldn't bear it so soon after leaving Jack. She felt she couldn't ever bear any man to make love to her again but Jack.

She said, 'It's so late, David. Can I see you tomorrow, have lunch perhaps?'

'I'm tied up tomorrow.' He sounded disappointed. 'I'd love to see you. Are you put off by that maniac, or is it . . .' He paused.

She knew he was going to say something about Jack so she rushed in, 'No, it's just, well, I'm quite tired, wrong time of the month, you know.' It was the easiest excuse to keep him from her bed. 'I'll come down to the pub . . . wine bar . . . wherever, see you there.'

'It's almost closing time. Can't I just come and see you? I won't stay the night.'

In the end she agreed to let him come round. She felt afraid of Colin and wondered if he was still standing by her door waiting to bring down the wrath of Heaven on her. In a short while she heard the ting of the front doorbell. She waited a moment in case Colin was still there, but hearing nothing she opened her door and went out.

The front passage was empty but as soon as she let David in, Colin appeared from behind his door at the foot of the stairs to his flat where he'd obviously been waiting. He stood there staring at them, his face heavy with disapproval.

David said pointedly, 'Good night,' and shepherded Miranda back into her own flat. When she was in he turned back and she heard him say to Colin in a menacing voice, 'Just you mind your own business and stop hassling her.' He shut the door firmly before Miranda could hear if Colin had replied.

'What a creep,' David said. 'What do your neighbours think of him? Does he harass them too?'

'I don't know. The people next door, Maureen and John, are not married, and the two women further down are lesbians, and Paula, this side, is a single mother. Plenty of souls for him to save,' she said sourly. 'I don't like to ask them. They live quietly enough and their living arrangements are surely their own business. Why should I suggest that what they are doing might be considered wrong, and so encourage people like Colin to preach to them?'

'I agree. Sin seems to be obsolete these days. No doubt it's politically incorrect to accuse anyone of it,' he laughed. 'But perhaps, if you're chatting to any of them, you could sort of hint at what he's saying to you. Then they might open up, say he does the same to them and then all together you could do something to stop him. But how are you, Miranda?' He looked at her critically.

'Fine, and you?' She busied herself in her tiny kitchen, getting him a drink. She didn't want him to ask about Jack. In her chest round her heart was a large, sore, empty place. She knew that their affair must be over but she couldn't bear to face it.

But as if he could read her thoughts David said, 'What happened about the married man?' His words dropped into the silence, into her pain like sharp stones.

She handed him a bottle of wine to open, a brittle smile clamped to her face.

'I don't want to talk about it, David.'

'Fair enough.' He took the bottle from her and opened it. 'I'd hate to see you hurt,' he said, filling a glass. 'These things so often end in tears.'

'I know,' she said, close to tears now. 'I'll tell you about it sometime, but not now. Tell me about you. How's the job going?'

She sat down opposite him and forced herself to listen while he told her about the complete muddle of paperwork he'd inherited in the Geneva office to be sorted out. She could tell that he was bored regurgitating these details, but that he was only doing it to fill in the awkward silence that would otherwise yawn gloomily between them.

She felt very sad. Their easy camaraderie seemed to have vanished since she'd told him about Jack. But more serious still, she thought, was that making love with Jack had put her into a sort of limbo, keeping her from taking other lovers but without the public evidence that she was committed to someone else. She had gone down an impossible road: she could not see Jack again and yet she could not slip back comfortably with her old lover. After a little more talking, and warning her to be careful about Colin, David left her.

He kissed her, holding her to him a moment. 'Ring me if you need me, Miranda,' and he was gone and she was left feeling lonely, missing him as he had previously been to her, missing their easy relationship, missing Jack.

Miranda struggled through the week, working hard, painting in the evenings, trying without much success to seal her mind against Jack. One evening, cleaning her flat in rather a hurry, she opened Colin's dustbin instead of hers and noticed a whole pile of newspapers and magazines with bits cut out of them. Intrigued, she looked closer and saw that the order forms for various goods – lawn mowers, electric garage doors, conservatories – had been cut out. Odd, she thought, he could hardly have much use for those here. She closed the bin, opened her own to empty out her rubbish and didn't think any more about it.

She didn't see Colin that week but on the Friday she saw Maureen from next door coming up their road and they walked together.

After praising the hot sun, and wondering when there would be a hosepipe ban, Maureen suddenly said to her, 'How well do you know that chap who lives in the flat above you?'

'Not well, why?' Miranda looked into Maureen's over-made-up face framed by copper-coloured hair.

Maureen looked embarrassed. 'You know John and I are not married?' she stammered, her eyes flicking up and down in Miranda's direction as if waiting for her disapproval.

'I'd heard you weren't but it's none of my business and these days—'

Maureen sighed. 'You see, John is not divorced. His wife refuses to give him one and though we could now, we haven't and . . . well, it doesn't bother us, we don't need a marriage certificate to prove we love each other,' she finished defiantly.

'Of course not,' Miranda said, feeling she knew what was coming. 'What's Colin been up to?'

Maureen stopped, stared at her. 'So my question about him doesn't surprise you?'

'It depends why you're asking it. But if it's about giving you and John warnings from the Bible about living in sin and adultery, then I understand. He's done the same to me.' She felt a great sense of relief that she was not the only person he was plaguing.

'Oh, he hasn't spoken to us, just sent letters.' Maureen trembled, bit her lip. 'Look, have you a moment? Come in and have a cup of tea.'

Miranda followed her into her house. Maureen led her into the kitchen, a pleasant room with a large table in the centre and green stained wooden chairs with stripy covers.

She made them some tea and pushed some biscuits towards her, all the time saying, 'I feel so bad about it. John says he's mad and not to worry so, he can't hurt us. But I hate it. It makes me feel . . .' she shivered, 'dirty. Though I know we're not doing anything wrong. John's ex-wife,' she dropped her voice to a more conspiratorial tone, 'she made his life hell. She drank, had other men. He stood it as long as he could, then he left her. I met him a couple of weeks later, he was very lonely.' She poured Miranda some tea. 'We hit it off straight away,' she smiled, remembering. 'Well, you do with some people, don't you? Feel as if you've known them before, belong as one?'

'Yes, you do,' Miranda said, thinking of Jack.

'We met in Bury St Edmunds, both of us were living there. After about a year we decided to move to London. I'm an accountant and John's in computers so it wasn't difficult to find jobs. We wanted to start again, just us.'

'I can understand that,' Miranda said. 'How long have you been here?'

'Four years at Christmas. We've been so happy,' she coloured, looked as if she might cry, 'until, that is, until . . .' She couldn't speak any more for tears. She got up, dabbing at her eyes with a handkerchief, then opened a drawer, took out a piece of paper and handed it to Miranda, holding it with the tips of her fingers as if it were contaminated.

'Read it,' she said, turning away.

Miranda unfolded it. It was written in neat handwriting on cheap paper.

Maureen and John,
   You cannot hide your sin from the Lord. He knows all. Repent while there is time. You are breaking the seventh commandment, Thou shalt not commit adultery.
   A well wisher.

Miranda folded it and pushed it from her. 'Do you know it's from Colin?'

'I can't be sure. But one night when John came home late he said he'd seen him skulking round our door. I had just picked up this letter that had been pushed through. John confronted him, but he stayed silent. I don't know what to do.' She sat down at the table, her face wrinkled with worry.

Miranda told her what he'd said about her and David.

'It must be him. How horrible,' Maureen said. 'I want to go to the police, but John doesn't.' She paused, then burst out, 'His wife doesn't know where we are, you see. She kept trying to get money out of him, just for her drink, you know.' She looked awkward and Miranda guessed there was more to it than she was prepared to say.

'Colin doesn't know her, does he?' Miranda asked.

'I hope not.' Maureen looked startled. 'I mean, we don't exactly shout it from the rooftops but people know we're not married. I've kept my name, after all.'

They discussed it some more, both relieved that they had spoken about it, that it was out in the open. Maureen said she'd ask some of the other neighbours, though she did feel she might be seen to be prying, suggesting that they were perhaps at fault for living as they did.

'You can't appear to be judgemental these days,' she said. 'Live and let live as long as you don't frighten the horses, that's what I say.' She attempted a laugh.

'If you can bear to, keep the letter for evidence,' Miranda said. 'If he does this to everyone in the street, well, some of them might feel like doing something.'

'I suppose so.' Maureen eyed the letter as though it was decomposing and would stink out her house.

By the time Miranda left she'd resolved to be more forceful with Colin, demand he stop his Biblical warnings. She was about to go into her own house when she saw Jack.

They stood and stared at each other a long moment, as if neither could believe that the other was there. He took one step forward and she was in his arms. They held each other as if they would never let go.

At last she said, 'Oh, Jack, I can't believe it's really you. Can you come in, just for a moment?'

'Only a moment. I'm on my way to Heathrow to go back to France. I just had to stop by your house. I did so hope to see you but I didn't know how you would feel about seeing me, after everything that has happened.' He linked his hands behind her waist, devouring her with his eyes.

'I feel the same, more so. I love you,' she said, pulling him inside, her whole being yearning for him.

Colin stood there in the narrow passage, a look of disgust on his face.

Miranda felt giddy with excitement. 'Go back to your Bible and stop spying on us,' she said fiercely, all fear of him gone with Jack here beside her.

'Do not mock. The end is closer than you think,' Colin said darkly. She heard a scraping noise and he produced a large wooden crucifix from behind his door and brandished it at them.

'What on earth . . . ?' Jack began, but Miranda, averting her eyes from the cross as if it condemned them, pulled him into her flat and shut the door firmly behind them.

'He's mad. He must have been making that the other night. I heard some dreadful thumps,' she said, laughing, though in truth she felt rather shaken by the sight of it.

'I can't bear to think of you living under a mad person,' he said, taking her in his arms.

'Forget it. Oh, it's so good to see you. I thought I'd die without you.' She kissed him, holding him close to her, all thoughts of sin and doom forgotten in her joy at being with him again.

Chapter Twenty-Three

'I'm so sorry, darling, but I must go or I'll miss the plane,' Jack said, giving her a quick kiss before jumping out of bed and retrieving his clothes. Their lovemaking had been frantic, almost desperate, as if they must snatch as much from each other as they could, before they were parted again. It left Miranda feeling sad and discontented.

She forced a smile. 'I'll come to the airport with you. I can take the tube back.'

'You don't want to do that. It will be miserable for you.'

'I do. It will give us a few more moments together.'

He buttoned up his shirt, his eyes troubled. 'I don't want it to be like this, darling. You know that, don't you? I've just got to put Tom first at the moment.'

'I know.' She touched his arm as she passed him on her way to the bathroom. She felt part of him had left her already, was away thinking of Tom. 'How is he?' She left the door open to hear his answer.

'He's OK. I went down to Pilgrim's Court . . . Oh, by the way,' he came and stood by the bathroom door, 'wasn't it extraordinary when I rang Ralph and you were there? God, how I wanted to talk to you, but Sonia was in the room with me and I couldn't face any more dramas. I never dreamt you'd be there.'

She came out of the shower and wrapped herself into her towelling dressing gown. He tied the belt round her waist, holding her to him, nuzzling her neck. 'I couldn't believe you were really there. What were you doing?'

'I was staying with Tessa and Simon. We'd been invited up for a drink. I nearly died when Ralph told me you'd been on the phone.' She didn't tell him how desperate it had made her feel at their situation.

'I don't know what we're going to do,' he said. 'I don't want to live without you, yet I don't want to hide you away, have a secret affair. If Tom hadn't . . . wasn't so . . .'

'I understand,' she said, wanting to spare him the pain of discussing Tom's overdose. 'So what did the headmaster say?' She slipped out of his arms and went into her room to get dressed. She pulled on jeans and a shirt.

'He wasn't much help. It seems these days that these special schools have a lot of severely emotionally disturbed children. They may come from rich families – well, the fees are steep enough – but as we know, that doesn't guarantee a stable family life.' He came and stood by her as she brushed her hair, picking up a strand in his fingers, watching the light pick up the gold in it. 'I think we're going to have to take him away from there, find somewhere else. I can't expect him to put up with those sort of children. I must find a "normal" school, if there is such a thing, one that has a dyslexic unit. There are a few, I believe. It's just a question of finding the right one.'

They went out to his car. Miranda half expected Colin to be lurking in the passage, waiting to throw a sermon after them or brandish his crucifix. He was not there but she felt sure his eyes were on them, watching from an upstairs window, though she did not look back to confirm it.

As they drove to the airport, Miranda showing him a short cut past Queen's Club out to the Cromwell Road, he asked her about Chandos Hall.

She told him about Bunny and Ralph's baby, then added, 'You know, it was funny – well, you must know about this – Simon researched into the Gillard-Hardings. He was interested because he lives on their estate. He thought you might be the next heir. Only, of course, if this child is not a son and after Sir Quentin and Ralph's deaths.'

Jack laughed, turned to her. 'I don't think so. Where did he get that from?'

'One Gillard-Harding in Australia died recently – he was childless – and the only other one is in a mental institution for life. The Lamberts are blood relations, aren't they?'

'Yes, but my great-grandfather had a row with them – I don't really know what it was about, money probably or marrying the wrong person – and changed the family name. I doubt I'd have any legal standing. Anyway,' he laughed, squeezed her hand as it lay on his thigh, 'I don't want to be a baronet and most of the house has been made over to the National Trust. Let's hope, anyway, for poor Ralph's sake that this child is a boy.'

'Of course, but it is quite funny, isn't it? That you *could* be the next baronet?'

'I suppose so, but Sir Quentin is bound to live for years and Ralph's only a few years older than me so if it ever *did* happen I'd be ancient. Anyway, by then there will probably be no monarchy nor hereditary titles anyway, and if there are, daughters will be able to inherit them.'

'That's true.'

He said, 'I never thought I'd see you today. I couldn't resist driving past your house just to be near you. I couldn't believe it when you were suddenly there, in the street.'

'I couldn't believe it either, and Colin ranting about sin and depravity.' She told him what Maureen had said and then, feeling a little awkward, she told him about David coming. 'Just for a quick visit, he didn't stay long,' she said, so as not to hurt Jack's feelings. Then she scolded herself thinking, am I to spend my life not seeing my friends in case Jack minds, when I cannot live with him, love him openly?

'You ought to go to the police. I don't like to think of you living alone in that house with someone like that upstairs,' Jack said.

'I don't think he'll hurt me. He just thinks I'm a sinner, need to repent.' She wondered now what he thought of her having two lovers, David and then Jack, calling on her in the same week. No doubt now she was truly damned in his eyes.

'I think you should ask Maureen to have a meeting with the rest of the neighbours and see if anyone else has been harassed. Collect as much evidence as you can and get one of the men, her partner perhaps, to confront him. If he doesn't stop, you go to the police.'

'I'm sure you're right,' she said reluctantly, not really wanting to get too involved.

'Do something, please, darling. I hate to think of you living close to such a pervert.'

'Don't worry about it, I will do something,' she promised to reassure him.

There was a long queue to get into the terminal at Heathrow. Jack became more and more agitated as they inched forward.

'Really, this is one of the major airports of the world and you miss your plane trying to get into it,' he complained. 'Ever since they've put up those traffic lights it's been murder.'

'It is awful,' she said, wishing he would miss the plane but knowing how much he wanted to be on it to get back to Tom, though he also had an early business meeting in Paris before he went to join him. She knew with a stab of guilt that if they hadn't made love he would be checked in already.

At last they arrived at the car park. Jack said, 'I've got to rush if I'm to catch it. I hate to leave you. I've a busy week, but maybe I can come round one evening. Shall I ring you?'

'Please,' she said, feeling him distancing himself from her as he sprang from the car, got his case and briefcase from the boot.

They walked together from the car park to the walkway to the terminal. Suddenly he froze, said under his breath, 'God, there's a chap I know.'

They were not touching each other and other people were walking down the same way. Before either of them could say any more Miranda heard a male voice.

'Jack! Where are you off to?'

'Oh, Michael, hello. Paris.'

'Me too. Cut it a bit fine tonight. Held up at a damn meeting.' He glanced round. Miranda, walking behind, kept her eyes away from them. 'Sonia with you or are you travelling alone?'

'Alone. She's in France, in the country, with my mother and my son. I'm joining them for the weekend.'

'Shall we travel together? *If* we get on the flight?'

'Yes, let's do that,' Jack said. He did not dare turn round to look at Miranda.

She followed them a little way. Michael talked incessantly about his business, his wife, how he had no time to join her on holiday this time. She longed to touch Jack, in some way to let him know she loved him, but she could not, and she knew he dared not acknowledge her as this man knew Sonia.

Jack and Michael were walking fast now, impatient to catch the flight. She let them go and melted into the crowd, her heart aching. This is how it will always be, she told herself, you in the shadows waiting for him to come to you, hoping no one who knows his wife will see you.

The tube was crowded. A group of young people, laughing and chattering about the holiday they'd just had, stood in front of her. A pale waiflike girl wound herself round a waiflike boy like bindweed. Miranda envied her. Their happiness and good humour seemed to compound her misery and her loneliness. But even as she felt the melancholy descend on her like a clinging mist she felt Jack's love was worth it.

The trick is not to think or wonder when you will be together again, she told herself determinedly. Just wait for the good times and devour them greedily when they come. She thought of her mother, stoically getting on with her life while her father still kept on with Linda. Both of us waiting in such pain, in the hope that everything will work out, she thought sadly, and resolved to ring her mother that evening to cheer her up.

As she walked up the road to her flat she felt a sudden fear of a confrontation with Colin. Would he be waiting for her, his huge wooden crucifix in his hand? His warnings were one thing, but making and brandishing a huge crucifix at her was quite another.

Her fear made her feel Jack's absence even more. She had no one to protect her, she thought pathetically, and the idea of having to be in her flat alone all night with that maniac above her made her edgy with panic. She suddenly felt terribly alone, felt as if she couldn't bear to go inside and shut the door on herself. As she passed Maureen and John's house she saw the soft glow of their light in the front room and had a sudden urge to talk to someone, to be included in that warmth. Before she could stop herself she went up to their door and rang the bell.

'I'm so sorry, John,' she said, when he opened the door, 'but could I come in for a minute? I'm being silly, but Colin—'

'Come in at once.' John opened the door. 'It's Miranda,' he called to Maureen, who came through immediately, wiping her mouth with a napkin.

'Oh, I'm sorry,' Miranda said, now feeling rather foolish, 'I've disturbed your supper.'

'Nonsense, we're just finishing. What's happened?'

'It sounds so peculiar,' Miranda said, as John showed her to a chair, offered her some coffee, 'but he's made a large cross, you know like a crucifix, and he waved it at me, at . . . my friend who was visiting.'

'A crucifix?' John's dark brows came together in a frown.

'He's barmy,' Maureen said. 'We must call someone – the police, social services, someone.' Her voice was frantic. 'He's not safe. You'd better stay here, dear. The spare bed's made up.'

'No, thanks all the same, but once I'm locked in my flat . . . It's just, well, it's all getting a bit out of hand.' Miranda tried to reassure Maureen and herself.

'I'll say,' John replied, his pale, thin face seeming to go paler. He licked his lips, cleared his throat, then said with embarrassment, 'I know Maureen showed you the letter and we should go to the police but I'm afraid it will get in the papers. I don't want my ex-wife,' he shot Miranda a glance to see if she understood, 'to find out where we are. She'll give us hell otherwise.'

'I understand. I don't want to make too much of a complaint either,' Miranda admitted. 'You see, my . . .' What word could she use, she thought suddenly, boyfriend, lover? 'My friend,' she said lamely, 'is married.'

'I see,' John said. He gave a short laugh. 'So none of us wants to draw attention to ourselves. We must think of another way to stop him. He can't be sane to behave like this. I wonder if he's under psychiatric treatment.'

'They're always letting them out these days to roam the streets, poor things,' Maureen said. 'Just because some government ministers think it would be terrible to live in one of those hospitals themselves, they let these people out to live in the community. But it's cruel. They're not like other people, they can't cope.'

'True,' John said, 'but he's been in this road as long as we have and he's never given us any trouble before. Not that we've ever got to know him – he keeps himself to himself.'

'And something else strange.' Maureen stopped, flashed a look at John as if embarrassed to continue.

'Yes,' John said. 'I have no reason to suppose it is him but we've had strange people round, or telephoning us. Coming to measure for garage doors' – he laughed – 'we don't even have a garage – a new kitchen, a sauna. We've had a porcelain figure, part of a set they say we've ordered, with a letter telling us we have to send money to pay for them by instalments.'

'We never ordered any of it,' Maureen went on. 'We always prefer to look before we buy things, and some of the salesmen were quite offensive when we said we hadn't asked them to come. They insisted that we had.'

Miranda suddenly remembered the newspapers with the cut-out coupons she'd seen in Colin's dustbin and told them about it. 'I thought it a bit odd but I thought he was sending away for them for himself, but of course we don't have a garage either. I know one was a garage for there was a great picture beside where the order form had been cut out. Another was of a conservatory.'

Maureen went quite pale and clutched at John's hand. 'We had a whole book about conservatories and a particularly irate salesman accusing us of wasting his time. He insisted that we had telephoned for an appointment for him to come round at the weekend. Oh dear,' she gasped, 'I can't bear to think that man's giving our address to all sorts of people. We have had an enormous amount of junk mail recently.'

John looked serious. 'Anyone can get our name from the electoral resister, but this looks like more than that. We had some religious tracts too, printed, suggesting that we attend various meetings. At the time I didn't think much of them and just threw them away, but I suppose they came from him as well.'

'One time-share salesman rang us every evening for a week, until John threatened him with the police. He insisted that we had asked to buy a property abroad but we haven't. We couldn't begin to afford it, and we don't want to anyway.'

'I don't like it. It's as if he's taking over our lives, trying to control us, first with these letters using the Bible to frighten us, and now being bombarded by all these salesmen and unwanted purchases trying to get money out of us. It's got to stop,' John said, half rising as if he would go round to Colin at once and have it out with him.

Maureen pulled him back down on to the sofa beside her. 'We must think of Miranda alone with him in that house. Don't do anything to antagonise him now. But we must think of something.' She swallowed, her eyes swivelling nervously round at them. 'Go to the police if we have to.'

'I'll look in his dustbin again,' Miranda said, getting up to leave, 'keep some of the papers.'

'I suppose you could. Look, do you want to go? Are you sure you'll be all right? You're welcome to stay here,' Maureen said to her.

'No, I must go, but thank you for giving me support. I just felt I had to talk it over with someone.'

'John will go in with you, just in case . . .' Maureen stopped, stammered, 'well, in case he's there with his horrible remarks. But promise to telephone us, day or night, if there's any trouble.'

'I will, thanks,' Miranda said.

She felt rather self-conscious with John coming with her, and wondered wildly what Colin would say if he saw him. Would he accuse her of seducing him too?

'There,' John said, when she'd opened the door to her flat, 'all clear.'

'Thanks so much, John, and I'm sorry to be such a nuisance,' she said.

'Any time,' he said. 'Good night.'

'Good night.' She went back to the front door to shut it behind him, then something caught her attention on the other side of the road. She heard John close his front door while she peered out into the dim street. There, in the school garden opposite, she saw the tall, dark shape of a cross. She shuddered, shutting her door quickly, running into her flat and bolting the door, frightened that Colin was standing beside it, watching her.

Chapter Twenty-Four

Miranda lay in the garden in her bathing suit, finding the warmth of the sun on her skin curiously comforting. Sally and Roland played on a rug in the shade near her.

'I think your mother looks so well, don't you?' Sally said in between nibbling Roland's toes and laughing at his squeaks of delight.

'Yes, she does.' Miranda had only been here an hour. She had suddenly wanted to get out of London, away from her friends who all seemed to be paired up. She'd seen Jack once that week. He couldn't stay the night, telling her that Tom rang him every night before he went to sleep and he must be home for that. Miranda wondered to herself why Jack didn't ring him – he could have done it from her flat – and supposed that Sonia had worked out this ruse to be sure Jack was at home. No doubt she knew that Jack would not take her to their home. She certainly didn't want to be anywhere that he shared with his wife. He was now in Spain for two weeks with them and she didn't know how she would get through the days.

'I wonder,' Sally sat up on the rug, hugging Roland to her, 'if she has someone in her life?' She looked enquiringly over at Miranda. 'I mean, she seems so calm, so much happier than she was and we know Richard hasn't given up that girl.'

'Do we?' Miranda hunched over her knees, ready for a gossip. 'I haven't been down for some time, or dared ask when I ring. I'd hoped it had blown over, was a hiccup not to be mentioned again. She did say Daddy would be here for lunch.'

'He still sees Linda, I'm afraid. Marcus actually saw them together in the car.'

'What does she look like? Is she pretty?'

'You know Marcus's descriptive vocabulary only flowers when he sees a piece of furniture or a picture,' Sally laughed affectionately. 'I couldn't get much out of him, but your father looked embarrassed, so he knew it was the woman.'

'Oh,' Miranda said sadly. 'I thought it was over as Mummy does look good, seems happier. I thought that was the reason.' She remembered her mother's cheerful voice when she'd rung last night.

'Oh, do come down, darling, we love to see you. Marcus and Sally will be here with the baby. Marcus has a sale he wants to go to on Saturday but he'll be here for dinner.'

'And Daddy?'

'I expect he'll turn up,' she'd said briskly. 'So how are you, darling? Job going well?'

Miranda knew that as Julia could not boast of her daughter's marriage or a coming birth she boasted about her job in the village. No doubt they thought by now that she was the editor of the entire magazine.

Sally said, 'Julia is a very attractive woman, and I admire her for not turning into a victim over this. It wouldn't surprise me if she hasn't met another man. Oh, it may not be serious, but enough to boost her confidence.'

'I wonder who. Most of the men I know in the village are married to her friends, deadly boring, or far too young. The only single ones are children or ancient.' A thought stuck her. 'You don't think she's got a toy boy, do you?'

Sally laughed, blew raspberries on Roland's fat little tummy. 'Toy boy,' she said to him, blowing another raspberry as he squirmed with pleasure. 'You're my toy boy. I could eat you. No, well, I don't know, do I? Have you any idea who it could be?'

Before she could answer Julia came over to them with a jug of Pimm's in one hand, a stack of acrylic glasses in the other. She walked with a confident step, her hair newly washed and tied back with a green scarf. Her skin was tanned and she wore an open-necked white shirt and jeans. She was smiling. Miranda got up and took the brimming jug from her. Strawberries and borage, with its bright blue flowers, floated on the top.

'How lovely, Mummy,' she said, 'just what we needed. Shall I get a long chair for you?'

'No, the rug will do, with Roland.' She smiled and sat down beside Sally, who handed him to her. She hugged him, remarking, 'How well he looks, Sally, and so much hair now. Makes him look much more grown up.'

They sat round drinking, talking of nothing in particular, then they heard a car crunch to a stop in the drive and Richard walked over the lawn to them.

Miranda thought he looked rather awkward, but he said with forced cheerfulness, 'What a nice picture, three beautiful women sitting in the sun.'

'Hello, Daddy.' Miranda kissed him. She still felt uncomfortable with him, angry even, but she knew it wouldn't do to show it now. He smiled at Sally, whom he'd seen the night before, and did not acknowledge Julia.

She took no notice of him, singing instead to Roland, 'This little piggy went to market, this little piggy stayed at home . . .'

'So,' Richard turned to Miranda, 'been up to anything exciting?'

'Not really,' she said, not going to mention the most exciting thing in her life, Jack. This morning at breakfast she'd nonchalantly asked Marcus if he ever saw him.

'You once said you were at school with Jack Lambert, a good cricketer. Do you ever see him?'

Marcus looked at her curiously. 'No, why?' Then seeing her blush, laughed and said, 'Don't tell me you're going to make Mother's dreams come true and get married?'

'No, do shut up.' She heard her mother next door in the kitchen. 'No, I . . . well, once you said you'd been at school with him.'

'Yes. Does he remember me?'

'I haven't asked . . . I just . . .' she'd floundered, knowing she'd only asked him because she longed to talk about Jack with someone who knew him.

'I remember now,' Marcus said, giving her a sharp look. 'You said that his wife was having an affair with James Darby. So he's married and you are in love with him.'

Her expression had given her away. He reached over and touched her hand. 'Is it serious? Is he getting a divorce?'

'No, he can't. Oh, it's complicated. His son . . .' She kept her eyes on the door in case her mother came in.

Marcus sighed. 'Same old story. No, I'm sorry, love, but I'm sure I don't need to tell you, you're on rocky ground.' Julia then appeared, all bright and cheerful, asking if they had enough to eat as though they were starving refugees. Marcus, keen to be off to his sale and knowing it would be a disaster if his mother had an inkling of Miranda's affair with a married man, asked her the way to the house where the sale was. He knew this would divert her for some time. Her road directions were always far too involved, but he knew the route anyway.

Remembering this now and afraid she might inadvertently let something slip about Jack, Miranda launched into a discourse about her job and how she was so busy as Stella was on holiday. But even as she spoke she felt her father was not listening, would not even have heard if she had mentioned Jack; she sensed that he was looking at her mother surreptitiously while she ignored him and played with the baby. It would serve him right, Miranda thought, if she did have someone else, but then she felt afraid, afraid that this idyllic haven for her would go.

If anyone passing saw us now, she thought they would think it a wonderful scene. Three women, a man and a baby lolling in a sun-filled garden, surrounded by lush countryside, a beautiful house glimpsed through the trees. In reality there are shattered lives stuck together by deceit and good manners. How long would this last? Where would they all be next year?

Suddenly she shivered in the warm sun. Where would she and Jack be? Would they ever be together? He had said he would try and ring her from Spain in the evenings.

'We're staying in a villa with friends. I may be able to slip out and phone from the village,' he'd said as they dressed after a hurried bout of lovemaking. It had been spoilt by the knowledge that he had to get home to take Tom's call before bedtime, and her fear that Colin was listening at the keyhole. Even at the most intense moment she had felt apart from him, feeling that although his body was hers his mind was travelling on, making plans of packing for his holiday, getting back to Tom. Getting back to Sonia? She wondered if he enjoyed being with her too, was looking forward to their holiday, two weeks with her that could possibly cement their relationship together again. But she had not voiced her fears, too afraid he might inadvertently confirm them.

My father is doing wrong, she thought now, watching him. Mummy may be maddening but, unlike Sonia, she's always been loyal and there for him.

They had an awkward lunch, all of them making Roland their focal point – Julia wondering if he had enough to eat; Richard remarking on what a messy eater he was; Miranda just smiling at him, thinking how he had grown and how impossible it was to compare him with that tiny scrap she'd first seen, struggling for survival. After lunch Richard said he had some work to do and would be back to see them and Marcus for dinner. They all knew he was going to see his girlfriend.

Julia said with a smile, 'I've a few chores to do in Alton. I expect you girls will like to lie in the sun. I'll be back soon.'

'Can't I do them for you, Mummy?' Miranda said without thinking.

'No, thank you, darling. Have a relax, you deserve it after a week working in London.'

Sally caught Miranda's eye. She saw her father lick his lips, give a clumsy gulp of a cough. Julia took no notice of him at all, but left the room, and they heard her going upstairs.

Sally said, 'I'll put Roland down to sleep in his room. It's a bit hot for him in the garden.'

Left alone with her father, Miranda said, 'What work have you got, Daddy? Something from the office?'

'Y-yes.'

'And you can't do it here?' She felt angry with him, angry with Jack too for being away from her with his wife in the sun.

'You know I'm not here all the time,' he said, not looking at her.

'You want both,' she said acidly, wondering if Jack did too. 'This house, Mummy's cooking and a bit on the side.'

'Miranda, don't be so crude.' He looked offended.

'It's true, though,' she said. 'I'm in love with a married man, too,' she found herself saying, wanting to shock him. 'Only he has a young boy and doesn't want to break up the family.'

'Oh, darling, you're not?' Richard looked horrified.

'It's no worse than you. *You're* a married man, remember. Only I love Jack, really love him, and he has a selfish wife who's always had lovers, unlike Mummy. Do you love this girl, and she you, or is it just lust?' She wanted to torment him, hurt him for hurting her mother, for hurting them, for breaking up this home.

'I don't like the way you're talking,' he said as if she were a small child and had used swear words.

'Is it worth destroying all this?' She gestured round the garden, the flowerbeds sated with overblown flowers lolling over the lawn, the haze of heat shimmering on the leaves of the trees. She wondered if Jack was thinking the same as he sat with his family in some lovely garden somewhere in Spain, drowsy with the heat, lazy with the familiarity of closeness with Sonia. Sensuous with wine and sun. She felt suddenly helpless and hurt that he could, would probably be making love to his wife while she, Miranda, waited alone, yearning, for him to return for a hurried embrace, furtively concealed from his fuller, more open life with Sonia.

'You don't understand, Miranda,' her father said, and got up to go. 'But you,' he looked at her with concern, 'you are too young, my dear, to be involved with a married man. You will only have half a life if he doesn't marry you.'

'And your young woman, does she only have half a life?' she said coldly. 'Maybe she wants marriage, children.'

'Do you, with this man?' he said.

'Yes, anyway I want to spend the rest of my life with him,' she said, 'but he has this child.' She found herself telling him about Tom's overdose, wanting, needing, to tell him, quite forgetting for the moment that he had a lover; seeing him only as her beloved father whom she wanted to confide in, shift to his more experienced shoulders some of her pain and bewilderment.

He listened, then said quietly, 'It sounds quite a mess, darling. I think you should try and give him up or you will get very hurt. He has a duty towards his child, you know that.'

'Yes, I know that. But you . . .' she looked at him candidly, 'what about you, and your duties?'

He had the grace to look ashamed. 'It is something different. You have your whole life. Don't throw away your chance of having a family of your own. I don't want to see you hurt and I'm afraid you will be.'

'And what about Mummy and this . . . Linda, what about hurting them, us?'

'I am sorry to hurt your mother,' he said reluctantly, 'but you children, you're all grown up now, have your own lives.'

'We can still be hurt, humiliated by your behaviour.' She saw him flinch as if she had hit him. How hypocritical love or lust makes us all, she thought. We all make excuses as to why our own particular behaviour is all right.

'And Linda? Does she not want a family of her own?' she went on, wondering with fear if he would admit that he was not going to hurt her as he would not give her up.

'We understand each other.' He looked away. 'Unlike you there is no great love between us,' he admitted shamefacedly.

'Then it is not worth it,' she said sharply.

Her mother, now changed into a fresh cotton dress, walked past them to the car. 'See you at teatime,' she called cheerfully, not looking at Richard.

''Bye, Mummy,' Miranda said, looking after her.

Her father left her then, walking swiftly away. His head was bowed and Miranda knew he was not happy. Sally joined her, having put the baby to bed.

'Why do you think your mother has dolled up so, just to get a few things in Alton?' she said.

'There is something going on, you're right,' Miranda replied with a sigh. 'I know I'm selfish, Sal, especially when I have my own place and life but I don't want this house to go. If both of my parents go off with someone else they will have to sell all this.'

Sally smiled. 'You have to grow up, you know, Miranda. But I know what you mean. It's a lovely place for children and I like the security of the continuity of a place where one was happy as a child; wanting to recreate it for one's own children. I'd feel the same way about my old home, but that was sold long before I married.'

'I wonder who he is?' Miranda said, looking after her parents who drove away in separate cars.

Both parents returned at different times for dinner, but after dinner, awkward again as neither Richard nor Julia looked at each other, Richard left. He kissed Miranda and said, ''Bye, darling. Let's have lunch one day. I'll ring you next week.'

'OK, lovely,' she said, thinking what a farce it would be if he tried to tell her to give up Jack and that what she was doing was wrong. She hoped guiltily that he would not tell her mother about it. She would go overboard in her anxiety over her daughter's happiness and reputation, and drive Miranda mad with her well-meaning but exhausting advice.

Julia took them all to church the next day as if she wanted to show them off more than to enrich their spiritual lives. Miranda was polite with the people she knew – some had known her since she was born – and she answered their questions about her life cheerfully, until one, Deirdre Allsop, asked, 'And when will you be getting married, my dear? Both my girls are now. I have three grandchildren and another on the way.'

'I don't think I will get married. Far too busy,' Miranda said brightly, moving away before Deirdre could enlarge on her daughters' achievements.

It never changes, she thought. When they were children the parents all boasted about what schools their offspring had got into, what exams they had passed, how talented they were at music, sport, whatever; now it's what job and who they'd married and how many babies they had.

Among the milling parishioners Miranda saw a thickset man, his greying hair springing like an unruly bush from his head. He wore neat trousers and a jacket and he seemed to be looking for someone in the crowd. Then she saw her mother go over to him and his face lit up. She saw her mother curl her hand round his arm in a most familiar way.

She felt stricken. So it was true, Julia did have someone. But then she thought, why shouldn't she if her father was behaving so badly? She pushed her way through the chattering throng and went to stand beside them, feeling insecure, like a small child who has lost sight of her mother.

'Oh, Miranda.' Her mother looked bemused, as if she had forgotten that she had a grown-up daughter. 'This is Peter Chapman, my daughter, Miranda.' She smiled, fluttering her hand between them.

'Hello, Miranda.' Peter's voice was pleasantly deep. He gave her a searching, friendly smile. 'I hear you work on a magazine in London.'

'Yes,' she said, not knowing what else to say. She stared at him and found herself liking him with his merry blue eyes and open face. She wondered if he had a wife. Marcus, Sally and Roland then came up and were introduced. Peter seemed to know all about them and Miranda wondered if he was her mother's lover or if she just discussed her family with him, boasting as she did to the ladies in the church flower rota about her children's achievements. She wondered what they'd all say if they knew about Jack.

'I'll see you later, Peter, about six thirty,' Julia said to him, smiling at him rather regally and walking away. 'I must get the joint on. I've bought some beef in your honour,' she said to Marcus as if he was still a schoolboy who needed feeding up.

Miranda wondered why Peter Chapman couldn't be invited to lunch too, and when they had left everyone and were in the car she said, 'Who was that Peter? I haven't seen him before.'

'Oh, he's new here,' Julia said vaguely.

'Where does he live?' Miranda pushed on.

'Oh, not in the village. Look, there's Betty Wilson. Her boy has just got into the grammar school. You wouldn't believe it, would you? He seemed almost retarded to me.' She prattled on.

Miranda let her, but later, when they were clearing up the lunch, she said, 'You seem very happy, Mummy, even though Daddy seems to still be with this girl.'

'Oh, that.' Julia carefully dried a wine glass and put it in the cupboard. 'He's making such a fool of himself, everyone says so.'

And you're not? she nearly said, but at least this Peter was her mother's age. 'So what will you and Peter do tonight?' she said.

'Oh, there's the music festival. Perhaps music festival does sound a bit grand but there is a series of concerts given at a large house near Basingstoke.'

'I see.' She guessed her mother was not going to tell her much.

'It's just a small thing, but very good. Not like you get in London, of course,' she smiled. 'Have you been to anything nice lately?'

Miranda ignored her question. 'So is Peter taking you?'

'Yes, dear. It's very kind of him. It's horrid going to things on one's own.' She put down the dishcloth with a flourish and said, 'Let's leave the rest. It can go in the dishwasher next time round.'

'At least you're happier,' Miranda said lamely, wishing *she* was.

'Very happy, thank you, dear.' Julia smiled, left the room, then turned at the door. 'It's no good me wasting my life waiting for your father to sort himself out. You only get one chance, darling. I hope you know that.'

'I do, Mummy.' She suddenly wanted, despite knowing how she'd overreact, to confide in her about Jack. Say what agony it was thinking of him in Spain with Sonia for two whole weeks, but she sensed that Julia was not in a confiding mood.

'Just as long as you do, darling,' she said briskly. 'Now where is Marcus? I want him to explain this letter I've had from my stockbroker. Really, all these taxes they clobber us with, better to put one's money under the bed.' She went into the garden, calling for Marcus.

Sally and Marcus set off soon after he had tried to explain Julia's finances to her. Miranda, feeling that she may be cramping her mother's style, left too. She felt immeasurably lonely as she headed off back to London. Lately she'd hated leaving her mother after the weekend, imagining her alone in the large house, perhaps miserably reminiscing over the days when they were all young and the house was filled with life. But now Julia seemed to have found a new person in her life and was forging on, making the best of it. Only she herself was alone, static, waiting for a lover who would not come.

It was about six when she got home. The street seemed empty and when she let herself into her flat that too seemed desolate. She busied herself unpacking and then to relieve her loneliness got on with her painting.

She was working on a copy of one of the Persian pictures, a charging white horse with a rider in rich, flowing robes. Soon she was lost in it, painstakingly painting each fold in his garment, her wrist resting on a ledge of wood, the fine brush stroking on each minute line.

So absorbed was she in her task she did not hear something being pushed through her letter box until it snapped back, making her jump. She listened, heard footsteps going away, Colin's flat door open and close and him clump upstairs.

There had been rather a commotion when the huge cross was found in the school garden. Colin had immediately owned up to putting it there. He explained patiently to the young constable who came round to question him, and to the local press, that people needed to be reminded of the sacrifice the Son of God had made to save mankind. He had not been charged and though the rest of the street had gossiped about it among themselves, no one wanted to put their own lives up for inspection by admitting they had been troubled by him.

Miranda finished the bit she was painting, feeling her concentration waning, a stiffness in her back. She stretched, wiped her brush and went upstairs. A copy of the *Independent* lay on the floor. She had not seen it this weekend. She wondered why Colin had pushed it through. Perhaps it held some religious message. She picked it up, not really wanting to look at it. On the other side was a picture ringed round in red. When she looked closely she saw that it was Jack. She read 'Jack Lambert, one of the three directors of Rivers Holdings awarded an average 98 per cent pay rise last year.' The article went on to outline the profits the company had made.

Miranda put the paper down slowly, feeling shocked. It was not Jack's mention in the press, or his pay rise, that affected her – apart from the pang of love she felt when she saw his picture. But there was something sinister about Colin putting it through her door like that, Jack's picture ringed in red.

Chapter Twenty-Five

Jack let himself into his house just after lunch. The alarm wasn't on and he assumed that the daily must still be there. He put down his briefcase in the hall and flipped through the post that sat on the table, seeing if there was anything that needed his immediate attention. He'd take the evening flight to Frankfurt and with any luck he could be home tomorrow and he might have time to see Miranda. The trip was a bore but no one else could really go. Besides, he wanted to sort this deal out once and for all.

He went upstairs to pack his things for overnight and heard a noise coming from the spare bedroom. He opened the door to tell the daily that it was only him, and saw Sonia and a man naked in the throes of lovemaking.

She gasped, and the man jumped off her as if he could pretend he was doing something else, grabbing the sheet to cover himself.

For a moment Jack felt numb. He stared at them stupidly until the realisation sank in that here, stark and brutal, was the evidence of Sonia's infidelity. Being confronted like this unnerved him, made him feel ill, disgusted.

'So this is your work, is it?' he spat at her, his mouth curling in disgust, his heart thumping with anger and jealousy.

'Darling, I can explain.' She too had covered her nakedness. He wondered why she bothered when he knew her body as well as his own.

'I don't want to hear a word from you. I'm so sick of your lies,' he shouted, hating the feeling of humiliation that overwhelmed him in front of this other man, cowering by the bed. He turned away, but the picture of them both stayed in his mind. He felt impotent with rage, he wished he could kill her. He walked mechanically up the stairs to their bedroom, forcing himself to think of what he would need for the overnight trip, trying to block out the picture of his wife naked in another man's arms.

He heard a scuffling and a muttered conversation coming from the spare room. He wondered what the man would do: come and apologise or make a run for it? God, he hoped he'd just leave. He couldn't bear to hear his grovelling excuses.

He longed to be away from this house, the scene he had just witnessed. He could divorce Sonia for this, but there was Tom, and they had both promised to try hard to stay together to make a stable home for him. He knew he wasn't altogether blameless – he had Miranda – but he didn't see her often and never brought her here. Besides, she understood the situation, was prepared to wait in the wings. But this man – what if he wanted to marry Sonia? Take her away? Take Tom away? For there was no knowing who would get custody of him if they did divorce.

He threw some clothes into his bag, his heart like lead. The last time he'd seen Miranda she'd seemed content with their relationship. He had wondered if perhaps she didn't want to marry him after all, if things became easier with Tom; didn't want to take his son on and the possible worse problems he might have as he went through adolescence. She was good at her job and enjoyed it, maybe she didn't want to give it all up, her own flat, her independent life, for them.

Sonia came into their room and when she saw his open bag on the bed she said in horror, her expression like a frightened child's, 'You don't have to leave me. It meant nothing to me. You're not going, are you?' She ran to him, but he put his hands up to fend her off.

'I don't want to talk about your filthy behaviour. I have to go to Frankfurt. A sudden crisis has come up. I forbid you to bring these men here when I am away, or ever again,' he shouted at her. 'It is my house, do not forget that, and you . . .' he turned from her in disgust, 'are such a slut.'

'I didn't mean it. It just . . . well, he was very insistent . . .' she bleated. She was dressed now, but had an unkempt air about her, a grubby look that revolted him.

'Leave it,' he said. 'There is absolutely no excuse for you to be in bed with a man here, at this time of the day. You are hardly an innocent little girl who didn't know what she was doing.' He threw his pyjamas into the bag and zipped it up.

'I know, but I can explain . . .' she tried again.

'I don't want to hear.' He pushed past her roughly and went downstairs.

'You had that woman in France,' she threw after him, angry too now.

He ignored her and saw as he went downstairs the man skulking in the spare room. As he passed him Jack said with contempt, 'Leave my house this instant.'

The man, younger than Sonia, tall with blond hair, looked contrite, rather foolish. 'I d-don't know what to say,' he stammered.

'Don't bother, just go. By the way, you know, you're not the first one,' Jack threw at him before going into the drawing room to ring for a minicab.

Sonia stood on the landing outside the spare room. 'Do you still see that woman?' she shouted as she came down the stairs. 'If you do, why shouldn't I have someone?'

He forced himself to ignore her, fighting to control his anger at her speaking of Miranda in that sneering voice. He longed to telephone Miranda but he wouldn't ring her now; he felt it would degrade her in the middle of this sordid scene.

He dialled the minicab firm and ordered a car to take him to Heathrow. He didn't need to leave for another hour or so but he asked it to come now and thought, I'll go and see Miranda on the way. He felt he needed to hold her, breathe in her honesty and her love after catching Sonia at one of her sordid trysts. The thought of seeing her excited him and he wished she too could take off with him and they could go together to Frankfurt.

He heard the front door close behind the man and then Sonia came into the drawing room.

'You have that woman, so why can't I?' she began.

'I don't want to talk about it,' he said, not looking at her.

'Well, I do. You never gave her up, did you, after Tom's overdose? He could have died while you were with her, pretending you were somewhere in France on business.'

'We couldn't get hold of you, remember,' he said coldly.

'You still see her, don't you?' Sonia insisted.

'I don't want to talk about it.' He looked at her now. 'I hope to be back tomorrow. I'll collect Tom from school on Saturday morning.'

'Darling,' she put on her wheedling voice, 'look, we're both being silly. If you give her up I promise you I won't look at another man. Perhaps,' she smiled, took a step towards him, 'we could have another baby. What do you think?'

'Just go,' he said in anguish. 'I can't bear to be in the same room as you after this.'

Sonia's face went hard. 'If you keep on with that woman, that woman who wormed her way into our family by taking advantage of Tom, I'll tell him.'

'Shut up,' he said, pushing away the coil of fear that wound in him at her words.

'I'll tell him you're going to leave us, run away with that woman, that you no longer love us.'

He almost hit her then. He had to clench his fists to keep them by his sides. 'You would frighten your own son, a child who is emotionally unstable at the moment, with lies like that?' He looked at her with such contempt, she shrank back. 'You make me sick.'

'I didn't mean it,' she said near tears. 'You made me say it. I'm so afraid of losing you, breaking up our family.'

Knowing this was just another of her wiles, he made to leave the room. To his immense relief he heard the doorbell.

'My taxi,' he said, gathering up his bag and briefcase, and making for the door.

'Not even a kiss goodbye?' she said.

'No.' Jack opened the door and went out into the street.

Once in the car he asked to go to Miranda's office. He rang her on his mobile as they drove.

'I've got to go to Frankfurt. I'm coming to see you now on my way to the airport. Have you a minute?'

'Yes.' She sounded pleased. 'I'll meet you by the entrance. How long will you be?'

He glanced at the traffic. 'Fifteen, twenty minutes. I wish you could come with me.'

She laughed. 'So do I.'

When he got to her office she was waiting outside for him. He kissed her in the street, not caring who was looking.

She said, 'You're bold. I hope no one saw us.'

'I don't care if they do. I love you.' He kissed her again, feeling a surge of desire for her, a longing to be alone with her.

She smiled, taking his hand. 'It's lovely to be told that in the middle of a rather dreary day. I can't stay with you long. Stella, my boss, will be looking for me soon.'

'Let's just go in here, out of the way.' He took her into a small restaurant next to her office. They sat down in the corner, still holding hands. A waiter hovered. Neither really wanted anything to eat but they settled on a couple of cappuccinos.

'So what's up in Frankfurt?' she asked.

'Just a deal we thought we'd clinched and now at the eleventh hour they've thrown up some more clauses. I have to go. I wish you could come. You haven't your passport with you, I suppose?' He smiled, kissed the palm of her hand, holding it against his cheek.

'No,' she laughed, 'sadly not.'

'Perhaps we could meet at the weekend. Tom's out, so perhaps we could meet at the Science Museum?' They had met there by contrived 'chance' one weekend. It had been very difficult to hide from Tom their exuberance at being with each other.

He seemed to guess anyway because later he had said to Jack on their way home, 'Miranda makes everyone happy to be with her, doesn't she?'

'Yes, she does,' he'd said, looking at his son and wondering how much he knew and how much he minded. He'd wanted to warn him to say nothing to Sonia. He felt bad about involving him in this deception, although of course meeting at the museum like that was deceitful enough. He never knew if Tom did say anything to his mother, for she certainly never let on that she knew.

'I can't see you this weekend,' Miranda said regretfully. 'One of my friends, Davina – you met her skiing in Verbier that time – is finally getting married to Piers.'

'Finally?'

'They've been engaged for ages. He's often away in submarines. Anyway, they are getting married in Scotland on Saturday. I'm taking the night sleeper up with some friends tomorrow night.'

'Oh, did you tell me? I must have forgotten.' He felt hurt, he knew he had no right to be.

'I think I did tell you.' She frowned, then said a little sadly, 'It's difficult to remember what I said, our meetings are so short and we so like to make love and . . .' She tailed off. She hadn't meant to complain.

'I know.' He wanted to tell her about finding Sonia with a lover, about her threats to frighten Tom about him leaving him, but he felt it was not something to say to her now, just before he was about to go away. On reflection too he thought Sonia wouldn't say those things to Tom, no mother could. But then again, he thought with fear, her tempestuous insecurity made her hit out, cause damage to the people she professed to love.

'I wish . . .' Jack leant closer to Miranda. 'I do want more than I can give you at the moment. I want to spend time with you without having to look at the clock. Days, weeks, my whole life.'

'So do I, but there's Tom. I really do understand, darling, about disrupting him. They say that divorce, however amicable, is disastrous for a child.'

He realised they had never mentioned divorce before. He said, 'I know, but in a few months, when he is really settled at this school – I told you he seems happy there, didn't I? He's made friends and is in the football team – then I would like us to be together always. What do you say?' He looked into her face, searching for confirmation of her love, wondering if his fear of her valuing her independence too much was true.

'What's brought this on?' she said, smiling. 'Just going to Frankfurt for the night?'

'No. I . . . I went home early to get my bag and found Sonia,' he swallowed, the scene looming in his mind, 'in bed with someone else.' The words he'd wanted to keep to himself seemed to be forced out from him.

'Oh no, oh, darling, how dreadful.' She held him, biting back the insults she wanted to heap on Sonia, wondering with fear how much Jack cared about finding his wife in bed with another man.

209

He said, 'Our relationship is a farce. I've always known it but I preferred not to admit it. Since meeting you I've seen it for what it is. I really want us to make our lives together, darling. As soon as Tom is ready, I'll leave her, come to you. We'll find somewhere to live, take you away from that pervert with his Bible bashing.'

She held him, not daring to believe that her dream was to be realised. She'd told him about Colin circling his picture in red in the newspaper and pushing it through her letter box, and also a few notes he'd pushed through, warning her of her 'adultery'. A few times Jack had confronted Colin but all he had said was, 'Your conscience surely tells you you are doing wrong, or you would not be so angry.'

Lately Colin had been away on a retreat 'to pray for your soul', as he'd told Miranda darkly as he left, and she and Jack had enjoyed passionate, uninhibited lovemaking together, knowing he was not upstairs.

Now Jack kissed her and said with despair, 'I've got to go if I'm to catch that plane. I'll ring you tonight.'

'OK.'

'So when are you back from the wedding?'

'Sunday, late. It will be quite a party,' she said.

'Have a good time,' he said, wishing that she wasn't going. He wondered if David was going too, would be one of the 'friends', but he didn't like to ask.

We are so intimate, he thought, and love each other so much, we share so many thoughts and fears, but still we live such separate lives. We do not know each other's friends, go to the same social events, or if we do, it is as strangers. But soon, he thought, this torture of wondering where she is and what she is doing will be over. We will be together and everything will be wonderful.

He kissed her goodbye and watched her go back into her office before getting back into the waiting minicab. Things had finally come to a head, he thought. In a few months he could leave Sonia and spend the rest of his life with Miranda.

Chapter Twenty-Six

'It's getting rather like *Four Weddings and a Funeral*, but let's hope we don't have a funeral,' James Darby said to Miranda. 'You and I have escaped this mania to get married so far, or are you about to tie the knot with someone?'

'No, are you?' Miranda asked him. They were standing together at Davina and Piers's wedding reception, held in a castle that stood on a cliff looking out to sea.

'Not me, I'm far too selfish. I have so much I want to do, and girls, well,' he smiled apologetically, 'not you probably, Miranda, but other girls when they become your girlfriend always want you to do things with them.'

'That's natural, surely?'

'To a certain extent, but if I suddenly want to go sailing, or to Paris or something and they don't want to, they then moan if I go alone.' He drank down his champagne and held his glass out to a waitress to refill it.

'I don't see you settling down, mowing the lawn, pushing the pram.' She laughed at the thought of it. She had known James for ever, been at university with him and for one year had shared a house with him among a crowd of others. Girls always milled round him, spoiling him shamelessly. They often got hurt, really because they, without him asking, or to be fair, him refusing, did far too much for him. They became wounded when he moved on, feeling that he owed them nothing. Having lived with him at such close quarters, Miranda had no wish to be romantically involved with him. He was far too fickle for that.

She was glad she was staying in a house party nearby with him, not only because she felt comfortable with him but also because she wanted subtly to quiz him about Sonia.

Tessa and Simon joined them, remarking on how pretty Davina looked and how sweet the little bridesmaids were dressed in white with tartan sashes. Henry was supposed to be a page, in tartan trews and a white shirt with a jabot.

'I don't like it,' he had screamed when his mother had dressed him. He had refused to walk up the aisle and she'd had to sit at the back of the church with him. Now he seemed to have forgotten about his horror of the clothes and was running around happily with the others.

Miranda was not staying in the same house party as the Gardiners so they had not had time to catch up on gossip.

'Bunny still pregnant?' Miranda asked her.

'Yes, due in March, I think, five months' time.'

'No one knows what sex it is?'

'No, but Ralph . . .' She lowered her voice, her eyes gleaming gleefully. 'You remember that good-looking chap who handed out drinks that time at the Hall?'

'Sort of,' Miranda said.

'He's called Chris. He looks after Sir Quentin's old hunters, helps in the garden, things like that. Anyway, people say—'

'*Mrs Busybody* says,' Simon broke in, overhearing their conversation.

'Yes, well, that's true, but the thing is some of the local ladies have gone for him and he takes no notice of them at all.'

Simon said in a bored voice, 'He's probably got more taste than to get involved with the likes of Marsha Pitney and Emma Mills, and so not to lose face they say he's gay.'

'I had a girlfriend once who swore her husband was gay,' James said. 'It turned out he didn't fancy her but was sleeping with his secretary.'

'Village gossip is deadly,' Simon said. 'I just hope that poor man has a son this time and everyone will shut up.'

Tessa giggled. 'You know they won't shut up. There's bound to be something else to speculate on.'

'True, but come and stay again, Miranda, see what you think of it all.'

'I'd love to, thank you.'

'You come too, James,' Simon said. 'Come and shoot. I'm quite friendly with Ralph now. I'm sure I can fix something.'

Tessa said quietly to Miranda, 'So how are you? How's Jack?'

Miranda smiled, feeling warm hearing his name. 'I saw him the day before yesterday. He'd just caught his wife in bed with another man.'

Tessa's eyes widened. 'No! What did he do?'

'He didn't really say, we didn't have much time, but he did say,' she paused, so hoping that she had read him right, 'that he'll leave her, live with me.'

'Oh, Miranda,' Tessa hugged her delightedly, 'I'm so glad for you. You deserve to be happy, be married like all of us,' she laughed.

'Oh, don't say anything, Tess,' Miranda hushed her. 'We have to wait until his son, you know Tom, is completely settled. He likes his new school, but Jack wants us to wait a few more months.'

Tessa frowned. 'He always seems to be making excuses,' she said. 'You like the son, he likes you, you'll be good for him – better than his own mother who always seems to be having affairs, I'd say. I can't see it makes any difference if he leaves his wife this month or Christmas. Better to get on with it, I'd have thought.'

Miranda chased away the prickly unease in her mind that Tessa had a point. 'The circumstances with Tom are tricky. You know he took an overdose. We must wait until he's really strong again.'

'How many months ago was that?'

'Just about three.'

'I'd give it till Christmas. If Jack's really going to leave his wife for you then he must do it by then, or anyway by New Year,' Tessa said firmly. 'Don't let him fob you off with endless excuses.'

Before Miranda could reply Davina waltzed up to them and any more talk of Jack was finished.

There was a dance in the evening. Miranda, who had forgotten most of the Scottish dances she'd learnt in her youth, soon picked them up again.

'It's such fun, I'd forgotten,' she said, twirling round with James. She realised that she felt very happy, exuberant with the music, being with her friends and the general good humour and gaiety around her. It was, she thought, the first time she had been conscious of being truly happy without Jack.

The music finished and James said, 'I'm so hot, shall we go outside?' He took her arm, laughed, and said, 'I really am hot. I'm not going to jump on you unless you want me to.'

She laughed back. 'Please don't,' she said, 'it would complicate our friendship.'

'It would,' he agreed.

She fetched her cashmere wrap and they went downstairs and out into the garden. The air was fresh and cold. They walked arm in arm to the edge of the sea. The moon and lights in the garden gave out a soft, ethereal glow. They stood on the cliff watching the waves as black as jet pulsating under the sky.

Miranda thought, Oh, Jack, you should be here with me. But she did not feel sadness, just a delicious melancholy that she was without him but that soon they would be together again, with any luck, for always.

James said, 'So here we are, a couple of unmarried people, not romantically involved with each other, standing by the sea in the moonlight.' He smiled at her. 'Wasted on us, do you think?'

'I was thinking that in a way,' she said, 'but it's lovely all the same. We can still enjoy it.'

'That we can. Have you anyone in your life at the moment?' he asked her in the same tone of voice he might ask what make her car was.

'I have, but . . .'

'But?'

She laughed awkwardly. 'He's married.'

'So are most of *my* girlfriends. You know, Miranda, perhaps we ought to stay together. We're two of a kind. Neither of us wants real commitment so perhaps,' he looked at her quizzically, 'we go for people who are committed already, but just want a bit of a fling.'

'Oh, I don't think that,' she said, almost horrified at his remark. 'I've never been in love with a married man – an engaged man either, for that matter – before.'

'Oh, sorry, love, I didn't mean to upset you.' He squeezed her arm.

'You didn't – well, not really. It's just rather a fragile relationship and Tessa has already quizzed me on it today.'

'Do you love him, really I mean, want to marry him?' James asked her.

'I want to be with him for the rest of my life, however it works out,' she said.

'Then that is serious. Does he want to be with you?' He looked at her intently in the dark. 'Or does he want both, you and his wife? There won't be much in it for you if he does.'

'He wants me,' she said, remembering the scene with him in the restaurant the day before yesterday. 'He has a child, you see – Tom.' She explained everything to James about Tom.

He said, 'That's rough, poor kid, but children are resilient and if he likes you,' he laughed, 'I can't see you as the wicked stepmother. I'd say you're good with children.' He paused, said suddenly, 'It's rather a coincidence but I had an affair with a woman who had an only son called Tom.'

'I know, it's his wife.'

'Good God, you mean Sonia? Sonia Lambert. You're in love with her husband?' He looked at her incredulously.

'Yes. I saw you both at Anna and Jonathan's party, remember?'

'I did meet her there, I think,' he frowned. 'So how long has this been going on?'

Miranda told him everything. Then she said, 'But what about you and Sonia? That's over, isn't it?'

'Oh, yes. It was only a game, for both of us. I knew she didn't want to leave her husband and I certainly didn't want to be saddled with her. She's a lovely woman, sexy too, but—' Then he stopped, clapped his hand over his mouth. 'Sorry, love, I forgot for a moment that I was talking about your lover's wife. I suppose it would be easier if I said she was horrible, longed to leave him, or that I wanted to marry her. But even for you, of whom I'm very fond, I don't want to take her off his hands.'

'Of course not, I didn't mean that. She had another affair, lots perhaps since you.' Miranda felt suddenly rather nauseous. What had she hoped he'd say? Sonia was beautiful and no doubt sexy as he'd said, but the way he'd remarked that she didn't want to leave her husband made her feel ill with fear. Suddenly the happiness she'd enjoyed all evening disappeared, leaving her feeling fearful and alone.

James put his arm round her shoulders. 'There are lots of wives like her, bored out of their minds. Perhaps they feel unloved, their poor husbands working too hard to provide for them to give them enough attention. They don't want to give up their lifestyle but they want a bit of fun on the side, and here,' he caressed her shoulder, 'dreadful old roués like me have a field day. Lots of action with no commitment.'

'I know,' Miranda said, feeling as if she might cry.

'It's a terrible thing to say, especially as here we are at a wedding of two people who are now obviously in love with each other, but I'm afraid there is a lot of it about. Sonia certainly didn't want to leave her husband for me, and I admit I'd have severely discouraged her if she had. She's too manipulative, immature, the eternal teenager. It gets a bit wearing after a while. But that's not to say she won't leave him for someone else.' His voice was not convincing.

Miranda said, 'I'm too naïve. Most of my friends seem to be still happily married. I know Laura had a bad experience first time round, but I haven't noticed all this unfaithfulness.'

'You're too nice, and no, of course it's not everyone. I exaggerated. I just seem to meet a lot of these women,' he laughed. 'I probably subconsciously seek them out so I know I won't have to become too committed to them.'

'You might be cited in a divorce.'

'I was once, very tricky,' he sighed. 'I don't want to upset you. I haven't seen Sonia for quite a few months and I don't know her husband at all. I'm sure he loves you and he has good cause to leave her, it's just in my experience – and not especially thinking of Sonia – most of these errant wives don't want to leave their husbands at all.'

'But if he wants to leave her!' she cried out.

James hugged her to him. 'Then he will. My poor, sweet Miranda, I can't bear to see you hurt. Just don't count any chickens, my dear. So many of these men are the same as their wives, you know. They don't really want to break up their family, their lifestyle. Besides, they might lose custody of the children, and a difficult wife might deny them access.' He sighed as if he hated to upset her with this reality. 'Also divorce is terribly expensive these days, you know. But with a wife like her, Jack would be mad not to change her for you.' He kissed the top of her head, but she did not feel comforted.

'He said he'd leave her, that their life together is a farce,' she intoned, remembering the look in his eyes, the touch of his hand.

'I'm sure he means it,' James said. 'I'm just a cynical old slob, you know. Far too selfish to find one nice, decent woman like you and marry her and stay with her. I'm sure Jack's not like that, but I just want to warn you. I know you're not the type to have affairs just for the sake of a bit of fun. I've always admired that in you, you know.' He grinned at her. 'I'm a complete hypocrite, as you know. I want to seduce every pretty woman I meet yet I respect the ones who turn me down because they're already committed or they're not in love with me.'

She smiled in spite of her pain. 'You are,' she said.

He hugged her to him, laughing. 'I could easily fall in love with you, Miranda. Perhaps you'd be my saviour, only I don't expect you want to be that.'

'No,' she said, trying to match his light-heartedness. 'You have too many beautiful curvaceous skeletons in your cupboard.'

'True.' He took his arm from her shoulder, looked intently into her face. 'Just don't get hurt,' he said seriously. 'These divorces can be very nasty.'

'I know,' she said, feeling the chill of fear in her heart.

She shivered and he said, 'It's getting cold. Let's go back and dance again to warm us up.'

She followed him back into the castle and even though the party was still in full swing, the music urging them on to dance, the guests brimming with good humour and *joie de vivre*, she felt out of it. Even as she danced, being caught up first by one partner then by another, even as she smiled into the faces of her friends, she felt isolated. She thought of Jack alone in his hotel bedroom in Frankfurt and yearned to be with him, but James's words filled her with foreboding. Maybe when it came down to it Jack would not want to give up his lifestyle, would stay with his wife.

Chapter Twenty-Seven

'Oh, do come to *Swan Lake*, Miranda. I'd love you to and I'd hate to miss it; the tickets were so expensive,' Laura begged down the telephone.

Part of her jumped at the chance to see the ballet at the Royal Opera House, the other part stalled, wanting to wait in until Jack rang her. He was meant to be coming back from a business trip to New York either today or early tomorrow and he might just have time to see her.

'Neil has this dreadful flu and we bought the tickets ages ago, so please come. I don't want to go alone with the baby so near,' Laura continued.

'I'd love to,' Miranda said quickly, knowing she'd feel mean if she didn't accept. Jack hadn't said he'd definitely be back that evening, nor would he definitely come and see her. She arranged to meet Laura in the bar at the Opera House. It was not worth her going all the way home after the office, and then setting out again. She wished almost immediately after Laura had rung off that she wasn't going. If Jack rang her at home and left a message on her answerphone, she wouldn't know until she got back later that night. She hoped that if he was coming back today he'd ring her at the office. She sat at her desk and stared vacantly ahead.

Her whole life was now one of waiting. She'd been warned about it by enough people but somehow she'd thought, or perhaps kidded herself, that she and Jack would be different. Ever since that night two months ago when he'd found Sonia in bed with someone, he had seen her more often. He'd been away a lot on business but once or twice she had been able to sneak out to places in Europe to join him for a weekend. She had put her whole being into these weekends, determined to forget their real life back home. They spent much of their time in bed, holed up against the rest of the world, talking and making love and just being together. She chased away any thoughts that suggested that he did not want to go outside in case they were seen by work colleagues or someone who knew Sonia. She did not talk about their situation, telling herself it was because she didn't want to spoil their magic hours together, but knowing deep in her heart she didn't want to listen to the doubts in his voice about whether breaking up the family would hurt Tom, or whether Sonia would get custody of him and put up barriers to stop him seeing his son.

'If she doesn't get her own way she can be very vindictive,' he said. 'That day I caught Sonia in bed with that fellow, she . . .' He paused and she could see the pain in his eyes. 'She said if I didn't leave you, not that I think she definitely knows we still see each other, but that she'd tell Tom, tell him I didn't love him, was leaving him.'

'What a bitch! Sorry, she is your wife, but what a thing to do to a child, especially when it isn't true,' Miranda burst out.

'I know, but I can't risk her doing it. It will finish him after my grandfather's heart attack and all that happened at school.'

They were in her flat. He came to her there sometimes, had even stayed the whole night with her, when Sonia was away. 'After Christmas,' he said, his face tight with decision, 'I'm going to tell him, tell him I love him, want him to share our home. I'll leave Sonia, buy another house and move in with you.'

'I'd love that,' she'd said, feeling that she would give up everything for him. She no longed cared so much for her flat or valued her independence with the enthusiasm that she used to. Her girl friends were right, she thought: once you met the right man all you wanted was to be with him, to please him. It was just nature's trap, she supposed sardonically, but at this moment it was one she longed for.

Her trysts with Jack had not gone unnoticed by Colin, but Jack had soon put paid to his dire warnings. One morning as they both rushed to work he was there in the hall, hovering, mothlike, by the door

'You are sinning,' he said, standing in their way in the narrow passage, waving his arms feebly in the air as if shooing away their sins so that they would not contaminate him. 'Repent now before it is too late.'

'Move on, old chap,' Jack had said, mildly at first, in a voice one might use to someone deranged.

'Your mortal soul is in danger. The sins of lust are—'

Miranda opened her mouth to protest, to tell him to mind his own business. He made her feel afraid. Jack, possibly suspecting this, suddenly went rigid with anger. She saw his hands clench at his sides as if he were afraid he would pick up Colin and throw him out on to the road.

'I have had enough of your sick remarks,' he thundered. 'I am going to the police. You have no right to harass people like this. It's got to stop. You are making Miss Farell's life hell, and no doubt most of your neighbours' too. We will all go to the police unless you stop it at once.' He shouted so loud Miranda was sure the neighbours would hear on both sides and, she hoped, would applaud him.

Jack towered over Colin, his anger somehow filling him out and making him appear even bigger. Colin opened his mouth once more to speak but Jack was quicker.

'One more word of this nonsense and I go to the police, understand?' His voice was commanding, his eyes fixing Colin against the wall. 'Do you understand?' he demanded again. 'Not another word.'

Colin nodded, cowering against the wall. Jack yanked open the front door and she followed him out, but as she passed Colin she heard him mutter under his breath, 'The Lord sees all. You shall not escape.' His words stung as if they were stones thrown at her. She took Jack's hand and hurried up the street to the tube with him, quite forgetting that they usually walked a little apart in case they were spotted together.

The ballet with Laura was wonderful but sometimes, especially during the first act, Miranda couldn't help wondering if Jack was ringing her at this moment, if he was perhaps outside her flat on his way back from the airport. But when the lovers met, the haunting melancholy music seared her heart. She watched Odette and, later, Odile and her prince perform their memorable *pas de deux*, perfect as a pair, each complementing the other, the man always there to support the ballerina, she so sure of him, knowing as she launched herself into the air or into a spin that he would be there to catch her.

'Like a good marriage, knowing each of you is there for the other,' Laura whispered dreamily to her.

'I suppose so,' she answered, thinking of Jack. Would Jack always be there to catch her? Did everyone need someone there to catch them? The thought saddened her. Was it really so necessary to be part of a pair?

Odile came to the party, disguised as Odette. Transfixed and deceived, the prince danced with her. Then each dancer danced alone. The ballerina pirouetted and leapt, full of joy and independence, gloriously, magnificently, on her own. When she'd finished the applause was deafening. The man came back on stage and did his bit on his own, leaping higher and higher, round and round the stage. Again the audience applauded. Then again the ballerina danced alone, and the joy in her of her body, her power over him, the music, the rhythm and her dancing, filled Miranda with hope. You could get joy, perhaps a different joy, dancing alone. Music, life, could be enjoyed on one's own; one could make one's own rhythm. Once she had known that – been happy with her flat, her work, her painting, with friends and lovers there when she wanted them. Being with Jack had made her forget the pleasure of just being oneself. It had made her discontented with her old life and that, she thought now, was a mistake.

Halfway through the third act Laura gasped and clutched at her frantically. 'My waters have broken.'

'What?'

'My waters! The baby is coming.' She gripped Miranda's arm with her fingers, her eyes wide with fright.

'Are you sure?' Miranda looked at Laura's stomach as if expecting a fountain suddenly to rise above it.

'Shh,' the man beside her insisted.

'Yes,' Laura said, nodding her head at the same time.

Miranda didn't know what to do. Would the baby be born there under the seat at any moment? Laura stood up, much to the annoyance of the people behind. Miranda followed her, half bending so as not to obstruct the view for the other people, and awkwardly they pushed their way out.

Miranda, her new understanding of life now shattered with Laura's devastating predicament, did her best to pull herself together. 'Shall I call an ambulance?' she said, taking her arm, looking anxiously into her face.

'No, I want to go home.'

'But if the baby's coming, Laura, you ought to go to hospital.'

'I don't know if it is or not, but the waters have broken and I have a sort of pain.' She moaned and one of the staff came over to them. 'If only Neil didn't have the flu.'

'I don't see what difference that makes. Anyway, you've got another month to go, haven't you?' Miranda said, as if the child would hear her and stop coming.

'Three weeks, but when the waters break . . .' Laura said helplessly.

Another person came over to help, a man this time, and they all hovered round rather ineffectually, Laura refusing to let them call an ambulance in case they took her to some hospital she'd never heard of. Finally, at Laura's insistence, Miranda drove her home in her own car, leaving her to the care of the Opera House staff while she went outside to get it.

All the way back to their house at Notting Hill, Miranda waited anxiously for the child to appear, but as there seemed to be no real pain, Laura reassured her.

'I don't think it's being born. Well, it's meant to be agony, isn't it?'

'I don't know. You hear of women going to the loo and suddenly finding they've had a baby.'

'I don't want to go to the loo.'

'Keep everything crossed,' Miranda said firmly. 'Think of something else. Though what will you do at home? Neil won't be able to deliver it.'

'I've got my suitcase packed,' Laura said mysteriously, as if without it the baby could not be born.

They arrived at last and Miranda took her inside. She settled her on the sofa, then went upstairs and woke up Neil, who had just fallen asleep. He at once began to panic.

'It's terribly dangerous for the baby not to have the amniotic fluid,' he began. 'Is she having contractions?' He spun about, looking dreadfully ill, pulling on some clothes, and ringing the hospital at the same time, calling down to Laura to explain her symptoms word for word.

The hospital told them to come in. Miranda fetched the famous suitcase. Laura went to the loo, panicking Neil further by airily saying she hoped the baby wouldn't fall down the pan. Then, because Neil was too hazy with his flu – not to mention general panic, quoting gynaecological terms with such alarm that both women told him to shut up – and Laura was obviously unable to drive, Miranda drove them all to St Mary's, Paddington. Here they were scooped up by the night staff, Laura clutching her back, saying she was having a terrible pain; Neil holding on to her, looking as if he'd die of pneumonia even before his child saw the light of day.

'Oh, Miranda,' Neil remembered her suddenly, 'take the car back, do you mind? I'll only get it towed away or something. Thank you so much for all of this.' He swayed in the doorway.

'You should be in bed, not her,' Miranda said, wondering how the nursing staff felt about an expectant father filling the ward with flu germs.

Miranda hovered in their room for a moment, watching the nurse lie Laura on the bed, another offer Neil some tea, but he wouldn't leave Laura, who was by now in some distress. Miranda felt unwanted in this scene and muttering, 'Good luck,' she left them, knowing they had not seen her go.

Once out on the street again she took a deep breath of the cold night air. She felt strangely apart from the human race. She thought briefly of Laura and Neil's hours ahead while presumably the child would be born. They, she thought, would never be free again. The world would change from an exciting place for them to a place of menace that held all sorts of terrors to harm their child. Yet she almost envied them, going through this experience together, so common, yet so unique to each person.

She drove their car home and parked it in their street in the residents' parking place and pushed the keys through their front door. Then she hailed a taxi and went home, all the time feeling as if she were an actress playing out a part in another time, quite alien to her.

As she opened her front door she found a note from Jack on the doormat. It was written on a piece of paper torn from his diary. She felt lucky she had found it and that Colin had not thrown it away.

'Called by on my way back, but you were out. Ring you tomorrow. J.'

Vainly she looked back up the street in case he had just left and was still there, but it was empty. Loneliness hit her like a sledgehammer. She forgot her earlier optimism, during the ballet, about the joys of life alone.

She let herself into her flat, went into the bedroom and threw herself down on the bed. It was past midnight and she was tired, hit now for the first time by shock at the way the evening had ended. That was life, real and raw, and she somehow didn't feel part of it at all.

'A bit on the side' – the words sprang into her mind. That's what their affair was, a bit on the side of real life, where people who loved each other made babies, struggled in fear and ignorance, and despite sometimes being struck down with flu, supported each other through it. Of course there was a bad side too – babies born without love and support – but she did not think of that now. To her the world seemed full of couples like Laura and Neil, going through life supporting each other, and she felt out of it.

She was angry now, sad, that she had missed Jack, felt the worm of resentment probe into her. *If* as her instinct had warned her she had refused Laura's invitation, *if* Laura's waters hadn't broken, *if* Neil hadn't got flu . . . on it all went, the barriers building up, stopping her seeing Jack. She turned her head this way and that in anguish. This way madness lay, she told herself. She must not allow herself to get like this, let life go by while she holed up here waiting for him.

The phone rang, cutting through her thoughts. She grabbed the receiver by the side of the bed.

'Hello.'

'Miranda.' His voice was soft.

'Oh, darling, when did you come? I went to the ballet with Laura and her baby started and . . .' Words and tears tumbled over each other, making her gasp and stop.

'About two hours ago. I wanted to see you.'

'I want to see you. Where are you?' She forced herself to speak coherently.

'At home. I can't talk long. I'll see you tomorrow, after work.'

'I want you now.' The words were wrung out of her. The events of the evening swept away her rational thoughts. 'I cannot go on waiting for you, I need you now.' Tears enveloped her.

'What is it? Darling, what is it? What's happened?' She heard his voice grow frantic at the other end.

She fought to remain calm, to pull back her panic and her need for him, but she could not.

'I . . . it's Laura's baby and . . .' She couldn't tell him, couldn't explain how much Laura and Neil's closeness had affected her, how the simple birth of a child had made her feel apart from the rest of the world. Not that she wanted a child, did she? She suddenly knew she wanted something of Jack's, to go through some deep experience with him.

'I'm coming round,' she heard him say, and the phone went dead.

He was with her almost before she knew it. He took her in his arms, held her close, then led her back into the bedroom, sitting with her on the bed.

'What is it? What has upset you? Laura's baby – is something wrong with it? With her?'

'No.' She leant against him, feeling drained, foolish, feeling she'd let him down. 'I just felt so out of it. Then when I found your note and I hadn't been here, had missed you . . .'

He stroked her shoulder, kissed her on her face. 'I know. I missed you too. I felt terrible when you weren't here, jealous, even.' He gave a bitter laugh. 'I thought you might be with David, or someone else, and why not? I told myself. You haven't much life waiting around for me.'

'It's all right,' she said, comforting him now, clinging to him. 'I love you. I don't want to go out with anyone else. But Laura wanted to go to the ballet and Neil is ill.' She went on telling him about the evening.

He held her, lying down together on the bed. He sighed. 'It can't go on like this,' he said. 'I want to be with you all the time, not snatched meetings, secret calls. Listen.' He turned her face to his. 'There's Christmas in two weeks. You're going to your family and we, as you know, are all going to France to my mother. Then I promised Tom we'd go skiing. We'll be back mid-January. He goes back to school then. I'll tell Sonia the minute we get back that our marriage is over, that I want a divorce and to marry you.'

'And Tom? When will you tell him?'

He hesitated. 'I'll tell him before I tell Sonia, make sure he knows the truth of it.' His brow furrowed. 'But I'll have to play that by ear, judge when it is the best time. After Christmas Day, or during the holiday. As long as he knows for certain that I love him, am not abandoning him, I'm sure he won't be upset, especially as it's you I'll be with and he can be with us whenever he wants.'

'Of course he can.' She kissed him and he held her close. 'I'm sorry I was so upset earlier. It was just such an emotional evening. Perhaps it's delayed shock or something.'

'My poor darling, I hate not to be with you when you need me.' He kissed her.

'Surely Sonia knows about us. Where does she think you go at night?' Her agitation changed course. She could not believe it would be so easy for him to leave her.

'I only come here when she's away. Sometimes her office promotes something in another town and – well, hardly ever, more's the pity or I'd be with you more often – she's away for the night.'

'Where is she tonight?'

'At home, asleep. I'll have to go quite soon.'

'I still can't believe she doesn't know we still see each other,' she said incredulously. 'After all, she better than most must know the signs of an affair.'

'After I found her in bed with that man she's behaved impeccably. Hasn't asked me anything, and I've said nothing.' He laughed ruefully, caressed her arms. 'I don't mind telling you I'm petrified she'll find out, drive Tom to . . .' He did not finish the sentence.

'It's all right, it's not long until Christmas,' she said, the strong one now. 'I can be patient, if I know there's going to be an end to this secrecy, know we'll be together soon.'

'We will, I promise. Tom breaks up the day after tomorrow, but I think it's best to tell him after Christmas. I don't want Sonia to cause any ructions in France with my mother and her family. But we'll be together in a couple of months, I promise,' Jack said, stroking her hair. 'I want you more than anything. I want to be with you for the rest of my life. You do believe me, don't you?'

Looking into his eyes she did believe him, but somehow she felt afraid. He went on to tell her how Tom's near suicide had unnerved him, made him feel paranoid about how to tell him about the breakup of the family, fearful that Tom might try it again if he felt cornered and out of his depth; fearful that Sonia would get custody of him and he would never see him again.

'I do understand,' she said, holding him in her arms again, praying that his nerve would not falter and that they would be together before too long.

Chapter Twenty-Eight

'I'm so glad you all came out, darling,' Cynara said to Jack. 'You never know, with people the age they are in this family, who will be here next Christmas.'

'Mother, don't sound so depressing.' Jack squeezed her arm against his side. They were walking beside the fields on a path crunchy with frost. The dead twigs of the hedgerows were white and there was a blue-grey mist rolling over the ground in the distance. Tom ran on ahead, his warm breath coming out in little puffs from his open mouth.

'I don't mean to,' she smiled, 'but Father is not any younger and he's had a bad year. He's still not really well and I suppose at his age one has to accept that he won't ever be truly fit again.'

'I know, but he may outlive us all,' he said encouragingly, but in his heart he agreed with her. The general had deteriorated quite a lot since his heart attack.

But as he walked, arms linked with his mother, Jack thought ahead to next Christmas. He would be with Miranda. He looked at Tom, who was wiping the frost off the long reeds by the pond. He wondered when would be the best time to tell him. Not now, not here, further upsetting his mother and grandfather. Where would Tom be next Christmas? With Sonia?

For the first time since he'd decided to leave Sonia and go to Miranda, Jack saw how it really might be. Saw past the dream of waking up every morning with Miranda by his side, finding her every evening at some house he'd buy for them. Where would Tom go? Who would have custody of him? It was this that gave him nightmares, haunted him at this family time.

Nowadays he knew parents were often granted joint custody, but would Sonia agree to it? Knowing her she would pull out all the emotional stops and demand to keep him herself, saying she was his mother, that he needed his mother after taking an overdose, she needed to help him with his dyslexic work, she could after all put her job on hold, Jack could not.

At sixteen, Jack thought, a child could choose which parent he wanted to live with. But he could not ask Miranda to wait so long for him to be free. He too was sick of the secrecy of their relationship. He wanted to tell the world he loved her, wanted to take her out, abroad, be seen like everyone else, not hide in the shadows like villains.

'Why are you so quiet, Jack?' Cynara said. 'Everything's all right, isn't it? Tom seems fine, happy in his new school.'

'Yes . . . I was just thinking.'

'Don't dwell on what I said about Father. None of us knows how long we've got. It's pointless to worry about something you can't do anything about,' she said briskly. 'Live life for every day, that's what I try and do.'

'You're right.' He forced himself to smile at her. He longed to confide in her, ask her what to do for the best. But he sensed that she knew he wanted to confide in her and that it was about Miranda, and she did not want to talk about it and give the subject life. She had the courage to face some things full on, such as accepting that her father might not live to see next Christmas, but he knew that she sometimes refused to face other things that might upset her life, as if by not mentioning them they would get bored and go away. So he said nothing, joining in now with her dissection of her stepdaughter and her family, knowing as well that it would be unfair to tell his mother about his plans when he hadn't even told his wife. Knowing too it would kill her if Sonia kept Tom from her.

Sonia was being extra nice to them all at the moment. He knew it was because she was afraid he would tell his mother about finding her in bed with another man. There had been a tricky moment at dinner the other night when Etienne was discussing the marriage of two of their neighbours.

'His wife brought her lover home, quite against the rules. She deserved to be horsewhipped,' the general had barked, looking as if he would be happy to horsewhip her himself.

Sonia had kept her eyes firmly on her plate. Jack had said nothing, but the general, the bit now well between his teeth, had thundered on: 'It is against all the common rules of decency for a woman to entertain another man in bed in the marital home. She should be put out on the street immediately without a penny.'

'Father, what a chauvinist you are. What about if a man brings his mistress home?' Cynara said jokily.

'A gentleman would never do such a thing,' the general said firmly. 'Play away if you must, that's the thing; it's something different away from the home.'

'So then it's all right,' Cynara continued, 'to have affairs when one is married?' She gave Etienne an amused glance as if to say, what did the old boy get up to when he was married to my mother?

'It happens,' the general said, 'but it must not happen in the marital home.'

Jack thought that at any minute his grandfather would guess that Sonia had committed this offence and he himself would be blamed for not keeping her in order. For not throwing her out at once into the street. But he *was* throwing her out, he thought, watching her discomfiture. He was getting rid of her because he wanted Miranda more than he cared whom Sonia bedded. His heart sank at the thought of the trouble in store. He knew however he played it it would turn out to be an expensive and painful affair.

Later that night Sonia had said, 'Really, your grandfather is such an old fool.'

'I think he's right,' Jack said, and went into the bathroom. When he came out Sonia was waiting for him in bed, her dark hair round her shoulders, her pale blue silk nightdress showing off her creamy skin.

'Jack,' she purred, holding her arms out to him, 'let's be friends again. It is Christmas.'

He had tried to resist her but her charms had been too potent, but as he made love to her he thought of Miranda and longed for her. How weak I am, he thought later. It is only lust that made me succumb to Sonia, nothing more. It was the first time they had made love since he'd found her with that man and he knew with sinking heart that she now thought she was forgiven and all would be well between them. The next two nights he had pleaded a sick headache and was relieved that he had to go to Geneva the following day for a couple of days' business before they set off to ski.

On a sudden impulse he telephoned Miranda and asked if she could meet him in Geneva. He'd used his mobile phone when he knew Sonia had gone to the local town to shop.

'I might be able to get the Friday off,' she said. 'Will you be there for the weekend?'

'Saturday, I could be. We go skiing on Monday. How I wish you could come there.'

'Another time,' she said.

'Next year, I can't wait. So come to the hotel, can you, darling? Friday.'

When he'd rung off he felt between two worlds. Here he was with his wife, son and the rest of the family, and there was Miranda waiting for him. He longed to be with her and yet he did not want to leave his family. It was not a question of changing Sonia for Miranda, he thought, it was also changing one sort of life for another. It would be a happier life, he thought, knowing she was there loving him, not cheating on him. He wondered if they would have children and realised that they had never spoken of such a thing.

His thoughts came back to Tom again and he wondered if he would mind having to share his life with half-brothers or -sisters.

The complications that lay ahead frightened him. It was like awaiting a major operation which one knew would be unpleasant but in the end would give one a pain-free life. Only would it? How would Tom react to his news? What mischief would Sonia create?

Etienne came out of his study to find him still standing in the passage. He came silently in his soft-soled shoes. Jack started guiltily, wondering if Etienne had heard his conversation with Miranda.

Etienne just looked at him as he passed. Then he said, 'You should have good snow in Méribel.'

'Yes, I hope so.' He walked with him along the passage. 'We go on Monday.' He took a deep breath said evenly, 'I'll be back from Geneva Saturday evening, I think.'

Etienne gave him a shrewd look. 'Good,' he put his hand on his shoulder, 'we have some friends for lunch on Sunday who I think will amuse you.' He gave him a quick smile, then went upstairs, calling for Cynara.

Jack met Miranda at lunchtime on Friday. It was very cold and clear and she looked beautiful and glowing in a red coat. They barely touched when they met, waiting until they got upstairs to his room. He shut the door and took her in his arms, letting the familiar shape of her mould into his body, smelling the scent in her hair.

'God, I've missed you.'

'Me too.' She held tightly to him.

Even as he held her, kissed her, he found himself thinking: I have to go tomorrow afternoon. How wonderful it will be when we are together for always. He took off her coat then, laughing, her jersey, and kissed her breasts.

'A whole week without you,' he said, 'it's far too long.'

'But soon we'll be together, won't we?'

He thought her voice a little hesitant, then she laughed, kissed him hard, pulling at his scarf, his coat. But even as they undressed he heard that plea in her voice echoing in his mind. Did she not believe that he would leave Sonia and live with her?

He stopped kissing her and took her arms, looking intently into her face. 'We will be together in not much longer than a month. You do believe that, don't you, darling? You do, don't you?' He wanted her to believe it as dreadfully as he wanted to believe it himself.

'Yes,' she said, he thought a little too eagerly. 'Have you told Tom yet?'

'No. My mother's concerned about my grandfather. I think it's better to wait until we've left the château. I've been thinking . . .' he pulled her down on to the bed with him, wanting to have more bodily contact with her as he told her his anxieties, 'about who gets custody of him and what you think of that and—'

'You know I'd love to have him, I'm so fond of him,' she said at once. 'He can make his home with us.' She laughed. 'It might take a little while for me to get used to looking after a child but I've plenty of friends with children who can give me tips.'

'I know you'll be wonderful.' He kissed her, happy that she cared so much for Tom. 'But it's not you I've any qualms about, it's Sonia.'

'Sonia? She can see him whenever she wants to, of course. She is his mother.'

He felt her stiffen beside him. He tightened his arm around her, caressing her arm. 'It's not that. She might not want us to have him. She might—'

'She has had affairs too, lots of them, so she can't pretend she is the virtuous wife and mother, sitting at home with her child while her husband is out with other women,' she said tartly, sitting up smartly, giving him an intent look. 'I'm sure it is going to be difficult, just at first. I don't think this sort of thing is ever easy and I appreciate that you are the one who is going to have the most flak thrown at him. But I love you, and Tom, and I'm sure in the end it will work out.' She said it seriously, with conviction, then added, 'I've thought this through long and hard. I hate the idea of breaking up a marriage and if I thought yours was a good one, I wouldn't do it . . . well,' she said with a sardonic laugh, 'I hope I wouldn't do it. I'm so crazy about you that I might be guilty of riding roughshod over a wife and a whole nursery full of children.'

He smiled, wishing suddenly that he felt happier at her words. He gathered her in his arms and caressed her. 'I love you, and whatever we have to suffer I'll do it for you. It's just Tom I don't want to hurt.'

'I won't hurt him, I'll give you time to be alone together, do things . . . all boys together,' she grinned. 'He is after all at boarding school so we can be alone then.'

'You're a wonderful, wonderful girl.' He kissed her passionately, wishing everything was already resolved and that they had started out on their new life together. 'I feel very lucky to have found you.'

After they had made love and been a while together, she said, 'Let's go out. I feel like a walk, getting out under the sky. I don't think I could bear being cooped up with room-service dinner, do you?'

'No,' he said, although he wanted to. Would have much rather stayed in the room with her in their private love nest.

She took his arm in the street and they walked along by the river, watching the lights glint in the darkness, dancing on the black, sinuous water. Jack felt very close to her as they moved as a couple through the other people. It was sharp and cold, but he felt warm with her, pleased to have her by his side.

Jack chose the restaurant, complaining with a laugh that he was cold and, after all their activity, ravenous. He dropped her hand and opened the door for her and she went in and walked straight into David.

'Miranda!' He noticed her before she noticed him.

'David . . . what a surprise.'

Jack, behind them, watched them both take a step towards each other, then back, then David went up to her firmly and kissed her on her cheek, letting his hand rest on her shoulder for a moment.

'It's so good to see you. What are you doing here?'

At that moment the maître d'hôtel came over to them to take their coats and she turned to Jack, smiling, and said, 'Do you remember David March? We were all skiing together in Verbier.'

'I do,' Jack said, giving him a sharp look and feeling a ton of jealousy falling on to him.

David gave him a critical look, seeming unconsciously to back off. He gave him a stiff smile and nod, then putting his hand on Miranda's arm said, 'Good to see you. We'll get in touch,' and walked quickly past them into the street.

Miranda stood puzzled for a moment – like a child excluded from a game, Jack thought, watching her, searching each facet of her face, yearning yet dreading to read her feelings at seeing David again. He did not know if she still saw David when he was not there, and having just witnessed the pleasure on David's face at their unexpected meeting, he now felt threatened.

Then she smiled at the maître d'hôtel, took off her coat, handed it to the youth who waited to take it and, taking Jack's arm and squeezing it gently, said, 'I'm hungry too, and this looks a great place.'

But she hardly ate anything and Jack felt the warmth had gone out of the evening. They did not mention David once. She laughed and talked of other things: the Gillard-Hardings, her job, her parents and how both now had new lovers. Her hand, like a slender butterfly, caressingly dropped on his many times but he felt that he had lost part of her and that that part was with David as he walked out into the night and back to wherever he lived.

Chapter Twenty-Nine

'That feature was your best yet,' Spike said to Miranda as she packed away the clothes after the fashion shoot. 'You have more style than Stella, though don't tell her I told you,' he laughed. 'You ought to go higher, you know, branch out, work for *Vogue* in Paris or New York.'

'Oh, Spike,' she laughed, pleased at his compliment, but also taking it with a pinch of salt. 'I'm fine where I am.'

'You're vegetating there. It's a great magazine in its way, but you're young, should spread your wings a bit. I happen to know,' he dropped his voice as if they were being overheard, 'that Paris *Vogue* will be looking for a new fashion editor in a couple of months. I think you should apply for the job. I can put in a word for you.' He winked. 'I've lots of friends out there.'

'That's sweet of you, but—'

He took her arm, said with an exaggerated bored sigh, 'I know, darling, you're in love and the boyfriend lives in London.'

She blushed, euphoria breaking in her like a wave. 'Yes, actually I am, but all the same I don't know that I'd be good enough to work for *Vogue* in Paris.'

'Don't ever underestimate yourself, darling. And is this man worth it?' He fixed her with a penetrating gaze, made more ferocious by the brutality of his shaved head.

'Yes, of course. He's married but going to get a divorce this month, or anyway tell his wife it is over.' She blurted out the words like a child caught out in some misdemeanour.

His face screwed up. 'Oh, darling, not a *married* man,' he said contemptuously. 'They are the worst, all that guilt. Is he really going to leave his wife? Are you sure?'

'Yes,' she said, 'I am. He's in Moscow this week but he's back next week then he's going to tell her. He's asked me to look for a house for us both to live in. I haven't had much time so we'll live in my flat until we find somewhere,' she told him triumphantly, remembering Jack's last telephone call when he'd said he was counting the days until they could be together for always. She had told no one else, thinking it unfair until Sonia and Tom knew all about it.

She said rather apprehensively to Spike, 'Don't say anything, will you, Spike? His wife doesn't know yet and although you don't know who I'm talking about, I don't want to risk her finding out before he tells her.'

'Are you certain she doesn't know?'

'She doesn't know he's leaving her.' Then seeing his incredulous expression, she went on, 'Oh, it's so complicated but they have a son, who's . . .' she paused, not wanting to go into the overdose drama, 'who's not very confident, and we have to be sure that he knows his father's side of the story, knows he loves him and wants to keep seeing him, as I do. Not let his mother upset him before he knows that he is loved and wanted by both of us.'

Spike looked very serious. He said in a voice of doom, 'Darling, I think you have got yourself into one hell of a domestic crisis. Ask yourself if any man's worth this aggro. Damaged children, vindictive wife . . .' He rolled his eyes theatrically. 'Sounds like an Ibsen play to me.'

'It will be fine,' she said quickly, his words making her feel uncomfortable. She didn't want to lose the happy optimism she'd been feeling these last few days. Jack had had to go unexpectedly to Moscow the second they came back from skiing, so his break with Sonia had been postponed for a little while longer, but he was back in a few days, and then he and Miranda would be together at last. Spike couldn't possibly know the story and she wasn't going to start to tell him now.

'I must go,' she said. 'Thanks again. I'm dying to see the pictures.'

'I'll bring them round to Stella in a day or so.' He looked at her. 'Take care, dear, but don't forget that job at *Vogue*. If you change your mind about trying for it, let me know.'

She took a taxi back to her office with the suitcases of clothes and accessories. Spike's words, both about her affair and the job at *Vogue*, spun through her head. Everything happens at once, she thought. She had given Davina one of her miniatures for her birthday and it had been seen by someone she used to work for who had a gallery off Bond Street. He wanted to meet her to see if she had enough good pictures to exhibit there. Davina had only rung her about it yesterday.

'He's called Charles Westwood and he thinks you're so talented and wants to see more. I told him you had dozens,' she said excitedly.

'Oh, Davina, I haven't . . . well, I haven't painted many lately. But how exciting! I don't know what to say.' Then, curbing her excitement, she said, 'It may come to nothing. Perhaps he was just being polite to you.'

'No he wasn't. I know him well. He kept looking and looking at it, saying the work was exquisite and there weren't enough good miniature painters around – all the spiel, you know. He said he'd love to see more of your work. You may well be on your way, Miranda,' she laughed.

Miranda, trundling back to her office through the icy London streets, thought of all this now. They stopped in a queue of cars waiting to get past some road works. The driver grumbled and she agreed with him that the whole of London seemed to be filled with deep holes, dug out, then surrounded by striped barriers and left yawning open, seemingly having no other function than to snarl up the traffic.

But none of this mattered to her now. She felt so happy, so complete somehow. She'd spent Christmas with her parents and Marcus and Sally, 'the paramours', as they'd been nicknamed by her brother, having gone to other relatives for the holiday. Richard and Julia were still involved with their lovers, both slept in separate bedrooms while at home, but Miranda noticed that they had a certain respect for each other that she had not seen before. It gave her hope that Jack and Sonia's break-up could end in similar amicability. At New Year she had made a silent plea: let this be the year Jack and I get to be together for always. It seemed that it was going to come true in a matter of weeks if not days, and if that was not enough this friend of Davina's was interested in her pictures and Spike had told her about this job at *Vogue*. She smiled, her mouth running away across her face with it. She couldn't live in Paris now, there was too much to keep her here.

Back in the office she hung up the clothes ready for them to be taken back, and checked her captions against them, noting the fabric and the cut.

She was just finishing when the telephone on her desk rang and the receptionist from the front desk said, 'Miranda, there's someone waiting to see you. Will you be long?'

'No . . . Who is it?' She thought at once of Jack, a quick burst of pleasure soaring through her.

'They'll wait,' the girl said. 'OK?'

'Fine, I'll be about ten minutes,' Miranda said, thinking it was probably a designer, or a model with her portfolio of pictures, mistakenly thinking she had some influence in using her. Then she fantasised and thought it might be Jack, though he wasn't due back for four more days. She finished the last caption, tidied away the last shoe, then went to the ladies', checked her make-up and hair and went downstairs.

Sonia stood up as she came out of the lift. Miranda's heart stopped. Jack, she thought in panic; something has happened to Jack. She knew Russia was dangerous at the moment. Businessmen had been caught in gangster crossfire and killed. She had a momentary vision of Jack lying in the gutter bleeding to death.

Sonia was dressed in a dark suit with a yellow silk blouse, her glossy hair wound back, her make-up impeccable. She had an icy smile on her face.

'Miranda.' She stated her name as if she were arresting her.

'Sonia.' Miranda stared at her, trying to read in her beautiful face what she had to say to her, why she was here.

'I would like to speak to you for a few moments,' she said. 'I see there's a wine bar on the corner. It looks quite quiet, shall we go there?'

Every fibre in Miranda's body was screaming no, don't go, but she knew she had to. She forced herself to remain calm, thought frantically of Jack's warm endearments, how he loved her, wanted her. She must remain dignified, do, say nothing to antagonise his wife.

'Of course.' She smiled at the receptionist. 'Night, Clare.'

'Night,' Clare called cheerfully after them.

They walked without speaking to the corner. Miranda got to the wine bar first and opened the door for Sonia, who ushered her in. They sat down in a secluded corner.

'What will you drink?' Sonia said as the waiter hovered by them.

Miranda's mouth was dry, her throat had a huge lump in it, making it difficult to swallow. She couldn't think. 'White wine,' she said at last as it was the first thing that came to mind.

They sat in silence while they waited for it to come. Sonia made a great play of lighting up a cigarette. Miranda wished she smoked so that she would have something to do while she waited to hear what Sonia was going to say. At last their glasses of wine came. Sonia took a sip, then put down her glass and looked at Miranda intently.

'I know you're having an affair with Jack and that it is probably serious,' she said, her dark eyes pinning her to her seat.

'I love him and he loves me,' Miranda said firmly. Her mind was spinning. Had Jack told her already? Had someone seen them together, informed Sonia? They had been so careful, Jack had been so insistent that they do it his way to protect Tom and she had agreed with him. She hadn't even told her girl friends he was about to leave Sonia to live with her. She hardly ever mentioned his name to them.

'I don't care about that,' Sonia said dismissively, 'but I'm not losing him. I will not have him leaving me for you. Do you understand?' Her voice was very calm.

'What has Jack told you?' Miranda said, wondering what he'd said, how she knew.

'He has told me nothing. I've had this.' She opened her bag and took out a letter. As Miranda read it, recognising the same handwriting, the same cheap paper he had used for Maureen, she felt as if the blood was draining out of her and she would collapse.

Dear Mrs Lambert,
 Your husband is committing adultery with Miranda Farell. He spends the nights with her in her flat. Their souls are in mortal danger and you are being sinned against. The marriage vows state categorically that a man must forsake all others.
 From a well wisher.

Miranda knew who the well wisher was. Colin had destroyed them.

'Can you deny it?' Sonia asked her.

'No. But the man who sent you this is an evil, sick pervert,' she raged. 'He sends letters like this to other neighbours, causing untold trouble and misery.' She scrunched it up in a ball and threw it down, seeing suddenly the newspaper picture of Jack ringed in red that Colin had pushed through her door.

'But it's true?' Sonia persisted.

'Yes.' Miranda looked hard at her. 'I'm not a marriage breaker, Sonia. I love Jack and he loves me. I know . . .' she paused, wondering how to put it, then ploughed on, 'it is none of my business, but you've had affairs, haven't you? That must mean you're not really happy with Jack. Must mean you need something more from your life with him.' She tried to sound calm and reasonable, feeling sick and terrified inside, not knowing how to handle this terrifying situation.

'I may have affairs,' Sonia said, 'but they mean nothing. I like men, like the attention they give me, I like sex. But Jack is my husband. I don't want to lose him, I will not lose him.'

'But do you love him?' Miranda burst out.

The pause before she answered was too long. Sonia said quietly, 'In my way. But he is my husband and we have built up a life together, and I want it to stay like that.'

Miranda fought to control herself, fought to stop herself screaming what a selfish woman she was. Did she ever think of Jack and how she was using him, and their child? Did she care how he was hurt by her callous, greedy behaviour? But she did not want a scene, wanted to remain calm until Jack got back and sorted all this out. She could have killed Colin for throwing this deadly spanner into their carefully constructed plan to make everything go as smoothly and painlessly as possible.

'We must see what Jack says when he gets back,' she said levelly.

'It is you who must stop this,' Sonia said icily.

'I love him. Why should I stop it if he loves me?' She took a long drink of her wine, not knowing what else to do, feeling her emotions churning inside.

Sonia stabbed out her cigarette, took a long, cool sip of wine. Then, looking Miranda full in the face, she said firmly, 'You will stop the affair because otherwise I will tell Jack what I have kept to myself all these years.' She paused, then continued with an air of defiance, 'He is not Tom's father. He thinks he is, his mother thinks Tom is her grandson, his grandfather his great-grandson. Imagine the havoc it will cause when they find out that it is not true. That Tom is genetically nothing to do with any of them.'

Miranda could not speak. She opened her mouth a few times, but nothing came out. She could not believe the treachery of this woman.

'Jack adores Tom, the knowledge will shatter him. If you do really love him you won't want that, will you?'

Miranda found her voice. 'But Tom, how would it affect him? He dotes on Jack. You can't say these things, you are his mother. You couldn't do that to him, to the family.' She pleaded with Sonia, hearing her voice rise in panic. It was an evil lie, Sonia was desperate, making up this preposterous story to stop her taking Jack and her lifestyle from her.

'I had an affair – well, just a one-night stand really – with an American. I can tell you his name, but I won't.' Sonia watched her dispassionately. 'I got my dates a bit wrong, thought I would be safe, but I wasn't. What could I do? I was married, didn't want to lose Jack, give him up for this man who'd gone back to the States. I didn't want an abortion either. I'd had a couple already and they're not much fun.' She lit another cigarette. Miranda thought, this can't be true, it's like a terrible play, she must be making it up.

'So I told him it was his. I had a few fearful moments wondering if he would look like . . . like his father. But Tom is dark like me. You couldn't tell he wasn't Jack's, or was Jack's for that matter, could you?'

'I can't believe you could do this, Sonia.' Miranda felt defeated. She didn't want to believe her, couldn't believe anyone could do such a thing. 'You know how much Cynara loves Tom, and Jack . . .' Her voice wobbled, then she burst out, 'You couldn't do that to Jack. He adores Tom, you'll kill him. Are you sure you're not telling me this story to make me give up Jack?'

'It is true,' Sonia said, 'and if you take Jack I'll tell them all. Jack can have a test to prove it, if he doesn't believe me. I can name Tom's father. I haven't heard another word from him but he comes from an influential family in the States. I can easily track him down for a paternity test if I have to.' Her voice and face were hard, as if she didn't want to do this, and blamed Miranda for making her do it.

Sensing this Miranda tried again. 'I know you're upset, it was horrible to receive a letter like that and I'm really sorry about it. I'll give you more time, won't hassle you or Jack, but we do love each other, want to be together. But think, please, Sonia. Think how terrible this will be, what damage it will do to everyone's lives. It will ruin them. You wouldn't want that, I know you wouldn't.'

'It is all up to you, Miranda. If you tell him it's over I'll keep quiet, otherwise I'll tell him.' She shrugged, took another pull on her cigarette. 'It's in your hands.'

Miranda was stunned. She managed to say, 'I can't believe you'd do this, to your own son. Think how it would destroy him. You know how vulnerable he is.' She frowned, trying to make sense of it. 'What sort of a person could do such a thing?'

Then she saw the raw hurt on Sonia's face. She said, 'All my life the people I love have been taken away from me. My mother died when I was a child. My brother, whom I adored, fell in love with this woman and lives the other side of the world with her. I haven't seen him for years. I was seduced and let down by a man I fell in love with when I was seventeen. Two years later my father died. I will not lose Jack too.'

Miranda stared at her, seeing a deeply hurt and resentful woman. A woman who in her insecurity could not bear the men in her life to love someone else better than her. But she could not feel sorry for Sonia. All the joy and happiness she had felt these last few days, thinking of Jack and her being at last together, had gone. She thought she would never feel happy again.

'So,' Sonia said, opening her bag, taking out a five-pound note, then getting up from the table. 'Jack is back on Saturday. Tell him it is all over or I will tell him about Tom. Their happiness is all up to you now.'

She threw down the money for the drinks with contempt, as if she were paying off Miranda. She walked out of the wine bar and did not look back.

Chapter Thirty

Miranda lay on Davina's sofa, utterly spent. She felt swollen with too much crying, empty as if all life had been taken from her with Sonia's threat. It was as if an electric current that had kept her buoyant with vitality and joy had been cruelly pulled out, leaving her exhausted.

Davina sat on the floor beside her, holding her hand, sometimes stroking it, sometimes giving it little tugs to emphasise the sympathetic and positive words she was trying to comfort her with.

'Remember what a hopeless wreck I was when Ian dumped me, and how good you were to me and told me I would get over it? And I did, though I didn't believe you at the time, and now I've got Piers and I couldn't be happier.' She tugged her hand gently. 'Or I could be if he wasn't away so much in his dratted submarine.'

After Sonia had left Miranda had felt so shell-shocked she had just sat there in the corner of the wine bar as if in a catatonic trance. The waiter had finally asked her if she was all right and she felt she had to leave, get away from this place where Sonia had destroyed her life.

But where could she go? Not home where she might see Colin, who had engineered this nightmare, ruined her life. Killing him slowly would not be good enough, she thought weakly, knowing she hadn't the strength to kill a mouse, let alone a man. Then she'd thought of Davina and gone blindly there, arriving on her doorstep in a complete heap, the tears pouring down her face, incoherent with grief.

It had taken Davina a lot of careful probing to get the story out of her, but she had not told her the whole truth of Sonia's blackmail.

'It's something about Tom which will kill Jack, I can't tell you exactly what,' she sobbed, 'but I'll have to do what she says; I can't do that to him.'

Davina, who had a shrewd idea what the truth of it was, just said, 'She's a bitch, especially as she plays around. If she'd been the pure little wife waiting at home while her husband messed around, that would be different, but she's a scheming bitch. But it's you I'm worried about, Miranda. How will you tell him that it's over so that he doesn't guess his wife has engineered the whole thing and carries out her threat?'

'I don't know,' Miranda said, calmer now, 'I really don't know.' The utter pain of it all hit her again and the tears coursed down her face. 'Oh God, what can I do? We really do love each other. How can we live apart?'

'Maybe in a few months, years . . . I know that sounds awful but when Tom is older, you could be together. Or maybe once Sonia's got what she wants she'll be bored and go after someone else,' Davina said, fishing frantically round for some shred of comfort. 'It's just now, this moment, which is such hell, and it will be hell telling him, but it may work out all right in the end. You have to believe that.'

'I don't see how it can,' Miranda said. The shock of it all had subsided now into stark despair and pain. However much she railed against Sonia's threat and Colin's wickedness with his poison letters she knew she had to let Jack go. She could not destroy him with the knowledge that Tom was not his, could not break up his family and destroy Tom with such a revelation. She knew Sonia meant what she said, she'd seen the ruthless hardness in her eyes.

She spent the days with Davina leading up to Jack's return. Davina took her back to her flat to pick up some clothes. 'If I see that pervert I'll ram his religious ideals down his sanctimonious throat,' she said darkly when she arrived. But there was no sound from his flat. Once inside Miranda saw that the light on her answerphone was flickering, informing her that she had some messages. She felt the tears rise in her again and turned like a bewildered child to Davina.

Davina said, 'I'll listen to them. You go in your bedroom and pack some clothes. I promise I'll tell you who is on it and what they say.' Firmly she pushed her into her bedroom and then came back into the living room and shut the door.

There was a message from Tessa ringing for a gossip and one from her mother saying the lampshades Miranda'd ordered from a local shop were in, and there was Jack. Halfway through his message Miranda came into the room as if drawn by him.

Hearing his voice was like a drug, she thought as she curled up in a chair and listened to the voice she loved so well.

'. . . So, darling, I'll be back Saturday afternoon. I'll come straight round and be with you, then go home. I think it better to tell Sonia first. I fetch Tom from school on Sunday and I'll tell him on the way back, so, soon we'll be together. My number is . . .'

Davina had her finger over the cancel button ready to snap it off if it became too much for Miranda to bear, but Miranda motioned to her to leave it on. She copied down the telephone number, then played it through again, all the time feeling what was left of her heart splinter into painful shards, piercing the last scraps of hope that something would work out for them. She felt like a condemned prisoner, knowing that there was no way out but the gallows, and however much one might rant against it, there was no going back.

'Please,' she said to Davina, 'can you leave me a moment while I ring him?'

'Of course, if you're sure, Miranda.' She came and put her hand on her shoulder. 'Oh God, I wish I could do something. I can't bear to see you so broken by this, when that dreadful woman . . . sorry,' she bit her lip, 'I know I'm not being at all positive saying that. I know you must break up with him for the moment . . .' She squeezed her shoulder again and said, 'I'll be in the garden. Call if you need me.'

Miranda rang his number in Moscow immediately, before she lost her nerve. He answered quicker than she'd expected. She couldn't speak for a moment, hearing his voice, yearning for him.

'Darling, how are you?' He sounded cheerful, full of love.

'Listen, Jack . . . I . . .'

He sensed the pain in her at once. 'What is it? What's happened, darling? Are you all right?'

She took a deep breath, felt this would kill her, wished it would, quickly now. 'I want to see you away from the flat. I've something I want to say. It must be outdoors, I think . . .' She knew she was rambling but she had the strange feeling that telling him outside would be less painful than in the confines of a room where their pain would ricochet off from the walls, suffocating them.

'What do you want to tell me?' His voice was panicky now. 'Miranda, you must tell me now. We'll talk more on Saturday, but you must tell me now.'

There was a long silence while she fought to remain calm, fought to stop words of love, of wanting to be with him, to beg him to escape somewhere, anywhere, with her. She said in a small voice, 'I feel we ought to wait a while to be together. Tom—'

'What's happened to Tom? Has he—' There was terror in his voice.

She broke in quickly, 'No. He's fine, as far as I know, but I just feel he's still so young, needs you . . .' She swallowed a lump that felt the size of an orange in her throat. 'I feel . . . that at the moment, with his Common Entrance and all coming up, you and Sonia should stay as a family. Perhaps . . . in a few years we'll have a chance to be together.' She knew she was comforting him as well as herself, but she also knew that he must never know that Tom was not his, even when Tom was grown up. He may be his father in every way but biologically, but the knowledge that another man's seed had made the child he believed was his own would destroy him.

'Darling, we must talk about this. I mean, it's so sudden, and I thought we'd decided I'd leave Sonia, live with you.'

He was obviously shaken and she said, 'We will talk more, but, having thought seriously about it over these last few days, I do feel very strongly, darl— Jack, that Tom must come first in this. We must put our feelings aside until he is older,' she finished lamely, feeling as if she'd run a marathon with lead weights on her limbs.

There was a long silence his end while he digested her words. Then he said, 'We've talked of being together, longed for it so often, Miranda. I can't understand this sudden change. It's not . . .' his voice became hard, 'it's not because we saw that chap in Geneva, is it? That David? You don't feel life with him would be easier than with me and Tom, do you?'

'Of course not. Oh, darling, I love only you, I want to be with you.' The words poured from her and she knew she should stop them.

'Well then, what's happened to change it? Has Sonia said anything?'

His question acted like a brake on her emotions. She forced herself to say, 'No, it's just that . . . seeing other children who have been hurt by their parents splitting up, and feeling pretty awful and insecure myself because of my parents fooling around with other people, I don't think it's fair on him. I don't think we can be truly happy together knowing we might damage him for life.' She felt as if she was an actress, saying the words of a character, not wanting to say them but having to for the progress of the play.

'We'll talk about it,' he said, his voice full of sadness. 'Where shall we meet?'

'I don't know . . . Yes, why not that temple thing in Hyde Park, you know, behind the Serpentine Gallery?' They had been there once before on a long walk through the park, having been round the gallery.

'It might be raining, or snowing.'

'Then we'll go somewhere else, but let's meet there,' she said, wanting to finish this agony, yet unable to bear to let him go.

He told her the time of his flight and what time he could be there. Then he said, 'I love you. I love you more than any woman I have ever known before, remember that.' And he put down the telephone, leaving her devastated.

After a few moments there was a knock on her door and at the same moment Davina came in from the garden. She opened the door. It was Maureen.

'I . . . do hope I'm not intruding,' she said hesitantly, creeping round the door into the room. 'You'd left the front door on the latch. You haven't been here for a couple of days and I've been looking out for you.' She stood in the middle of the room, looking awkward, wringing her hands in front of her, an embarrassed smile on her face. 'I . . . I'm sorry . . .' Now seeing Miranda slumped in a chair, her face pale and drawn, she moved to go out again. 'I can see I've called at an inopportune moment. I'll come back.'

'Do stay,' Miranda said. 'What is it?'

Davina came and stood beside Miranda as if to protect her from any more bad news.

Maureen, looking nervously from one to the other, said haltingly, 'It's only about Colin.' Then, seeing Miranda and Davina's sharp look, went on, 'He sent . . .' she paused as if she were going to say something obscene, swallowed and went on, 'he sent one of his nasty letters to Audrey and Carol . . . you know.' She looked significantly at Miranda as if she didn't want to spell out in front of Davina that the two women were lesbians.

'What did he say?' Davina asked, then, seeing Maureen's surprise, said, 'It's all right. I'm an old friend of Miranda's. I know all about that pervert upstairs.'

Maureen visibly relaxed. 'These ladies . . . live together.'

'As lovers, you mean,' Davina said.

Maureen blushed. 'Well, yes. They are very nice actually,' she added as if she was surprised that gay people were nice, 'but he sent them a letter, full of terrible things . . . things from the Bible. Really, to misuse the Bible like that.' She frowned. 'I'm not religious, but I think it's dreadful.'

'So what happened?' Davina urged her on.

'Well, they weren't going to put up with it. They went straight to the police and then John and I and various other people in the area came forward. It seems he's been sending letters to lots of people, and organising catalogues, salesmen and so forth, and not just people he knows either.'

'How did they find all this out so soon?' Miranda said.

'They'd had a lot of complaints over the last couple of years. Like I said, poison letters, giving out people's names and addresses to all sorts of companies, so that they were bombarded with leaflets, letters and calls asking for appointments to measure up for the things, just as he did to us.'

'But how did they know – the people who had all these brochures coming through their letter boxes – they were a result of Colin's nastiness? One gets enough junk as it is,' Davina asked.

Miranda shivered. 'Maureen and John had them and when they told me I remembered that I'd found lots of newspapers and magazines with forms cut out in Colin's dustbin, so we know it's him. What a ghastly man he is.'

'I know. The police came and I told them all I knew. Now Colin's disappeared.'

'Been arrested?' Miranda perked up a little.

'No, but he's disappeared. Hasn't been seen since Sunday. You weren't here that night, and I was out yesterday until late so I didn't like to disturb you, but I saw your light on now, so I hope you don't mind my telling you.'

'No . . . I'm so glad he's been found out. What will happen to him?' Miranda looked at Maureen. She felt too empty and defeated to care much what happened to him, but after his letter to Sonia she felt she couldn't bear to see him again.

'The police are collecting evidence and if they find enough, which I'm sure they will, he'll be sent for trial. They know the religious group he belongs to and some firm that they run that he works at. He harassed you, didn't he? You can tell the police that, add to the evidence against him.' Maureen brightened.

Miranda could feel Davina take a breath, was certain she was about to say, 'Yes, and he sent a terrible letter to someone which will ruin so many people's lives,' so she said quickly, 'I'd rather not say much, if you don't mind, Maureen. There seems to be so much evidence without mine. You see . . . well, I was in a rather delicate position and I don't want to have to go to court and be questioned. There are too many other people involved, do you see?'

'All right,' Maureen said reluctantly, 'but the police might ask you a few questions. After all, he did live above you.'

'Then I'll answer them,' Miranda said exhaustedly. 'I'm staying with Davina for a few days. I'll leave you my number. I just hope Colin doesn't ever come back.'

'He'll be hounded off the street if he does,' Maureen said, making for the door. 'We don't want his sort here, poking his nose into our lives.'

When she'd gone Miranda said, 'I can't say anything in court about the letter to Sonia. It might get into the papers and then . . .' She trembled, said with a broken sigh, 'Well, I can't, but let's hope there's enough evidence to nail him.'

'It's terrible, sick,' Davina said. 'You hear of people, don't you, parents of murdered or missing children getting letters telling them it served them right, they deserved it, all from cranks like him? Really sick,' she shuddered. 'What a relief you're staying with me. He might come back in the night, do *anything*,' she said dramatically.

Miranda went back to her flat on the Saturday morning to tidy up and do her washing. She felt as if she were living in a sort of limbo, just passing the hours until she saw Jack that afternoon. She had kindly but firmly turned down Davina's suggestion that they spend the time until she had to meet Jack doing something, going shopping or to an exhibition, to take her mind off it. She wanted to be alone to prepare herself for the ordeal ahead.

Last night Davina had laid out, like gifts before her, her talents and the good things in her life.

'Charles Westwood is really keen on your miniatures and I know he will get in touch with you,' she said in an encouraging tone. 'Then there's that job in Paris that photographer told you about. Think of living in Paris. We'll all visit like mad. We can pop over on the train, meet for lunch,' she'd said, getting more enthusiastic by the moment, making Miranda, despite her misery, smile at her.

'Oh, love, I know this is terrible now, but think of the good things and gradually you'll get a life you'll be happy with.' Davina had hugged her. 'Hold on to that.'

Miranda thought of this now as she emptied her rubbish bins, wiped endlessly round her kitchen surfaces, picked at a splash of burnt food on her cooker. But all I want, she thought, is Jack. The rest isn't important at all. Her hopeless yearning was disturbed by a sound above her.

She felt her skin prickle. She strained her ears but there was nothing. Then just as she was about to relax, telling herself she had imagined it, it came again, the sound of something being dragged over the floor.

She felt sweat breaking out on her skin, terror tighten like a wire inside her. The noise came again, then something thumped down the stairs and she heard Colin's door open.

She picked up her mobile phone and began to dial the emergency number and opened her front door. He was in the front hall, a huge sports bag bulging beside him. He jerked up, threw her a look of terror. His face was ashen. He licked his lips, his tongue darting in and out like a reptile's.

'You were away,' he said. 'I've been watching so I can come back.'

'Come back?'

'I live here.'

'I don't want you here, nor does anyone else after what you've done.' She felt the anger rise in her, the pain of losing Jack, losing him because of Colin's letter. 'How dare you take it upon yourself to judge us?' she cried. 'How dare you spread your vile rumours around, frightening people, ruining their lives? I'm ringing the police,' she pressed one more digit on her phone, 'and they can take you away and put you with other mad people.'

'Please . . . please, don't.'

She didn't hear him at first, hearing only her anger, letting it pour out, hitting him with her accusations. Then when she paused a moment for breath she saw him, cowered like a cornered rat against the wall. She raged on, but her words were losing their fire. He was weeping.

'Don't, don't say those things, I didn't mean it. But your soul, I had to save your soul.' He squatted down, head bowed on his knees, and she suddenly couldn't bear it any more.

He was nothing, she thought, despising herself for a feeling of sympathy that crept into her. A weak, pathetic creature whose only way of making his mark on life was by terrorising vulnerable people with warnings from the Bible.

'Are you leaving?' she said firmly, wondering where he would go.

He snivelled and finally, at her insistence, said with a touch of defiance, 'I have friends. I'm going to them, they will put me up.'

'Go then and don't come back.' She marched to the front door of the small house, yanked it open, and walked out into the street so that he could pass with his bag without touching her.

She saw John sweeping up his front garden. He looked up.

'Miranda, are you all right?'

'Colin is here. He's just leaving,' she said, walking down to him, feeling safer beside him.

'Leave him to me,' John said and, brandishing his broom, he marched into her house.

She was about to call after him to leave him, he was so pathetic, when she heard John shouting, 'Get out, you miserable wretch. Leave this street, leave us alone.'

As Colin ran out, his bag got stuck in the doorway, bringing him up short. There was a cry as John either collided with him or hit him, then he was out in the street. The noise brought out some of the neighbours he had victimised and they all booed him as he slunk off down the street.

'You're safe now,' John said, smiling rather proudly at her. 'I don't think he'll come back.'

'Thank you,' she said, hearing the other neighbours congratulate John for ridding them of such a man. Miranda's anger had left her, and some of her fear. To her surprise she could only feel sorry for Colin, a misplaced creature, floundering viciously in a society he didn't fit into.

Chapter Thirty-One

London was clear and bright but cold. Jack told his driver to drop him at the Albert Hall, then take his luggage home and tell Sonia he'd called in at the office and would be home soon. He walked across Hyde Park to meet Miranda.

He felt detached, bewildered, as if he was not part of the world at all. Since her telephone call he had not known what to think. He had geared himself up to tell Sonia he was leaving her to live with and eventually marry Miranda. He had planned – being tortured by exactly what words to use, fearing the wrong approach would be devastating – what to say to Tom. He'd even planned in his head a meeting between Tom and Miranda so that Tom could see how much Miranda wanted him to live with them too. But now it seemed all this was going to change and he had lost her.

At the back of his mind was David March. Miranda had seemed so pleased to see him in that restaurant in Geneva. She hadn't spoken much about him again that evening but he felt, and now his feelings were reinforced, that she was regretting breaking up with him.

There was, he knew, no easy, painless way with divorce. He'd seen it with friends, however much they might boast that their ex-spouses were still their best friends – something in itself he found hard to understand: why, after all, divorce your best friend? Or say how their children simply loved their new partners, when he had seen the bewildered trauma in their eyes. Had Miranda realised this too, and felt that Tom could not cope with it? Or was it that she preferred to be with David, who came unencumbered with an ex-wife and a child?

As he walked over the grass towards the small temple-like building in the park, he saw Miranda sitting huddled there. She got up, paced back and forth, and then sat down again. He felt his heart would burst he wanted her so much. He felt he couldn't make his legs cover the ground quick enough to reach her, to take her in his arms and hold her and beg her not to leave him. But also he felt fear, fear that she no longer loved him and would have put up a fence of icy remoteness around her so that he could not touch her.

Then he saw that she had seen him. She sprang up and for a

moment his heart soared as he thought she would run to him, thud into his arms, laughing, kissing him and holding him as if she would never let him go. But instead she sat down again and his heart plummeted for he knew she meant what she'd said to him on the telephone.

He stood before her, hands in pockets, looking into her white, anxious, beloved face. 'Hello.'

'Hello.' She was looking at him as if she would devour him, keep him for ever, and yet he saw the firmness of her gaze, the pain in her eyes.

'How was Moscow?' she said.

'Fine.' Still he stood there looking at her, unable to move closer to her, feeling in the air and the trees around him that she was leaving him.

She looked at her slender feet in their dark stockings and black leather loafers and said, 'I want to say this quickly and then I want you to go and not look back. OK?'

'No,' he said. 'I love you, you love me. Don't you?'

'That's not the point,' she said. Her voice was ragged.

'I think it is.' He took a step forward but, seeing her involuntarily shrink into herself, he stepped back again.

'The point is . . . must be, that we cannot live together for Tom's sake. You and Sonia must keep together, keep his home for him. He has . . . adolescence and all that . . . and I'm sure,' her mouth went firm as if she was determined to convince him, convince herself, 'we are doing the right thing. I do love you. I will always love you.'

'Oh, stop it,' he cried out in pain. 'If you love me stay with me. Tom cares for you, he'll be fine with us. It may be difficult for a little while, but you are so good for him. I wouldn't chuck up my marriage, his home, for anyone else.' He clenched his fists as if he would tear these words from her, expose the love they felt for each other.

'I can't. Jack, please.' She lifted her eyes to him, imploring. His heart felt as if it was being torn from his body. He sprang forward, pulled her to her feet and into his arms, burying his face in her hair.

'I love you, I will not let you go.' He felt her relax a little into him, felt the warm curve of her body against his, felt his desire for her. He knew then there was a sliver of hope that she didn't mean what she'd said and would stay. He caressed her back, kissing her neck, feeling as if she was coming back to him like a frozen person gently thawing in the sun. Then she stiffened, pulled herself away from him. He could feel her take a deep breath as if rallying herself to break away.

'I must go,' she said calmly now, looking deep into his eyes. 'We are doing this for Tom, remember. I really feel, especially after what happened to him this summer, that I am right about this

and you, when you think about it, will know that I am. After all,' she swallowed, did not look at him while throwing out her trump card, the biggest fear he had, 'you may lose custody of him, and Sonia might keep him from you, that would be devastating for both of you.'

She was out of his arms now and he saw her standing so strong, so resolute in front of him. He could not bear it and yet she was right, they could not risk harming Tom. He could not bear to lose him.

'When he is older, after Common Entrance . . . We can't just leave like this.' He appealed to her once more, at the same time feeling the hope drain from him. Something had gone from their relationship, he thought sadly. They could not be so close again.

'I will always love you,' she said, her face like death. 'Nothing will change that. Perhaps something will happen to change things in the future, but let me go now, please.' She gave him a smile, a smile that was so brave, so full of courage and resolve it broke his heart again.

'All right. I'll let you go because you ask me to, because I love you. I will always love you. My marriage will continue to be a sham but I'll continue with it for Tom's sake, until he is older, anyway. But if ever,' he fought to be as resolute as she was, 'if ever you need me. Come to me.'

'I will.' Her eyes were bright under her tears. He put out his arms to her to comfort her, to comfort himself, but she raised her hand to ward him off, turned and walked away from him.

He stayed there a while, watching her go until she disappeared. He felt as if all the colour had gone from his life. Yet deep in his mind he wondered if perhaps she wasn't right. Tom was an extremely vulnerable child and he remembered Sonia's threat. He was sure now that she would damage Tom further, especially if she got custody, by telling him lies about Miranda and no doubt himself, turning his son against them.

He walked slowly across the grass, feeling the wind bite his face. Her decision had been such a shock to him that he hadn't thought it through properly, but the more he reflected on it now the more he suspected there was something deeper. He was certain that Sonia was behind this. There was something desperate about Miranda's plea for them to part that was unlike her. She was more rational. She had admitted, faced up to the fact that Tom might be hurt, and asked him what they could do to minimise it. They had faced and discussed the custody problem, both perhaps with more optimism than they felt, reassured each other that Tom would move freely between both parents. Yet suddenly, on the eve of Jack's leaving Sonia and coming to her, she had backed out.

He came out of the park and took a taxi home. He opened the

door and heard Sonia's music blaring from the kitchen. His suitcase stood in the hall. He closed the door, glanced through the pile of mail waiting for him on the table, but hardly saw it, then went straight into the kitchen.

Sonia, in a blue and white striped apron, was cutting up vegetables. A leg of lamb wrapped in rosemary stood on the board. She looked up when he came in and smiled.

'Oh, darling, you're back.' She wiped her hands on her apron, turned off her music and came to kiss him.

He could smell the onions and rosemary on her hands. He did not kiss her back.

'So how was the trip?' she asked brightly. 'Would you like a drink or something?'

'No . . . well, yes, I might.' He went out into the drawing room and to the drinks tray. He poured himself a whisky, telling himself it would help warm him up after his time in the park, but knowing it was for courage.

He went back into the kitchen and said, 'Have you said anything to Miranda Farell?'

He saw at once that he had hit home. She blanched, then gave a quick laugh, frowning. 'Miranda Farell?'

'You know who I mean.'

'Yes, that woman who helped Tom and who we saw in France. Why should I speak to her?' She was in command now, he saw. Busying herself with putting the vegetables in a deep dish, putting the lamb on top.

'I want to know what you said to her.' His voice was firm.

He saw her mouth clench. Her movements were fierce as she sprinkled salt and pepper on to the lamb, added some red wine. 'She is two-timing you,' she said, not looking at him. 'She has other lovers. I know because I know someone in her street. She could break up our marriage, unsettle Tom for life, then dump you for one of these other men.' She faced him now, her face hard.

'*You* have lots of lovers,' he said, raw with pain. 'You cannot point a finger at anyone else.'

'But I always come back to you. They mean nothing to me, not like you do. You know that,' she said.

'That is no excuse.' He wanted to say that Miranda loved him, only him, that they wanted to live the rest of their lives together. 'She did have a boyfriend but she gave him up for me.'

'Are you sure? Oh, darling,' her voice was light now, 'I'm sorry if she duped you. She probably just wanted a good time, was seduced by your mother's château in France. That sort of girl always falls for that sort of thing.' She had a sneer in her voice and he hated her.

'Miranda isn't like that at all,' he said. 'She is used to France, her brother lives there. We love each other. That you can't, *won't*, understand, will you?'

'If you don't believe me, I've got proof,' she said, and she went to the painted cupboard in the corner, opened a drawer and took out a letter which she handed to him.

Feeling sick with apprehension he opened it. He was not to know it was Colin's writing. It was not dated; it said:

Dear Mrs Lambert,
   Your husband has got into the clutches of this woman of sin. He is not the only man she spends the night with. She is a whore and you should be warned. In the Bible it is written, 'To be carnally minded is death.'
   From a well wisher.

Jack crushed it in his hands and threw it on the floor. 'You believe such rubbish?'

'Why else would it be sent to me?'

'It's from that man who lives in the flat above her. He's sick. I'm sure it's from him. I shall inform the police. He can't do this.'

'I'd be very careful about doing that.' Sonia's voice was quiet. 'If it gets to court all sorts of unsavoury things might come out, and think of what that will do to Tom and your mother.'

'What unsavoury things?' he demanded.

'About her, of course – how many men go to the flat . . . things like that. You know how the press love these stories, and whether it's true or not it won't look good on you. And Tom, think how he'll be bullied at school. Remember what happened last time he was bullied.' She fixed him with an iron gaze and he felt his resolve to fight to clear Miranda's name shrivel and die.

'It is not true,' he said. 'She is a wonderful girl and I love her.'

'You love her more than you love Tom?' Sonia's voice was sharp.

He turned away from her, despair and frustration surging through him. He should have known that Sonia would fight to keep him. She could not bear to be abandoned and in her fear she would be vindictive, do, say anything to keep him and their way of life.

'I wonder if she is afraid that you'll find out about her love life,' Sonia went on.

'Why should she be?' he demanded, but a sliver of uncertainty flickered inside him.

'Where there's smoke there's fire,' Sonia said, retrieving the letter and smoothing it out. 'I'd better keep this in case there is a court case against this man. Evidence, isn't it? Won't we get into trouble for destroying it?'

His pain was almost unbearable. 'You're a bitch,' he said. 'Whether I stay with you or not is not because I care for you. I do it only for Tom.' He left the kitchen and went upstairs to his study, slamming the door behind him and giving himself up to his misery.

Chapter Thirty-Two

Almost a year had passed since Miranda had parted from Jack. The pain and the emptiness without him were terrible. Her grief crouched like a silent panther in the shadows, waiting to pounce on her when she least expected it.

She found she couldn't stay in her flat – the home she had once so loved. The flat upstairs was being gutted and redecorated to be put on the market.

'Shocking state, the way some people live. Pigs live better,' the builder had informed her one morning. But she was not interested. John was treated like a hero for seeing Colin off and now that all trace of him had gone, taken over by noisy and cheerful builders, she ceased to worry about him.

She found to her despair that the ghost of Jack and their love-making upset her. She had thought that she'd find comfort remembering their rapturous times here but instead she found it reinforced his absence and she longed for a new start. To get away from London, where any moment she might see him and her resolve to stay away from him would weaken her and cause more agony. Or worse still, she might see Sonia, who would no doubt flaunt him as her trophy, knowing Miranda loved him too well to try to get him back and risk her telling him about Tom's paternity.

She kept on working, doggedly going through each day, but she was forced to tell Stella she was suffering from a broken love affair when she made some mistakes in her work.

'Don't let it ruin you life,' Stella said firmly. 'You're a great editor, should really be higher up than you are here, but,' she grinned, 'that means getting rid of me, and I'm not going. But don't let this spoil your prospects.'

But the most decisive push to get her life together came from her parents' situation. She went down one weekend about three weeks after leaving Jack. She told her parents she was suffering from a broken love affair and Julia, perhaps having learnt from going through her own trauma, offered only comfort, not interrogation. She respected Miranda's wish not to talk about it, and instead merely spoilt her with kind gestures such as breakfast in bed, nurturing her as if she were recovering from major surgery.

But, returning from the car wash, Miranda heard, as she entered the house, her father shouting: 'But you can't go away with your lover like that. It's not right. You'll be the talk of the village.'

'It'll be no worse than your behaviour. At least Peter is a respectable age,' her mother retorted.

They were in the drawing room, the doors open to the rest of the house. Their voices were so loud it was impossible not to hear every word. Miranda felt sick and unsettled at their arguing. She didn't know whether to go out again and make a great commotion coming in, or just go upstairs and leave them to get on with it.

'I can't have it,' Richard said firmly, 'it's just not on.'

'Too bad,' Julia said, with a note of triumph in her voice. 'I've always wanted to go on one of those cruises with lectures on the places we visit, and Peter and his friends have asked me to join them. Your . . .' she paused, and Miranda, still dithering in the hall, heard the sneer in her voice, 'bit on the side can wash and iron your shirts and cook for you every day. See what real life is like. I know you get round Mrs Davis, sneaking her your laundry, but I've given her time off. She'll just keep an eye on the house, not look after you.'

She came out from the drawing room, saw Miranda, and said with an air of defiance, 'There you are, darling. I was just telling your father of my holiday plans. I'm going on Friday for two weeks. I'll send you a postcard.' She began to go upstairs, saying as she went, 'I'm coming up to London on Monday to buy some new clothes. Any suggestion where I should go?'

'What sort of things do you want? I'll think . . . Where are you going?' Miranda, seeing her father standing by the door looking shell-shocked, felt the same.

'On a cruise to the Greek islands. I've always wanted to go there. I've been asked by these friends, and as your father is occupied and you children settled it's time I took some time for myself, do things I want to do.'

'Of course.' Miranda had felt rather lost at the new direction her mother was taking. She was reminded of Sonia in her fight to keep Jack at any cost. I admire it in my mother but despise it in Sonia, she thought wryly, but my mother's tactics are less destructive.

As the weekend progressed she admired her mother's more positive way of dealing with her father's affair, for seeing her father's anguish, treated by her mother as no more than the tiresome temper tantrum of a difficult child trying to spoil her fun, she was emerging the victor instead of the victim. This determination to ignore his affair and do her own thing was the only way that might bring her husband back to heel, Miranda thought, fearing that it might also work with Sonia and Jack.

'You brought it upon yourself, Daddy,' she said to Richard when he appealed to her to bring Julia to her senses. 'Why should you be allowed to have an affair and she not? Anyway, she's going with other people, not just him, so it sounds more respectable than you staying alone overnight with your Lolita,' she said impatiently.

But Julia's cruise brought everything to a head and a month later her parents were back together again. Ironically, this made Miranda decide to put her own life in order.

'We realise that we have so much – you children, our way of life – it's too good to just throw away,' Julia said to Miranda when she went down to Hampshire to lunch at their request. Sally and Marcus were there too and Miranda, seeing them exchange happy, secret smiles, felt doubly alienated from the mysterious state of marriage.

'We went through a bad patch, which was, I admit, my fault, but we've weathered it, and I hope will be stronger because of it,' her father said with a tender look at her mother. 'We're going to rethink our lives, travel, do more things together now we have more time.'

'That's a relief, isn't it, Miranda? I don't think I could have handled stepparents at my age,' Marcus said, lifting a glass to them.

Miranda, though relieved at their reunion, felt stunned by the strength of the marriage ties. Their strength may be wonderful in cases like her parents', but it showed that they could sustain Jack and Sonia against her love and she must cut loose from hoping that somehow he might come back to her. She must get on with her own life.

Urged on by Spike, she made enquiries about the job on *Vogue* in Paris. She then found out that Nicole had a friend working there who put in a word for her. Stella sent a reference and without much difficulty the job was hers.

'Good,' Nicole said, when she heard that she'd got it, 'you can come and live in Paris and fall in love with a Frenchman. Stay with us until you find somewhere of your own.'

Miranda wasn't looking for love when she still felt it so keenly for Jack. What was the point, she thought, when love from anyone else would be second rate? By the end of March she was in Paris, where the work kept her busy, finding her way around, networking with the fashion designers and shops, forcing herself to speak better French. Living with Edward and Nicole for the few weeks before she found her flat eased her into her new life. She found that the warmth of their family life helped to soothe her pain. It helped too that she'd never been in Paris with Jack so there were no memories waiting to jump out at her with unbearable melancholy.

She found another source of help too in the shape of Davina's old boss Charles Westwood. He was a man in his early sixties, round and twinkly, and she liked him at once. He was very impressed with her miniatures.

'They're exquisite,' he said. 'You have a wonderful touch, control of the brush. But,' he smiled, taking the glass from his eye, 'I want you to do more like this.' He picked up the Persian-style picture she'd interpreted in her own way. 'How are you with portraits?'

'Not very good.' She showed him one she'd done of her niece Clair, trying to capture her young, rosy complexion, her light blonde hair.

'Work on it,' he said. He explained in more depth what he wanted and now, in her spare time, of which there was a fair amount, she worked for him, motivated by his praise. There had even been a small article about her in a Sunday magazine. She wondered if Jack had seen it.

She told herself she was happy, she had a good life. The job was a challenge and she liked the people she worked with. Her old friends often came to visit her, sleeping on her sofa bed in the tiny sitting room. She became fond of the flat, which was near Sacré-Coeur, the rooms arranged in a circle. The sitting room led to the bathroom, which led to the bedroom, which led into the hall/kitchen and back into the sitting room. Her friends brought her news of London, and very occasionally she heard about Jack.

Laura, now the proud mother of a pretty little baby, Portia, had seen him at a party with his 'frightful' wife, she said. Davina cut out and sent a newspaper cutting on how well he was doing for his company, but it was Tessa who told her the most.

One weekend Tessa, leaving the children with Simon, braved the Eurostar and arrived at the flat, flushed and excited.

'Paris!' she cried, arms outstretched as if she would embrace it all. 'I can't believe it after so long of my country mouse existence. Oh, Miranda, what a darling flat. It's like being a student again. How I'd love to stay and study something, anything.' She was overcome with it all.

Miranda was thrilled to see her. It was the first time she'd seen her since she and Jack had parted, and somehow her being alone, unencumbered with her husband and children, made it feel as if they were young again. In their excitement at being together they gossiped like schoolgirls, each vying with the other to cap each piece of gossip with something better.

'I simply *must* tell you about the Gillard-Hardings,' Tessa said at last.

'How are they?' Her words brought Jack back to her, hitting her like a dash of cold water.

In her excitement Tessa didn't notice the pain in her eyes, the dulling of her exuberance.

'The baby was another girl – you know that?'

Miranda nodded.

'Well, you know I told you about Chris, the boy of all trades.' She giggled, then dropped her voice to a more sober level. 'He's very ill, people say it's Aids.'

'Oh,' Miranda said, not really interested.

'Ralph was, still is, I think, in love with him.'

'What?' Miranda now did become interested.

'They've been lovers for ages, apparently. He lived in Salisbury and they saw each other there. Chris didn't know, or didn't let on that he was HIV positive.'

'So don't tell me Ralph has it? And what about the baby?'

'The baby's fine, so is Bunny, but Ralph . . .' Tessa sighed. 'It's terrible, isn't it, this modern plague? They say he does have it. Sir Quentin is shattered, but Bunny's been marvellous over it. I know she said she'd go home to America when the child was born, but she's staying here, anyway for the moment, with him.'

'Will he die? I've read that various new drugs keep people going for a long time,' Miranda said, 'but I don't know how true that is.'

'I don't know. He's not that ill yet. He's living at Chandos Hall but it's all pretty gloomy.'

'What will happen to your cottage?'

'So far things are staying as they are. Sir Quentin could go on for years yet, so could Ralph. They might even find a cure.'

The conversation drifted to someone else they knew who had Aids.

Then Miranda could not resist asking, 'Have you seen Jack there? There was some talk of his being the heir, if everyone else dies.' She laughed awkwardly.

Tessa looked at her. She said quietly, 'I did see him once at church. I was waiting for a good moment to tell you. I don't know if you want to talk about him.' She touched her arm. 'I know you've been through hell and I'm so glad you have another life now. It was jolly brave of you to push away like this, not sit and mope at home.'

Miranda knew she was going on talking to give her a chance to decide if she wanted to hear about Jack. She said, 'Tell me, I would like to know.'

'I only saw him once. I don't know how often he comes down. As you know, tucked away as we are we can go for weeks without knowing who is at the Hall. Anyway, it was about two months ago, he was at church, he came up to me afterwards . . .' She paused.

Miranda, feeling she could hardly breathe, said, 'Go on.'

'He said good morning, talked to Henry, then, under his breath he asked how you were, did you still come down? I told him – I hope I was right, Miranda, but he did look so miserable for a moment – that you were fine, working in Paris.'

'What did he say?' Miranda had a sudden picture of him; she felt she would die wanting him.

'His wife then came up,' Tessa scowled, 'made some sickening remarks about Luke, pretending she thought him sweet. He moved away then and the moment was lost. It was too difficult to say any more to him.'

'How did he look?'

'Pretty good.' Tessa hugged her. 'I wish it had worked out for you. I know he'd have been far happier with you, and his son. Poor child, moping about, disinterested in everything.'

'So they were all there?'

'Yes, but as you can imagine all the gossip is centred on Ralph, his relationship with Chris, who's been put in a cottage, by the way, in the village, much to some people's disgust. Some of them think you can catch Aids from just walking past his window.'

When Tessa left, Miranda felt a bit deflated. She enjoyed seeing her old friends here on their own, away from their familiar circles. She felt she saw a more relaxed, independent side to them. She lurched between missing them dreadfully and feeling rather free without them. All their questions about Jack, while kindly meant, were also painful, reopening wounds that she yearned to heal. Two evenings after Tessa had left, David rang her from Geneva.

'I haven't seen you for so long, can I come for the weekend?' When she hesitated, he said, 'Don't worry, I won't push myself on you. I'd just like to see you for old times' sake.'

They met for lunch, then spent the afternoon at the Louvre. They kept their conversation light, discussing the new, to both of them, glass pyramid and layout at the Louvre; they talked about their jobs, the pictures. Neither mentioned their past affair, or Jack. When she took him back to her flat they both became suddenly shy. Miranda fussed round opening wine, spreading herb cheese on to rounds of baguette to eat with it. David kept on praising the flat, wandering restlessly round, picking up a book here, an ornament there, but after quite a few glasses of wine the atmosphere between them became easier.

'I heard where you were from Davina and Piers, when I was in London the week before last,' he said, lolling now on the sofa beside her. 'I asked after you.'

She turned her eyes to him. They were luminous for a moment, with a core of pain.

He laid his hand on her arm. 'It must be hell for you, but everyone admires you for getting away like this. Starting a new life.'

She smiled sadly. She thought, I wonder what they are all saying about me and Jack. She could imagine them, even her dearest friends, passing round gossip like a tray of sweets. Would she ever get away from it? She imagined years hence people still whispering, 'Poor Miranda, she only ever loved one man, you know. It's quite ruined her life.'

'But you enjoy your job?' he asked. 'And Paris?'

'Yes.' She drank some more wine. She felt sleepy, comfortable with him here. She leant back, a little against him, and he put his arm round her and kissed her on her mouth.

They made love gently, familiar like old friends.

Later David said, 'You must let him go, you know, before you can love again.'

'I know,' she said, her body curled round him, comfortable beside him. 'I find it so difficult. I look at the men I meet and find them wanting compared to him.'

'I see.'

'Oh, not you,' she said quickly, guiltily, knowing that she had slept with him for comfort, to feed a yearning for warmth and tenderness.

Perhaps he guessed this. She wondered if he minded, felt he had been used. She put her arm over his chest, her face in the hollow of his neck.

'Thank you,' she said, 'for being here.'

He sighed, put up a hand to stroke her hair. 'It should have worked for us, but . . .' He paused and she lifted her head to look into his face.

'But?'

He smiled, a sorrowful smile. 'People today,' he said, 'drifting, meeting, drifting again like leaves in a river.'

'Ships in the night.' She tried to sound cheerful.

'In business nowadays we never stay anywhere long enough to really have a chance to nurture a relationship. One meets so many people and some come close and then a relationship one is having with someone else is further eroded. No wonder this way of life leaves so many lonely people in its wake.'

She sat up, swinging back her hair. 'It's true. We all have too many choices, I suppose. It's no longer frowned upon to have affairs, so we have them but they too erode commitment to one person.'

'We want it all, but so often we don't realise until it is too late that we've lost what we were looking for.' He stroked her back gently with his fingertips.

She wondered if he was testing her, to see if they could get back together, make a commitment to each other. Then he said softly, 'We lost it, didn't we?'

She felt relief, then sadness. 'Yes. But I'll always be fond of you, extremely fond of you.' Then with a brittle laugh she added quickly, 'I know that sounds trite, but I mean it. I love Jack, I can't love anyone else even though I know it's hopeless. I'm very fond of you, but I don't want to use you. I care for you too much for that.'

'And I'm fond of you,' he said, 'but I do recognise that we can't make a go of it together. How wonderful it would be if we could.' He smiled at her and she felt overwhelmed with affection for him.

'We can always be friends. I'd value that,' he said.

'Friendship is tougher than love,' she said. 'I don't think it demands so much or is so easily bruised. I think it is a more generous feeling.'

'Not so possessive,' he laughed, and pulled her to him.

Their weekend was then a success with this new openness, both knowing and accepting that one part of their relationship had passed.

At the end of October Miranda went back to England for a fortnight's holiday. She first went to see her parents, who were now well settled in their 'new, improved life', as Marcus called it. Through telephone calls and letters they had kept in touch with her, but, apart from enquiring about her health, had not questioned her on Jack. Now seeing her, and perhaps recognising that the worst of her pain had healed, Julia could not resist tentatively broaching the subject.

'So he is married,' she said gently.

'Yes, he decided he must stay with his child.' Miranda did not want old wounds re-opened by her mother's dissection, however kindly meant.

'I wish he hadn't hurt you so much,' Julia took her hand, 'but I do admire him for keeping his family together.'

'Jolly sensible,' Richard said brusquely, and she saw the relief jump in his eyes.

'As you were,' Miranda said, feeling how ironic it was to commend her parents' reunion while at the same time mourning Jack and Sonia's.

Miranda braved a few more days of her mother's nonchalant questions about whether she'd met any nice Frenchmen. They were proud of her getting this new job on such a prestigious magazine as Paris *Vogue*. One in the eye, as her father had joked, for the other ladies in the church flower rota, who could only boast of the fecundity of their daughters.

All her friends wanted to see her and it was difficult fitting them all in. She had a round of dinner parties to go to and felt the time slipping past to when she must go back to Paris again.

She stayed with Davina, did not go back to her flat which she'd let since she'd moved to Paris. Unconsciously she found herself avoiding places she'd been to with Jack. Her friends pointedly did not mention him and she did not ask about him – though she felt his presence between them like a shadow over their laughter. Often, too, she found herself looking for him in the streets and in bars, yearning, yet dreading, to catch a glimpse of him.

A few days before the end of her holiday Laura and Neil persuaded her to come to a charity evening with them.

'It will be wonderful, a concert at Hampton Court, in a few of those lovely rooms. Do come,' Laura begged.

'What do I wear? I've nothing smart,' Miranda said, having left most of her clothes in Paris.

'It's black tie. Shall I lend you something?' Laura said. 'Since Portia's birth I've put on pounds, but you're still so sickeningly slim,' she said with affection.

Miranda borrowed a deceptively simple blue dress from her.

'You look sensational,' Laura said. 'It never, ever, even at my thinnest phase, looked that good on me.'

Their party consisted of other friends too. They all planned to meet there, and Miranda went with Laura and Neil.

Hampton Court was teeming with smartly dressed people. Miranda looked round, thinking how beautiful it was, how perfect the palace was for such a gathering. She saw James Darby, who greeted her with delight. 'Wow, Miranda, you look fantastic. Paris must suit you,' he said, taking her arm and leading her to the bar. 'Have a drink, then we'll go on the wander. I want to see who's here and you can tell me about your new life.'

She took a glass of champagne and together they wandered through the beautiful rooms opened for the evening. They left one room and were about to enter another when Miranda heard Sonia's commanding voice, speaking as if she was on the stage.

'So the title looks like falling to Jack, and we have a son so it will go on to him too.'

Mesmerised by her voice, Miranda went on into the room. A group of people were sitting close to her, their chairs pulled up in a semicircle. Sonia was holding court.

'It will mean having to rethink Tom's upbringing, of course,' she continued. 'I'm determined to groom him to make sure he knows his responsibilities. It is a very old family, after all, and the estate, though rather run down at the moment, is very large.'

She looked up and saw Miranda standing there, staring at her. There was no doubt in either of their minds that both knew that she had heard every word.

Miranda glanced quickly through the group but Jack was not there. She looked back at Sonia, seeing the horror in her eyes.

261

Someone said, 'So you said that the old baronet wants to make Jack his heir just because you have a son and he can see that the line will go on for another generation?'

Miranda watched Sonia, challenging her to answer. If she denied that Tom was Jack's son, would Sir Quentin block the inheritance? Was he able to by law? She did not know but as she stood there in the magnificent room she felt calm, a power come over her. She knew enough about Sonia's ruthless determination to go for the main trick. Her son could be the heir to a baronetcy; she would not give up that in a hurry.

She smiled, a sudden joy touching the dull ache of pain she'd carried with her for so long. Sonia would never tell Jack about Tom now. Jack would be spared the torture of that.

'Hi, Sonia. So you'll be a lady, my dear.' James went forward and kissed her extravagantly. 'I can hardly wait.'

Sonia gave him a deadly look.

James didn't seem to notice, but went back to Miranda saying, 'Come on. The concert will start any minute. We ought to find the rest of the party.' He took her arm and forcibly steered her out of the room and back the way they had come. 'Poor you,' he said. 'Do you want to see her husband? I heard you'd broken up; it will be damned awkward for you.'

'Do you think he's here?' she said, her eyes searching the crowd for him.

'I don't know. He may have left her, for all I know. She's having an affair with someone from my office. He's besotted, poor sod. I did warn him. Been there, done that, as have half of London, I said. But he wouldn't listen to me.'

'*Has* Jack left her?' She turned to him, tugged on his arm.

He thought a moment. 'Well no, I suppose he hasn't if she's talking about him inheriting a title. Shouldn't think she'd miss out on that, do you? Perhaps he doesn't know she's having an affair. Perhaps he doesn't care.'

Before she could ask him any more questions they were whisked up by their party and they all went into the room for the concert.

Miranda searched the crowd for Jack, but she did not see him. She could hardly listen to the music she was so agitated, wondering if she would see him, if he could see her, if he was here at all. Not until the very end, as they were all leaving, streaming out to their cars in the dark, did she see him. He was with Sonia and some other people. He looked the same, perhaps a little drawn. She felt overcome with love for him. She had a desperate need to touch him, to speak to him, to know if he still loved her as she did him. He did not see her. She started, heart pounding; she may even have called out his name but in the noise and muddle of people leaving, no one heard her.

As the audience walked through the cloisters and the courtyards in a body to go to the car park outside the gardens, Miranda found herself walking fast, trying to get closer to him. There were so many people it was impossible. She saw his head, then it disappeared, swallowed up in the crowd.

James caught up with her. 'What's the rush?'

'I've just seen Jack. I . . . I'd so like to see him, see how he is,' she said, having glimpsed him, now overcome with a desperation to make contact with him again, even if it was only for a second.

'Are you sure that's a good idea?' he said, and when she nodded he took her arm and steered her quickly though the crowd. They reached the garden and on out through the gate to the fields beyond, where the cars were parked. It was dark and there were so many people struggling over the uneven grass looking for their cars. Miranda thought she saw Sonia but then she'd gone.

'We've lost him,' she said desperately. 'I can't see him, can you?'

'It's damned difficult, light's not good, sorry, Miranda.' James squeezed her arm. 'Can't you ring him?'

'I don't think so,' she said, feeling drained and defeated. If only she had caught up with him. If only they had seen, talked to each other, except what would that have achieved? Probably just more pain.

'Hang on. Where are you two rushing to?' Laura and Neil reached them.

'I'll tell you tomorrow,' Miranda said, feeling too dispirited to go into it now.

'Are you two going back together?' There was a gleam of amusement in Laura's eyes.

'Yes, we can,' James said.

'Shall I give you a key?' Laura said. Miranda was staying with them for the night.

Miranda, knowing that Laura was hoping that she and James had suddenly decided, after all this time, to become an item, said, 'No, he only lives round the corner, we'll be back as soon as you are.'

'Or sooner,' James said, steering her to his car.

On their way back James asked, 'So I take it you still love Jack?'

'Yes, but . . . well, as you know he's married and has a child to consider. Tom's a very vulnerable child and . . .' She wished she could confide in James, tell him everything about the situation, but she was so afraid of Jack ever hearing even a hint that Tom was not his that she forced herself to say nothing.

'It can't be much of a marriage if she has to have affairs all the time,' James said. 'I mean,' he coughed awkwardly, 'there's nothing wrong with him, I take it, in the bed department?'

'No, not at all.' She felt a sudden rush of desire for Jack.

263

'I think she's a highly mixed-up woman, looking everywhere for love when all the time it was probably there in her own backyard. I bet Jack did love her once, would still if she'd behaved.'

'Maybe.' Miranda didn't want to think of that. She felt a wedge of resentment hammer through her. Sonia looked like having it all: affairs, a child and Jack. Even though she'd heard Sonia boasting about her son being the heir to the baronetcy, there wasn't anything Miranda could do about it. The title would surely make Sonia hang on to Jack even harder.

Chapter Thirty-Three

Tessa rang Miranda at Laura's house the following morning. She sounded forceful. 'You simply must come for the weekend. Or at least for a day, before you go back. You can't return to Paris without seeing us.'

Miranda laughed. 'You do sound bossy, Tess. I don't know if I can. You know I'd love to but I've so much to do.'

'I insist. You can't come over without seeing us, your best mates and your godson,' Tessa went on. 'I was so disappointed not to get up to see you last week.'

'But you said you'd come up on Saturday,' Miranda reminded her. The plan had been vague, but they'd arranged to meet somehow.

'I can't, I want you to come here,' Tessa went on, then hurriedly explained something complicated about the baby's inoculations and not being able to leave him.

'I'll try, but I must go back Sunday, I've got to work on Monday. It's getting close to the Paris collections – no sleep for two weeks, I'm told.'

'Come tomorrow, go back Saturday. You simply must,' Tessa insisted.

Miranda had a sudden urge to go back to Chandos Hall, even if she stayed in Tessa and Simon's cottage and never saw Chandos Hall itself at all. She wanted to be back where Jack had been, feel the ghost of him, of them, together there. She knew it would hurt, but somehow having glimpsed him last night she yearned to be somewhere close to him again. She also felt it may help her to lay their affair to rest once and for all. She fetched her diary and saw that by jiggling things round she could get down on Friday afternoon, stay until Saturday and return to London that night ready to drive to Paris on Sunday.

'You ought to come over more often,' Laura said, picking up Portia, who sat placidly on the floor, to take her up for her rest.

'I know. I do miss you all, but, well . . . it's better I'm in Paris for the moment and I do enjoy it. I'm making a few friends through Nicole and Edward and the people I work with are fun.' She gave her a quick smile.

She had not slept at all well last night, wondering and worrying if she should ring Jack and what reaction she would get, *if* he wanted to see her at all. Surely, she'd wondered stupidly, if he still loved her he couldn't have helped but feel her urgent demand for him to turn round, stop, so she could catch him up? She felt wrung out and agitated. She had got up late and, having listened to Laura's ecstatic praise of Portia's progress – no other baby had ever been so intelligent – hadn't yet got round to telling her about seeing Sonia and Jack at the concert.

Laura, balancing her child on her hip, gave her a searching look. 'How long will you escape for?'

'I'm enjoying it, it's a challenge and—' The call of the telephone interrupted her. Laura went and answered it.

'Yes, she is here, who shall I say it is?' She eyed Miranda. Miranda felt a lurch in her stomach. Only her friends and family knew she was with Laura today and Laura knew all of them, so who could it be? Laura put down the receiver, tiptoed closer to Miranda as if the caller could hear, Portia clinging to her like a limpet. She whispered, her eyes wide, 'It's Sonia Lambert. Shall I say you're out?'

'Sonia?' Miranda felt a thudding panic. How had she found her here? Had she told Jack that she'd seen her at Hampton Court last night? Her first instinct was to say she was out, could not speak to her, but then she thought of last night and the remark she'd overheard, and Jack.

Slowly she went to the telephone and picked up the receiver. 'Hello.'

'We must speak. Where are you now?' Sonia said sharply.

'I'm with a friend.'

'I know, I got your number from James, I meant where exactly?'

The tone of her voice irritated Miranda. She said, 'I can't see that it's any of your business. Why should we meet?'

There was a short pause, then Sonia said defiantly, 'It's what you overheard last night. You shouldn't take it literally, you know.'

Laura, though looking fascinated, was forced to leave the room with Portia, who had started wailing.

Miranda sat down on a kitchen chair and said carefully, 'I think you're contemptible, Sonia, using your son as you do. First you tell me he's not Jack's, now that there may be a title and estate involved you say that he is. You can't have it both ways.'

'I need to talk to you. Where can we meet?' Sonia insisted.

Miranda did not want to see her, but the pain she had suffered over giving up Jack, the unfairness she felt in Sonia's manipulation of them all, surged through her.

'Holland Park, by the Orangery,' she said curtly. Laura's house was close by.

'In half an hour?'

'Fine.' Miranda put down the phone, her thoughts and emotions whirling. She yearned to know how Jack was. She had thought she had come to terms with the situation, could just about live with the pain of his loss. But since seeing him last night she knew her love for him, her hope of some sort of life with him, hadn't died. Part of the reason for going back to Chandos Hall was to try to recapture some memories of him. She knew with a sudden clarity what it was she'd been trying to hide all these months: that she was still waiting for him, giving up any chance of love with someone else in the impossible hope that he would come back to her.

'So, do tell.' Laura came back into the room and saw her sitting at the table, head in hands, lost in thought. 'What does she want? Is Jack after you?'

Briefly Miranda told her about the night before. She didn't tell her, hadn't told anyone, that Sonia had insisted that Jack was not Tom's father. 'She'll hold on to him in case he gets the title, but old Sir Quentin may go on for another twenty years, and some of the treatment for Aids now gives people a long life, and a cure might be found for it. She may have to wait for ever,' she finished.

'She's such a selfish woman,' Laura said, pulling up a chair at the table beside Miranda. It was littered with the remains of their meal: breakfast cereal packets, marmalade, toast and a plate of parma ham and salad.

Laura poured them both some more coffee. 'I would fight to the death if anyone tried to get Neil,' she looked fierce, 'but Sonia doesn't deserve a decent husband, the way she treats him. Her affairs are common knowledge. I must say I don't know why he stays with her.'

'It's Tom.'

'Of course, you told me about him, poor child. But she can't use that to mask her outrageous behaviour and blackmail Jack to stay with her.' Laura went on at some length about both people in a marriage having to work hard at it.

When Miranda left for the park to meet Sonia, spurred on by Laura's strident opinions on fairness and consideration in a relationship, she felt strongly that she was in the right. She had not snatched Jack away from the warm stability of a good marriage. Sonia had had her chance with Jack but had squandered their love with her affairs and had forfeited her rights to him.

She marched into the park and made her way to the Orangery. She was determined to fight back, to have it out once and for all with Sonia. She hadn't really thought about what sort of relationship she and Jack would have. She'd made her new life in Paris and couldn't suddenly give it up, and no doubt with his job, Tom's school and all, Jack couldn't suddenly up sticks and come to live with her in Paris. But if he still wanted her they would manage something. She felt buoyant for the first time in ages.

Mothers and nannies pushed prams, small children and dogs ran about on the grass, a shabbily dressed man with a bottle beside him snoozed on a bench. Then she saw Sonia walking restlessly up and down. She was dressed in a pale brown tweed jacket with a blue thread running though it, matched by a shirt in the same blue and a tan skirt. Her dark hair was swept back, she looked beautiful. She turned at once, saw Miranda and came over to her.

'Where shall we go where we can't be overheard?' she said briskly.

'I doubt anyone will listen to us if we walk,' Miranda said, feeling she wanted to keep on moving.

Sonia looked quickly round at the children and the tramps; no one seemed to be interested in them. 'OK.' She started walking through the park and Miranda kept up with her.

'I was a bit silly last night,' Sonia said defiantly, 'boasting about this title. We might never get it. Quentin looks as if he'll go on for ever, the old bugger. It's as if this business with Ralph has made him determined not to die himself, hold on to everything. He might even marry again, father more sons.'

'I rather doubt it,' Miranda said, 'but it is true it's not exactly going to fall into your lap.' She almost said Jack may die first but the thought was so awful to contemplate that she didn't. She felt suddenly ill, as if thinking it would precipitate his sudden demise. She said fiercely, 'I love Jack and he loves me. I cannot bear the way you treat him, this sort of dog-in-the-manger business. You may not want him, really want to stay with him and stop having lovers, but you're too selfish to let him go, give us a chance to be together.'

'He's my husband. We love each other in our own way.'

'You don't,' Miranda said. 'He doesn't want an unfaithful wife. You're just greedy, you want it all, but worst of all,' her voice was hard, hard after all the pain she had suffered these last months, 'you lie about his son, using him to get what you want.'

Sonia stopped. 'He may not be his son,' she said, 'I meant what I said: I'll tell him if he leaves me for you.' There was a tinge of desperation in her voice, her shoulders sagged. 'He is everything to me, he must stay with me. Whatever you've heard, he wants to stay with me.' She looked into Miranda's face, her eyes wide, gullible like a child's.

To her annoyance Miranda felt a prickle of pity for her. She remembered Jack saying how spoilt Sonia was, almost using it as an excuse for her behaviour. It was true, she was just like an adolescent, pushing, pushing all the time for attention, for love. She remembered what James had said, how some women craved love all the time, but perhaps were incapable of giving it back, or seeing that it was there all the time at their feet, they were too busy trampling over it in their greedy desire to get more.

'I do love him, and I need him,' Sonia said, her voice quiet now, almost pleading.

'You should stay faithful to him and not tell such lies about his son,' Miranda said, but the fire had gone from her voice. She had come here ready to fight the bitch of a woman who treated her husband with such contempt and had found instead a lost, sad child-woman who, through some strange aberration, was incapable of giving love. But why, she thought, should Jack continue to suffer for this? Why should she make his life such hell, when he could be happy with her?

She turned away, such anguish in her heart. It would be so easy to go with Jack, be part of the breakup of his family if Sonia was a wicked woman. But she was not, only a sad, insecure one, though destructive all the same.

'How is Jack?' she said.

'Fine.' Sonia's voice was hard.

'And Tom?'

'Struggling at school.'

'But he is well?'

'Of course. Why wouldn't he be? His father and I are good parents to him.' She was on the defensive now.

'Whose son is he?' Miranda turned back and confronted her. 'If he's not Jack's will you still pass him off as the last heir to Chandos Hall? Might his real father not come back and claim him? Some men are not good with babies but get quite possessive when they see a grown-up child, especially such a good-looking one and a son.'

Sonia looked uncomfortable. Her eyes skittered away from Miranda's steady gaze. She said in a small voice, 'He probably is Jack's. Anyway, what does the moment of conception mean compared to a lifetime of bringing him up? Jack is his father in all the important ways.'

'They may not work legally, for inheritance. You can't keep making up such damning stories just to get your own way,' Miranda said as fiercely as she could. To her dismay she found her determination to win Jack, should he still want her, waning. It wasn't that she didn't want him, had stopped loving him, but she realised with sickening pain that Sonia was more to be pitied than hated. But why should Jack suffer, and Tom too from this woman's insecurities? She suddenly felt very weary and wished she was back in Paris, living her new life that was so easy, so uncomplicated without all of this.

Laura had asked her when she would stop escaping and she realised that it wouldn't be for a long, long time. If only the situation was as cut and dried as Laura, and indeed she, had thought it was, with Sonia as a hateful woman, purposefully cheating on her long-suffering husband and not loving him. Over the last months Miranda had been helped by the spectre of Sonia's treachery as the whole cause of why she and Jack could not be together, absolving her of all guilt at breaking up the family. But now Miranda saw Sonia as she really was: a sad, disturbed person on an endless search for love, with Jack being the nearest she'd get to it.

Sonia looked at her. There were traces of tears in her eyes. 'You have everything,' she said quietly, 'a wonderful job, you're beautiful, kind, easy to love, surely you can find another man.'

'I don't want anyone else.' Miranda didn't look at her. She let her eyes run over the park, took in the children on the swings, the trees with their fading leaves blowing down in the wind. She felt the deep, bitter pain of loss seep through her, pushing itself into every corner of her being.

She heard Sonia say, 'He will be happy with me, with us. Ever since you finished with him he's been relieved that you made the decision.'

Miranda looked at her sharply. '*You* made the decision for us,' she said. 'I would never have finished it if you hadn't blackmailed me with that story about Jack not being Tom's father. You know I love him too much to hurt him so, hurt his mother and grandfather. But when I heard what you said last night . . .' She felt the full force of her pain and anger come back to her. 'Sonia, I can't go on with this charade. I think Jack should make up his own mind on what to do,' she said, wishing so much that he was here. She couldn't stop the tiny fear that festered inside her that maybe Sonia spoke the truth and he had been glad that she had finished their affair, afraid that what she'd said about upsetting Tom would be true. He had, after all, made no attempt to make her change her mind, get in touch with her. What was the point, she thought dejectedly, of fighting for him if he didn't want her after all?

'He has made up his mind,' Sonia said. 'Since this . . . this thing at Chandos Hall, he must stay close to Tom, teach him his responsibility.' She did not look at Miranda.

'I thought you were going to do that,' Miranda said. She wanted to get away, go back at once to Paris, leave all this behind. Even if Jack did love her, did want to be with her, she thought, we'd have to put up with all of this. She imagined frantic telephone calls and constant hounding from Sonia, ruining any life they might snatch together.

'Tom needs us both.'

'You should have thought of that before you started on all your affairs,' she said. 'I'm leaving, I've had enough of all this. You're just a selfish child really, destroying everyone who loved you. I suggest you get help before you muck up your son's life.'

'I'm not mad,' Sonia said angrily. 'You just keep away from us, leave Jack alone.'

Miranda walked away from her, feeling tears clutching at her throat. She wished she hadn't come. How foolish she'd been to let this woman get to her. If only she'd caught up with Jack last night, seen for herself how he felt about her. For one mad second she thought she'd ring him, tell him she'd been at Hampton Court, seen him there, but then she thought it would only make it worse. She heard Sonia call after her, she broke into a run, ran out of the park and along the road to Laura's house.

Laura, seeing her face, just offered her some tea, 'or coffee and brandy, or just brandy?' she said.

'I'll start with tea, thanks,' Miranda said, throwing herself down on the sofa, utterly exhausted.

Laura made some tea and brought it into the drawing room on a tray with some biscuits. Miranda knew she was longing to hear what had happened, but she said nothing, poured her tea, and put a biscuit into Portia's hand.

'Don't get it all over the carpet,' she said, then scooped her up and put her on her lap. 'She wouldn't sleep, just cried all afternoon,' she said with a sigh. 'I hope we'll have a peaceful evening.'

Miranda drank two cups of tea, mechanically answered Laura's comments about Portia. She felt utterly spent and empty.

At last she said, 'I've got to face up to it, I can't have Jack, however much I want him. I can't have him.'

'Why? Does he want to stay with her? Even after all her affairs?' Laura looked incredulous.

'I don't know, but Sonia's one of those . . . oh, it sounds so ridiculous, I don't know how to explain it. Those sort of people who can't settle, flutter here and there looking for something that doesn't exist. I don't think she can help having affairs.'

'Oh, nonsense, Miranda,' Laura said. 'What psychological rubbish have you been fed? She's got a fabulous husband and a child and she rushes off having affairs, making the excuse that she can't help it. Oh, Miranda,' she said sadly, 'don't be fooled by that garbage.'

'I know it sounds mad. I've hated her all these months I've been without Jack. I thought . . .' she paused, remembering Laura didn't know it all, 'after something she said last night, that everything would be all right. If Jack still loved me we could be together. I went to the park hating her, determined to get him, but when I saw her . . .' She chewed on her lip. 'Oh, it sounds stupid, but I felt sorry for her. She's like a child craving for love, only she'll never know when she finds it.'

'She's miles past being a child. I suggest she grows up fast and stops manipulating people like this,' Laura said crossly. 'You're too kind, Miranda. If I'd been there she'd have found love, all right, the selfish bitch. No one takes responsibility for their actions any more. It's always someone else's fault, or some tragic flaw in oneself that one can't possibly help, so everyone must be understanding, condoning these people as they destroy everyone in their way.'

'I know it seems like that,' Miranda said weakly. 'If Jack came to live with me she'd torture me with those huge, hurt eyes and desperate begging to let him go. She'd bother Tom with lies too, or make him think I'm the only reason she's so hurt, and that might send him off again . . .' She trailed off, feeling devastated at the scenario now laid out before her.

'You deserve him, you'll make them both happy,' Laura said fiercely. 'Why should these dysfunctional people go on wrecking people's lives? For whatever happens she'll wreck Tom's, and he in his turn will muck up some poor woman's life and no doubt his children,' she sighed heavily, 'so on it goes. But someone like you could stop it, give Tom and Jack stability and happiness.'

Miranda agreed with her but she couldn't say any more. It had been such a wonderful affair but if she was honest things had been against them from the start: the marriage, Tom's vulnerability, his attempted suicide. And all Jack's family – his mother, stepfather and grandfather – all their lives would be affected if Jack left Sonia and took up with her. They may blame her, though she felt that Cynara was on her side, but that too would make its own problems.

She thought longingly of Paris. Somehow she felt free there. Apart from Nicole and Edward there was no family to worry her and although she loved and missed her friends, they were not there to urge her into marriage, or commiserate or pass comments on her love for Jack.

'Do you remember *Swan Lake* – the night Portia was born?' Miranda said suddenly.

Laura laughed. 'Could I ever forget it? Wasn't it terrifying?'

'It was Odette, Odile, dancing on her own. I feel like that, quite happy, complete, on my own.' She said it musingly as if she didn't really mean to say it out loud.

'That sounds so sad. Oh, love, don't let this get you down,' Laura said, rising from her chair and coming to sit beside her on the sofa. Portia, still in her arms, made a grab for Miranda's gold chain, her hands sticky with biscuit crumbs.

'If I can accept now that it is over I'll have a chance, if I want it, to meet someone else,' she said. 'Up till now I've measured every poor man I've met against Jack.'

'What's wrong with that? I'd do it with Neil if I lost him. That's what loving one person is, otherwise why not have a string of lovers, ring the changes?' She untangled Portia's fingers from Miranda's chain and wiped them on a none-too-clean handkerchief from her pocket. 'That woman's unhinged you. Ring Jack now. Go on, ring him, then make your decision.'

'I can't.'

'Why not? Are you going to ruin your life, his life and Tom's by just listening to her side? The side of a raving nympho by the sound of it. You must discuss it with him for all your sakes.'

'I finished with him, remember. That's why I went to Paris.'

'If you'd really finished with him why were you in such a fuss after seeing him last night? Why did you go to see Sonia?' Laura demanded.

She went on at some length and finally, in exasperation, Miranda rang Jack. Her whole body seemed to home in on the telephone, waiting for the sound of his voice.

A woman answered and she asked for him. Her mouth was dry and she could barely get the words out, so deep was her longing for him.

'Mr Lambert has left the office for the day. Can I take a message?' the cheerful voice replied.

'No thank you, it's not important,' Miranda forced herself to say, feeling swamped with disappointment and despair.

Chapter Thirty-Four

Miranda didn't want to go down to Tessa and Simon. She wanted to pack up and head back to Paris, to sanity and an uncomplicated life. The Paris collections were about to start and she was looking forward to them. She and her other colleagues had to cover the shows all day, marking off the clothes they wanted to photograph, then spend as long as it took all night photographing the clothes in the studio. It was, by all accounts, very exhausting, but she would welcome it gladly as balm to soothe her raging heart.

It was as well, she told herself, that Jack had not been in his office. Sonia had rung her again at Laura's, but Miranda had anticipated this and told Laura to say she'd gone back to Paris.

'Don't say anything else,' she said firmly, not wanting Laura to stir it up further with giving Sonia a piece of her mind.

'Why so glum?' Tessa said a few minutes after greeting her. 'Got that going-back-to-school feeling? Don't leave us then, stay here.'

Miranda smiled. 'I'm fine, just a bit weary. I seem to have done so much these last couple of weeks.' She didn't want to hurt Tessa's feelings and admit that she longed to go back to Paris. Her new life there seemed suddenly so attractive, so exciting, free from the rather claustrophobic life in London, with everyone knowing what everyone else was doing, and all the advice she'd been given by her friends. It had been kindly meant, she knew, but just because they were all happily married with babies, it didn't mean she wanted to be too. There was none of this in Paris, the people she'd met there were interested in her for what she was.

They sat together, having a drink, waiting for Simon to come home from London. Henry was in his pyjamas having a very noisy and destructive game with various toys in the corner of the room.

'Henry, I can't stand any more of this. You'll have to go to bed,' Tessa kept saying exhaustedly from the sofa.

'I'm waiting for Dad,' he said before pulverising some unfortunate toy into the carpet.

'It's television, I'm afraid,' Tessa said, seeing Miranda flinch. 'It's all so loud and violent, I'm trying to stop him watching it.'

'You can't,' Henry said mildly, staging a spectacular car crash over the edge of a table.

Miranda felt her head pounding. She longed to get away, go outside into the cold, fresh air. She was about to get up and go when Simon appeared. Henry threw himself at his legs and she could only sit there, smiling at them weakly.

'I'm sorry to desert you but I'm off shooting tomorrow,' Simon said to her at dinner.

'At the Hall?' Miranda vaguely wondered if Jack would come down for the shoot.

'No, there's nothing like that there now,' Simon said. 'It's very quiet there. Everyone's a bit shell-shocked with the events, or to be truthful,' he gave her a shrewd glance, 'I think there's a lot of ignorance about Aids and the old boy thinks, probably rightly, that no one will want to come here now, so he never organises anything.'

'That's sad. How are the children, and Bunny?' Miranda felt she must go on talking to stop the feeling that everything to do with Jack was closing down, coming to an end.

'Fine. I do see them from time to time,' Tessa said. 'I don't know how long they'll stay. I have them here sometimes. Bunny and I are becoming quite good friends.'

The conversation continued but there was no mention at all of Jack. Miranda, who had been gearing herself up for yet another explanation to a friend as to why their relationship could not work, was relieved. Perhaps, she supposed, Tessa thought that any mention of him would too hurtful. Well, tomorrow there'd be time for gossip, tonight she was too tired.

She was woken in the night by the baby crying, then later by Simon leaving for his shooting. She heard the car drive away and settled back to sleep, but she was disturbed by her door opening and looking up she saw Henry peeping round at her.

'Did you wake up when Luke cried in the night?' he asked her solemnly.

'Yes, and now by you. Henry, can't I sleep, please?' she begged him.

'If you want,' he said, coming in and walking over to the window, pulling back the curtain and looking out.

'Henry, be a good boy and leave me for a little while longer,' Miranda begged, looking at her clock which said twenty past eight.

Henry hummed to himself, still looking out of the window. Then he suddenly became animated and said, 'There's that man,' and ran out of her room and down the stairs, leaving her door open.

Luke then began to howl, she heard Henry chanting something and Tessa snap at him. With a deep sigh, Miranda heaved herself out of bed and went to the bathroom. When she came out she found Henry in her room.

'Come down now,' he said, 'it's important.'

'Is something the matter? Have I time to get dressed first?' She made for the door, wondering if Tessa needed her.

Henry whizzed past her, shrieked, 'Mum, must she get dressed first?'

Miranda heard Tessa call back, 'Yes. You come down here and leave her in peace, Henry.'

Miranda dressed quickly, wondering what could be so important. Perhaps it was just Henry exaggerating. She pulled on her jeans and a pale yellow polo-necked jersey, brushed her hair and went downstairs to the kitchen.

Tessa was feeding Luke. She looked rather agitated.

'Are you all right? Henry said it was important,' Miranda said to her. Luke was eating and grizzling at the same time. He kept trying to get out of his chair, but when Tessa lifted him out he whined to go in again.

Tessa gave her an agonised look, chewed her lip. 'Miranda, I don't know if I've done the right thing. You seemed so tired yesterday. I meant to come up earlier and explain, but Luke is so fractious with his inoculations and, well, it's about Jack . . .'

'Jack?'

'He's here, next door with Henry. He insisted on seeing you. I'm sorry, I should have warned you but . . .' She looked agonised.

Miranda stood there in the warm, untidy kitchen, feeling completely numb.

'I shouldn't have let him come without asking you, but he rang me on Thursday and insisted that I get you down here. He said I was to say nothing to you in case you wouldn't come and . . .' Her voice went on and on but Miranda ceased to listen to it for Jack, preceded by Henry who was pretending to be some sort of screeching space craft, stood in the doorway looking at her.

'Miranda, I just had to see you,' he said, or she thought she heard him say over Henry's noise.

Tessa came over and took her arm. 'Go in the drawing room, or out for a walk. You can't hear yourselves think here.'

Miranda fought to pull herself together, but Jack took charge. He strode across the room and took her hand. 'Let's go,' he said, tugging at her.

'I can't,' she said, but she felt her legs moving with his.

'Have you a jacket? It's cold,' he said, and Tessa thrust one of hers at him and he pulled it round Miranda. In a moment they were outside the cottage and with his arm in hers he marched her away from it towards the Hall.

'How can she live with that chaos?' he said, and when she didn't answer he went on, 'I heard from James Darby that you were at Hampton Court. I wish I'd seen you.'

'Did he ring you?' She felt a flicker of annoyance as if all her friends were pecking at her life like inquisitive chickens.

'Yes. I understand you saw Sonia. She rang him to find out where you were. I didn't even know you'd come back.' He looked at her keenly. 'God, I've missed you. How are you? You look wonderful.'

'I'm going back tomorrow,' she said, not looking at him. 'I have my life there now.'

'Does that mean that you don't want me in your life?' His voice was ragged with pain. It smote at her heart. 'Do you? Tell me, Miranda.' He stopped, faced her, pulled her to face him. 'Tell me now.'

She forced herself to look into his face, the face she loved so. It was drawn, paler than she remembered. 'I can't,' she said, 'you know I can't.'

'Why not? Have you someone else?'

For a moment she thought it would be easier to say yes, she had, but she couldn't lie to him. 'I saw Sonia yesterday, as you know,' she said. 'James seems to have got very involved in this.'

'He thought I should know that she wanted to see you,' Jack broke in. 'It was embarrassing, him having an affair with Sonia and all, but he's fond of you and he thought it unfair that Sonia should hassle you. He said . . .' Jack paused, looked searchingly at her, 'that you were frantic to see me at the concert and how you tried so hard to catch up with me.'

She looked away from him. He let go of her and said gently, 'He said it was obvious that you were still in love with me and he felt you needed a break and that if I wanted to see you, I should get on with it as you were about to go back to Paris.'

'It won't work,' she said dully, 'we can't be together. We must accept that.' She looked away from him and saw through the golden leaves the towers and roof of Chandos Hall, magical through the mist of the autumn morning.

'Tom understands. I've talked to him about it,' Jack said. 'He's made friends at school now, he's not doing that well academically, but he's good at games, and art, thanks to you. He's much happier.'

Her heart ached. She felt it would break but she thought, I'll have to get used to it. She moved away from him, feeling the chill of the morning air on her face, and deep inside her. 'It's Sonia,' she said quietly. 'I've hated her for hurting you. All these months that has kept me going in a way, but when I saw her yesterday I saw what a lost person she was, how she needs you.'

'Oh, darling.' He snatched at her hands, pulled her to face him again. 'She puts that on. She wants it all, don't you see – me, Tom, affairs, this place?' He jerked his head towards the Hall. 'She's like a spoilt child, but I've had enough. I've left her.'

She stared at him, seeing the taut line of his jaw, the grim glint in his eyes. 'I've had enough,' he repeated, 'being tortured by her affairs, her manipulation of me, of Tom. Then I met you and my whole world changed. You loved me, you did, you know you did, for myself, not my money, or . . .' his mouth went sour, 'this place and possible title.'

'Oh, Jack . . . but—'

'You've got to listen,' he said frantically. 'From that moment in the park when you said it was over I knew I couldn't stay with Sonia, stay as a proper husband, I mean. I thought for a while I'd be there in name for Tom's sake, but I soon realised that even if I never saw you again, I couldn't stay with her. I had a lot of business trips, I volunteered to go on them.' His smile was raw. 'I come here fairly often too. They need me. You've heard what's happened?'

She nodded.

'Sonia came once, before I'd left her. I saw Tessa, did she tell you?'

Miranda nodded again.

'I brought Tom down here many times, and I told him that I could not love his mother any more. I told him that it wouldn't change my love for him. He helped me choose my flat, choose the decorations. His room is full of posters of the Spice Girls and anorexic models.'

'How did he take it?' she asked, feeling as if she was sleep-walking.

'He took it fairly well. As I said, he has more of his own life now he has friends. He has one he often stays with, dyslexic like him. I said I might take them both skiing in the Christmas holidays.'

'I'm glad.' She wanted to ask what Tom had said about her, but she couldn't. She felt it was all so unreal. Instead she asked, 'So what's Tessa to do with all this?'

'I wanted to see you. I rang Tessa, hoping you were coming here. I had already made plans to come. They are trying to get back into life, wanted me to help Ralph organise a shoot. I persuaded Tessa to make you come here,' he smiled. 'I am so happy to see you, Miranda. I missed you so terribly, I thought I'd die without you.'

His hand reached gently to her face, his fingers caressed her cheek. 'I love you.' His voice was soft. 'I'll never stop loving you.'

She felt her blood surge through her and yet part of her held back. 'I . . . I don't know what to say,' she said at last. 'I feel so much damage will be done if I . . .'

'Weren't you listening to me, darling? I've left Sonia. I've been living apart from her for over a month now. We only went to that concert together because the tickets had been bought ages ago and it was a business thing and I had to go.'

'No one told me you were living apart and Sonia made it sound as if you were still together when I saw her yesterday.' She stared at him, not knowing what to think.

'I wanted to have everything a *fait accompli* before I tried to get in touch with you, and we haven't told many people. I don't know what Sonia says about it,' he sighed, lowered his eyes. 'She keeps ringing me, asking me things, behaving as if we *are* still together, but we're not. We have to talk about Tom, of course, but she's still with her lover. This one seems mad about her, might even take her on.'

'She said you'd get the title here and that Tom would have to be groomed to take after you. It just sounded like you were all together and—'

He laughed. 'Maybe it's self-delusion. She's dreadfully keen on the title and this estate so that's another reason why she's trying to hold on. Because I've got money she thinks I can restore the Hall to its former glory.'

'But she looked so desperate, said you were the only person who loved her, would stay with her,' Miranda said, seeing Sonia's sad, desperate face in her mind. 'Jack, I'm so sorry but I just feel I can't be part of the breakup, put up with her mental anguish, and her making Tom feel guilty, unhappy because of me,' she cried. 'Please see that, Jack. Please make it easy for us. See that we have no future together.'

His face looked taut again, his eyes impatient. 'If she really cared for me, wanted me back, she'd give up her lover, wouldn't she? She's a spoilt, manipulative child, I told you. I can no longer live with her. I try to remain on good terms with her because of our son. I have a flat in the Brompton Road. Tom has a home with both of us. I have a very nice housekeeper, but when he's there I try not to go away on business trips.'

'But she looked so desperate.'

'She is, but I've had enough. I've given her enough chances. Perhaps I should have been tougher in the beginning like my grandfather suggested. I can't pretend it's all her fault. I was away a lot on business, maybe she was lonely.'

'But when she talked of the title, it was as if you were still together,' Miranda insisted.

'As Tom's mother she will always be part of it,' he said, 'but only as his mother.' He drew her to him. 'Please, darling, don't put up so many objections. Tom wants you, I promise you that. He suggested it. "Let's ask Miranda to visit us," he said.' He smiled, but his face was tight, wary, as if waiting for a blow. 'Have you stopped loving me, is that it?'

He had his arms loosely round her waist, holding her to him. His eyes, deep with apprehension, searched into her soul. She did not know what to say. If she admitted that she loved him, would he expect her to drop everything and live with him? Make her part of it all: Sonia's spoilt histrionics; Tom, whom she liked but who needed so much care; and Chandos Hall with all its dramas?

On the other side there was Paris: her little flat that ran round like a circle; her job that gave her such a buzz, and the feeling for the first time in her life that she was really independent, away from her family, her own country, complete, whole, dancing on her own.

'I love you,' she said, 'and always will, but just for the moment I want to stay as I am, living my new life in Paris.'

'Without me?' His voice was bleak.

She could not answer him. If only she could have him and not all the baggage that came with him. But life was not like that; there was always a price to pay.

'Things have changed,' she said gently, 'we cannot go back as we were.'

'Nor can we finish,' he said desperately.

The wind blew round them, catching the leaves from the trees and chasing them across the ground. There was a feeling of nostalgia, the end of a season in the air. They stood there silently in each other's arms, their hearts too full, both understanding the dilemma of their love.

But with the end of things, it came to Miranda suddenly, there was also a beginning. Perhaps they would begin a new life together. Only time would tell.